Born in Sunderland, Barbara enjoyed twenty fulfilling years teaching History and Classical Civilisation in sixth-form colleges before leaving to pursue her love of story-telling. She has a passion for hiking and dancing, the perfect antidotes to long hours of historical research and writing, as well as for travel, and wherever possible, she walks in the footsteps of her characters. *Beyond The Shetland Sea* is Barbara's third novel, following *Secret Lives* and *Discovery*.

Beyond the Shetland Sea

Barbara Greig

Beyond the Shetland Sea

Vanguard Press

VANGUARD PAPERBACK

© Copyright 2024
Barbara Greig

The right of Barbara Greig to be identified as author of
this work has been asserted by her in accordance with the
Copyright, Designs and Patents Act 1988.

All Rights Reserved

No reproduction, copy or transmission of this publication
may be made without written permission.
No paragraph of this publication may be reproduced,
copied or transmitted save with the written permission of the publisher, or in accordance
with the provisions
of the Copyright Act 1956 (as amended).

Any person who commits any unauthorised act in relation to
this publication may be liable to criminal
prosecution and civil claims for damages.

A CIP catalogue record for this title is
available from the British Library.

ISBN 978 1 83794 065 3

This is a work of fiction. Names, characters, businesses, places, events and incidents are either the
product of the author's imagination or used in a fictitious manner. Any resemblance to actual persons,
living or dead, or actual events is purely coincidental.

*Vanguard Press is an imprint of
Pegasus Elliot Mackenzie Publishers Ltd.*
www.pegasuspublishers.com

First Published in 2024

**Vanguard Press
Sheraton House Castle Park
Cambridge England**

Printed & Bound in Great Britain

In memory of my grandfather, Harold Greig Thompson, whose foresight inspired this story

A big thank you to all who enriched my experience of creating *Beyond The Shetland Sea*. For me, the enjoyment of research equalled the pleasure of writing the story. I fulfilled a long-term ambition to visit Shetland, where I encountered a warm welcome wherever I went. My feeling of coming home was overwhelming. Many thanks to the wonderful volunteers of the Shetland Family History Society, and to my newly discovered cousins, whose knowledge was much appreciated. Please be tolerant of any mistakes I have made in using dialect. As in Shetland, my time in Canada was rewarded by helpful people enthusiastically answering my questions. In particular, the Parks Canada staff at Lower Fort Garry and Fort Carlton, and the archivists at the Archives of Manitoba. Special thanks to my husband, Mike, for his patience and critical eye, and finally, to all those at Pegasus Publishing whose expertise made my dream a reality.

ONE

Roker, Sunderland, March 2019

It was time. Three months had passed since she had received the box, almost thirteen weeks of avoidance, and on this Saturday morning, as Eve lay in bed listening to the rain beating on her window, she decided she was strong enough to open it. Her certainty lasted while she showered, ate a quick breakfast of coffee and toast, and then climbed the two flights of stairs to, what her mother had always referred to as, the box room.

Opening the door, she flicked the light switch and the single bulb shone yellow in the gloom. Rain lashed against the mansard window, blowing directly off the sea on a fierce easterly, and obscuring any light that had the temerity to filter through the grimy glass. Eve, fully aware that window cleaning was not one of her priorities, welcomed the rain. At least, the outside of the glass would receive a good dousing, but as for the inside, it would take a herculean effort to clear a passage to the window. Stacked in order of arrival, boxes of all shapes and sizes had been placed in front of it, and for three generations, anything not immediately needed, but still wanted, had found a home there. She glanced nostalgically at her dolls' house and her rocking horse; her chest tightened when she saw her father's old tool chest and the vacuum cleaner kept in case any parts could be recycled, and finally, when her eyes alighted on her mother's sewing machine, left to gather dust, she had to blink away tears.

The box in question was very large, made of transparent plastic, and brand new. For a moment, Eve almost turned tail and retreated to the warm kitchen and a second cup of coffee but she held firm and snapped off the lid. The smell of a musty damp attic was overpowering despite some of the contents being no more than a few years old. There was no order to the items at the top; brown foolscap envelopes bulged with photographs and partially covered some others which were still in their frames, bundles of letters and treasured greeting cards lay higgledy-piggledy with a thick album. She lifted out the latter and knelt back. It was the type which had an adhesive film to keep its contents in place but it had deteriorated with age. She opened it gingerly and read the inside cover. The simple instruction, "For Eve Cummins" in Hannah's distinctive writing threatened to undo her.

Her cousin's death, so soon after Eve's own mother's, had been so sudden, so shocking, that Eve had not yet come to terms with it. She closed the album and held it close to her chest, thinking of Hannah painstakingly organising it. The action dislodged a couple of photographs and a single piece of folded card which fluttered to the floor. Eve leant over and picked them up. The photographs were sepia, family groups from the late nineteenth century by the clothes, and as she eased the folded card open, a young voice called from the bottom of the stairs.

'How much of this coffee can I have?'

'Just leave me enough for another cup.'

'Will do.' There was a pause. 'What are you doing up there?'

'I'm coming down.' Eve carefully replaced the album, slotting the photographs in the front ready to be returned to their original position later, and pressed the lid firmly back on the box.

Lara, her niece, was leaning against the kitchen counter, still wearing her pyjamas; her lively face showing no signs of a late night.

'What is that?' she asked, nodding towards the card in Eve's hand.

'I think it's a homemade valentine.'

'Let me see.'

Eve opened the card, noticing the ragged, worn edges. Inside, someone had drawn a heart and surrounded it with indistinguishable shapes. There was a message written in neat script, the ink almost faded to illegibility. She held the card closer.

'Can you read it?'

Eve struggled but her many years of reading different scripts helped.

'Though I be beyond the Shetland Sea, my heart will always be with thee.'

Lara snorted a laugh. 'Victorian sentimentality!'

'You think so?'

'Yes, they invented the valentine. Is there a date?' Lara peered over Eve's shoulder.

'I can just make out eighteen something.'

'There, I was right. That is a five, I believe.'

Eve agreed. 'It isn't signed,' she commented, almost to herself.

'Of course, it is not, Auntie Eve,' responded Lara. 'That is the whole point of a valentine. Haven't you ever received one?'

Eve held her peace and ignored Lara's emphasis on her name. Hiding her irritation, she asked, 'How come you are an expert on valentines?'

Her niece delivered one of her beaming smiles. 'I took an option on the Victorian poets last term and they popped up in some background reading I did.'

Lara, daughter of Eve's eldest sister, Kate, had arrived from Berkshire the previous autumn to start her first term at the university. Eve had suspected a family conspiracy, a plot cooked up between her three elder sisters, to help fill the void left by their mother's death. The Edwardian terrace, their family home, had been far too large for two people, let alone one. Years ago, it had been up to Eve, the mistake child of the menopause as her sisters used to tease her, to care for their widowed mother. It was the obvious choice, her sisters had argued; Eve had no family, she had recently returned home after four years away studying, and her doctorate could be put on hold temporarily until a more convenient time. Eve had acquiesced, and now, nine years later, she still worked in the local library.

She ignored the question about receiving a valentine. Her dreams had been dashed by black ice on a cold January evening but she doubted Lara was aware of that. After six months of living together, they were still finding their way. Her niece had been a stranger when she had arrived, a relative Eve only saw a couple of times a year, a child who had grown into a young woman without her aunt noticing.

The first few weeks had been awkward; Eve adjusting to another person in the house, worrying about Lara when she was late after a night out, concerned about whether an eighteen-year-old would want to live with her aunt, yet, somehow, it had started to work. Lara came and went as she wished, shopped and cooked for herself when need be, and Eve had started to relax. She no longer lay awake at night waiting for the front door to click open and she found that she had missed Lara when she went home for the Christmas vacation.

'Where did you find the valentine?' Lara had started to spoon yoghurt onto some sliced banana.

'In the box Hannah's partner brought.'

'It must have belonged to someone in the family then.'

'I suppose so,' replied Eve, cautiously.

'What else is in the box?'

'I've only glanced at the items on the top—an old album, bundles of letters, and some photos in frames.'

'That should be enough to be going on with. Perhaps you'll find a clue as to who received the valentine? I presume it was sent?'

'There is no way to tell.' Eve scrutinised the card. 'What do you think these are?'

Lara loomed over her shoulder again, the spoon of yoghurt perilously close. 'They look like animals of some sort.'

'Yes, they do.' The drawings were very faint, but here and there, Eve could make out what looked like a bear. 'Why would a lovelorn admirer draw animals on a valentine?'

'Don't ask me. The Victorians had some very strange valentines.'

Eve looked up at her niece, who was a full head taller. 'I thought you were the expert?'

Lara had the grace to look slightly sheepish as she placed her bowl on the counter. 'Coffee?'

Later that morning, after Lara had disappeared into the bathroom for what her aunt knew would be a long time, Eve climbed back up to the box room. She picked up the album and sat down, leaning against the old, battered trunk which held bedding. Stretching out her legs, she balanced the book on her thighs and found the slots for the loose photos. Before she replaced them, she scrutinised each sepia face, wishing that somehow they would speak to her, but the stiff figures kept their secrets, not even offering their names. Eve carefully lifted the film and eased out another photograph but that, too, was frustratingly blank on the reverse. She spent a few minutes looking through the album and then laid it to one side when it became obvious that there were no photographs early enough to be of either the valentine's author or its recipient.

Rather than choose items at random, Eve decided to be methodical; she would empty the box completely, and then sort its contents into photographs, letters, souvenirs, and miscellaneous. Before long, when she was already surrounded by memorabilia spanning several generations, Eve came across a worn blanket wrapped around a collection of sharp objects and tied with string. Tentatively, she placed the bundle on the floor and tried to undo the knot without success. The string, although frayed in places, was too thick to snap so she gathered up the blanket and its contents in her arms, switched off the light with an elbow, and made her way to the dining room, collecting the scissors from the kitchen as she passed.

An assortment of tarnished silver pieces stood forlornly on the table when Lara popped her head around the door.

'I'm just off out.'

Eve turned around. 'Are you eating here tonight?'

Lara took a step into the room to reply. 'Ugh!' she exclaimed. 'What a manky blanket!'

Eve smiled at her niece's northern jargon which often peppered her speech after only being in the area for six months. 'It is not so bad. It is only old.'

'And moth-eaten,' added Lara, pointing to the tell-tale holes.

'True but it has been a fine covering in its time.'

They both studied the blanket laid out on the parquet floor. Originally white, it had yellowed with age but the green, yellow, red, and dark-blue stripes at one end still held their colour. Just above the bands, three black lines were woven into the wool with a shorter one finishing the set.

'Where did it come from?' wondered Eve. 'It's so unusual.'

In reply, Lara reached into the back pocket of her jeans and pulled out her phone. Seconds later, she announced, 'It's a Hudson's Bay blanket.'

Eve reached down and ran her hand along the selvedge. Lara pointed to the dark-blue stripe. 'That is indigo. Hudson's Bay Point blankets have green, red, yellow, and indigo stripes.'

'How old is it?'

'This one looks incredibly old but you can still buy them today.' Lara passed Eve the phone whose screen was filled with the image of a blanket exactly like the one at their feet.

'How amazing!'

Lara eyed her aunt questionably. 'You have just found an old blanket, Eve. It isn't that remarkable!'

'But it is,' argued Eve. 'Can't you see it might be a piece of the puzzle?'

'What puzzle?'

'The valentine,' replied Eve.

'Oh, I'd forgotten about it.' Lara turned her attention to the selection of silver. 'What about those? They might be worth a bit.'

'I'll clean them later,' Eve stated by way of an answer, in the full knowledge that she would do no such thing as she very much doubted that any silver polish could be found in the house. She was more interested in the blanket. 'What does it say about the black lines?'

'You'll need to read about that yourself. I'm late!' Lara moved towards the door and then remembered her aunt's first question. 'Don't make me anything to eat. I'll be with Ed,' she called over her shoulder.

Eve glanced around the room, now somehow desolate without Lara's infectious energy, and realised how dowdy it appeared with its heavy oak furniture. 'Like me,' she thought in a moment of self-pity as the day loomed long in front of her while Lara was having fun with her latest beau. Then her eyes were drawn back to the blanket. 'Pull yourself together, girl,' she ordered. 'And do something useful.'

The kitchen was bright and cosy. The rain had stopped and the sun, with a promise of spring, shone through the window, warming Eve as she sat with her eyes riveted to the information on her laptop.

The Hudson's Bay Company (HBC) was set up as a trading company in 1670 in, what is now, Canada. The territories granted to the HBC by King Charles II were named Rupert's Land after the first governor of the Company, Prince Rupert of the Palatinate, who was the King's cousin. In 1821, the HBC joined with its rival the North West Company of Montreal and continued under the former's name. The principal activity of both companies was the trade in furs, especially beaver which was highly prized for its water-repellent quality.

The HBC had a network of factories and forts (trading posts) which stretched south from York Factory on Hudson Bay to the present-day border of the USA and as far west as the Pacific Ocean. In 1870, the HBC relinquished its territories to the new country of Canada but it continued with its business ventures and developed the large department stores now associated with its name.

She scrolled down the page and had just started to read about the blanket when the doorbell rang. Lara pushed past her without a word and Eve's question about using the key was lost in the face of such anger.

Two

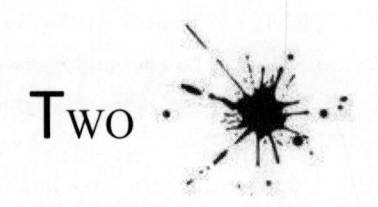

Lerwick, Shetland, January 1849

He was running, adrenalin coursing through his body. Every muscle screamed, demanding respite, but he did not falter. The gap was closing, the flames in front of him bobbed and bounced as the sledge ground its way downhill towards the harbour, and he took his chance. Without consulting his companion, Gideon Thompson broke his stride, grabbed the burning barrel from their sledge, and in an action which seemed to defy possibility, heaved it above his head. Shouting in glee, John Gray abandoned the sledge and ran after him, matching him stride for stride. They separated, skirting around the lead sledge pulled by Angus Duncan and William Cattanach, before meeting again for the final few yards.

They skidded to a halt with a triumphant roar, swinging around to meet the unsuppressed indignation of their rivals. Angus Duncan spat out a tirade of abuse while William Cattanach stood by, speechless. Gideon took a step backwards, to avoid the spraying spittle, and calmly lowered the barrel. The acrid fug reddened the young men's eyes and caught at the back of their throats as they faced each other. Nobody moved, each one of them determined to stand their ground. The arrival of the other sledge teams went unnoticed but not the swish of skirts as the girls approached. Gideon suppressed the urge to turn, to try and see if she was there, and to check that she was watching him. Angus, his face contorted with rage, started to address the crowd, and was rewarded with a spasm of coughing.

Gideon, accustomed to the atmosphere of the forge, covered his mouth with his scarf and eyed his opponent. 'Just because you didna think of it!'

Mutterings circled around the gathered spectators, while the barrels were being carefully stowed near the water, ready to be doused. The night was still young. The heat from the flames kept the creeping cold away and their light played across the expectant faces. All eyes were on the two young men when the thud of military boots, from the direction of Fort Charlotte, announced an impending arrival. Eager for entertainment, the soldiers quickly joined the crowd and were rewarded by giggling and whispering as the girls ogled their uniforms. Gideon and Angus still stared at each other but both experienced an ebb in their heightened emotions. A silent understanding passed between them: they were not equal to the draw of the young troopers. Angus's fury flared again briefly as he witnessed Grizzel Cattanach and her bevy of friends walk away towards the Market Cross, followed immediately by four soldiers.

'Sooth-moothers,' he hissed as he turned away to address William Cattanach. 'Are we away after the lasses?'

'Aye,' his friend replied. 'Best keep an eye on Grizzel. You coming, Gideon?'

'Nae, I'll be gyaan wi John for a peerie dram.'

William looked sceptical. 'I thought you'd be wanting ta see the lasses?'

Gideon shook his head. 'Too much competition.'

Will nodded in agreement. 'See you in da morn, then.'

They parted ways. Gideon and John, after dousing their barrel, made their way back up the hill to their lodging in Tait's Closs. 'Sooth-moothers, incomers, and all others who interfere be damned,' grumbled John as they approached the sign.

Gideon clapped him on the back. 'You canna fight progress.'

'You can try. You canna give a street a new name and expect everyone ta use it.' He glanced up at the sign, which informed all those who passed that Tait's Closs was now Reform Lane, and spat.

They stopped talking as they picked their way up the narrow alley, avoiding the rubbish left by the inhabitants of the overcrowded dwellings, thankful for the moonlit night. As they neared their door, Gideon picked up the conversation with his characteristic reasonableness.

'Without Craigie's soldiers, there would be nae new roads and nae food now the tatties have failed again.'

'Aye, I give you that but they turn the lasses' heads.'

'There be plenty of lasses ta choose from.'

John looked sideways at Gideon and tapped his nose. 'Not if you have yer eye on a certain lass.'

Gideon paused before answering but he failed to mask his discomfort. 'Why do you say that?' His admiration of Grizzel Cattanach was so nascent, so private, that he had never contemplated John uncovering his secret.

'Nae reason,' replied John, as he tapped his nose again and leapt up the final set of steps, leaving Gideon to catch up.

The house was strangely quiet as everybody, except the old and the infirm, was enjoying the final celebration of the Christmas season, including the three men who shared the cramped room Gideon and John called home. They climbed the two flights of stairs, permeated with the reek of too many people, and crossed their threshold to see a feeble fire smouldering in the grate. John cursed while Gideon inched past him.

'Are you going down ta the peat heap or me?'

John, his appreciation of Gideon's trouncing of Angus Duncan still fresh, offered more readily than usual and clattered back down the stairs.

'I'll have me dram when I get back,' he shouted over his shoulder.

The fire did little to dispel the gloom. There was just enough light next to the hearth to do without the lamp, and enough warmth for the men to take off their coats once John had returned with the peat. Gideon stared morosely into his glass, watching the flames reflected in the amber liquid. After the temporary excitement of the festivities, reality had returned.

'A'll need to be away to Scatness to see me grannie afore too long. She'll have some haps to sell. We canna wait until voar. Me daa will also need some help.' Gideon's grandparents struggled to survive on their croft in the south despite his grandfather deep-sea fishing, the dangerous haaf, for the laird, as well as farming the land. The shawls his grandmother knitted provided vital income which would be needed before spring.

John tilted his head in acknowledgement and then downed his whisky. 'Now we've wet our whistles are we back out again?'

'Nae, you go and see what's happening by the Cross.'

Gideon waited until he was sure his roommate had definitely departed before he rose and lit the lamp. The wick took easily and the smell of fish oil filled the room, mingling with the earthiness of the peat. He reached under his mattress and retrieved the hidden book. Carefully, almost reverentially, he opened it and found the page he wanted. He began to read to the empty room, slowly and with measured pronunciation. The evening may have palled, but Gideon's mind was on a greater goal. As the Reverend Murray had placed the grammar book into the young man's hand, the clergyman had said, 'A learned man is a man with the world at his feet.'

The day dawned raw and damp as the young blacksmiths set off for work. Mist rolled in from the sea and both of them increased their pace as they made their way to the dock at Freefield with its shipyard, workshops, and warehouses. As they walked, they gathered companions, all employed by the Hay family in their various enterprises, until their group numbered at least a dozen. Once the young men reached Freefield, their ranks were swelled by those who lived there, including William Cattanach and Angus Duncan who were apprentice boatbuilders. Will shouted out a greeting,

'I wish I be cosy and warm in a smiddy today,' as he joined them and gave Gideon a friendly punch.

'So do I,' replied Gideon grinning. Then he pretended to remember, clapping his hand on his forehead. 'I forgot! A'm a blacksmith.'

Angus, who had heard the exchange many times before in the winter months and who had not quite forgiven Gideon his prowess of the previous evening, grunted in derision. Will glanced meaningfully at Gideon, it was always better not to antagonise Angus, especially early in the morning, and he changed the subject.

'Did you ken they are recruiting for Rupert's Land, again?
'Nae,' replied Gideon and John in unison.
'Aye, Robbie Dunbar has signed up. He told us last nite.'
Gideon digested this information. 'Are you and Angus thinking of it?'
'Nae, we have wark but for those who dunna, it's good money.'
'How good?'
'Robbie says he gets half a year's money even afore he's left Shetland.'
'Half a year's pay?' queried John. 'That would be something!'

There was no time for further discussion as they had reached the blacksmiths' workshop, but all that morning, as he worked in the heat, Gideon mulled over Will's words. He was still thinking about Robbie Dunbar leaving behind all that he knew, as he was working an anchor until a movement caused him to glance up. She was standing, framed in the doorway, with the sea behind her. It was the same colour as the iron on his anvil. He turned to see if she was looking for somebody else, but the other smiths were all busy. He placed his hammer down carefully and walked towards her.

'You'd best come in out of the cold.'

She accepted his offer and stepped just inside the workshop. She smiled a greeting and held up the tongs she was carrying.

'Me midder needs her tengs mending,' she explained, shouting above the strikes of the hammers.

He reached out and took the tongs. The iron was old and the break was not recent. A thought, too exciting to contemplate, flashed and was immediately suppressed. Yet, the evidence was there: the tongs Grizzel Cattanach had brought him had not been in a fire for a very long time. He met her eyes, grey and guileless, and replied,

'Yer midder will be needing these or she canna turn the peat.'

'Aye, that she will.'

'Who's yer midder?'

'You ken very well who me midder be, Gideon Thompson.'

'And who be you?'

For a moment, she was disconcerted. 'Grizzel Cattanach, you do ken my bridder, William.' Then realisation dawned. Merriment danced in his eyes as he watched her, the intense blue made brighter by his blackened face, and she exclaimed, 'You be mocking me!'

'Nae,' he chuckled and pretended to examine the tongs. 'These will be easy ta mend. A'll do it after wark.'

'I'll come back in da morn.'

Testing her, he said, 'I can give them to Will.'

'Nae. A'll come.'

He wanted to shout, to tell the world that Grizzel Cattanach had sought him out, but instead, he said, 'I can bring them around this evening. You live hereabouts and your midder will be needing them?'

She did not refuse. 'We live on Roadside,' she said as a slight blush coloured her cheeks.

'I ken,' he admitted, with a hint of a smile.

Gideon returned to his anvil but he was no longer preoccupied with imaginings of Rupert's Land. Instead, he thought of the unexpected turn of the afternoon and of Grizzel's face with its faint wash of colour just discernible in the fading light. John, who had kept an eye on the couple as he went about his work, grinned to himself and thought of all the fun he would have teasing Gideon.

It was late by the time Gideon finished the tongs and he needed to hurry if he was not going to be too late to call at the Cattanachs' house. Taking a burning peat from the forge to light his way, he ran the short distance to Roadside. Although he counted William a friend, Gideon had never visited his home, and the cottages with their distinctive dormer windows, were all identical. It was difficult to remember which cottage he had seen Will enter. The dock was deserted, the boatsheds shut for the night and the warehouses locked, so he walked along the row peering at each door.

Light pooled onto the ground as Grizzel opened the door, a cluster of family behind her. Gideon held out the tongs and made to turn away but Will, from the back of the group, called out, 'Come in and have some meal, we were about ta eat.' The younger Cattanachs stood to either side of the door and Gideon stepped across the threshold into welcoming warmth, handing Will his burning peat.

'Who comes a knocking at this hour?' a light voice asked, its owner obscured by the crush of children.

'It be the blacksmith, Mammy,' shouted one of them, a small boy who bore a striking resemblance to Will.

'Why I thought it might be Angus Duncan coming a courting our Grizzel!' Janet Cattanach skirted around her brood and appraised Gideon nervously clutching an old pair of tongs.

Disconcerted by her mention of Angus, Gideon bent his head and studied his boots. A howl of laughter ensued, Gideon's head shot up and his eyes met Grizzel's.

'What be so funny?

The culprit was reprimanded by her mother, but the little girl continued to laugh and he was mortified to see that Grizzel was trying to contain herself, without much success. Will came to his rescue.

'It's yer eyes, Gideon. When you look down, the lids be very white compared to the rest of yer face. Elizabeth meant no harm. I doubt she's seen a blacksmith so close afore.'

Gideon shifted from one leg to the other. He could feel a dampness in the palms of his hands and under his arms. The room suddenly seemed too hot, his scarf too tight around his neck, and his throat very dry.

'I shouldna have come straight from the forge.' He scanned the parlour with its comfortable chairs and dresser, and his grandparents' croft flashed before his eyes. He knew Janet Cattanach was the widow of a master mariner, who had died at sea like Gideon's own father, but she had obviously not suffered as his mother had. The Cattanachs had supported Janet until her two eldest sons, Laurence and William, had been taken on as apprentice boatbuilders.

'I shouldna have come straight from the forge,' he repeated, twisting the tongs in his hands.

Grizzel stepped forward then. 'Thank you kindly for this,' she said as she reached out and took them, willing her mother not to comment. 'I found them by the peat pile and thought it would be useful to have another pair of tengs.'

An awkward moment followed while Gideon waited for Janet to respond for, although he would refuse the offer to eat with them, he wanted the opportunity to do so. Grizzel looked from Gideon to her mother and back again.

'Perhaps Gideon could come another day?'

'Aye.' Janet's tone conveyed a hint of reservation, or lack of interest, which caused Gideon to study his boots once more. They were his most expensive possession, made of good, thick leather, and he was proud of them. His grandparents had eyed them with interest, the last time he had visited, comparing them to their own sealskin rivlins. The boots were badly scuffed from his work, and suddenly, he saw them as Janet Cattanach would. He cursed inwardly, furious with himself for rushing round to the house without a care for his appearance, and mumbled, 'I must be away hame.'

As he spoke, Gideon's words were lost, masked by a confident knock. Janet bustled past him and opened the door wide to reveal Angus Duncan, dressed to impress. With a broad smile for Mrs Cattanach, an appreciative glance towards Grizzel, and a curt nod for Gideon, Angus eased past his rival who departed through the still-open door.

Three

Lerwick, February 1849

It was Sunday, the day of rest, and Gideon had just returned from the kirk when a loud knocking interrupted his moment of peace. Annoyed, as he had the room to himself, he opened the door to reveal a small boy.

'That's a mighty noise from such a peerie lad!'

'You're ta come ta the dock.'

'Why?'

'Dunno—I was just told ta get dee.'

Before Gideon could gain any more information, the child disappeared down the stairs, his sealskin boots making a slight slap on the stone as he went. Reluctantly, Gideon pulled on his coat and hurried after the boy.

As he neared the end of the closs, he had a clear view of the jetty, and of a diminutive figure with a large basket on her back. He began to run, flooded with the joy of seeing her. She turned and her face mirrored his, pleasure lighting her eyes as she purposely walked towards him, ready to be embraced.

Gideon's greeting died on his lips as he encircled her bony frame. Always slender, his grandmother had never felt so unsubstantial. He dropped his arms, drew back, and studied her closely. Her weathered skin was drawn taut across her cheekbones, her hands, devoid of flesh, were those of a very old woman, and her auburn hair, her crowning glory, was lacklustre. Akin to a physical blow, the truth hit Gideon and guilt consumed him: in the six months since he had seen her, his grandmother had been gradually starving and he had done nothing.

'Give me the kishie,' he demanded, trying to take the basket from her back. She batted his hands away and turned back towards the jetty. He watched her determined figure for a few seconds and then followed.

'What have you gotten there?' he demanded, pointing to the bag she was carrying as she emerged from the smack's cabin.

'Me haps.'

'You have the kishie full and this.' It was a statement rather than a question.

'Aye.'

'You've been busy since simmer.'

She shot him an unfathomable glance which could have said anything from, surely you know how I spend my days when I am not working the land, to, this is my last chance to keep the wolf from the door.

'How many do you have?'

'Not enough.'

Gideon met his grandmother's eyes, noted the weariness on her face, and was the first to look away. 'Are you hungry?' As the question slipped through his lips, Gideon immediately regretted it. Margaret Thompson had survived so long on so little food that gnawing hunger was her constant companion.

Conscious of her grandson's stricken expression, Margaret replied affectionately, 'Aye. I brought a bannock wi me but I ate it a while back.'

'You had best come hame wi me.'

They walked slowly, Gideon matching his steps to Margaret's, and maintained a difficult silence until they started to climb up Tait's Closs.

On reaching the second flight of steps, their attention was caught by a flicker of movement in an adjacent doorway. A filthy blanket was thrown to one side to reveal a woman and two children of indeterminate age. Remaining seated, the woman held out her palm with little optimism. Money was scarce and most people bartered for their needs. She silently appealed to Margaret, woman to woman, and watched as the older woman turned to the young man. He nodded, after indicating his pockets were empty, and she reached into her bag. Knowing she would be haunted by the children's hollow eyes, Margaret placed the krappen in their mother's outstretched hands.

'That is all I can spare.'

They carried on, Gideon's emotions warring with each other. 'You shouldna be giving meal away.'

'I couldna ignore the bairns.'

'I ken.'

'Who is she?'

'Mary Christie. She be from Northmarvine so canna always get poor relief in Lerwick. She has battles with the board and has appealed against its decision to stop her relief. She even went to the Sheriff's Court which ruled against the board but there be a new inspector who feels she doesna qualify for relief.' Gideon saw Margaret's indignant expression. 'Folks try and help her where they can, a meal here, a bed there, but they have to look to their own kin.'

'Aye, the taatie blight has bitten deep. Canna she go hame to Northmarvine?'

Gideon shrugged. 'She's been in Lerwick long afore I came.'

They reached Gideon's room and he carefully placed the basket, which his grandmother had allowed him to carry, on the floor as far away from the smoky fire as possible.

He laid some more peat on the hearth and reached for the brand iron. 'Would you like some fish, Grannie?'

Margaret, knowing Gideon would just cut his piece of salted cod in two, reached into her bag, once again. 'I've brought this for you. I boiled up four. I left two for yer daa and I did have two for us,' she said, with an apologetic smile.

He returned her smile and took two plates down from the cupboard. She watched him carefully assess the fish head before he cut it neatly, the stuffing of chopped fish livers and oatmeal staying solidly in place. Precision was part of his nature and had been since he was a small boy. When he handed Margaret her fish, she sliced a piece off and slid it onto his plate.

'You need it more than me.'

The love behind the gesture was not lost on Gideon. He was sure she had been doing the same with his grandfather.

'I dunna think so.'

'Aye, you do. Otherwise, you canna work the iron.'

He eyed her keenly. 'How bad is it, Grannie?'

Margaret took some time to answer, debating how candid she should be. It was clear that Gideon had sufficient food at the moment, evident by his muscular arms and the brightness of his eyes, but the potato crop had failed again and it was a long time to the next harvest.

'We have fish, mutton, and oatmeal, but without the taaties, it will be hard to last until hairst.' She watched the frown form, knitting his brows together, and continued, 'We canna survive another year like this. Yer daa is troubled by his chest, and if he canna do the haaf this simmer, we canna pay the rent.'

'What about your haps?' Gideon said nodding towards the basket.

'You ken there will be nae money, Gideon. A'll get some of the merchant's goods in exchange but it's money that I need. I need some for the dresser to whiten the haps ready for sale—nae lady will buy them as they are. We canna survive on lines although I'm off to see Mary Arcus in the morn to see if she will take them for her work. I also want some more worsted to wark with.'

He walked over to his bed and retrieved his purse from under the mattress.

'Nae, lad. Keep your coin.'

'You need what you need, Grannie.'

'Nae.'

'Take it,' he ordered, forcing the shillings into her palm.

Diminished by his action, Margaret studied the money, her heart crying for her to refuse again but her head willed her thin fingers to slowly close.

'Eat yer fish,' he said kindly, conscious of the shift in their relationship.

Gideon waited for his grandmother to speak while he made a pot of tea but she resolutely stared into the fire. Eventually, he broke the silence.

'Where are you sleeping tonight?'

'With Ann Hardie. I sent word last month that I would be in Lerwick this week, if the weather be kind.'

It was what he had expected. Ann was a distant cousin who had left Scatness as a bride to settle with her new husband in Lerwick. Now a widow, she kept a boarding house but was always happy to share her bed when Margaret was in town.

'You'll visit awhile longer?' he asked, worried she might take his question the wrong way.

'Nae, I'd best be off after I've drunk me tea.' Margaret nursed her mug. 'A'll pay you back.'

He reached down and touched her hand. 'I dunna want you to.'

'When have you ever told me what to do, Gideon Thompson?'

He chuckled. 'You can knit me a new gansey.'

His laugh was infectious. Margaret reached into her bag and produced a pair of socks with a flourish. 'I dunna have a gansey with me but I've brought you these.' Tossing them to him, she added, 'You canna be getting cold feet.'

Footsteps were heard ascending the stairs and the door opened without a warning knock, while Gideon was still examining his socks. John Gray led the group, seeing no reason why he needed such formality at his own door. Five lively young people spilt into the room, all dressed in their Sunday best. Margaret knew Gideon's roommate but the others were strangers. They spread out to fill the narrow spaces between the beds, circling Gideon and Margaret in front of the fire.

After greetings had been exchanged and introductions made, an expectant air filled the room. Margaret glanced at her grandson and he was trying, without success, to appear nonchalant. His eyes kept being drawn to one of the girls who stood by the nearest bed, a picture of composure. Margaret noted her clothes which were of good quality, although they had seen some wear and the girl's hands which bore no signs of manual labour. Grizzel Cattanach registered the appraisal and shifted position slightly just as Kitty Hart nudged her and announced,

'Gideon, we be away to hear the visiting preacher.'

Margaret stood up. 'You go, me lad.'

'Are you sure?'

'Aye, A'll come by the forge afore I leave on Friday.'

'We'll walk wi you to Ann's.'

Margaret was about to refuse: she already felt a spare part but Will Cattanach reached for her basket, lifting it as if it weighed nothing.

'Thank you, kindly,' she said, gathering her bag to her.

They left in a chattering cluster with Gideon and Margaret bringing up the rear. Waiting for the moment when he was distracted, Margaret placed the cloth of bannocks onto the table, before slipping in front of him as he closed the door.

Once they had said goodbye to Margaret, the young people naturally drifted into pairs. Kitty linked her arm through Will's and John offered his to Jessie Gilbertson. By the time they reached Hillhead, Grizzel's arm fitted snuggly through Gideon's.

'Where's yer grannie travelled from?'
'Scatness.'
'Today?'
'Aye?'
'How long did it take?'
'About three hours.'
'Has she come to sell her haps?'
'Aye.'
'Who does she go to?'
'The merchant, Laing.'
'He'll try and give her some lines and tea in exchange.'
'I ken. And it's money she needs.'
'A've heard it's bad down there in the sooth.'
'Aye, the taaties and the bere have been bad for years. It's three years since they started sending meal up from Edinburgh and there's still no sign of better days.'

Grizzel felt the rigidity in his arm and rested her free hand on it. Gideon looked down at the small mitten, bright against the dullness of his coat, and a spark of optimism flared briefly. John, just in front of them, turned round. He had obviously been listening to their conversation instead of Jessie's gossip and his expression, fleeting though it was, made Gideon feel uncomfortable.

Four

Tension, rising with each passing minute, became tangible now that the crew no longer battled against the wind. The six men rested, arms aching, initially welcoming the respite. Gideon strained his ears, willing the sounds of approaching oars to drift towards him, but none came. Beneath his feet, the boat rocked on the swell while, above him, a sickle moon rose high in the sky. Not for the first time, he questioned the wisdom of manning an oar.

John had been so persuasive, working on Gideon's need for money. 'It'll be an undemanding night's wark,' he had argued. 'Just ta row out a few miles to meet wi the Dutch, load up the goods, and then be back in Lerwick afore the sun is up.' Gideon had agreed. He needed the money desperately for his grandparents. The crew were a man down so he would be amply rewarded and it would be easy: he had been around boats since he could walk and he doubted anyone was stronger.

The minutes passed slowly, cramp threatened in his left calf, and a fine mizzle blew on the prevailing wind. Gideon pulled his hat on more firmly and massaged his leg. He stretched his back and tried not to think of the Revenue Cutter patrolling Bressay Sound. His mind wandered to the last time he had seen Grizzel and he lost track of time. At first, the splash of oars was hardly discernible, but gradually, a boat loomed out of the darkness. The craft, a similar size to their sixareen, deftly pulled alongside.

Despite a quickening wind, the contraband was passed from boat to boat with a skill honed by practice, and as Gideon heaved the boxes, he closed his mind to their contents, concentrating on stacking them, evenly distributing their weight. If he had had to take a guess it was tea or tobacco as he could discern no clanking bottles, but it was best not to know. He comforted himself with the thought that the wind would blow them home directly once the captain had raised the sail. The mizzle had changed to needle-pricking rain, not icy cold but uncomfortable in its intensity, and Gideon pulled his hat even more firmly over his ears.

Once they had turned west towards the coastline, with the rain now beating on his back, Gideon stifled a sigh of relief. The sixareen powered through the waves, the brisk easterly ensuring the men would reach their goal of making landfall well before dawn. As the towering cliffs of Noss emerged out of the darkness, an earnest discussion erupted as the captain, Magnus Burn, suggested a change of plan: instead of landing at the lodberries, where the jetties led directly to the merchants' houses and their tunnels, it might be wiser to enter Bressay Sound from the north and land at Hay's Dock where the customs' men would least expect. There, the boat could be hidden in plain sight until an opportune time to transfer the cargo presented itself.

Argument was batted back and forth until it was decided to take the southern route and scout out the position of the Revenue Cutter which, if luck was on their side, would not expect any activity that night and would be safely berthed. If the coast was clear, why risk approaching the lodberries on another night? They stowed the sail and rowed in silence, eyes peeled for any movement in the Sound. The rain had abated slightly and the smugglers, sheltered by the island of Bressay, welcomed the calmer conditions.

Inching past South Ness, the boat hugged the coast before staying a safe distance from the lodberries. The six men shipped their oars and waited. The town rose out of the darkness to their left: pinpricks of light sporadically winked along the shoreline and on Hillhead. Not everyone in Lerwick was asleep.

Lamplight flashed in a lodberry window ahead of them and the sixareen glided towards the pier. The smugglers waited, the only sound the gentle lap of water against the stone, until the beam was extinguished. Silently, the door opened and four figures emerged from the warehouse, ready to help unload with accustomed speed.

Suddenly, there was chaos. The customs' men swooped, their lanterns lighting up the night. For one heart-stopping moment, Gideon feared all was lost, yet even as he fought to control his dread, the order to man the oars rang out. Four of the smugglers responded, leaving Laurence Duncan and Magnus Burn to face the wrath of the officials who had cut off their escape route. As most of the cargo had been seized on the pier, the four men managed to control the boat; Gideon, like his shipmates, pulled on the oars until his muscles screamed. Knowing it would be too dangerous to land near the town, they rowed south towards Quarff where they would find shelter and help.

Gideon's heart continued to race even after they had hauled the boat onto the narrow beach adjacent to the Grays' croft. He was not alone. The four men stood, collecting their breath, before John led the way across the meadow, keeping to the edge of his family's cultivated patch which lay to the east of the neighbouring croft. All appeared to be quiet except for the whoosh of the wind and the sound of sheep on the scattald: no sign of movement could be seen until they were almost upon the croft.

A faint glow marked the edges of the byre door and John lifted the latch cautiously, conscious of the tales of customs' men raiding homes. The rush of cold air hit his mother as she rested against the cow's warm flank, rhythmically filling the milking pail. Janet Gray and Bessie turned their heads simultaneously to see four dishevelled young men slide into the byre. The cow turned back, disinterested, but Janet's eyes flicked to her son. There was no need for explanation, and with a slight nod of her head, she invited the men to pass through and enter the house, without pausing in her task.

Although Gideon had never been in the Grays' croft, it was instantly recognisable. Like his grandparents' home, the byre led directly into the but end, the main room of the house, where a central fire filled the area with peaty smoke. Here, five chairs were grouped around the hearth, left in position from the previous evening when Janet had hosted a carding for the neighbouring women so that they could chat while working the wool. Joan, John's younger sister, was busy stirring a pot of gruel, made with as few handfuls of oats as possible, her face an open book as she registered four extra mouths to feed before she quickly masked her worry with a welcome smile.

John flopped down into the nearest chair, indicating to his companions to do likewise. As they did so, a shuffling could be heard above them in the lemm, where the two youngest boys, David and Andrew, slept alongside the seed, fishing tackle, and anything too precious to be stored in a damp barn. David was the first to appear, running his hands through his sleep-tousled hair, immediately followed by his older brother. Speaking together, their words tumbled out in their eagerness to hear the smugglers' news.

'What happened?'

John reached out for the mug of tea Joan had just poured. 'Best if you dunna ken,' he said, as he wrapped his hands around the steaming warmth.

'You've been caught!'

'We wouldna be here, then.'

Joan cut off the conversation by spooning a dollop of gruel into a bowl for each man and the two boys. 'Eat,' she ordered. 'And then ta wark. It may be Sunday but there's much ta do.'

Watching the two boys demolish their breakfast, Gideon realised how tired he was as his own porridge began to warm his stomach and the adrenalin which had pumped through his body all night started to seep away. He caught John's eye, who turned to his brothers and said, 'The hens canna feed themselves and we need more peat.'

Once the boys had reluctantly left to do their chores, James Sinclair voiced the concern on all their minds. 'Do you think Laurence and Magnus will talk?'

'Nae,' announced Willie Duncan, convinced that his brother, Laurence, would keep his peace.

'The customs have the goods. Surely that should be it?'

John did not share James's optimism. 'Aye, but they will still be sent to the Sheriff's Court.'

Gideon's porridge began to sit uneasily. Even if the best possible outcome occurred at the court and Laurence and Magnus were fined, their four companions would need to help them and contribute to the payment. The alternative horrified him. If all six men had been recognised and he was found guilty too, it would be impossible for him to pay his fine.

They left as soon as they had finished eating, a wintry sun weakly making its appearance in the east. It had been decided to leave the sixareen and use the yoal, which Janet had inherited from her family in the south, as it needed fewer rowers. They would be able to take turns resting. It did not take long to launch the boat and set off for Lerwick, the two remaining boxes of contraband neatly stowed in the stern, out of sight under Willie's legs. As he rowed, Gideon continued to fret about what the future might hold and he recalled a conversation he had had with Robbie Dunbar.

They had met one evening the previous week as he was walking home from the forge. He was alone as he had tarried, in the hope of bumping into Grizzel Cattanach, and John had grown tired of waiting and had gone on ahead. Although not friends, Gideon was sufficiently acquainted with Robbie Dunbar to stop and pass the time of day. However, that evening, he had wasted no time in getting to the point.

'I hear you be going ta Rupert's Land.'

'Aye.' Robbie nodded his head, his shock of bright red hair rising in the breeze. He patted it down and eyed Gideon. 'You be thinking of it?'

'I maybe.'

Robbie, a man of few words, nodded again and waited for Gideon to continue. 'I hear they pay you half a year's money in advance?'

'Aye.'

Gideon studied Robbie, trying to ascertain whether he would be open to telling him the amount but rejected the thought. 'How'd you go aboot it?' he asked, instead.

'You need ta have a certificate of good character from the kirk or you dunna have a chance.'

'And then what?'

'The Company's always recruiting.' Robbie eyed Gideon keenly. 'But they dunna take weaklings.'

The young blacksmith visibly bristled and stared back making his companion laugh.

'I ken you'll be successful,' admitted Robbie, 'for A've heard it said that we be the hardiest of men. The hardiest in all of Europe.'

Gideon pulled on the oars, a plan forming in his mind. He would go and see the Reverend Murray as soon as they docked in Lerwick. The minister would be at home resting after the Sunday service, and now was the time to ask about a certificate before any hint of smuggling came to his attention. He thought about the clergyman's kindness and generosity in helping him to improve his reading and pushed the worm of guilt to the back of his mind. He glanced at the contraband in the stern, now protected by John's legs, and wondered whether the good Reverend would be averse to some smuggled tea.

Five

Lerwick, March 1849

With a smile on his face and a spring in his step, Gideon Thompson walked towards the Tolbooth. It was three weeks since the smuggling trip and he was beginning to relax. There had been no visit by customs' officials, Laurence Duncan and Magnus Burn had obviously held their peace, and he had the Reverend Murray's certificate, declaring him to be of good character, safely tucked into his inside pocket. He was on his way to see Dr John Brown who was acting as the Hudson's Bay Company agent charged with recruiting young men as servants. On hearing the term, Gideon had felt a temporary reluctance to fulfil his intention but Robbie Dunbar had allayed his fears by stating that there were many different opportunities for skilled men.

Gideon had listened carefully as Dunbar had reeled off a long list of jobs which dismissed the labourers who would crew the canoes and concentrated on the Company's need for seamen, or sloopers as they were known, as well as the highly prized carpenters, stonemasons, and blacksmiths. As he heard Dunbar continue with what Gideon believed to be the Company's recruitment speech, the young blacksmith could not help but experience an idea so fledgling, so audacious that he squashed it immediately. However, Dunbar's words echoed as he approached the Tolbooth. 'It be a known fact that men can rise in the Company. Even labourers can rise to become clerks and shopkeepers. One great Orkneyman, William Tomison, had long ago been hired as a labourer yet he rose to become Inland Governor.'

It did not take long for Gideon to sign away five years of his life. He exited from the Tolbooth ten pounds richer and daydreamed his way back to his lodgings, imagining his grandparents' joy when he told them that they would have enough money to pay their rent and to see them through the 'hunger gap'. His grandmother would be able to buy the raw materials to make her shawls and his grandfather could choose not to join a crew rowing forty miles out to the fishing grounds as he, Gideon, had given them a shield against starvation. If he was fortunate, his contribution to the smuggling fine would be counted in shillings and his grandparents would receive nearly all of his advance payment.

He was still lost in a reverie when he approached the Market Cross. Someone spoke, and his attention caught, Gideon registered two familiar figures. Grizzel Cattanach and Kitty Hart were coming towards him, arms linked and wearing their best shawls. He quickly glanced around for any sign of Will or Angus Duncan but the girls were alone. Capitalising on his good luck, Gideon hurried to meet them.

'Where have you been, Gideon Thompson?' asked Kitty with her usual directness. Grizzel waited next to her, wearing a wide welcoming smile.

The truth died on his lips as Gideon met her eyes. A sense of betrayal, unwarranted, as no understanding had passed between them, threatened to engulf him and he found himself mumbling some nonsense about going for a walk.

Both girls eyed him suspiciously although Kitty's held a challenge as well.

'Perhaps I be going to buy a certain person a keepsake.' He had no idea where the statement came from, and he was already reprimanding himself for mentally spending some of his precious money, but Kitty's reaction made it worthwhile.

'And who might that be?'

He gave her his most enigmatic stare, locked eyes meaningfully with Grizzel, and nodded a goodbye. He started to walk up the hill but he was still within earshot when he heard Kitty's loud voice. 'Who does Gideon Thompson think he be?'

Once home, the reality of his action hit him. He sat on his bed and felt the strange sensation of panic rising in his chest. For a moment it was difficult to breathe and his hands trembled, so he forced himself to inhale and exhale slowly. The panic eventually abated to be replaced by a feeling of sickness deep in the pit of his stomach. His grandparents were safe for now but he would not see them for five years, during which time anything could befall them, and any admiration he had for Grizzel Cattanach appeared futile as, in a few weeks' time, he was due to sail into the unknown.

The next morning was work as usual which gave some semblance of normality. He fielded John's questions about his whereabouts on the previous day and kept his intentions to himself as he worked with an intensity that caused the other blacksmiths to glance at him over their shoulders. As he heated and hammered, heated and hammered, Gideon worked out the order of his next actions. He would visit his grandparents the following Sunday and then hand in his notice to the Hays. After that, the news would travel quickly and Grizzel would soon hear of his plans.

Such organisation was not to be. That evening, as he and John were leaving the smithy, a small figure stepped into their path; Grizzel Cattanach, without the forthright Kitty Hart. Her face spoke volumes. John looked from the girl to Gideon and back again before deciding to hurry on ahead.

Without preamble, she asked, 'Be it true that you're gyaan to Rupert's Land?'

He was too taken aback to answer immediately. He kicked an imaginary stone with his boot and looked out over the Sound. The sun was sinking, painting the grey sea silver, although it would still be some time before twilight. Two thoughts flashed through his mind in quick succession: firstly, that she had been waiting for him, and secondly, and much more significantly, that his recruitment had unsettled her greatly.

'Aye.'

Grizzel seemed uncertain how to continue so he filled the silence. 'There be money to be made. A man coming hame efter five years… ' He left the sentence unfinished, reluctant to commit himself but giving her enough to realise that he would be a good provider.

She looked at him, his eyes still on the water, and willed him to turn towards her. 'You canna expect a lass to wait five years,' she stated, trying to keep her tone neutral.

'Aye,' he agreed, much to her chagrin. Then, he did turn towards her and smiled ruefully, pushing his hands further into his trouser pockets.

She took a step forward, and then another, until she was close enough to smell the forge on his clothes. He watched her speculatively, his eyes deep blue in his blackened face. She rested a hand on his lower arm, sensed its strength through his gansey's sleeve, and said,

'A'll miss you, Gideon Thompson.'

She walked away then, back in the direction of her house. He watched her neat, dejected figure guiltily.

'How did you ken I was gyaan?' he called.

She turned, a half-smile on her face. 'Why would you geng to the Tolbooth?'

It was the following Sunday when Gideon saw Grizzel again. He had just arrived back from visiting his grandparents, his head buzzing with emotions. Their relief at knowing that they would survive the coming year had been tempered by the shock of his recruitment. Margaret Thompson's hands had flown to her face when she heard the length of his service.

His grandfather had patted him on the back, understanding what needed to be done. As a young man, he had spent several separate years on the whaling boats in the waters around Greenland, making good money so that his family could eat. His own son, Gideon's father, had tried it but had then preferred the deep-sea fishing which meant trips of three days rather than many months. It was returning from one of these trips that he had drowned, the victim, like countless others, of a treacherous summer storm.

Margaret was not so phlegmatic. Having lost a father, and then, a son to the sea, she had determined to keep Gideon safe. On an island where women noticeably outnumbered men due to the seafarers' death toll, gaining an apprenticeship with a blacksmith for her grandson was, in her view, her greatest achievement. At eight years of age, Gideon had started to work with her cousin, learning his craft, and had seemed destined for a life away from whaling boats and the sixareens used in the haaf. Of course, he knew his way around a boat but it was a world of difference sailing around the Shetland Sea to experiencing the North Atlantic. She had accepted his move to Lerwick as spreading his wings, but now, he was going to cross the Atlantic to a wild, inhospitable place with dangers she could not imagine.

Tired, physically and mentally, Gideon's aim was to eat a light supper, his grandmother had insisted on giving him some fresh krappen, and then retire to bed.

'Gideon!'

He swung round to see his friend, Will Cattanach, with Kitty Hart on his arm. A thought, which popped into his mind, was that Will's choice of companion was questionable. Kitty was usually so outspoken that she made Gideon uncomfortable especially when he was in no mood to cope with her bluntness. She started speaking before they exchanged greetings.

'Have you bought that keepsake yet?'

Gideon chose not to answer. Will's eyebrows raised in interest before he took pity on his friend. 'Where have you been?' he asked, as it was obvious that Gideon was coming from the quay and that his voyage would have nothing to do with Kitty's query.

'A've been to see me grannie and me daa.'

Kitty piped up. 'Gideon be gyaan to Rupert's Land.'

'I ken,' replied Will who had been slightly aggrieved that Gideon had not shared his plans with him.

By way of apology, Gideon stated, 'It were a quick decision.'

'When do you geng?'

'End of May to Orkney to pick up the ship and then away from Stromness.'

Gideon waited for Will to say more but there was an awkward silence. He was so preoccupied with this uncommon situation that he failed to notice that Will and Kitty were in the company of another couple who had been lagging behind. Angus Duncan rolled up wearing a very self-satisfied expression, accompanied by Grizzel who stood demurely at his side when they stopped. Everything about his rival's stance told Gideon that Angus knew he would be leaving Shetland. He could barely look at the carpenter and inwardly cursed his predicament when Angus took Grizzel's arm and linked it through his. Under other circumstances the gesture would have been of little significance; Angus was merely escorting Grizzel on a Sunday stroll, but Gideon knew he was being sent a clear message. He glanced at Grizzel, noted her calm demeanour which gave nothing away, and swiftly took his leave.

The next day, after work, Gideon immediately went to the boatyard. He stood some distance away, watching the men leave until he saw Angus among them, and then he joined the remaining boatbuilders who were still tidying away their tools.

Will looked up at the sound of his approaching footsteps. 'What brings you here?'

Gideon studied the neatly stacked piles of Norwegian timber. 'A'm looking for a peerie piece of wood.'

Will laughed. 'You'll be lucky.'

On a virtually treeless island, wood was such a valuable imported commodity that every scrap was spoken for. Will eyed his friend keenly. 'What do you want it for?'

'Carving.'

'How big?'

Gideon demonstrated with his hands.

'About six inches long?' confirmed Will.

'Aye.'

'I canna help you. All we have are shavings.'

Gideon nodded, it was as he expected, but not what he had hoped. Now, he would need to comb the beaches for driftwood instead of using a pristine lump of wood.

'Why dunna you use bone?'

Gideon shrugged, he had his mind fixed on wood. He could see the object already, its sleek lines and smooth patina, and Grizzel's face when he presented it to her.

Will looked at his friend askance, unused to the faraway expression on his face, and offered what he could. 'You should go to Willie Smith.'

Six

Lerwick, April 1849

It was longer than Gideon expected before he had time for a visit to Willie Smith. Thus, it was on a fine April Sunday that he found himself walking towards Gremista at the northern end of the town. Since his conversation with Will, he had visited his grandparents again, conscious of how fast his departure was approaching, and he and his grandfather had taken the yoal out to fish. Sailing around Quendale Bay and up the coast towards St Ninian's, they had passed freshly greened cliffs carpeted with a riot of wildflowers and quiet beaches littered with driftwood. Now, he clutched a piece of the latter under his arm, disguised by his coat.

Willie, a cooper who had long thought his useful days were over, greeted Gideon with enthusiasm. The young man stepped off the street into what would normally be the kitchen and living room, but the Smiths had turned it into a workshop. He was overwhelmed by the smell of wood and the sight of the old man's tools, all carefully arranged. Barrel heads and truss hoops were stacked against the wall under a range of implements including an axe, a putter, a brander, a truss hoop driver, an adze, and several hammers. Through the open door at the back, he could see where the family ate and slept.

'What can I do for you, lad?'

'I ken you be able to help me carve?'

'Aye—although me eyes aren't what they used to be.'

Despite his caveat, Willie Smith was proud of his skills and proficiency. Learnt from his father, a lowland Scot who had been lured north by the rich fishing grounds firstly to Aberdeen and then to Shetland. He had married and settled in Lerwick, never to return to his roots, but he had continued to yearn for the trees of his homeland, and every chance he had, he could be seen whittling wood. Eschewing fishing as his main source of income for coopering, his father-in-law's trade, Willie Smith, and his wife, Elizabeth, had raised three sons in the cottage in Gremista. Two boys had been claimed by the sea, and after Elizabeth's death, it was Isaac who had followed in his father's footsteps and who kept the roof over their heads.

'Come through, lad, and have some tae. A've just refilled the stroopie.'

Gideon followed the old man to the ben end of the cottage which was so cluttered that there was little room to move. Willie poured two mugs of thick black tea from an old, chipped teapot and said,

'Dip in the restin shair.'

Gideon plonked himself down on the settle reserved for guests, which could be converted to a bed when required, placed his wood down and took a sip of the strong tea. Willie pottered around the restricted space, tidying this and that, before he squeezed himself into one of the other chairs which abutted against the two box beds. As a big man, Willie had mastered the use of the room with nifty precision and Gideon wondered whether his son was of a similar size, and was interested in how they did together in the cottage. Besides the beds, the settle, a table, and the chairs, there was a kist, presumably for storing clothes, and the usual cooking accoutrements.

Willie's eyes lighted on the driftwood. 'Pass it here, lad.'

'What be it?'

'Oak, perhaps,' replied Willie, but as he turned the wood over and assessed the shape, he corrected himself. 'I think what you have here be pine—a section of mast.'

'It will be easier to carve than oak,' stated Gideon, keen for Willie to realise he was not completely ignorant of the qualities of wood.

'Aye, lad.' Willie smiled to himself. He had noticed Gideon's eagerness and the faint whiff of smoke which permeated his clothes: the lad obviously worked with iron.

'I want to make a... '

Willie held up a hand to silence the young man. 'You must listen to the wood. It will speak to you. The wood decides what it will become.' Thwarted, Gideon could only watch the old man examine the piece of wood by running his hands over its outlines before he said, 'How big were you thinking?'

'About six inches in length.'

'This timber be too wet still. If it dries out efter you have carved, it will split. You can have a peerie bit of mine. I have a section of mast.'

Gideon nodded his thanks, disappointed that the wood he had recovered from Rerwick beach was not suitable.

'Drink your tae, lad, and then we'll get started.'

Once back in the workshop, Willie selected some wood from his stock and reached for his axe.

'I thought I had to listen to the wood,' Gideon remonstrated, with a hint of sulkiness.

Willie did not reply. He swung the axe, splitting the wood in two, one length considerably thicker than the other. He lifted up the narrower of the two. 'You need to practise first,' he said as he trimmed the wood into a shape.

'What is this to be?' he asked.

'A spune,' replied Gideon, feeling like a foolish child.

'Aye, lad. I can see it's not what you want but do this first.' He passed the half-finished object to Gideon along with a bent knife whose blade, which curved back on itself, would gouge out the bowl. 'Clamp the spune under your arm and use the action of your elbow and forearm to shape it. Your hand will hold the cutting edge steady.'

Willie watched Gideon concentrate and thought how young he looked. A memory, long forgotten, surfaced: his youngest son, Jamie, focusing on his carving. Willie almost expected the tip of a pink tongue to appear between Gideon's lips.

'Is it a keepsake for your lassie you want?'

A faint blush warmed Gideon's cheeks and Willie slapped his knee in triumph. He laughed. 'She'll like a wooden spune. It'll be better than the horn ones folks have.'

Gideon's expression told a different opinion.

'You dunna believe me. Did you ken that in Wales spunes are given as love tokens?'

Gideon, who knew little about Wales other than where it was, was too polite to be disrespectful of his elders, but very much doubted the truth of the cooper's words. He definitely had another carving in mind for Grizzel.

Willie left him to his task while he fetched more tea. 'It be thirsty wark,' he commented on his return, as he selected a spokeshave ready for the next phase of shaping the back of the bowl.

It was some considerable time, after much frustration, before Gideon had produced a useful spoon. He had stopped before the trimming stage as Isaac had returned home for his midday meal and the Smiths had kindly asked him to share the fish Isaac had caught that morning. Once they had eaten, Willie and Gideon repaired to the workshop to complete the job while Isaac left to visit friends. When the spoon was finished, Gideon studied it dubiously for so long that Willie announced sharply,

'She be a lucky lass to have such a keepsake. You ken how folks treasure their Skovi Kapps, always showing them off on their mantelpieces.'

Gideon was slightly heartened. Even his grandparents had one of the patterned wooden bowls brought back from the Baltic by sailors. The one in his own family had been a present from his great-grandfather to his wife. Gideon had noticed that the Smiths had no such souvenirs, but while he had been eating his dinner, he had seen a row of beautifully carved animals arranged along the top of one of the box beds. He looked up from his crudely carved spoon and pointed out,

'This be not a kapp.'

'Nae, it be not a kapp—but come back next Sunday and we'll see what we can do.'

It took five consecutive Sundays with Willie Smith for Gideon to produce another carving. He felt inordinately pleased with himself, and whenever he was alone in his lodgings, he would unwrap Grizzel's gift and run his hands over its sleek lines. He compared it to the spoon and experienced the thrill of progress made. Soon, it would be time to present it to her but he needed to think carefully about finding the perfect opportunity. He had seen Grizzel several times over the last few weeks but often she was with Kitty, or with her mother and her younger siblings. On such occasions, they chatted politely but with a reservation that made Gideon long for their exchange in the forge over the tongs.

It was towards the middle of May, only a couple of weeks before he was due to leave, when Gideon took his chance. Approaching Will, he asked whether it was possible to meet with Grizzel, explaining that he had something to give her. To Gideon's surprise, Will chuckled and asked why it had taken so long for him to speak up.

The day had dawned dull and miserable with a dense sea fret, making a mockery of any notion of early summer. The grey mist rolled in waves onto the quay and Gideon found it difficult to distinguish the small figure emerging in front of him. As Grizzel stopped, he saw Will behind her and it was he who held up his arm in a friendly greeting.

'It be a stumba,' he said, commenting on the weather.

'Aye,' replied Gideon, whose hair was already very damp.

Will came to a halt, looked around him, gave Gideon an encouraging pat on the back, and then continued walking, waving as he went.

Now that he was face to face with Grizzel, all of Gideon's well-planned words deserted him. He thrust the package at her with such a lack of ceremony that she, too, was rendered speechless. He watched her turn it over, wishing he had been able to use some pretty wrapping and ribbon instead of the plain material. He had cut up his best shirt, worn but still with a good square of cotton in the back, knowing that he would have no need for such an article in the wilderness of Rupert's Land.

She took her time, picking at the knots in the string, for he had tied it too tightly, until he wanted to grab it from her and use his knife. He forced himself to be patient, keeping his arms by his side with fists clenched, until she eventually passed him the material to hold while she examined his gifts.

'A selkie,' she exclaimed, as she cradled his carving in one hand while she ran her fingers from the tip of the seal's nose, across its back, and down to its feet. She felt the striations he had used to depict the fur and then examined the face. Gideon had chosen to carve the rounder, dog-like face of the common seal rather than the grey seal, both of which were abundant in Shetland's waters. The carving was of a pup, its round face dominated by huge eyes, stretching forward with its flippers splayed. The mammal was almost smiling.

Grizzel glanced up, joy suffusing her face. She did not ask if it was his work, for the pleasure on his face told her it was, instead, she said, 'This be the best gift. Thank you.'

Gideon found his voice at last, and suddenly, he wanted to tell her everything: his visits to Willie Smith, the practice spoon, and finally, the frustration he overcame each Sunday trying to carve a gift for her. She listened, her eyes never leaving his face, realising with each word the true affection he felt for her.

'What aboot the spune?' he asked, pointing to his practice piece.

'It be a bonnie spune, Gideon Thompson,' she said, her face lit by a wide engaging smile.

'You be mocking me!'

'Nae.'

'You can use it,' he said, defensively.

'Nae,' she responded, serious once more. 'A'll keep it with me always. It be too good to use.'

'Walk with me awhile?'

'Nae, A've to get back.'

Gideon shuffled from foot to foot, unsure of what to say next.

Grizzel regarded him earnestly. 'Are you faird of gyaan so far?'

He met her eyes and studied her keenly, debating whether to bear his soul. He was afraid; he was apprehensive about the voyage, intimidated by tales of the wilderness with its great expanse and extremes of climate, anxious about his grandparents and how they would fare without him, but most of all, he was afraid that she would be married by the time he returned. He could not ask her to wait for there had been no intimate exchange between them, just an overpowering certainty on his part that Grizzel Cattanach had captured his heart, making it useless for anyone else.

For a moment, fury, hot and intense, flashed at the injustice of it all. Then it subsided as quickly as it had come. He had no alternative.

'What wirries you?' The shadow across his face had not passed unnoticed.

'A'll be there and you be here.'

Grizzel thought carefully before she reacted. It was well known that, of the men who travelled to Rupert's Land, more stayed than returned, taking advantage of the opportunities of a new land. Despite her feelings, how could she promise to wait? She studied his gifts, made with such care, and knew she should offer something in return.

'How well do you ken your letters, Gideon Thompson?' she asked, without a trace of irony.

'Better than many folks,' he replied, wondering if, by some uncanny means, she knew of the Reverend Murray's grammar book.

'You do, do you?' she queried, her mouth twitching at the corners.

'Aye.'

'Well, Gideon Thompson, you can scrit me letters.'

Grizzel wrapped her shawl more closely as dampness crept down the back of her neck. She waited. Gideon looked at her, lingeringly and intensely, committing every feature of her animated face to memory. The silence dragged out.

'Aye, Grizzel Cattanach, A'll scrit.'

Seven

Roker, March 2019

Eve returned to her laptop and continued reading about the Hudson's Bay blanket, trying to ignore Lara's feet stomping up the stairs followed by the banging of more than one door. Her niece would calm down in time and would probably emerge at lunchtime, lured by the aroma of homemade soup. What interest Eve lacked in housekeeping, was more than compensated by her culinary skills. Honed over the previous nine years, with the primary aim of tempting her ailing mother to eat varied nutritious food, Eve had developed into an adventurous and talented cook.

While she read, Eve discovered that each of the black lines at the end of the blanket represented a beaver pelt given in exchange. This seemed logical, but when she consulted another site, there appeared to be a difference of opinion about this. She leaned back in her chair and thought about the discrepancy, experiencing a frisson of excitement that reminded her of researching for her doctorate. She clicked on another site, hoping to cross-reference the information but she found herself reading a general history of the Company. The words leapt off the screen.

From the early eighteenth century, The Hudson's Bay Company recruited men from Orkney and Shetland for service in Rupert's Land. By the end of that century, these men constituted three-quarters of the Company's workforce. The numbers peaked in the mid-nineteenth century when disastrous economic conditions forced many to leave their homeland. These Orcadians, as the men were collectively referred to, were ideal for work in the Canadian Fur Trade. Known as the hardiest in Europe, they could cope with the extreme conditions involved in the Company's service.

Although these men faced hardship, the monetary reward was significant, making it a great incentive. The majority of the recruits chose to settle in the new land, once their contracted time expired, and it was rare for a man to return home. Initially against Company rules, many men secretly lived with indigenous women who were vital in helping the newcomers to adapt to the challenging circumstances of their new surroundings. After their service was completed, they could live openly with their wives and children.

Eve stopped reading, the bubble of excitement growing in her chest. She clicked off the site and brought up a genealogy one. It had been over a year since she had last logged on, and for a moment, she could not recall her username, but after the first failed attempt, it came back to her. She quickly typed it in, with her password, and pressed 'Enter'.

Disinterested in finding unknown ancestors or relatives, Eve's interest had been in her own DNA. Her sisters had clubbed together and had bought her a test for her thirtieth birthday, hoping to lay to rest the question of how much Viking heritage she possessed. Eve had been disappointed in the result, regarding the findings with a jaundiced eye and she had never bothered with the site since.

Now, she navigated through the site as quickly as she could before she reached the page 'DNA Story for Eve Cummins'. Then, she skimmed past a couple more pages until she reached the map with the colouring indicating her areas of Irish/Scottish ancestry. Her eyes focused on Shetland where she could see two small yellow circles. Excitement rising further, Eve pushed back her chair and ran to the top of the stairs where a large bookcase dominated the first landing. Finding it easily on the bottom shelf which housed the large books, she grabbed the atlas and retraced her steps, hardly noticing the ominous vibrating music coming from Lara's room.

She opened the atlas on the kitchen table next to her laptop, and compared the two maps. She had never realised Shetland was so far north, in fact, it had been placed nearer Orkney in the atlas so that it fitted on the page. She leant over the book, and there, on the larger map, she could clearly identify the areas shaded yellow. One circle was over the capital, Lerwick, and the other was on the most northerly of the islands, Unst. She looked from the atlas to the screen and back again, and a wide smile to rival the Cheshire cat's spread across her face.

Against all expectations, Lara did not surface for lunch despite Eve calling up the stairs twice. After a mumbled reply on both occasions, Eve gave up and decided to go for a walk to clear her head.

On leaving the house, she cut across the park and was on the seafront in a matter of minutes. A strong wind was whipping across the waves creating spumes of spray which glistened in the spring sunshine. The sea was a rare deep blue, and although the sun possessed some heat, the wind was biting. Eve pulled up the hood of her duffle coat, thrust her hands in her pockets and resolutely set off in the direction of Whitburn.

As she strode out, Eve tried to bring some order to what she had discovered. She had the valentine, the blanket, and information to suggest that one of her forebears had a connection to Shetland, the Hudson's Bay Company, and Canada. Was the blanket a gift, perhaps given by the sender of the valentine? Was the sender or the recipient her forebear? What had happened to the sender, so far away from the Shetland Sea?

Eve continued to ponder these questions until she realised she had reached Whitburn without taking any notice of her surroundings. She stopped by the fishermen's cottages and stood for a while, looking out to sea. A thought crept into her mind, fanciful but true: it was the same sea that her forebears in Lerwick would have seen every day. She waited, hoping for a feeling of affinity but nothing happened: instead, she was reminded of the solid stone of sadness lodged in her heart. Her mother was not here, she could not answer her questions nor help her uncover the past. Neither could Hannah.

She sighed, focused on the beauty of the water, and the stone, which was her permanent companion, shifted slightly. Her thoughts roamed over possibilities. She chided herself for being whimsical: she possessed research skills which she needed to use. Evidence was paramount, and in a flash of illumination, she knew exactly where to start.

Lara was in the kitchen hugging a mug of hot chocolate when Eve arrived back at the house. One look at Lara's shoulders, which appeared to have folded in on themselves, told her aunt that all was not well.

'Don't even ask,' warned her niece.

'I wasn't going to.' It was the truth. Eve, being a novice herself in affairs of the heart, knew she was ill-equipped for coping with the vagaries of an eighteen-year-old's love life.

Lara took a sip of chocolate. 'Where have you been?'

'Just along to Whitburn. It's lovely out there.'

'Oh yes?' She noted her aunt's windswept hair; half of the bouncy curls, initially tied back in a scrunchie, had escaped, and now framed Eve's face with a halo of frizzy tendrils. Lara placed her mug on the worktop and reached for another biscuit.

There was a long pause. The packet of biscuits, which had been unopened that morning, was half empty. Eve resisted the temptation to remind Lara it was almost time for tea: she would have sounded like her mother. Instead, she decided to lead by example so she began to collect together the ingredients to make a pasta sauce.

Eventually, Lara asked, pointing to the laptop still open on the kitchen table, 'Did you find anything else out?'

'A bit about the Hudson's Bay Company.'

'Interesting?'

'I think so.' Eve started to chop the onions and tomatoes. When she had finished she turned to Lara. 'Pass me some basil, please.'

Lara was leaning against the counter in front of the spice rack. 'I thought you'd have some fresh.'

'Not today,' replied Eve as she took the proffered jar. 'Thank you.'

'You're so methodical. You always gather everything together before you start cooking.'

Unsure whether this was a compliment or a criticism, Eve carried on with her preparation without responding. It was what she did. She was an organised, methodical person when faced with a task but was the opposite in many other aspects of her life. She tossed the onions into the hot oil. 'I'm going to Saltburn tomorrow.'

'Why?'

'To see Ada. I haven't seen her since Christmas.'

'Ada?'

'Yes, Auntie Ada—my mum's aunt.'

Lara mulled over Eve's words. 'That would make her my great-great aunt.'

Eve nodded as she turned the onions, assessing their transparency.

'How old is she?'

'Well into her nineties.'

'Can I come?'

Eve failed to disguise her surprise and Lara responded tetchily. 'It's not as if I've got anything else to do.'

The budding romance with Ed had obviously come to a very acrimonious end.

The following morning, Lara remained glum for the duration of the journey south with Eve receiving occasional grunts in response to her comments. By the time they were cruising past the Middlesbrough skyline and Eve pointed out the famous Transporter Bridge, which elicited a disdainful glance from her niece, she decided to give up and the rest of the journey was completed in silence.

If Lara had expected a little old lady, she would have been surprised. Ada Thompson greeted them dressed in a fetching boatneck sweater and tailored ankle-skimming trousers. A single string of pearls lifted the outfit from functional to elegant, as did the pearl drops which bobbed in Ada's ears as she invited her visitors to come up to her apartment.

They followed her across the foyer of the complex; a bright modern building designed to provide luxury living for the third age, through an assortment of comfortable sofas, and into the lift, which would take them to the second floor. On exiting, as they continued along the corridor to Ada's flat, Lara lost some of her ill humour. Light flooded in from the end window which framed a magnificent vista of the sea. Lara, having grown up in land-locked Berkshire, exclaimed,

'Everywhere I look there is sea!'

Ada chuckled, deep and throaty, a sound at odds with her short stature. 'Come on in,' she invited, stepping back and sweeping them into her front room. Furnished with new furniture when Ada had moved into her apartment, the room was decorated in soft neutrals allowing the rich green velvet sofas to make an arresting statement.

'Wow,' said Lara, as she walked to the bay window and let her eyes roam from the long pier which stretched out to sea, to the cliffs which fell steeply to the beach.

'The pier was even longer,' Ada announced, proudly, 'until a china clay vessel chopped it in half in the 1920s.'

'Wow,' Lara said again, as she turned around and sank into one of the sofas.

Ada had made cheese scones in honour of their visit and she served them still warm with a generous dollop of butter: the coffee was strong and complimented them perfectly. Lara leaned back against the copious cushions and felt an overriding feeling of calmness. She caught Ada's eye and returned her smile, warming to the keen blue eyes which were appraising her.

'You remind me so much of your mother,' stated Ada. 'Although it is a long time since I saw her, I remember her well.'

'People often say that but I don't see it myself.'

Eve watched as her niece sat up straighter and settled her long, willowy legs into a more graceful position and she did, indeed, resemble her mother, Kate. Not for the first time, Eve questioned the lottery of genes which had produced her three tall, slender sisters before she was born, small and curvy.

The conversation moved to everyday things; what Ada was doing, how much Lara was enjoying her course and news about other members of the family. The latter eventually gave Eve her opener.

'Did any of our family in the past go to Canada?'

Ada accepted the change in conversation without missing a beat. 'Why do you ask?'

'I found some interesting things in a box Hannah left me.' At the mention of Hannah's name, Eve saw the old lady's eyes mist over. She swallowed and fought for composure. 'There was an old blanket from the Hudson's Bay Company.'

'Let me think. There was a distant cousin who emigrated in the 1950s. I remember he came back for a visit and I met him at my parents' house.'

'No, earlier than that—with perhaps a connection to Shetland.'

'How much earlier?'

'Mid-nineteenth century.'

'I'm not sure. I often wish I'd asked more questions of my grandparents.'

The old lady remained quiet for several minutes, thinking. An old clock, sitting incongruously on the ultra-modern mantel, ticked loudly. Eve waited, expectantly, while Lara, becoming bored, picked up a magazine from the side table and started flicking through it.

'There is something but it might be hearsay. You know what families are like.'

'Tell me.' Eve found she was leaning forward on the plush velvet.

'There was somebody in the past who lived with the Indians. My father once told us this nugget of information when we were watching Laramie on the television.'

'First Nations,' corrected Lara, obviously still listening.

'Do you know who it was?'

'Eve's bloke is a Victorian who sends soppy valentines,' Lara interjected, never raising her eyes from an article about the latest lipstick colours.

'Um,' said Ada. 'And if the blanket was in Hannah's possession, he must have been a Thompson?'

'I know I'm making too many assumptions, but if he was, can you tell me any family names from back then?'

'Let me see,' said Ada, taking her time, again. 'I believe there was a Hugh and a James and one of them had a biblical name but I can't remember what it was.'

'The names were often used from father to son,' added Lara who was calculating whether a rather striking red would suit her lips.

Eve reeled off a long list of biblical names but to no avail.

'None of those rings a bell,' admitted Ada.

Lara put down the magazine with a flourish. 'Good luck with googling them.'

A tilt of Ada's head indicated slight puzzlement. Lara clarified. 'It's hardly an unusual surname!'

Eve, who had realised this before their visit, was disappointed: she had hoped for more. It was obvious Ada could help no further and the conversation, led by the old lady, moved on to reminiscences about more recent family. Half an hour later, Lara started to fidget, taking out her mobile phone now that she had finished the magazine. Ada regarded the girl indulgently but Eve decided it was time to leave.

'Ada, would you like to join us for some fish 'n' chips? I thought we would eat lunch before we set off home. I can drive to the car park at the bottom of the bank.'

'No, my dear, I will be fine. I believe the cliff lift is running today.'

'Cliff lift?' Lara looked up from the screen.

'Yes, it's exceedingly rare. In fact, it's the oldest water-balanced funicular in this country. I used to love going on it,' replied Eve, scowling at Lara, sending her niece the message to pocket her phone.

They set off at a leisurely pace, and on seeing what looked like a small railway carriage perched at the top of the steep cliff, Lara exclaimed in surprise and increased her speed. There was a queue of people waiting to board so they watched the water tank system which controlled the lift while they waited.

'Is it safe?' asked Lara peering down the cliff as one car descended while the other climbed.

'Of course,' Ada reassured her, pointing out the safety cables.

After two journeys, it was their turn, and once seated, Lara reacted like the child she had recently been, turning her head in excitement to check the view from every angle, tracing the outline of the birds in the stained glass windows with her finger, and even standing up, which was forbidden, and caused the other passengers, an elderly couple, to glower.

The sun made a brief appearance during lunch, long enough to tempt Ada to walk along the pier after they had finished eating. The tide was coming in and a smattering of surfers was taking advantage of the waves while the beach was busy with families and dog walkers making the most of their Sunday afternoon. They stood at the end of the pier, staring into the roiling sea before they raised their eyes towards the distant horizon.

'I don't like it,' admitted Lara.

'You won't make a sailor, then.' Ada patted the girl on the back. 'Come on, let's go.'

Eve was of a different opinion: the urge to travel, to explore, and to broaden her own horizons had lain dormant for so long but now she saw infinite possibilities. The waves were inviting her. What if she crossed the sea to Rupert's Land, to Canada? What would she find? She had no ties, no responsibilities now, and she had accrued enough holiday for three weeks. The excitement she had experienced during her searches about the Hudson's Bay Company resurfaced and it took considerable control not to blurt out her intention, there and then, to her aunt and her niece. Instead, being Eve, she said calmly,

'I think it is time we started back.'

Eve's enthusiasm continued during the journey home when Lara was in a much better frame of mind. It did not diminish throughout the evening as they ate a light supper and caught up with a box set, and it was still bubbling inside Eve's chest when the phone rang just as she was about to go to bed.

'Eve,' said a familiar voice, without any preamble. 'I've remembered the biblical name. It's Gideon.'

Eight

It was almost lunchtime and the library was quiet so Eve took her lunch to the office, leaving Aidan Clark on the front desk. She ate the cheese and pickle sandwich quickly, boiled the kettle to make a fennel tea, and then sat down at the computer. The excitement of the previous day had abated slightly but she was eager to use her new knowledge at the first opportunity.

Bringing up 'Google', she typed in 'Hudson's Bay Company Archives' and clicked. The list filled the screen and she chose the 'Archives of Manitoba'. Reading meticulously, she learnt that the Hudson's Bay Company Archives, for the first two hundred-and-fifty years of its existence, had been added to the UNESCO Memory of World Register in 2007. She scrolled down, noting the contents of the Archives, a cornucopia of official records and ledgers, of ships' logs and journals, and of letters, both official and personal.

Eve spent some time navigating through the available online resources before, eventually, settling on a section about the contracts of the Hudson's Bay Servants. Searching for the relevant surname, she was rewarded with several hits: Thompson in its various spellings was a popular name. Narrowing it down to the mid-nineteenth century reduced the field, but disappointingly, there were no matches to the forenames Ada had provided.

Thwarted but not disheartened, Eva took a sip of tea. It was still warm, having started at boiling point, so her search had not taken up too much of her lunchtime. She clicked on the next list, that of the details of the Hudson's Bay Servants' recruitment, which recorded the men's names, the position they held, their place of origin, and in some cases, their age on joining the Company.

The first name she tried, produced no result so she typed in 'James Thompson' and a match popped up. A person with that name had been engaged in 1850 to be a labourer. Her heart started to hammer when she saw the place of origin, Walls. Taking out her notebook, she jotted down the details, closed the page, and googled Walls, just to confirm what she already knew—it was a port in the west of Shetland. The name had caught her eye when she had been studying the atlas. She returned to the details on the screen, leaned back in her chair, and sipped her tea which had cooled considerably.

'What are you doing?'

Lost in thought, Eve jumped at the sound of Aidan's voice, spilling some of the tea.

'Sorry, I startled you.'

'It doesn't matter. It's only water really.' She rubbed the wet splashes into her skirt and looked up to see Aidan peering over her shoulder.

'I didn't know you had the ancestry bug!'

She bristled at his tone, as Aidan had the ability to make a simple statement sound like a criticism. 'I haven't—I'm looking for one particular person.'

'That's okay, then?'

'I don't know why you are against people researching their family tree.'

'I'm not.'

'It doesn't sound like it.'

'Why are you so prickly this morning?'

Eve shrugged her shoulders and waited for Aidan to move towards the kettle. She re-read the information on the screen while he was making an instant coffee, heaping two spoonsful of sugar into it.

'You shouldn't have that much sugar. In fact, you shouldn't have any.'

'Yes, boss,' he replied and pulled a chair next to her. 'Let's see.'

Aidan read the details, noting the surname which meant nothing to him. 'Who's he?'

Eve turned towards him and admitted, 'I don't know. I'm searching for someone in the mid-nineteenth century who went to Canada from Shetland and could well be related to me—on my mother's side.'

Aidan took a bite of his sandwich and eyed her quizzically through his rimless spectacles, his warm hazel eyes full of humour. 'Not what I expected!'

Eve told him about the box and its contents and her determination to find who had sent the valentine.

Aidan looked back at the screen. 'Do you think that's him?'

She explained about her DNA story and the connection to Lerwick and Unst, pointing out that the capital was on the east coast and that Unst was the most northerly island. 'The yellow blobs were definitely over them.'

Aidan raised his eyebrows. 'You wasted a hundred quid to find that out!'

'It was a present,' she countered, negating to mention that, initially, she had not been impressed with the findings. 'Anyway, why are you being snippy—don't deny it?'

'I think you should look to the future, not to the past,' he said, being serious for once. 'DNA testing can reveal all sorts of hidden family secrets.'

Eve regarded her friend. They did so much together; concerts at the Baltic, theatre visits to the Theatre Royal and the Empire, cinema trips to see the latest releases and she had stood and cheered him on as he ran towards the finishing line in the last three Great North Runs, yet they never discussed anything of consequence.

'What do you mean?'

He was evasive. 'You know.'

She wondered whether he was speaking personally or generally but decided not to pursue it. She glanced at the clock on the wall. She had seven minutes left before she needed to relieve Jennie on the front desk.

'I have one more name to try.'

Distracted by Aidan and in a hurry, Eve did not type in Gideon Thompson with the same flutter of expectation as she had with the others. The match showed up instantly, almost without her registering it: one of one out of over five thousand plus names.

She did a double-take and then read the information slowly: Gideon Thompson; aged nineteen years; 1849; Blacksmith; Lerwick.

Eve sat motionless, stunned. Aidan followed her line of sight.

'Bingo?'

'Bingo!' she shouted, raising her arms and nearly whacking Aidan in the face.

As the afternoon passed, Eve started to doubt whether she had actually found her ancestor. Surely it had been too easy? How many Shetlanders had that name? Was she jumping to conclusions based on very few facts? What should she do next? Where should she start? These questions buzzed in her brain until the end of the day when Aidan found her, once again, in the office at the computer.

'I thought you'd left.'

'No, I'm doing the evening shift tonight for Jennie, we swapped last week,' she replied, without taking her eyes from the screen.

'What are you reading about now?'

'I need more evidence to prove I've found the correct person.'

Aidan started to put his coat on and was fastening the zip when Eve instructed, 'Look.' He leaned over reading as she continued, 'There is much more information available on microfilm than online.'

'Where are these archives,' he asked, still checking the screen.

'Winnipeg.'

'And you are just going to nip over to Winnipeg and do some research?'

'Yes,' she confirmed, her eyes alight with possibilities.

'You would just go?' he repeated, his voice laced with doubt. In the four years he had worked with Eve and had become her friend, he had never known her to do anything impulsive.

'I know what you're thinking!'

'You do?'

'That I won't go—I'm too timid.'

'I would never call you timid—steady, cautious, or even, unadventurous, perhaps.'

'Aren't the last two the same?'

'No—there are nuances.' He said, with great authority.

'Anyway, I have worked it out. I've been thinking about it all afternoon. Mum had a friend in Canada, an old school friend, I believe. She wrote a lovely letter when Mum died, all about when they were young, and she invited me to come to Canada for a holiday.'

'People always say things like that but they probably don't mean it.'

'Stop being so cynical.'

Aidan pulled a face. 'Where does she live, this friend?'

'Calgary.'

'That's in the west. Winnipeg is in the centre—and it's a huge country.'

'I can get an internal flight. I've looked it up. There are several flights a day—it takes about two to three hours. I can't work it out exactly because of the time zones.'

'When did you find this out?'

'In my tea break this afternoon.'

'You have been busy!'

'Yes.'

'You've made your mind up, haven't you?'

'Yes, I can stay with Anne for a holiday and have a few days in Winnipeg to break it up. I have three weeks' leave owing.'

Her excitement was infectious. Aidan chuckled and gave her a friendly pat on the shoulder. 'Go for it, Cummins!' were his parting words.

After he had left, Eve followed the instructions on the screen and composed an email to the Archives of Manitoba explaining her quest. She glanced at her watch, it would be mid-morning in Winnipeg.

Three hours later, Ruth Henig, sitting at the reception desk in the hushed public room of the Archives on Vaughan Street, glanced around at the handful of researchers lost in a bygone world. All was quiet, nobody needed her help. She opened the 'Enquiries' emails and one popped up from the UK. She read it carefully, walked over to the shelves which lined one wall and pulled out a drawer. '1849; Gideon Thompson,' she reminded herself as she searched for the relevant roll of microfilm.

NINE

June 2019

Eve sat rigidly, her eyes riveted on the blank screen in front of her now the safety video had ceased. Once she was in the air she knew she would relax but the take-off still had the power to unnerve; the thrust of the engines and the steep climb to cruising height, the clunk of the wheels being retracted, and the dizzying view through the window glimpsed out of the corner of her eye. Determined to see as much as she could on the journey, Eve had deliberately reserved a window seat. The plane would fly over the North Atlantic, Greenland, Baffin Island, and Hudson Bay before crossing swathes of land on a journey of just under nine hours. Eve braced herself against the back of the seat, her thoughts turning to Gideon Thompson and his voyage. What would he have endured?

York Factory
August 1849
Dear Grizzel,

I trust you are in good health. As promised, I have writ you a letter which I trust will be one of many. I know that it will be nigh on a year afore you read this but I thought to tell you about my journey afore I forget it.

We set sail from Stromness on the first day of July, having waited for a fair wind to set us on our way through Hoy Sound. There was much lamentation as we left with the gathered crowd on the shore waving hats and handkerchiefs. There was more than one pair of eyes filled with tears as we said our goodbyes. I was heartened to have Robbie Dunbar by my side and I thought of you, Grizzel, at home in Lerwick.

As Shetlanders, Robbie and I berthed with the crew and took our turn climbing aloft to set and furl the sails. We were glad of this as it kept us warm when we weren't tramping the decks to keep out the cold. The only fire is in the cook's caboose on the deck, although the finer folk can enjoy a small fire in the saloon, I believe. There is so much gunpowder on board that it is unsafe to have more fires.

You may be interested in the finer folk. Among the better sort who travelled with us on the "Prince Rupert" were two clergymen, one with his daughter, a young man who is the son of a chief factor and Dr John Brown who is the ship's surgeon. He hails from Lerwick so he may be beknown to you. There are also some educated men who are to take up positions as clerks in the Company and will travel on further with us servants.

I did not want for food, Grizzel, and enjoyed fresh meat as, under the longboat, there were pens for pigs and sheep as well as coops for fowl. Nor did I need the ministrations of Dr Brown as we were provisioned with lime juice to prevent us developing scurvy. There was also a goodly supply of liquor.

Two weeks after we departed from Orkney, we reached Cape Farewell in Greenland. The sea was very choppy as three cross swells meet there. Betwixt the strong currents from the Atlantic and those from the east and west coasts of Greenland, the ship pitched and tossed. Later we endured a gale from the north and water got into the bunks. Shortly afterwards I saw my first iceberg.

Grizzel, icebergs are impressive but dangerous as you will know. Perhaps you do not know that they are usually bluish-grey and rather dirty looking. Once we reached this part of the voyage, we hoisted the crow's nest to the mainmast head so that the lookout could spot them. Some icebergs appeared to be a mile long. Think of that, Grizzel. Now our journey became extremely uncomfortable, cold, and foggy with ice as far as the eyes could see, which at times, was truly little. We were glad of our ship's iron cladding as she inched her way through the floes, her masts and decks rimed with ice.

You can understand our delight when, six weeks out of Stromness, we entered Hudson Bay. No longer was there ice, but a beautiful sea, smooth and green. We sailed across this magnificent water for eleven days until we came to York Factory.

Of my new home, I will say little as I write to you almost on arrival. Nevertheless, I will tell you the two things I have noticed the most, mosquitoes and the scent of spruce.

It will be a surprise to you that I do not write as I speak. For several months, I have been perusing the Reverend Murray's grammar book which he has kindly allowed me to bring to Rupert's Land. Be assured that this letter is sent to you, Grizzel, with best wishes from

Gideon Thompson

It was nine o'clock Calgary time, when Eve had finally cleared customs and collected her baggage. The artificial light was harsh on her tired eyes and she felt disorientated with exhaustion. While waiting, she had tried to estimate how many hours she had been awake but failed, her befuddled brain refusing to calculate the number. All she could do was remember arrival and departure times just in case she wanted to work it out later. Aidan would be interested. He had picked her up at five in the morning for the early flight from Newcastle, his familiar face helping to allay her nerves as he encouragingly waved goodbye. She had spent what seemed an interminable eight hours at Heathrow, where the designer shops of Terminal Five did little to alleviate her anxiety before she left for Canada.

Eve walked into the Arrivals Hall to be greeted by two smiling figures holding a placard on which her name was hastily scribbled. Swiftly enfolded into Anne Lennon's welcoming arms, while her husband, Andrew, grabbed Eve's luggage, the weary traveller was whisked off to the Lennons' truck and driven through the fading light to their home on the outskirts of the city, where she, thankfully, collapsed into bed.

Eve woke the next morning to the delicious aroma of freshly made coffee.

'Hi, honey! Are you up?' called Anne from the base of the stairs as she heard Eve's door open. 'Don't worry—come down as you are. Andrew is making pancakes.'

Unaccustomed to being a guest, Eve apprehensively descended the stairs reminding herself that Anne had been one of her mother's oldest friends and that, although she was a stranger, they shared the bond of both having loved her.

'Come, sit down, honey,' invited Anne as she pulled out a chair. 'Did you sleep well?' she inquired as she handed Eve a mug of steaming coffee.

'Yes, thank you,' Eve replied, eyeing the large number of pancakes Andrew was lifting off the griddle.

'There,' he said, passing her a plate.

Eve was hungry but the stack of pancakes was high. She valiantly worked her way through them: they were delicious, topped with maple syrup and perfectly crisped Canadian bacon. Anne sat opposite her with a mug of coffee, watching her eat.

'That was wonderful,' Eve said, truthfully. 'Normally I make do with a slice of toast.'

'You want toast?' Andrew hurried towards the bread bin.

'No, no,' Eve answered emphatically, with a hint of panic in her voice. 'The pancakes were quite sufficient, thank you.'

'Andrew, love, I think Eve's eaten her fill.' Anne rolled her eyes towards the kitchen table.

He came to join them. 'What would you like to do today, Eve?'

Their guest hesitated a second. 'We have several activities planned,' announced Anne, without waiting for Eve's reply.

She laughed. 'Show me everything. But leave enough for me to see when I come back.'

Andrew clapped his hands. 'Ready in half-an-hour?'

It was an hour before Eve had unpacked, showered, and made herself presentable, but that first morning, set the tone for the three days she was to stay with the Lennons before she flew to Winnipeg. She enjoyed her visit immensely as they were excellent hosts. Both in their mid-seventies, Anne and Andrew were sprightly and full of enthusiasm, taking Eve to the top of the Calgary Tower where she saw the majestic vista of the snow-capped Rockies, to the Glenbow Museum, and to the Heritage Park. On the final day, Andrew drove them out to Banff and Lake Louise.

Eve had appreciated her time so much with the couple that it was with genuine sadness that she wished them goodbye at Calgary Airport. She knew she would see them on her return, but uncertain of how long she would stay in Winnipeg, she had purchased a single ticket.

The scene that greeted Eve that lunchtime reminded her of a British bus station. The Internal Departures Hall was packed with people moving purposefully; businessmen and women, older people, and couples with only young children as it was a school day. Several passengers had pets with them, mostly dogs, which seemed to be allowed on the plane with their owners. Eve stood for a moment, getting her bearings, and taking a deep breath before she wound her way forward.

The Lennons had explained to Eve about the automated system—how she would need to print off her boarding card and luggage label—and she had assured them that, as a librarian, she was technologically savvy. Anyway, when she arrived in Calgary there had been several elderly people dressed in red and white western wear who were on hand to help travellers: two of them welcomed her as she left the plane.

Eve looked around the Departures Hall, trying to spot a red and white uniform in the melee but to no avail, so she made for the nearest machine and started to read the instructions. She tried keying in her details and nothing happened. They appeared to be invalid. She pressed 'cancel' and started again. Still no success. Eve glanced at her watch, she had left plenty of time for check-in as she hated being under pressure, so she told herself to be calm and try again. After the third attempt failed, her hands started to tremble.

'Do you need help, ma'am?'

Eve swung round, expecting a neat pensioner in red and white, and almost collided with another traveller. She looked up as the man was tall, although compared to her most men were tall, and met a pair of amused eyes just visible under the brim of his cowboy hat.

'Help me?'

'You seem mighty agitated, ma'am.'

Flustered, she started remonstrating. 'I'll get it right soon.'

He stood, exuding an aura of calm, completely silent.

Eve, whose guilty secret was a predilection for flicking through the romance section when the library was quiet in the evening, had read about twinkling eyes but she had never witnessed the phenomenon.

He continued to study her as if time were irrelevant and neither of them had a plane to catch.

She capitulated first. She stepped back from the machine. 'Thank you.'

She handed him her e-ticket. 'Winnipeg,' he said, and in an embarrassingly short time, he had printed off her boarding card, slapped a luggage label on her case, and had pointed her in the direction of the baggage drop-off.

'Thank you,' she replied, torn between humiliation and relief.

He nodded his head imperceptibly, touched the brim of his hat, and was quickly swallowed up in the milling crowd.

Ten

When Joel Baxter had seen a woman in the Departures Hall struggling to print off her boarding card he had assumed, by her clothes, that she was middle-aged. Her hair was completely covered, from the back, by one of those hats British tourists of a certain age tend to wear on sunny days in the Rockies, and her sensible sandals, just visible beneath a skirt which, due to the stature of its wearer, fell well past her calves, were similar to those his mother favoured. The mismatched outfit was completed by a denim jacket, smartly cut and modern, yet it managed to be the opposite due to a white blouse which hung a good ten centimetres below its hem.

His surprise and subsequent amusement when she swung round and almost winded him was, in part, the result of his lucky escape, as he had swiftly stepped back, but mainly because he was mistaken. She was young, easily younger than him, and very fetching in a dizzy, dishevelled way. What hair he could see from the tendrils which framed her face, was fair and wavy, while the eyes which were assessing him were of a blue so dark, they were almost indigo. He found the conflict in them, between choosing independence and accepting his help, beguiling so he allowed himself to stand silently and watch. Her face was like an open book and the smile she eventually bestowed on him as he handed her the boarding card embodied the perfect combination of thanks and embarrassment.

By the time Eve reached the waiting area next to the departure gate, there was not a free seat in sight. Too weary to stand for the next hour, as suddenly jet lag and her three hectic days were catching up with her, Eve leant against the wall. From habit, she reached into the pocket of her flight bag and retrieved her book. She tried to read it but felt her eyes drooping.

'Good book?'

She looked up with a start. It was the cowboy, still sporting his hat.

Instead of answering his question, she asked the first thing which came to mind. 'Do you always keep your hat on?'

'Until I get on the plane, ma'am.'

Uncertain about continuing the conversation, Eve glanced down at her hands clutching the book. She was about to tell him about it when he asked his own question.

'What about your hat?'

Believing that he was laughing at her, Eve whipped off the offending article, freeing her mass of unruly curls. She had begun to hate it: every time she had caught a glimpse of her reflection this holiday, Lara's words came back to haunt her. It was true, she did have a roundish face, but her niece's comment that the hat made her look like Winston Churchill had stung. However, it had been too late to buy a new hat and Eve had never bothered about what she looked like. Until now.

Chastened by her reaction, he held out his hand. It was large and callused. 'Sorry, ma'am. I meant no disrespect.'

Eve held out hers. His apology appeared genuine.

'Joel Baxter,' he said.

'Eve Cummins,' she said as he firmly shook her hand.

He smiled, crinkling the corners of his eyes.

'You look as if you could use a sit-down.'

'If only,' replied Eve, gesturing towards the full seats.

'Come with me?'

She hesitated, checking the desk which showed no sign of any boarding activity.

'It's not far.'

She followed him, at a distance, to the next but one departure gate which, when she looked back over her shoulder, had a view of theirs.

He sat down in the nearest seat of the empty area. 'The flight to Regina has just boarded.'

'You've done this before!'

'More times than I can remember, ma'am.'

'Eve,' she corrected. 'Ma'am makes me feel as if I'm a hundred years old or the Queen!' This, she felt, was unreasonable as he was older than her. It was hard to work out his age. His face was weathered with deep lines fanning out from his eyes, caused by too much squinting in the sun, but his build was youthful and athletic. He could have been thirty-five or fifty or any age in between.

He laughed. 'You're obviously British.'

'Yes,' she affirmed, deliberately choosing a seat opposite him.

He leaned back and rested one leg across his thigh, totally relaxed, giving Eve a glimpse of his finely tooled leather boot.

Eve stared at its pointed toe and square heel and then at its owner. She had rarely met anyone who seemed so comfortable in his own skin.

'You on holiday, Eve?' he asked conversationally.

'In a way, yes.'

He waited, she paused, he was in no hurry.

'I'm on a quest.'

'That's a new one.'

Eve took a moment to consider her answer, her search for Gideon Thompson had started to feel personal and she was reluctant to be too candid. She had told the Lennons the minimum, explaining that she was doing some research on her family tree, and they had queried no further. Yet, inexplicably, the man sitting in front of her, although a stranger, elicited a frankness which she had never shared.

'I found a valentine in a box of family items my cousin left me. It was old with, to me, a heart-wrenching message. I desperately want to know who sent it, or even if it was sent, and I think the person who wrote it was in Canada.'

'Why do you think that?'

'It was decorated with animals which looked like bears. We don't have bears in Britain.'

'The US has bears. It could have been there.'

'I don't think so. I found a Hudson's Bay blanket in the box—also old and very worn.'

'You want to find this guy?'

'Yes—I already have a clue.'

'How come?'

'I found the name of a young man in the Hudson's Bay Archives online and I think he could be my ancestor. I wrote to them and an archivist called Ruth Henig contacted me. She did some initial research on my behalf. I'm going to see her tomorrow.' Eve finished her explanation with a wide smile, unaware that she had been leaning forward in her enthusiasm.

'You've come a long way.'

'I know,' she said softly, almost to herself.

'You should visit the Manitoba Museum on Rupert Avenue—it has a great Hudson's Bay gallery including a replica ship.'

To his further delight, she opened her shoulder bag and took out a small notebook before spending what seemed a considerable time to him, scrabbling around in the bag for a pen.

'Where's the museum again?'

'Rupert Avenue.'

'Can I walk from the Archives?'

He glanced down at her sturdy sandals, 'Yes,' he said, with marked assurance.

Eve ignored the action, determined to make use of his local knowledge. 'Where else should I go?'

'Lower Fort Garry—it was the Hudson's Bay Company's headquarters in the middle of the nineteenth century.'

'Is it in the city?'

'No, it's about thirty kilometres north. You'll need to take the bus.'

He noticed the quick and efficient way she jotted the information down, using very few words. 'There are other attractions in Winnipeg.'

Eve looked up from her writing, flashed him a polite but slightly dismissive smile, and repeated, 'I am on a quest.'

'Surely that is no reason to miss out on Winnipeg's highlights,' he pointed out before listing other museums and galleries; Chinatown, The Forks, and St Boniface with a short explanation about each one.

She put the pad and pen down. 'I'm only there for a short time—a week or so at the most.'

He changed position, stretching his legs out in front of him, and pointed in the direction of their gate, 'Boarding is about to start.'

Eve gathered up her things in a flurry. 'Take your time,' he said, his eyes twinkling. 'There's no rush.'

She met his eyes. 'Nice meeting you, Eve,' he said, touching his hat.

As she turned to go, Eve realised she knew nothing about him. Unusually for her, she had talked and her companion had listened, and in

Joel's case, he had listened with apparent enjoyment. Emboldened, she asked the question which had been on the tip of her tongue.

'Are you a real cowboy?'

'Yes, ma'am,' he chortled. 'There are real cowboys in Alberta.'

As soon as she had spoken, Eve was overcome with mortification. Fortunately, she did not see him again to speak to, although, once on the plane, she could see him across the aisle from her, four rows forward. As soon as the plane was cruising, he adjusted his seat, tilted his hat over his eyes, and appeared to sleep for the entire journey.

On landing, transit was so much quicker without customs' control, and as soon as Eve had collected her bag, she made for the hotel's shuttle bus stop. She had chosen to stay in the city centre, ideally placed near the Archives. Unable to stop herself, she scanned the crowd for a glimpse of a tall man in a cowboy hat, but when she saw him, she turned away swiftly. He was being kissed by an elegant woman with dark cropped hair, on both cheeks in the French way, while a boy of about nine was hopping excitedly from foot to foot next to her.

Eve woke bright and early the following morning, full of anticipation. After a delicious breakfast of fruit, yoghurt, and croissants, she walked the short distance to the Archives. Ruth Henig's email had told her how to prepare for her visit, explaining that she would need to leave her bag in a locker in the entrance next to the security guard, and that she must not wear perfume. She had her passport with her, as photo ID was needed to allow her to register as a first-time researcher, and a USB pen drive so that she could scan from the microfilm. The guard was just opening the front door when she arrived.

By noon, Eve had made significant progress. After making contact with Ruth, she had seen Gideon Thompson's entry in the Northern Department servants' engagement register and also the record of his salary in the Northern Department abstracts of servants' accounts for 1849. In both of these, he was described as a blacksmith from Lerwick. In that year, he had earned twenty-three pounds and five shillings which would have been a substantial amount of money compared to the six pounds he probably had made the previous year at home. Eve glanced at her watch. As she was only allowed one retrieval at a time, she would need to wait until after lunch before she could request the accounts for 1850, so she decided to go in search of a sandwich.

Eve collected her bag, had a few words with the guard who had once visited England, and stepped outside into brilliant sunshine. The light was so bright that she shaded her eyes and failed to see a tall figure, patiently waiting on the sidewalk.

'Howdy, Eve,' said a familiar voice.

She lifted her eyes from rummaging in her bag for her sunglasses. She knew what she was going to say. 'Hello, real cowboy,' she replied, having decided to embrace her embarrassment and turn it to her advantage. She could be humorous too. It seemed totally natural that he should be there.

'Thought you could use a coffee after all that beavering in the Archives.'

'Where's your hat?'

He laughed. 'Didn't bring it into the city, but seeing this sun, I might have made a mistake.' He ran his hand over his hair which was cut close to his head. 'I miss it.'

'We'd better find some shade then.'

'When do you want to get back?'

Torn between spending some time with him and returning to the Archives to look at the years following 1849, Eve was uncertain how to answer. She decided to be noncommittal. 'Why do you ask?'

'Depends how far you want to walk.'

'I want to go somewhere interesting.'

'Great—we'll go to the Forks.'

Joel led the way, chatting as he went, cutting through several streets until they crossed Main Street, skirted the Museum for Human Rights, and ended up in the busy plaza next to the Forks Market, by which time, they had covered Eve's accommodation, her initial impression of Winnipeg, and the morning's research.

Eve looked around her. 'Where exactly are we?' She knew he had mentioned the place but it was not what she had imagined.

'At the junction of the Red and Assiniboine rivers. In the early days, this is where the Red River Settlement started.'

'Oh,' she said, thinking that perhaps Gideon Thompson had stood on this very spot. She turned a full three hundred-and-sixty degrees slowly, determined to commit everything she saw to memory.

'Eve,' he called, to attract her attention. 'We need to grab a table. We can explore later.' Spare tables were clearly at a premium.

Joel sat down and waved her over. It was half in the shade so he had politely left the cooler side for her, she noticed. 'I'm having a burger.'

Eve looked at the menu, the invite was obviously not just for coffee. 'I think I'll have a salad.'

He looked at her keenly. 'You're not vegetarian?' There was a touch of reproach in his voice.

'No—I just fancy a salad.'

'That's okay then.'

She looked at him quizzically, and then asked, 'How come you know your way around Winnipeg so well?'

'I went to UW.'

'UW?'

'University of Winnipeg.'

It was not the answer she expected. Reading her face, he said, 'Don't you think cowboys go to school?'

She started to flounder, he sat back and relished her discomfort, amusement dancing in his eyes. Eventually, he relented. 'I studied Environmental Studies and Sciences concentrating on forest ecology, policy, and management. I used to work for Parks Canada but then my dad got sick and I had to return to the ranch.'

Her sympathy showed in her eyes. 'I can relate to that. I had to abandon my studies when my mum became ill. I was the youngest daughter, the only one without a family of her own.'

Wanting to concentrate on the present, not the past, Joel moved the conversation forward. 'What did you study then?'

'Classics.'

He looked at her with interest, causing Eve to continue. 'I'd just finished my master's and was planning on continuing with a PhD.'

'What were you researching?'

'Are you really interested?'

'Sure.'

'A poet—Cornelius Gallus. He was a love poet and we only have seven lines of his work. He's mentioned by other poets like Virgil and Ovid who acknowledged his influence.'

'Why is there so little of his work remaining?'

'That's an intriguing question. He fell out of favour with the emperor. He was forced to commit suicide by Augustus.'

'You did good?' He expected her to answer in the affirmative.

Eve just nodded.

'How good?' he probed, wanting to see her reaction.

'The best,' she admitted, a becoming blush tinting her pale complexion.

His face split into a triumphant grin, the sun burnishing his hair to the colour of the shiniest conker as it danced across his face, picking out the red in his stubble.

His delight was infectious and Eve found herself laughing, almost uncontrollably, shedding her cares, some of which she had carried with her for years until she had come to this moment. Sitting in a sun-drenched plaza, in a foreign country, with a man she felt she had known all her life.

They sobered as the waitress brought them their meals and they turned their attention to eating. Eve watched Joel's large hands as he picked up his burger and took a bite. There was no wedding ring; perhaps ranchers considered rings a hazard? Why was he being so friendly? Everyone she had met in Canada, so far, had been courteous and kind. She suppressed the niggle of the woman who had greeted him at the airport: Eve had skimmed through enough romantic novels on her quiet evenings in the library, to know that jumping to conclusions always caused misunderstandings. Then she chided herself for thinking of romance. It beggared belief. She was only in Winnipeg for a matter of days and had no intention of being diverted from her purpose. Enjoy the moment, she told herself and ask about the woman at a suitable opportunity.

After lunch, they wandered down to the meeting of the waters. Joel pointed to the Red River. 'Traders could come all the way from Hudson Bay via Lake Winnipeg, then travel west along the Assiniboine to reach the plains.'

'For furs?'

'Yes.'

'Where would the recruits land in Hudson Bay?'

'York Factory, or Churchill perhaps.'

Eve turned a full circle again, trying to absorb everything, totally unaware of the pleasure on her face. He watched her closely. 'What do you want to do now? We could climb the Forks Market tower. You'll get a great view of the city.'

'What else do you know about the Hudson's Bay Company?'

'Not a lot but I do know someone who does.'

'Can I meet them?'

'Wait a moment.' Joel took out his mobile. 'Are you free tomorrow night, Eve?' he asked as he scrolled down his contacts. She nodded and moved away to give him some space. The phone conversation was brief but appeared to be successful. He gave her a thumbs up.

'What's happening?'

'We're meeting a couple of friends of mine. Rach is a historian in the Archaeology and History Branch of Parks Canada. Her husband, Phil, was my roommate at UW. You'll like them.'

'When?'

'Tomorrow at seven? We can have dinner.'

'Can we eat at my hotel?' Eve asked, caution returning.

'Of course,' he said easily.

'I'll book a table for four then?'

'Book?' he queried.

She remembered what Anne had told her. 'I mean I'll reserve a table for four.'

'Great,' he replied, taking out his phone again to message the details to Phil.

Eve delved into her bag and found her phone. She snapped a couple of photos of the river and waited for Joel to finish. 'I'd better have your number in case anything crops up,' she said handing him the phone.

'Sure thing,' he said, and typed the digits into her contacts. He messaged himself. 'All set.'

'Look at the time,' Eve exclaimed, as she started to close her phone. She held it up for Joel to see. It was well after three. 'The Archives close at four.'

'Jeez, I've gotta go.'

It was not the answer she had expected or hoped for. 'Go, now?'

'Yeah. I didn't realise we'd been so long.' He ran his hand across his hair. 'I'm so sorry. Can you get back to your hotel?'

'Yes, of course. I have a map,' Eve replied, trying to keep her voice neutral.

'I can't be late. I promised Nate I'd pick him up from school.'

'Nate?'

'My son.'

Eve plastered a smile on her face. 'Thank you for lunch,' she said, as he had insisted on paying.

He smiled back at her; his smile reaching his eyes unlike Eve's. 'It was swell,' he said. 'Don't forget, seven tomorrow.'

And he was gone, hurrying towards the Provencher Bridge.

Eleven

Eve wandered back to her hotel slowly, trying to quash her feeling of dissatisfaction. She told herself that she had enjoyed a fruitful morning, eaten lunch with an interesting companion, and had the promise of learning more about the Hudson's Bay Company the following day. She meandered through the Union Station, recommended in her guidebook because of its Beaux-Arts design, and then crossed to the small park opposite where she studied a stone gateway which appeared to be all that remained of Upper Fort Garry, the fort in the centre of the Red River Settlement. From there, it was a short walk to her hotel.

Once she was in her room, Eve kicked off her sandals and lay on the bed, mulling over the day in great detail. After apparently staring at the ceiling for a while, she rolled over, pulled her bag towards her, and took out her phone. She looked at the two photos she had taken of the Red River, and then, as if a switch had been flicked, she jumped off the bed and opened her laptop. In no time, Eve had a map on the screen. Joel had said that goods arriving at Hudson Bay could travel all the way to Winnipeg or rather the Red River Settlement by boat. She traced her finger from York Factory on the edge of the Bay, following the rivers south until she came to Lake Winnipeg, and wondered if Gideon Thompson had made that journey.

Norway House
September 1849
Dear Grizzel,

As you can see, only one month has passed since I last writ you. It seems strange to me that you will receive all of my letters at once.

I am at Norway House on the shore of Lake Winnipeg, four hundred miles south of York Factory, after a journey of three weeks. It is here that I will find out my destination. Some of us will winter at Norway House before going into the interior, while others will continue on to the Red River Settlement.

Before I tell you of my journey, Grizzel, which was the hardest I have ever undertaken, I will describe to you York Factory, from where I writ my first letter. The fort is situated five miles from the mouth of the Hayes River. The site is damp and boggy, with moss being predominant. As I said in my letter, the mosquitoes are particularly troublesome. All of the buildings are constructed out of logs except for the powder magazine which is made of stone. The area within the pickets is large, about five acres, and all manner of things are made here. Outside of the pickets, there is a boatbuilding and repair yard and I thought I might be assigned to the forge here. But it was not to be.

You should see my new clothes, Grizzel. I cut a fine figure compared to how you used to see me. I have a blue pilot cloth pea jacket and trousers, and for outerwear, a warm blanket capote. It is white in colour, faced with blue and piped with scarlet. I have a pair of sturdy boots and a pair of hide moccasins which are not unlike our rivlins. As I think of you and write, there is much noise. The Highland recruits and the voyageurs are dancing with the local women, the Crees. Someone is playing the fiddle. It is a merry tune. The Highlanders call Robbie and I staid as we do not join in the fun. The Crees are a very friendly helpful nation, often given to laughter and they chatter to the Highlanders who seem to quickly understand them. We are left out because we do not understand Gaelic.

We left York Factory on the sixth day of September in a brigade of five inland boats. These boats are called York Boats and are modelled on our Shetland sixareens so I felt very much at home. I set off with great excitement, unaware of the trials of the journey ahead. In our boat, there were two gentlemen recruits who were to be clerks, two Crees, the native tripmen, and Robbie and myself. We also had cargo. All manner of items for the needs of the forts and for the settlement. Nails and tacks are worth more than their weight in gold in the interior and we also carried cups and bowls, blankets, capotes, and shirts. All the goods are divided into separate bundles and spread amongst the boats so that, if one bundle is lost through damage by water or wreck, a variety of goods still reaches its destination. We also had some mail and documents from home as the packet boat arrived at York Factory shortly after our ship. It comes once a year and it is odd to think that, next year, I hope, there will be a letter for me, from you.

Robbie and I, and the two Crees, were the crew on our journey upstream. I will not bore you with too many details, but for much of the time, we towed the boat, first of all up the Hayes River. On the whole journey, there are thirty-four portages where we had to carry the cargo and pull the boats overland. Towing the boat is called tracking. Two of the crew track while the other two stay onboard. After half-an-hour we swap. The oars are only used when needed to cross the river to the bank which has the best footing. We waded through mud and bush and the mosquitoes and black flies were almost unbearable. I often wondered why I ever enlisted into the service, although I know it is because of the money. My hands became blistered and my feet cut by the rough stones. We were always jumping into the water to lift the boats over rocks. Some days, my clothes were permanently wet, and at the start of the journey, the water was icy cold and the weather inclement.

It is a good thing that the boats travel in a brigade as, when it comes to the portages, we work with the other crews. A single boat could not travel alone. The Crees are very good-natured and show Robbie and me the ropes. We toil from dawn to dusk, eighteen hours of labour and six hours rest. We eat pemmican which the Crees explained to us is dried buffalo meat, partially pulverised and then mixed with its own tallow. I find it not to my taste but I have been told that I will get used to it. Sometimes we are allowed flour bannocks baked with water and these are a treat as, once we are in the interior, flour is also more valuable than gold. So betwixt the tacks and the nails and the flour, Grizzel, you can see that actual gold has less value here. One saving grace is the strong black tea which warms my heart and reminds me of home.

Once we left the Hayes River and then the Steel River, we no longer had to track but had to contend with the swift rapids on the Hill River which caused me much alarm. I consider myself an able sailor but I have never experienced such water. At one point, Morgan's Portage, the river, was almost a mile wide, and there are many low-lying islands in it. When we crossed the portage, the crews carried all the cargo and the gentlemen recruits did help for a change, they carried the oars.

As we journeyed south, the bush turned to larger trees, some of them beautiful in their autumn colours. Eventually, we came to two lakes where we could use the sail, and we did so with much relief. After the first days in the north, we were fortunate as the weather stayed mild for the time of year and we did not have too many nights camping in the rain.

Now I am here, Grizzel, and think of you with fondness, I wish I were dancing with you this evening. Please forgive my scribbling as I have no table on which to rest. My knees must suffice.

Gideon Thompson

After she had finished tracing the route on the map, Eve checked the time. It was later than she expected so she showered and changed. As she was towelling her hair, her phone bleeped. Rushing to pick it up, she was disappointed to see that it was Aidan, asking how her trip was going. Chiding herself for hoping it might be Joel apologising for rushing off, Eve sent a brief reply and then felt guilty. Aidan messaged every day with a few friendly words from home, usually when he was on the way back from work. Today he was late: it would be the early hours of the morning in England. Then she realised she had not replied to his previous message; he would be keen to know about her research in the Archives. Reluctant to explain about meeting Joel, but not acknowledging to herself the reason, Eve speedily texted a few details about Winnipeg and then she attached one of the photos she had taken at The Forks, before explaining that she was going to the Archives again the following day and would tell him more later.

The restaurant was quiet when she entered as it was still early. Before she was shown to her table, Eve made the reservation for the following evening feeling slightly uncomfortable that the group might be seen as two couples so she added that there may actually be five diners on the night. This did not appear to be a problem. Eve scanned the room, pleased to see that the waitress was leading her to a table against the wall. She was not alone in dining solo as, a few men, who looked like they were in the city on business, were dotted about the room. Unused to eating alone, Eve had brought a book just in case she felt self-conscious, but it lay unopened on the table for the entire meal.

Shortly after she had sat down and still while she was studying the menu, a middle-aged couple were shown to the table next to her. They struck up a conversation almost immediately introducing themselves as Kendra and Wallace: they were friendly, not intrusive, and gave her more advice on what to see while she was in Winnipeg. Several of the places Joel had already mentioned but many were new suggestions. Eve made a note to visit the Exchange District and the Old Market Square, the Royal Canadian Mint, the Manitoba Children's Museum, and the Legislative Building, and then, before she received any more options, she explained why she was in Winnipeg. Kendra Smith's reaction was enthusiastic. She was a genealogy buff herself and plied Eve with numerous questions, several of which Eve was unable to answer. At the end of the meal, after the Smiths had asked her to join them at their table for coffee, Kendra wrote down her phone number on the napkin and gave it to Eve.

'Look us up, honey,' she said, 'if you have time. Or need anything.'

Back in her room, Eve plonked herself on the oversized bed and keyed Kendra's number into her contacts. Then she sat back and took stock. In one day she had acquired more acquaintances than she had in the previous couple of years. She thought about the kindness of the Lennons, the open friendliness of Joel and Kendra and wondered whether being outgoing was a national characteristic. Her phone pinged, the sound unnaturally loud in the perfect quiet of the room. Her heart jumped. Perhaps it was Joel? She glanced down and was disappointed once again. It was Lara, asking which dustbin was due to go out the following morning. With a jolt, Eve realised that she had been away less than a week, and as she replied she realised how much she was enjoying her trip. In fact, enjoying it so much that she never questioned why her niece was messaging at four o'clock in the morning.

Twelve

Bright sunshine, escaping around the edges of the heavy curtains, played on the closed lids of Eve's eyes and forced her to stir. Feeling unnaturally tired, she was almost tempted to roll over but then she remembered where she was. She checked the clock on the bedside table: if she wanted to maximise her time, she needed to get going so, she flung back the covers, had a quick wash, and was down in the breakfast lounge within twenty minutes.

Eve had decided to be more adventurous that morning, eschewing the notion of repeating the previous day's breakfast, despite it having been very tasty. Many of the guests appeared to be enjoying, what her mother used to call, eggy bread topped with thin rashers of crispy streaky bacon. Eve progressed along the hot tureens, lifting various lids. She had worked her way along six of these before she realised there was a label next to each one, just as a waitress came up to her.

'Can I help you, ma'am?' she asked pointedly.

Flustered, Eve replied, 'I'd like a cup of coffee.'

The girl looked puzzled for a moment, and then turned and left.

Eve slid onto the nearest chair and placed her plate on the table. Then she realised she had forgotten to pick up some cutlery. She was just coming back to her seat when the waitress appeared with her coffee.

'Oh,' apologised Eve, 'I didn't mean for you to get it. I know there's a machine. I used it yesterday.'

The girl smiled at her. 'Just flown in, ma'am?'

Eve nodded an affirmative, embarrassed to admit that she had been in Canada for six days.

'From England?'

'Yes.'

'What part?'

'The North East.'

'Is that anywhere near Bristol?'

'No.'

'My grandma came from Bristol.'

'It's in the South West.'

'Oh, I thought you might know it. England being a small country.'

'No, I'm afraid I've never been to Bristol.'

The waitress stood for a moment, mulling over Eve's words. 'Are you on vacation?' she eventually asked.

Eve found herself explaining about visiting the Archives, mentioning Gideon Thompson in general terms. The girl appeared interested. 'Did he settle here?'

'I don't know,' replied Eve. 'I hope to find out.'

'Cool.'

Eve made an exploratory cut through her toast. As time passed it was looking less palatable. The waitress watched her, not in any hurry to move on, so Eve started to eat. The egg was flavoured with something sweet which she did not recognise nor was it to her taste.

'Good?' asked the girl.

Eve nodded again, not wanting to offend. She decided to eat the bacon.

'Think, you might have relatives here that you didn't know about.'

'I've never considered that possibility,' Eve responded. It was certainly food for thought.

The waitress smiled again, pleased with her suggestion. 'Have a nice day,' she said as she sashayed towards the tureens to check if they needed replenishing.

Eve hurried so that she reached the Archives just as the building opened. The security guard greeted her like an old friend, as did Ruth, and in no time at all, Eve was studying the microfilm of the servants' accounts for 1850. Immediately, she noticed a difference: whereas in 1849 it had stated, 'Fort to Change' in the district column next to Gideon's name, the following year it stated 'Saskatchewan'. Eve glanced over at the reception desk: Ruth was nowhere to be seen and her place was occupied by a colleague. She approached him. It took several seconds for him to look up and acknowledge her.

'Yes,' he said abruptly but not impolitely.

'Would you be able to help me with a query about the documents I'm studying?'

'I'll try.'

Eve started to explain but he rose from his position and waved her towards her monitor.

'What is it?'

Eve pointed to the column marked 'District' on the 1850 document. 'Look, it says 'Saskatchewan' here, and on the previous year's accounts, it said this.'

He looked at her notes. 'It means the person wasn't assigned anywhere yet.' The archivist studied all of the columns on the screen. 'In what capacity did he work for the Company?' The writing was faded. 'A blacksmith, I see. From Lerwick.' He turned to face her. 'Saskatchewan was one of the administrative districts for the HBC's fur trade. It was much larger than today's province and stretched all the way to the Rocky Mountains. There were several districts and their boundaries changed over time.' He glanced back at the desk. There was nobody waiting there. 'Do you have any more details about him?'

'Sorry, I know next to nothing. Would he stay in that district for all of his service?'

'Probably—it was a very large district.'

'Would I be able to find out which forts he was stationed in?'

'Not from these documents.'

Eve could not hide her disappointment.

The archivist glanced at the desk again. 'There is one thing we could try. We do have some lists of servants and their postings.' He invited her to follow him to the end of the room where the wall was lined with shelves. He took down a file and started looking through the pages.

'Look,' he said, pointing to a name. 'There was a James Thompson from Walls. Somebody has been here to research him'

'But no Gideon Thompson?'

'No, many of our records are incomplete. A lot haven't survived.'

As they spoke, another researcher was approaching the desk. 'I must get back. Look at the years up to 1854 and then you will at least see if he remains in the Saskatchewan District.'

'Thank you.'

Eve spent the rest of the morning scrolling through the microfilm of 1851 and 1852 and Gideon was still assigned to the same district. She noticed with satisfaction that his salary was increasing, year by year, and that he appeared to spend very little. She wondered how the accounting system operated and jotted down some questions she could ask Rach that evening.

Having worked through until mid-afternoon, Eve decided to call it a day. Her eyes were tired and her stomach was rumbling, and although she had planned an initial foray into the Manitoba Museum, once she was outside in the sunshine, the lure of more indoors had palled. Wandering down Vaughan Street towards Portage Avenue, which the security guard at the Archives had told her was the main shopping street, Eve opened the map she had found in the hotel's reception area. Highlighting all of the bookshops of Winnipeg, it was the equivalent of a treasure map to Eve. She could combine getting some exercise with more research. There were two second-hand bookshops within walking distance. She went into both, and an hour later, was the satisfied owner of three Canadian history books with sections on the nineteenth century.

By now, Eve realised she was very hungry, so she grabbed a quick cup of coffee and a sandwich in one of the malls on Portage Avenue and then made for her final stop of the day. She stood outside of the imposing building and studied the words across the façade. 'The Hudson Bay Company'. Half expecting, as part of a romantic notion, to be greeted by piles of blankets, furs, and the necessities of wilderness living, Eve actually found herself in a cosmetics hall which could have been transported home to Newcastle without anybody noticing the swap. There were the same perfume counters, the handbags and the gloves, and the list of departments and floors. For a moment, she imagined Gideon walking through the doors along with her. What would he think? Then she chided herself for her flight of fancy. She had only forty-five minutes before the store closed: she needed to stay focused.

Eve applied similar methods to those she used in her research to clothes' shopping. She knew what she was looking for, she had made a list, and she would recognise it when she saw it. She was also prepared for the unexpected. Following her plan, Eve walked at speed through the women's department, bypassing the expensive designer consignments unless there was a sale rail, weaving in and out of each clothes' stand. Searching for a particular colour, she would stop periodically, inspect the garment, and then move on. Eventually, when she was just about to admit defeat, she saw it: a simple cotton shift in bright turquoise, the colour which, according to her elder sister's fashion magazine, suited everyone. It was the perfect dress.

Back in the hotel, Eve assessed her appearance in the full-length mirror. She was inordinately pleased with her purchase, especially teamed with the toe-post sandals she had packed to serve as slippers, and for the first time, she acknowledged the notion that clothes could boost confidence. She glanced at her phone. Ten minutes to go until she was due to meet Joel. As she turned back to the mirror, ready to tie up her hair, the ping of a message arriving made her jump. He was waiting in the bar.

Joel stood up as she approached, and instead of feeling nervous, as she had expected, Eve experienced the sensation of déjà vu. He was so different yet so familiar.

'Howdy,' he said as his face broke into a wide smile. Instead of wearing the mismatched clothes she had worn on the two previous days, Joel watched Eve coming towards him in a neat shift dress. Uncertain whether he should compliment her on her appearance, Joel kept his peace. After all, he rather liked her disregard for fashion and was pleased to see that, despite the dress, she still appeared dishevelled. Her honey-coloured curls, instead of being scrunched up untidily on the top of her head, bounced in wild abandon onto her shoulders.

'Howdy,' she replied.

'Joel!' They both swung round to see a couple approaching. Eve appraised them with interest: a man's choice of friends said a great deal about him.

Joel and Phil shook hands, while Rach kissed Joel's cheek in a sisterly fashion. She addressed Eve before Joel had a chance to introduce her. 'Hi, I'm Rach,' she said, her eyes assessing Eve with open curiosity.

'And I'm her better half.' Phil's handshake was firm but gentle. 'I hear you picked this reprobate up at the airport.'

'Reprobate?' repeated Eve, already part of the banter. 'I'll take a rain check on that.'

'Let us know when you decide,' instructed Rach.

Joel stood impassively, waiting for them to finish. 'Let's eat,' he said.

The meal started well; Joel and Phil had a friendly debate about the quality of the steaks, and the three friends caught up with the news since

Joel had last been in Winnipeg. Eve was happy to listen and soak up the atmosphere.

After they had eaten their main course, Phil turned to Eve and said, 'Joel tells us you are researching some guy who worked for the HBC.'

'Yes, that's why I've come to Winnipeg.'

Rach looked up from studying the dessert menu. She glanced from Eve to Joel, who was sitting directly opposite her. 'Was I right in remembering that you can't request items for about an hour after eleven thirty in the Archives?'

Eve replied to Rach, missing the blush which coloured Joel's face. 'Yes.'

'It hasn't changed since I was at school,' stated Rach. 'I always went for lunch then.'

'I was ready for a break too. You can only look at so much microfilm,' commented Eve before she asked, 'Would you mind answering some questions for me, Rach?'

'Ask away.'

Phil held his head in his hands, jokingly. 'Let's order dessert first. Once Rach starts it'll be a long evening.'

'I'll have chocolate ice cream, thanks. Now, Eve, what do you want to know?'

Joel butted in. 'Eve?'

'I'd just like an espresso please.' Eve reached into her bag and pulled out her notebook. 'I believe my forebear was a blacksmith in the Hudson's Bay Company and I think I've found him in the Archives. He was assigned to the Saskatchewan District. Where is that?

'It's a very large area, stretching from just west of here all the way to the Rocky Mountains. It's interesting that you say he was a blacksmith. They were in demand and were paid more than other skilled tradesmen. In the major posts, blacksmiths had their own room while labourers and boatmen had to share.'

Eve jotted these points down.

'When was he here?' queried Rach.

'He signed up in 1849.'

'He would be in great demand. I know that in 1850 there was only a handful of blacksmiths serving so he would have to move around.'

'Where would he go?'

'I can give you the names of the forts in the Saskatchewan District. Give me your email and I'll send you them.'

Rach and Eve finished exchanging details just as the coffee and desserts arrived. Eve took a sip of her espresso. It was delicious, hot and strong.

'The Archives don't have a record of where Gideon was sent.'

'Is that his name?'

'Yes, Gideon Thompson.' Eve paused, took another sip of her drink, and asked, 'Could I visit the forts? They might have some information.'

'They might,' replied Rach, without enthusiasm.

'You don't think so?'

'Many of the forts no longer exist.'

'But some do?'

'Yes, some have been reconstructed.'

Rach watched Eve's face light up, and fleetingly, caught Joel's rapt expression before he composed his face, as she exclaimed, 'Then I could visit.'

'Do you have a car?'

'I can drive. But I haven't thought about a car.'

'You can't get anywhere easily by public transport. The distances are too vast. You would need to plan a trip with overnight stays.'

Eve's disappointment was tangible. 'How long are you here for?' asked Phil.

'Only about a week—maybe ten days. I expected to stay in Winnipeg.'

It seemed that topic of conversation was over. The four of them chatted for a while and then Joel announced, 'I'll get the check.'

There was some argument but Joel insisted on paying, it was his treat. While he went to the bar to settle up, Eve took the opportunity to visit the bathroom, as she was learning to call it. She had used the word 'loo' a couple of times earlier in the week to be faced with either total incomprehension or amusement.

When she returned, Joel was still at the bar, and as she was about to join Rach and Phil, who were sitting with their backs to her, Eve overheard the end of a conversation.

'That's a totally bizarre suggestion.'

'Why?' demanded Rach.

'It just is! He's just met her.'

'It's not. It's a great idea. He obviously likes Eve. She's the first woman we have seen him with since Colette.'

Eve doubled back and returned making more noise.

Rach looked up. 'What are you doing tomorrow evening, Eve?'

'No plans.'

'Come to ours.'

Eve did not have to think twice before she accepted.

'What are you three discussing?'

Phil looked up at Joel. 'Eve's coming to ours tomorrow.' Then he winked at Eve. 'I'll grill some steaks and show this Albertan cowboy just how good Manitoba beef can be.'

'Who said I was coming.'

'Suit yourself,' replied Phil.

Rach grinned at them all but she addressed Eve. 'I'll do some digging tomorrow and see if I can find out anything more for you.'

'Thank you.' There was an awkward moment. Who would make the first move? Eve felt panic rising and decided to be brave. She raised her eyes to Joel's. 'Will I see you tomorrow?'

'Of course, you will, Eve,' announced Rach, rather emphatically. 'He's visiting with us.'

Joel's eyes twinkled, creasing at the corners. 'I'll pick you up at seven.'

Thirteen

The following morning, when Eve switched on her phone, there were two messages for her. The first one, from Aidan, she skimmed quickly, laughing at the cartoon he had forwarded. Then, more carefully, she opened the second one. It was from Joel. Short and to the point, it asked whether she was free for lunch.

Eve sailed through the morning at the Archives. The large research room already felt like a second home as so much of it was similar to those she had visited whilst at university, and consequently, Eve had begun to question her lack of ambition over the three days she had been in Winnipeg. Why had she stayed working in the library while academia had always been her calling? She kept pushing the thought away and concentrated on the screen, scrolling until she found Gideon's name. Each time she came across it, she experienced a frisson of excitement mingled with frustration that she could not find more.

There was an extensive archive of photographs which she dipped into without too much expectation. Gideon had been in Rupert's Land at the dawn of photography and all those she looked at were at least a decade or two after he could have left. She peered at the grainy images of heavily bearded men who appeared indistinguishable. Perhaps, one day, she might come across a photo of him in later life and she would be able to see if the reality matched her imagination. Although, of course, it would be in black and white. In her mind's eye, she had started to see him: she had created a man of average height with a muscular body, especially his arms. She had given him light brown hair with a hint of sandiness and blue eyes set in a thin face. Had she but known, she was remarkably accurate.

Eve left the Archives full of anticipation, only to experience crushing disappointment. She looked left and then right. She scanned the sidewalk opposite. There was no sign of a tall figure. She checked her watch. They had agreed on noon and it was now five minutes past. She took out her phone. There was no message. Five more minutes passed and she was becoming increasingly agitated. Then she saw him walking casually towards her.

'Howdy,' he said, in his unhurried way.

'You're late,' Eve said, immediately wishing she had bitten her tongue rather than sounding accusatory.

If Joel was taken aback by her tone, there was no sign. He continued to regard her benignly, waiting without awkwardness. There was no apology.

'I thought you weren't coming,' she blurted out.

He looked at her, his eyes twinkling. 'Why would you think that?'

'You're late,' she said again.

'A few minutes,' he said reasonably. 'It can be difficult to judge the traffic.'

'I was worried.' Eve was appalled to hear a faint whine in her voice. She hated how this man made her feel. The weight of disappointment had been out of all proportion yet, four days ago, she had not known of his existence.

'Shall we start again?'

Eve nodded.

'Howdy, Eve.'

'Hello,' she replied, somewhat subdued.

Then Joel did apologise. 'Sorry,' he said. 'The traffic caught me out this morning.' He looked at her keenly. 'You know I'm more used to riding a horse than driving in a city.'

'I thought ranchers rode on those zippy things.'

He threw back his head and laughed. 'Zippy things—you mean quads?'

'Yes—we have them in Britain, too.'

'I do have zippy things, but usually, I ride a horse.'

She was interested, despite herself. 'Why?'

'Horses are much better with the cattle. A zippy thing can unsettle them.'

She smiled at him for the first time since he had arrived.

'Come on,' he said, 'something tells me you are hungry.'

They ate a quick lunch and then went to the Manitoba Museum. Together, they wandered through the Hudson's Bay Gallery. Eve spotted a chief's blanket with four end stripes of indigo, yellow, red, and green; she read about the Plains Cree and the value of the buffalo, the entire animal being put to use; she saw some pemmican, a mixture of buffalo meat and fat, which was a staple in both the Cree and the servants' diet. They took some time exploring a full-scale replica of the sailing ship whose voyage had led to the formation of the Company. The Nonsuch had an area of the gallery to herself and stood centre stage, surrounded by the reconstruction of a seventeenth-century port. Eve marvelled at the size of the vessel, envisioning her making the perilous voyage to Hudson Bay in pursuit of furs, and although she was from an earlier time than Gideon, Eve thought the ship that brought him to Rupert's Land would not have been too dissimilar.

Halfway through the afternoon, Joel turned to Eve and said, 'There could be a change of plans for this evening.'

The face she allowed him to see was totally expressionless, so out of character for her that, this time, Joel did feel wrong-footed. He hastily tried to clarify. 'I can still pick you up at seven.'

'Okay,' Eve replied, drawing out the word.

'But I was wondering if you'd like to come with me to pick up Nate from school?'

So unexpected was his question that she took a moment to respond. 'Where would we go then?'

'To Phil and Rach's.'

'Nate is coming too?'

'Yes—I have a surprise for him.'

'Okay, I'll come,' she said, more brightly.

An hour later, Joel drove into the suburb of St Boniface pointing out various points of interest to Eve. He leaned back in the seat of the truck, entirely relaxed, driving with only one hand on the wheel: a skill utterly alien to Eve who had been drilled to keep hold of the wheel in the 'ten-to-two' position. She was fascinated by his hand as he navigated a corner, confidently turning the wheel with the heel of his palm. He saw her watching him.

'This is the French Quarter—you'll hear many people speaking French.'

Eve studied the names above the shops and restaurants, noting the French names. 'Is this where the French-Canadians settled?'

'Yes.'

'And Nate lives here?'

'Yep—with his Mom and Jean-Claude.'

'That's a very French name.'

'He's from Quebec.'

Eve examined Joel's profile as he spoke but could ascertain no difference to his normal measured tones.

Not wanting to pry, Eve settled back to enjoy the rest of the drive, looking this way and that to make sure she missed nothing.

Nathaniel Baxter walked out of school solemnly and greeted Eve with a modicum of reserve after his father had introduced them. He was tall and slim, with deep brown eyes and a shock of hair the same colour. During the journey to reach Phil and Rach's house, the youngster managed to deflect all of his father's questions about the school day until, eventually, Joel gave up trying. Eve remained silent, biding her time. She liked children, had spent countless hours in the library running reading sessions, and was experienced enough to know when to give a child space.

Phil had already fired up the grill when they arrived, his cheerful face evidence of a man in his element. Fond of his beer and steak, Phil's solid figure was on the cusp of running to fat as its owner eyeballed forty. Rach had messaged to say she was running late but Phil, who worked from home, had chosen to finish early. He had brought forward the meal as Joel would need to take Nate home in good time.

'Come with me,' he invited Nate, 'while we wait on Rach.'

The boy looked dubious. 'You too,' added Phil, glancing round to Eve and Joel.

He led them to the other side of the house where a motorhome stood on the second drive. It was an impressive size. Joel rested his hands on Nate's shoulders.

'What do you think, bud?'

The boy shrugged his shoulders. Joel removed his hands.

Eve took a step back, aware of undercurrents. She glanced at Phil.

'Want to have a tour?' he said, addressing her.

'Please.'

Phil unlocked the side door and a step slid out. 'After you,' he said with a sweep of his arm.

Eve found herself in a well-designed living space. There was a kitchen on one side with a hob and sink while, on the opposite side, there was a dinette. Behind her, over the cab, there was a bed, large enough for two people, and in front of her, she could see what looked like another bed.

There was a wardrobe on the right, past the dinette, and on the left, a full-size fridge and a microwave.

'Wow, I've never been in a motorhome before.'

A young voice piped up. 'You've never been in an RV!'

'RV?'

Joel's voice drifted in through the open door. 'It's an abbreviation for Recreational Vehicle.'

'Watch this,' instructed Phil. 'Nate, can you come and press here?'

The boy eased past Eve and pressed the switch. The back part of the motorhome slid out sideways so that what Eve had perceived to be part of a bed transformed into a double bed.

'Cool,' admitted Nate.

'Cool,' agreed Eve and they both sat on the side of the bed.'

'Look,' said Nate, taking charge. 'There's a curtain.' He reached up to draw it but he lacked the technique and the curtain jammed halfway across.

'Shall I,' offered Eve as she reached up to help him.

They sat side by side behind the curtain, Nate grinning widely. 'Sssh,' he whispered.

Eve whispered back. 'I think they know we're here.'

'Dad's still outside. Pull your legs up.'

They waited and they waited, until Eve wondered whether Joel would ever come. Eventually, there was a creak on the step. Nate started to giggle soundlessly which Eve had never witnessed a child do before. His eyes danced, and for the first time, she saw a resemblance to his father. She heard Joel ask Phil about their whereabouts but Phil had obviously left to check the grill.

'I can't understand where they've gone.'

Nate placed a small hand on top of Eve's to stop her from speaking and held a finger to his lips.

The tension was palpable. Eve, ridiculously, found herself holding her breath, until a large hand crept around the edge of the curtain.

Nate screamed and scrambled to the back of the bed, half climbing over Eve and knocking her over. The curtain whipped back and she hastily righted herself.

'Got you!' Joel laughed as he lunged forward to catch Nate and swing him off the bed. Eve climbed off more sedately and followed them out. But not before she had checked out the neat bathroom at the foot of the bed.

'What do you think, bud?'

This time, Nate answered his father, 'Cool.'

'Phil says we can borrow the RV. Would you like that?'

Nate appeared to give this some thought. Joel added another incentive. 'We can take the tent as well and camp out under the stars. We'll take about a week to get home to Grandma.'

'Just me and you, Dad?'

'Yes, just you and me. Phil and Rach will fly to Calgary for the last week of the Stampede and drive it back here.'

They were all replete, relaxing in the early evening sun. Phil and Joel had cleared away the remnants of the meal while Rach had told Eve about her findings. Nate had sat quietly, listening to the conversation.

'I've checked out which forts were in the Saskatchewan District in the mid-nineteenth century. In no particular order, they were Fort Assiniboine, Fort Pitt, Fort Carlton, Lesser Slave Lake, Fort Edmonton, Jasper House, and Rocky Mountain House.'

'What's the difference between a fort and a house?'

'Nothing—the terms were interchangeable. For example, Fort Carlton is sometimes referred to as Carlton House.'

'And you think that is where Gideon Thompson would have been?'

'Yes—he probably would have moved around between them.'

'Which ones can I see?' asked Eve, unsure whether she could fit any visits into her schedule or even if she had the courage to leave the city.

'The nearest from here is Fort Carlton but you couldn't get there and back in a day.'

'Is there much to see?'

'Yes—it has been fully reconstructed.'

Phil and Joel had joined them at that point.

'What's been reconstructed?' asked Phil.

'Fort Carlton.'

Rach looked from Eve to Joel. 'What route are you taking home?'

'Thought Nate might like to go up through the Narrows, see a bit of Lake Manitoba and then we'd cut across to the Yellowhead. From there, we can take our pick which way we go.'

'Why don't you take Eve with you?'

Phil dropped the idea seamlessly into the conversation, having agreed with Rach's argument of the previous evening that Joel was more likely to take notice of his old friend's suggestion. Eve almost choked on her drink.

There was nothing to indicate that Joel was surprised. Eve felt his eyes evaluating her but his hat was tilted so low, due to the sun, that she was unable to fully fathom his expression. She found herself blabbering, providing a myriad of excuses which ended with the argument that the trip was a special one for father and son.

'I'd like you to come.'

Eve turned towards the voice. Nate was waiting for an answer.

She sought Rach's eyes, searching for an ally. 'I can't possibly go.'

Rach did not comply. 'Why not?'

'I've just listed them.'

Phil butted in. 'The main one has gone. Nate wants you to join them.'

'It's an ideal solution for you, Eve. You can go to Fort Carlton and maybe as far as Rocky Mountain House. Then, Joel can drop you back in Calgary before he and Nate head for Lethbridge.' Rach realised this would entail Joel taking a circuitous route, but if she had read the signs correctly, he would be happy to do so.

Phil pushed home the advantage. 'You've only got limited time until you fly back to England. It would be lonely trying to see one of these sights by yourself. The distances between places are much greater than what you are used to. Also, if you hire a car here, in Winnipeg, you'll pay a premium for dropping it off in Calgary.'

'You argue well,' complimented Eve.

Phil opened his arms, palms upward. 'What can I say? And you can travel for free in our RV.'

At last, Eve found the courage to meet Joel's eyes. The usual twinkle had been replaced by such intensity that she looked away.

'It's up to you, Eve.'

Fourteen

After Joel had dropped her off at the hotel, Eve paced the room trying to decide what to do. It was approaching ten o'clock but she knew she would not settle until she had contacted Anne Lennon. Making a decision, Eve quickly typed a message asking whether it was too late to call that evening. Immediately, her phone rang.

Anne's loud voice, full of concern, filled the room. 'Honey, is everything all right?'

'Yes.' Eve paused, concentrating on her own turn of phrase. 'I've had an offer of a ride back to Calgary.'

'Oh!' There was a long pause. 'You realise you can't drive back in a day, honey.'

'I know—I'll be in an RV.'

'Who with?'

Eve took a deep breath, suppressed her linguistic urge to correct Anne's grammar, and said, 'Joel.'

Anne's voice rose several octaves. 'How do you know this man?'

'I met him at Calgary Airport.'

'What are you thinking of?'

'It sounds fine—his son is with him.'

Anne ignored what Eve had said. 'You've only known him a few days.'

'Yes.'

'You're not thinking of actually accepting the ride?'

'I am. That's why I wanted to talk to you. It will take a good week to get back to you. Joel has offered to show me some of the old Hudson's Bay forts.' Eve quashed the uneasy thought that she was telling an untruth. In reality, she felt Joel had been press-ganged into taking her.

'What would your Mom say?'

Eve sighed inwardly. Her mother was dead and Eve had no idea what she would have advised, although, a part of her hoped that her mother would have encouraged her to grasp the opportunity with both hands. Eve wanted to shout the answer. She was thirty-one-years-old and for almost a decade she had put her life on hold and every fibre of her being wanted to accept the offer fate had placed before her.

Eve had not responded quickly enough. Anne's was obviously a rhetorical question as she immediately demanded more information. 'Is this man from Calgary?'

'Joel's a rancher from near Lethbridge, between there and a place called Fort Macleod.'

'A rancher? What's his name?'

'Joel Baxter.'

'Listen, honey,' replied Anne, thinking furiously. 'Don't do anything until I get back to you tomorrow. Andrew's second cousin, Lilian, is married to a rancher down that way. I'll see what he can find out.'

Eve agreed reluctantly and said goodnight. Still realising sleep would elude her, she sat at the narrow desk below the wall-mounted television and took a sheet of the complementary paper out of the drawer. She folded it in half, lengthways. At the top of one column, she wrote 'pros' and at the top of the other 'cons'. After a very short time, the 'pros' column was full and the 'cons' only had two words. Her exercise spoke volumes. She studied the two words, and then, picking up the pencil, scribbled out 'madman?' The remaining entry stood alone in its column. Slowly, with neat precision, she drew an arrow, leading from the word, towards the opposite column. Eve smiled, laughing at herself, as she read, 'seducer?' and then she scribbled that out too.

The following day was her own as she was free until the evening when Joel had suggested they meet up for dinner. Eve had decided to spend as much time as she could in the Archives and then wander over to the Manitoba Legislative Building which her guidebook had highlighted as not to be missed. Anne called her back, in the afternoon, while Eve was exploring its grounds.

'Eve?'

'Yes.'

'I'm glad I've caught you.'

Eve waited.

Anne launched into a potential monologue. 'Lilian knows Rose Baxter, Joel's mother, through a mutual friend but she can't recall meeting him. Rose has had a difficult few years. Her husband died a few years back and Joel left his job and came back to the ranch.'

Eve interrupted. 'I know.'

'Oh, honey! That's not all. Joel's wife became pregnant almost as soon as they arrived, but after the baby was born, when he was about nine-months-old, she announced that she couldn't stand another winter "in the middle of nowhere". She took the baby to her parents in Winnipeg. Joel tried flying backwards and forwards, trying to find a solution, but before Rose knew it, the wife was living with a Frenchman.'

'He's a Canadian from Quebec,' corrected Eve.

Anne hardly drew breath, she was in full flight. 'Apparently, Joel was devastated, and then, to make matters worse, the wife became pregnant again—twin girls. There was a divorce, of course.'

Eve glanced around worried that Anne might have been overheard, but the grounds were quiet with nobody in sight.

Anne had not finished. 'Rose doesn't see much of her grandson. He comes for his summer break, and once or twice, he's been at Christmas. The boy hardly knows his father. It's a tragedy. The Baxters have ranched that land for five generations and it looks unlikely that Joel's son will want to follow in his father's footsteps.'

'He's called Nate.'

'Is he? Lilian couldn't remember his name.' Anne had lost the thread of her thoughts.

'Is that all?' asked Eve feeling increasingly uncomfortable. Joel and Nate were just faceless names to Anne.

'Let me think. Lilian said Joel is known as a good son.' Anne paused for so long that Eve believed the conversation to be over and then the older woman remembered. 'I know what else she said—he was a handsome man but never socialised much—he'd dashed the hopes of a few local girls.'

'That's idle gossip,' Eve retorted bluntly.

Anne responded to her tone. 'Sorry, honey. I was only repeating what Lilian said.'

Eve softened. She knew Anne and Andrew meant well. 'I'll return to Calgary with Joel and Nate then.'

'It's still a bit unusual,' Anne started to say but Eve cut her off.

'It's vital research—visiting the forts,' she stated forcefully.

'If you say so.' Anne responded doubtfully.

Eve moderated her voice, making it light and breezy. 'Thanks for your help, Anne. Looking forward to seeing you and Andrew when I get back. I'll keep you posted en route.'

'Take care, honey. Don't lose touch.'

Eve slid her finger across the screen, feeling anything but upbeat. Instead, she felt grubby, as if she's been caught rummaging through Joel's personal possessions.

It was no better when she was sitting across the table from him having a candlelit dinner. He appeared to be totally relaxed, regarding her, once again, as if she delighted him. It could become addictive, thought Eve, as she made a concerted effort to concentrate on the menu. 'I think I'll have pasta.'

'Pasta?'

'What's wrong with that?'

'Nothing—there are just so many other choices.'

'I happen to be very partial to pasta.'

'Pasta it is,' said Joel.

'I expect you will be having steak?'

Joel grinned. 'No—I'm going to order the salmon.'

'Good choice,' said Eve, for want of saying anything else.

'Do you eat a lot of pasta at home?'

'Yes, it's a great meal if you live alone.'

Joel's expression changed. She met his eyes, so often full of amusement but serious now. The colour of the sea, when the blue gradually bleeds to green, they appeared to change colour noticeably depending on the light and what he wore. That evening, courtesy of his shirt, they leant towards green. 'You live alone?'

'Yes—well, no.'

'Interesting answer!'

'My niece lives with me during term time—she's at university.'

'There's nobody at home missing you?'

She tried to look affronted. 'What makes you think no one would miss me?'

'I didn't mean it like that.'

Eve understood exactly what Joel meant but she kept her peace. 'I know,' she said, softly, and then changed the subject. 'I'd like to come with you and Nate to Calgary.'

'Great,' he said. 'Nate will be pleased.'

'I'm glad. I hope he really doesn't mind. I had the impression he was looking forward to it being only the two of you on the trip.'

'No—he's cool with it.'

Eve took a deep breath. She could not continue without telling Joel about Anne's inquiries. She started hesitantly. 'I phoned my mother's friend in Calgary to tell her about my return.' Her mouth was dry. She took a sip of her red wine.

He looked at her over his beer glass, and then carefully placed it on the table.

'Her husband, Andrew, has a cousin who knows your mother.'

Joel's eyes lit up, crinkling at the corners. 'Did I pass muster?'

'So, so!'

'That's all right, then.'

Eve could not let the matter drop. 'I felt bad about Anne asking about you.'

'Why?'

Eve shrugged.

'It's a normal reaction. I would be concerned if one of my sisters hitched a ride with a strange man.'

Joel had sisters. She wondered how many. 'Are you a strange man?'

'I was a stranger until Monday.'

'And it's only Friday night now.' The enormity of what she was doing hit Eve. Yet it seemed so natural.

Joel read her face. 'Don't worry, Eve. You have a seven-year-old boy for a chaperone.'

'Nate is seven? I thought he was older.'

'He'll be eight in the autumn. He's the tallest in his class.'

Their meals arrived and conversation briefly ceased. Joel broke the silence. 'How did you get on at the Archives today?'

'Well, thank you. I now know that, from 1850, Gideon worked in the Saskatchewan District until his contract ended in 1854.'

'Did he go home then?'

'I don't know.'

'Rach said that most of the recruits stayed in Canada. Usually, the reason that they signed up was because conditions were so difficult at home.'

'I'll have to do much more research.'

'I was thinking that perhaps you'd come to Lower Fort Garry with Nate and me, tomorrow? I know it's not in the Saskatchewan District but you'd get a good idea of what a large fort would have looked like.'

'I'd like that.' Eve could feel the smile on her face widening.

'Bring your notebook.'

'Anything else?'

'Insect repellent.'

'I have some. When I was in Calgary people kept teasing me about coming to Winnipeg. They said I would see mosquitoes the size of moose!'

He looked at her gravely. 'They weren't teasing!'

'Where are they then?'

'It's a good year. There're not so many at the moment. You'll see more tomorrow perhaps, the fort is next to the Red River and you'll see plenty on our trip.'

Eve hugged the words "our trip" to herself. She felt she could cope with a million mosquitoes.

'When I drop Nate home you can meet his mom, Colette, and Jean-Claude. Colette would want to meet you. We'll be leaving on Sunday.'

Lower Fort Garry surpassed all of Eve's expectations. It was much larger than she had imagined and she was pleased that Joel had insisted they have an early start. Armed with the map provided by the Visitor Centre, Eve could clearly see what lay outside of the fort's walls and which buildings were enclosed within its perimeter. There were some areas of greater interest for her research but she had told herself to relax, it was not exclusively her day. Nate ran on ahead of them, darting this way and that, always needing to be reminded to stay in view. It was decided that they would restrict themselves to the five nearest exhibits and then take a break for lunch. Eve was heartened to find that Joel's dining philosophy chimed with hers: whether to go early or late was of no significance as long as the lunchtime rush was avoided.

First of all, they checked out the industrial complex, where the lime kilns, the miller's house, the brewery, and the malt barn used to stand before they made their way up the path to a cottage for visiting Hudson's Bay Company officials. The attraction of Lower Fort Garry was that it was not a reconstruction. The cottage had been built in the 1840s, and although as a craftsman, Gideon would not have lodged within it, he would have seen it if he had come to the fort. Joel pointed to the Men's House on the map, inside the walls, where the HBC labourers and craftsmen like Gideon would have lived. At each exhibit, there was at least one very knowledgeable guide dressed in period costume from the mid-nineteenth century, and Eve methodically jotted their salient points in her notebook.

'Why are you writing things down?' asked Nate.

The boy's question made Eve reflect. What would she do with the information? Gideon may never have been at the fort. 'In case I will have forgotten what I've seen when I get home.'

It seemed a good enough answer for Nate. He was bounding off before she could add anything else. 'Hurry up. I want to go to the wigwam.'

The encampment where the indigenous people gathered when they came to the fort to trade, circled a fire surrounded by stones. Eve noted the metal kettle, resting at its edge, and recalled what she had read about goods coming from England. As well as other imported metal objects on display, there were several baskets in various designs and a pair of snow shoes which were propped up against a tree, making an incongruous sight on a hot summer's day. The wigwam that had caught Nate's eye was made of thick material rather than hide, and adjacent to it, was a framework which allowed visitors to understand its construction. He wanted to run inside them and had to be restrained by Joel, resulting in a sulkiness which marred their visit to the next exhibit.

It was a blacksmith's shop, situated outside of the fort's walls for safety. Nate grumpily entered the wide double doors and the three of them squeezed into the group of people gathered at one end. There were two smiths, a master and an apprentice, dressed in shirts and trousers held up with bracers. One of the men wore the brightly coloured Assumption Belt, favoured by the voyageurs, around his waist. They both had kerchiefs around their necks which they frequently used to wipe their brows and cover their faces. The forge was hot, the atmosphere caught at the back of Eve's throat and she wondered about Gideon working all day in such conditions. She whispered as much to Joel who whispered back that at least the man would have been warm in the biting winters.

The two smiths engaged in good-hearted banter for the benefit of the visitors while the apprentice worked a large nail to show his skill. Nate lost some of his pique but soon started to complain about the smoke, so they crept out into the fresh air. It was only eleven o'clock but they wandered back to the restaurant. Joel and Nate went to find the bathroom while Eve browsed the gift shop. She found a selection of teas, artistically packaged, and picked up the one which caught her eye. It was the blend for blacksmiths who, it was written on the front of the packet, were the most skilled of the tradesmen. Then, the blurb stated that most men remained in Canada and raised a family. Eve bought a packet, remembering what the waitress at the hotel had said. Perhaps she did have distant relatives in the area?

'Who's that for?' asked Joel, leaning over her shoulder.

'Aidan.'

'Who is Aidan?'

'Someone who is missing me while I'm away!' Eve explained playfully.

Joel regarded her speculatively for a long moment and then said, 'Let's eat.'

Nate was already in the queue.

The afternoon passed in an overload of displays for just one day. Eve could not do them all justice. She skimmed through areas, of great interest at another time, which would not have been relevant to Gideon, leaving enough time to see where he would have stayed if he had travelled to Lower Fort Garry. There was a small room for tradesmen at the end of the house where the labourers lived. It was pleasant with a window and enough space for two narrow cots and a couple of small tables. On one of these, various objects were arranged including a lantern, a candlestick and candle, a polished piece of metal to serve as a mirror, and some shaving tackle. She studied the latter. Would Gideon have been clean-shaven? She needed to do some research. When did men in Victorian times begin to sport prolific facial hair? And what happened to men who lived in the wilderness? She had imagined Gideon as beardless, he was only nineteen, but that could be incorrect.

At the end of the day, as Joel drove back to St Boniface, Eve's stomach began to churn with trepidation, but when she arrived at Nate's, it rapidly disappeared. Jean-Claude met them enthusiastically and led them through the house to the garden. Two identical girls were playing on a set of swings and the lawn was strewn with toys abandoned in succession as the afternoon shadows had lengthened. Introduced as Amelie and Sophia, the girls were miniature versions of their father. Small and neat, Jean-Claude brimmed with energy, his intelligent dark eyes darting everywhere. His hair was black, tied up in a man-bun, with the first signs of silver threading through it. He was so different from what Eve had expected, so different from Joel, that she found herself staring.

'Colette has just gone to the store, she'll be back soon,' he announced, as he invited Joel and Eve to sit down. Nate had disappeared into the house. 'Would you like a drink?'

Colette arrived while her partner was in the kitchen. She was as Eve remembered from the airport. Tall and slim, she appeared elegant and cool in a crisp white shirt and very tight jeans. A pair of wedged sandals added to her height. When Jean-Claude arrived with their sodas, Eve noticed that Colette topped him by a good ten centimetres. She greeted Eve warmly as she sank into an adjacent chair, and asked,

'Did you have a good day?'

The conversation ranged from Lower Fort Garry to Eve's holiday, from the latest escapades of the children to current affairs and the price of beef. Eve felt herself becoming increasingly more relaxed and was reluctant to interrupt the flow of the conversation to ask where the bathroom was.

'I'll show you,' volunteered Colette.

The house was large and airy, flooded with light. Eve was surprised when Colette led her up the stairs as she was sure there must have been a downstairs toilet.

'It's just here.'

Eve opened the door to a spacious family bathroom. She took the opportunity to freshen up, splashing her face with water. After a warm day exploring the fort, she felt uncomfortable and sticky, convinced that, if Colette stood close to her, she might detect a faint trace of body odour. Her sandals felt tight, despite their sensible design, and at that moment, Eve longed to sink into a deep cooling bath. Instead, she loosened her hair, ran her fingers through it, and then tied it back up more tidily.

Colette was waiting for her outside the door and Eve felt an embarrassed blush warm her face. She had taken her time. They looked at each other, neither woman knowing quite how to begin.

Eve spoke first. 'Sorry.'

'Do you have children?'

The question was so unexpected, that Eve blurted out, 'I'm not married.' She felt her blush heighten: mortified in case Colette believed she was making a judgement.

'But do you have children?'

'No, but I often work with them.'

'What do you do?'

'I'm a librarian and I've introduced many activities for children.'

'I'd like you to take this with you.' Colette passed the object she had been fiddling with to Eve. It was an inhaler. 'Joel already has one but I'd feel better if you had a spare. Nathaniel is a very sensitive little boy. He often gets worked up and he hasn't seen his dad for six months. It's a year since he went to stay with his Grandma. That's a long time for a seven-year-old. He can be very babyish at times and Joel might not quite understand. He's worried about this trip underneath. Last night he wet the bed. I've got these for you to take.'

Colette reached out and took a pile of waterproof sheets off the hallstand. 'I think Joel hopes Nate will sleep in the tent with him but he's afraid of insects. He might want to be in the RV with you. Would you mind?'

'Of course not.' Eve reached out and touched Colette's hand.

'Good—Nate said last night how much he liked you.'

Eve followed Colette back down the stairs. Her ride back to Calgary had taken on a whole new dimension.

Fifteen

Lerwick, June 1850

It was almost midsummer, the time of the summer dusk, when the sun barely dipped below the horizon before it rose again, promising another long day. Grizzel Cattanach had worked into the night and now the heavy curtains kept some of the soft dawn at bay while she tried to sleep. However, it was not the light seeping from around the curtains' edge that interrupted her slumber but the myriad of heightened emotions which jostled for dominance and refused to subside.

In the morning, Grizzel was due to visit the merchant, Laing, and she tossed and turned, mulling over what she wanted to say. The fruit of her night-time labour rested on a protective linen sheet, hung over the back of the chair next to the empty hearth. Gossamer and white, the shawl was knitted so airily that it appeared insubstantial, the perfect accessory for a fashionable London lady. Popularised by Queen Victoria herself, who had been shown examples of Shetland knitted lacework by Arthur Anderson, Shetland's Member of Parliament of three years, the collars and shawls of Shetland were now greatly sought after by the London shops.

Grizzel, like all Shetland women, had been able to knit since she was a young girl, and now, with a demand for their finest work, she had abandoned knitting the coarser workday haps in favour of the luxury items. She had stayed up to complete the final process of removing the lines of contrasting yarn, threaded across the shawl after every pattern of intertwining flowers and leaves, which had allowed her to pull out a mistake without losing too much of her fabric. It was one of five perfect shawls that she would show Laing.

The merchant had provided her with the very fine yarn whose cost would be deducted from the payment she would receive for the finished articles. He would try and give her some tea and a selection of dry goods which she could then exchange for food, but Grizzel wanted to receive part of her payment in cash. If he was impressed by the quality of her lacework, and she bartered well, Laing might be persuaded to give her a shilling or two. She needed cash to buy paper and ink so that she could continue to write to Gideon Thompson.

The letter she had written since his departure had already started its journey to Rupert's Land. It would sail with the new recruits due to leave Stromness at the end of the month, and any day now, Gideon's letter to her would arrive. Mingled with her rehearsed bartering with Laing, was an anticipation which threatened to overwhelm her. A letter would arrive, or maybe several, the receipt of which would be the culmination of a year of longing. For what Grizzel had failed to realise until he had left, was that Gideon Thompson had become firmly lodged in her heart.

Finally, just when she would be able to read his words, her mother made an announcement. Grizzel was to take her younger brother, Adam, and sail down to Dunrossness to help her grandmother. No amount of argument could persuade Janet Cattanach to postpone their visit. Their grandfather would be returning in a few days from a fishing expedition and extra hands would be needed to preserve the fish. It was the time to salt the catch and dry it in the sun, as well as to wind-dry the fish without salt. Grizzel could help her grandmother while Adam would make the task of mending the roof thatch faster before his grandfather took him back out to sea. It was vital that the family earn enough to pay their rent as the fear of being thrown off the land was very real. News had recently filtered down from Fetlar, and from Tingwall and Weisdale on the mainland, of tenants being thrown off the land in favour of sheep.

Grizzel had argued, without success, until the moment she stepped into the boat manned by her uncle and Will, which would take them south. Adam, a small sturdy boy of twelve, was brimming with excitement, the level of which matched his sister's indignation. It was the first week of June and the letters from Rupert's Land would not arrive for at least two weeks. The previous day, Grizzel had run down to the post office on Commercial Street on the off chance that they had arrived early, but she had been disappointed. Her mother, tired of seeing Grizzel fretting over a man thousands of miles away, lost her temper and harangued the girl for selfishness. Janet's parting shot did nothing to ameliorate her daughter's resentment. 'You need ta get gyaan. Your grannie hasna started to roo the sheep yet.'

Later that day, as she alighted from the boat at Rerwick and made her way towards her grandparents' croft, Grizzel could see that the sheep had already been herded into a gated enclosure in preparation for their fleeces to be plucked. Everyone's animals were there, sporting thick fleeces of different colours: shades of brown, grey, and black, patterned with white. Her heart sank and she subconsciously stroked her hands. Softened by rationed applications of Kitty's hand cream and perfect for lacework, they were not the hands needed for all the chores Mary Petrie would expect of her. The summer stretched ahead as Grizzel's mother had suggested that she and Adam could stay until the oat harvest was in, by which time, her hands would be so rough that they would snag any delicate yarn.

Will, walking along next to Grizzel and carrying her belongings, glanced at his sister.

'Why be you out of sorts?'

Grizzel was tempted to deny her depressed mood but shrugged her shoulders instead. Rough hands paled into insignificance compared to being unable to pay the rent.

Will studied her profile. 'You used ta enjoy coming here. It's a change from Lerwick.'

Grizzel gave a second shrug, more pronounced than the first one.

Adam, catching up with them after leaving their uncle chatting to a neighbour on the beach, announced loudly, 'I ken. She's a fretting for Angus Duncan.'

She gave her younger brother a withering look but the boy just danced past them and hurried towards the croft.

'Is that how it be?' asked Will.

'Dunna be foolish,' Grizzel retorted crossly. 'I canna see me wi Angus.'

'Why not—he's been thinking of you as his lass.'

'A've given him nae encouragement.'

'Only walking out wi him on a Sunday.'

Grizzel shrugged again and Will reprimanded her. 'You canna lead a lad on.'

'A'm not. Am I supposed to stay hame when you and Kitty and me friends are gyaan oot?'

'Nae but if you dunna want to marry Angus you should tell him. There aren't enough lads on the island for you to be picky.'

Grizzel gave him a condescending look. 'I ken'

'It be a hard life for a lass without a husband.'

Grizzel acknowledged that her brother had her best interests at heart. Single women, whether widows or spinsters, were a greater proportion of the population than anywhere else in the country, and although Grizzel had no knowledge of statistics, she could see the evidence all around her.

'You speak the trath but I canna love Angus.'

'Love canna survive with nae food.'

'I ken.'

'And a boat builder is a good craft.'

She smiled at him then. 'You be trying hard. Did Angus ask you ta?'

'Nae,' replied Will, without conviction.

Should she speak to Will about Gideon? His name was on the tip of her tongue. Her brother could collect any post for her when he returned to Lerwick and bring it with him the next time he visited. Grizzel decided against it but the urge to mention Gideon's name was too great.

'It be a year since Gideon Thompson left for Rupert's Land,' she said, trying to infuse her voice with enough nonchalance to mask her feelings.

'Aye,' agreed Will. 'At one point I thought he might be the one for you but then he signed up.' He paused, stopped walking and swung around just in front of Grizzel. 'You canna be thinking of waiting for him?'

Grizzel's silence spoke for her.

'Grizzel, you canna wait five years.'

'It be only four now.'

'He may never come hame.' Will's concern was genuine. He reached out and touched her arm, the better to emphasise his words.

Grizzel's mouth set in a determined line. She increased her speed, hurrying to catch up with Adam, and left Will and his negativity far behind.

'Grannie,' she shouted as she came across the small figure just leaving the croft.

Mary Petrie turned at the sound of her granddaughter's voice, a welcoming smile brightening her face. 'Grizzel, hinny, it be good ta clap my eyes on you. Adam be inside. A'm away ta collect the washing. Is that Will, I see?' Mary raised her voice, several decibels, and shouted, 'Join your brother in the hoose. Grizzel be coming wi me to fetch the washing.'

Grizzel, suppressing the irritation that her brothers could help themselves to refreshments while she was expected to help immediately, dutifully fell into step with her grandmother. Mary chatted about this and that as they walked, a steady torrent of words washed over her granddaughter who was still incensed by Will's words. Her brother had not seen Gideon Thompson's face when he had given her his carving of the selkie. He had not heard the emotion in the young blacksmith's voice as he had promised to write and Will certainly had no idea how their relationship had developed, in Grizzel's imagination, over the last year.

Spread out over the dyke, the clothes were dry, benefitting from the warmth of the stones as well as from the midsummer sun. Mary and Grizzel folded them carefully and placed them in the basket. They were near the stream where the clothes had been washed and it was some distance back. Of the three crofts encircled by the dyke, her grandparents' croft was farthest from the stream.

'Give me the kishie,' instructed Grizzel as she took the basket from Mary, and slid her arms into the straps.

They made their way back slowly for the clothes were heavy. Grizzel felt that her grandmother must have saved up every article of clothing and linen to be washed, taking advantage of the glorious day. The weather changed so quickly, even in summer, and the following day could be dull and cool as the mist rolled in from the sea. As they walked past the two neighbouring crofts, Grizzel also noticed that their croft was the farthest from the well, and the nearest to the midden. She wondered why she had never thought about this. Her grandmother was still talking, asking about Janet and the other children, when Grizzel stopped and turned around, her eyes sweeping the terrain in a full circle.

'Grizzel?' queried Mary.

'I was just looking at the toun.'

'You've seen it many times.'

'I ken. Our croft is a good way from the stream and the well.'

Mary studied her granddaughter, a puzzled expression creasing her forehead.

'Aye.'

'And we be the farthest from the peat banks.'

'Aye.'

'It doesna seem fair.'

Mary chuckled. 'When was life ever fair?'

By the time they reached the croft, the notion of life's unfairness had ousted Gideon Thompson from the forefront of Grizzel's mind. It was strengthened further by the sight of her uncle and two brothers sitting outside of the door, waiting for them. George and Will acknowledged Mary warmly but they remained seated. They spoke together to neither Mary nor Grizzel in particular.

'We thought we'd wait for you ta make the tae.'

While the men sat outside enjoying the evening sun and Mary unpacked and placed the clothes in their kist, Grizzel placed the kettle on the brand iron to boil. The contrast to outside was marked. The smell of burning peat filled the room, and the gloomy interior, where even the summer light hardly penetrated the skin windows, matched her despondency.

Sixteen

Grizzel watched the muscles on her grandmother's arms, while Mary expertly plucked the wool from the sheep in front of her, and shifted uncomfortably. The grass was damp, slowly penetrating through her skirt, the consequence of a thick mist which had rolled in from the sea early that morning. Now, although the sun was gradually winning against the fret, it would be at least noon before it fully lifted. Grizzel sighed deeply which did not go unnoticed, but Mary decided to ignore her granddaughter. It was always the same, as if every treasured day of sunshine was required to pay a forfeit in the form of a blanket of foggy greyness, but the work still needed to be done, whatever the weather. A bit of damp did nobody any harm.

Mary firmly believed that her daughter, Janet, had not asked enough of her children. Leaving the croft at twenty to marry Andrew Cattanach, Janet soon adapted to a different way of life in Lerwick. As the wife of a master mariner, the young woman had enjoyed a degree of security unknown to her parents and it was this, Mary believed, that resulted in a granddaughter whose face could have curdled milk as she had struggled back from the well that morning. Even after Janet had been so tragically widowed, the Cattanachs had rallied around to ensure that Andrew's family could stay in Lerwick.

From Mary's perspective, it was all well and good to make fancy shawls and collars for folks in London, as both Janet and Grizzel now did, but it was no substitute for being able to survive on the land. Mary loved her home with a fierceness born of a sense of belonging, which had nothing to do with land ownership. She would meet the rent, the laird would have no reason to evict her, and if she had to use her grandchildren's help, which had materialised after asking her daughter more than once, she would make them work as they had never done before.

Mary looked from the sheep she was plucking to Grizzel. 'I think you be ready ta do yer own.'

Her granddaughter, who had been half-heartedly helping with Mary's sheep, eyed the assembled flock dubiously. She scanned the circle of women, all kneeling and leaning over an animal whose fleeces were in various stages of being removed. There were a couple of girls, younger than her, who were expertly working their way down the sheep's body from its head, a pile of wool growing at an impressive rate beside them. She took her time getting up.

'It's time ta get yer knees wet,' chuckled Mary, although she did have some sympathy for Grizzel. She could remember how she had felt at eighteen, when a brief spark of resentment had flashed at the tediousness of her life to be quickly extinguished by necessity. 'Take that one,' said Mary, pointing to a small ewe whose horns protruded at a jaunty angle. 'She be one of ours—but check her ear just in case.'

Grizzel grabbed the sheep by its horns and led it into the circle. Uncertain whether the beast was calmed by the other prostrate sheep or by her own handling, the animal willingly lay down. She started plucking, the wool coming away easily as the island sheep moulted naturally, and was pleased to see her pile of wool growing at a reasonable rate. The work was rhythmic, the wool soft, and Grizzel let the chatter of the women wash over her. She thought about Gideon Thompson and imagined his reaction when he opened her letter. She had only sent one, the culmination of several attempts over the previous months, whose tone and contents she had agonised over. She had taken her time trying to remember everything that Mister Balfour had taught her at the kirk school. A stern man who had come north from Stirling, he had regarded his pupils as rough clay in need of firm moulding and Grizzel had been nervous of him. Consequently, she had listened attentively and had applied herself diligently so that, even several years later, she could write to Gideon in formal English.

Roadside
Lerwick Shetland
April 1850
Dear Gideon
   I trust this letter will find you in good health. When you read it you will have been away for one year. After you left you were much missed by all. I

often saw John Gray outside of the forge and he looked most lonesome. My brother sends his regards. He and Kitty are still courting.

I hope your letter will tell me of your adventures, if I am so fortunate to receive one. I spoke to Agnes Dunbar last Saturday. She is keen to hear news of her son. We spoke of you and she hoped you and Robbie are together. We were at the graveyard. She was visiting her husband's grave and I was visiting my father's. They both perished in the sea.

I can write of life in Lerwick. It has not changed since you left. The harvest was poor again. More people have come into the town from their crofts. Kirk sessions have been busy with people wanting relief and with punishing petty thieving. The meal is sent from Edinburgh as before. The fort has some new troopers. Jessie Gilbertson is walking out with one of them. John Gray says he does not care. All we eat is fish.

I think of you. The selkie and spoon are by my bed. Agnes Dunbar told me a sad tale. William Robertson did not come home from Rupert's Land this year. He left the ship when it docked in London. His sweetheart went to Stromness to meet him. Her brother was with her and he was very angry. It is said William Robertson has gone to Liverpool. Agnes said it is a cruel thing for a man to break his word.

I am kept busy knitting lacework for Mister Laing. The ladies in London cannot get enough of our work.

May God keep you safe, Gideon Thompson
Your friend
Grizzel Cattanach

Grizzel could recollect every one of her words as her hands plucked the fleece and she recalled that, after re-reading the letter, she had still believed that it gave Gideon no understanding of her regard, despite the hours spent composing it. Yet, she remained uncertain about being more forthcoming. If only she could talk to him, she thought, and watch his face, she might have been able to convey her feelings. Although the letter was on its way to Rupert's Land, Grizzel continued to chew over what she had written. Would Gideon understand why she had included the tale about William Robertson? Should she have been bolder and said she was missing him rather than everyone was? How could she have signed herself? She was not his sweetheart for he had not declared himself and he owed her no loyalty. She sighed. Will was correct: five years was a very long time to wait.

Her grandmother's voice, full of reprimand, broke her reverie, 'Stop dreaming, hinny, and work faster. We need ta finish today.'

Grizzel nodded an acknowledgement and continued to be preoccupied with her reflections. William Robertson was dominating them. She thought about him disembarking in London and not returning to his island home and his sweetheart, wondering whether he went anywhere near the fashionable establishments which would sell her own delicate work. She could not envisage the nature of those shops but she was sure they must differ from the layout of most merchants' premises in Lerwick. Her mind jumped easily from Robertson to the ladies who would buy her lacework.

Conscious of her grandmother's attention, Grizzel rooed the sheep more vigorously, all the while, allowing her imagination to run riot. What would the lady who bought one of her shawls do all day? What did you do when your day was not filled from dawn to dusk with chores? For what occasion would she wear it? Kitty Hart's aunt, who subscribed to a lady's magazine, had told her sister and niece that ladies wore their lace collars every day. Grizzel found this hard to believe, although Kitty had argued that the magazine had clearly stated that it was the truth.

She paused briefly and regarded the women around her, all dressed in an assortment of work clothes. There was not a man in sight. Most were away fishing, leaving only the old men and young boys at home. Adam, by far the oldest of the boys, was with them helping to mend the dykes so that the sheep would not wander on the crops once they returned to the scattald. The able-bodied men had all left after the spring sowing, some of them to be away deep-sea fishing until the harvest, while others would return in midsummer, only to leave again until September. It had been up to the women to nurture the crops, hoeing away the weeds, spreading seaweed on the land, and heaping the potatoes while they prayed for a better harvest. There had been peat on the hills to cut and then to be carried on their backs back to the peat pile that served the three dwellings. The cows needed milking, although the run of poor harvests had reduced their number to one per household, and now, when some of the men were due to return, there would be the fish to preserve.

Grizzel returned to her rooin, and when she glanced up the next time, she realised she, too, was being studied. Marion Sinclair, whose parents rented the croft farthest from that of her grandparents, flashed her a conspiratorial smile, and when Grizzel responded, the girl walked towards her.

'Be you finished, Marion?' queried Grizzel who had only plucked as far as her sheep's haunches.

'Aye, for now. I just be taking a peerie rest afore I tackle him.' Marion pointed to a ram, resplendent with four horns, who was being shooed into the enclosure.

Grizzel's eyes widened, the result of a combination of apprehension and admiration, and she was about to comment when she realised Marion's mother was going to help with the beast. The girl had seen her expression and laughed.

'He be a strong un but he be no match for me mam.'

There was a pause, as though Marion was mulling something over, and then she said, 'A few of us be gyaan down to the beach later ta collect bait for the lines. The boats will be back in the morn.'

Mary Petrie had overheard. 'There'll be nae gyaan afore Grizzel has rooed another yowe,' she stated firmly, pointing to a small ewe nibbling the grass at the far side of the enclosure. 'And there be plenty of other chores afore then.'

With the promise of some young company, Grizzel's rate of production increased markedly until it was early evening. She completed her allocation of sheep, packed the wool into baskets ready for sorting, offered to prepare the meagre supper in order to ensure that she was in command of its timing, and generally, made herself useful with the everyday tasks needed to run a croft.

Mary smiled to herself. What did her granddaughter expect to do down on the beach? She watched the girl redo her hair, bending so that she could see in the small mirror, and brush the soil from her skirt. Who did she expect to see?

Mary sent Adam to fetch two buckets and the rake to harvest the mussels. 'You remember what ta do, hinny?'

Grizzel turned from the mirror to face her grandmother, at least in Mary's view her daughter had taught her children to be polite, and replied, 'Aye, I bring the mussels hame and leave the whelks in the pund.' Then she turned back to the mirror, spat on her fingers, and dampened some of the curls framing her face.

'Can I come,' asked Adam, returning with the buckets. 'I canna find the rake.'

Mary muttered under her breath, stating that she needed to do everything. 'Look again—it be the one wi long prongs.'

'I canna take him.'

'Why not?'

Grizzel did not reply, unable to explain that Marion's whole attitude had spoken of activity where younger brothers were a hindrance.

'Take him,' ordered her grandmother. 'You'll gather far more bait.'

Fearful of being late, Grizzel hurried towards the beach, the slope of the land giving her a clear view of the curve of the sand well before she reached it. Behind her, she could hear Adam panting and complaining as his bucket and the rack banged against his leg. She stopped, scanning the vista below, and at first, she believed the beach to be deserted except for a yoal pulled up at the tideline. Then she noticed a movement and picked out three figures stooping among the rocks.

'Come on,' she urged Adam. 'And remember what I said.'

Her brother scowled, scampered past her in his usual manner and headed down onto the sand, determined to ignore her strict orders that he was to be as unobtrusive as possible.

She increased her speed, resolute in her intention that she should reach the group first, and she was relieved to find Adam waiting for her at the near end of the beach. He was kicking the sand with his right foot, watching the cloud of white grains rise and fall. Without turning his head, Adam announced, somewhat sheepishly,

'I dunna ken them.'

'You shouldna have run ahead.'

He grinned then. 'I waited. I didna need ta.'

'Come on,' Grizzel ordered, crossly. 'A'm late enough.'

She set off at a rapid pace, half-running, half-walking, and Adam kept to her side like glue. Flocks of oystercatchers rose in their path, their loud communal piping filling the air with indignation.

Alerted by the sound, Marion, who was keeping an eye out for Grizzel, straightened up and waved, but the two youths with her continued to collect shellfish. Grizzel, now with a subdued Adam hanging behind, had almost reached the group when the taller of the two stood upright and openly appraised her. Flustered, she turned her attention to his companion who was obviously from the same family, evidenced by his dark hair and eyes. Both youths were square-shouldered and stocky, the majority of their height in their backs. They appeared to be nearer Marion's age of sixteen rather than her own. Marion was the first to speak.

'This be Malcolm Aitken and his bridder, Ted.' Grizzel immediately noticed the emphasis on Malcolm's name and the reason for her invite to the beach dawned on her a fraction of a second before Marion declared, 'Malcolm, it be time for our walk.'

His gaze intentionally lingered on Grizzel, before he answered, 'Aye.'

His interest had not passed unnoticed. Marion unceremoniously thrust her bucket at Grizzel and asked, 'Can you finish for me? A'd do the same for you.' But the disingenuous sisterly tone failed to mask the resentment.

Bewildered and outfoxed, Grizzel took the bucket, saw that it was virtually empty, and felt two bright spots flush her cheeks as she realised how easily she had been duped. Marion Sinclair had no intention of genuinely befriending her.

The chuckle behind her did not help. She whipped around and almost lost her footing. Ted Aitken reached out and grabbed her. 'You best be careful—these rocks be slippery.' He registered her affronted expression and laughed. 'That be Marion!'

Grizzel did not respond. Instead, she carefully walked away from the shore and placed the bucket a good distance above the tideline where Marion would be able to retrieve it. Then she returned to Ted and Adam at the same sedate pace. As she approached, she pointed to the boat. 'That yoal—it be yers?'

'Aye.' Ted replied cautiously. 'Why?'

A secret smile curved Grizzel's lips. She studied the nearest rocks and then her eyes were drawn to the water. A shimmering aquamarine with silver-tipped waves, the sea stretched to a mauve horizon with all traces of the earlier mist long dispersed. It was a glorious evening.

'Ted,' she said. 'I think there be better pickings across the bay.'

It took a moment for Ted to understand. 'You want ta geng to another beach?'

'Aye. We have plenty of time.'

'What aboot the others?' asked Adam, in innocence.

'I dunno think they'll notice,' said Grizzel wryly.

Ted laughed, admiration in his eyes. 'Not until they get back.'

'Do you ken another beach?'

'I ken every bit of sand and rocks from here, sooth,' confirmed Ted, with a hint of pride.

'Where shall we geng?' asked Adam.

'Where the boat canna be seen,' suggested Grizzel, looking very directly at Ted.

Their eyes met in total understanding. He was tired of being taken for granted by Malcolm. However, for once, he had the advantage and the appreciative gaze he bestowed on his companion held none of the salaciousness of his brother's.

'We do need plenty of bait.' Grizzel pointed out.

'We can do that.'

Ted turned to Adam. 'Come on, lad.'

Grizzel followed them, triumphant. Marion Sinclair had met her match.

Seventeen

Early morning light, muted by the skin window, cast its beams across Grizzel's face as she stirred. It reached her through the open door of the box bed, her grandmother had already risen, but instead of following, Grizzel turned onto her front and nestled back into the mattress. Now awake but unwilling to face the day, she rested her forehead on her hands and relived the previous evening.

The yoal had arrived back at the beach to see an irate Marion storming forwards and backwards along the tideline while Malcolm appeared relaxed, sitting at the edge of the dunes staring out to sea.

Ted had chuckled. 'Yon lassie is mightily put out.'

For a moment, Grizzel experienced misgiving but it soon passed when the younger girl unleashed her tongue while Ted made safe the boat. An enthusiastic spectator, Malcolm ambled towards the group with an appreciative leer on his face as he watched Grizzel hold herself very erect during the onslaught.

Adam, feeling uncomfortable and wishing he had not been so insistent on coming, tugged at his sister's sleeve. Only used to the everyday squabbles and the arguments among his siblings, he had never witnessed such venom.

'I wanna geng hame.'

Ted, sensing that retreat was the best option, had interrupted the tirade. '''Tis late', he observed, checking the sky which was softly glowing orange as the sun dipped towards the horizon.

There had been a pregnant pause that, as she now thought about it, Grizzel realised was of worrying significance. Malcolm had looked from one girl to the other and then addressed Marion. 'You better be away hame, as well.'

Still incandescent with rage, the thwarted girl had waited for him to offer to walk her part of the way back to the croft. He made no move, insolently studying Grizzel, until Adam whinged again,

'I wanna geng hame.'

'Aye, lad,' said Ted. 'We all be needing our beds.' He turned to his brother who continued to ogle Grizzel. 'You be coming?'

Malcolm nodded but kept his eyes riveted on her. He was difficult to ignore and despite herself, Grizzel turned to meet his gaze. He smiled provocatively and she instantly turned her attention to Ted. She held up her bucket which was full to overflowing.

'We have plenty of bait.'

'Aye,' he said, in his gentle way and Grizzel was struck by how different the Aitken brothers were. She glanced towards the dunes to see Marion rapidly disappearing, her empty bucket swinging angrily.

'We'll be off then,' she said, turning to follow Adam who had decided to set off without her.

Grizzel pushed up from the bed, slid her feet into the sheepskin slippers made for her last birthday by her grandfather, and joined Mary by the fire. Adam, who had been sleeping in the other bed, could be heard as he shuffled into his clothes, and as Mary placed two pieces of white fish on the gridiron, the bed's door was pulled across.

'Aboot time,' she grumbled. Adam looked at her blearily but did not speak. He tried a sunny smile, somewhat at odds with his tired eyes, and saw his grandmother soften.

'You did well last nite. A've seen the buckets.'

'And we filled the whelk punds, Grannie,' added Grizzel, not wanting to miss out on her share of the praise.

'I ken, hinny—but Adam be a peerie lad to be out so late.' Mary eyed her granddaughter keenly. 'And why be you so late?'

Grizzel, her guileless grey eyes a true reflection of her nature, told the truth. 'We did meet the Aitken lads and Ted showed Adam and me a better beach.'

'And what aboot Marion Sinclair?'

'She be walking out with Malcolm so they stayed on our rocks.'

Her grandmother seemed satisfied with this explanation and turned her attention back to the fish. 'Here, eat yer piltek and then geng to the well ta fetch the water.'

In the time between Grizzel rising and leaving the croft, mist had started to roll in from the sea, obscuring the sun and lowering the temperature noticeably. She hurried towards the well and stopped short as another figure was coming from the opposite direction. Indecision rendered her immobile for a full minute and then she advanced towards the pump; she would have to face Marion Sinclair at some point so she might as well talk to the girl sooner rather than later. The latter arrived at the well first and was vigorously working the pump handle. She spoke without looking at Grizzel.

'That be a mean trick you played.'

Grizzel thought before she answered. 'No worse than yers.'

'I dunna have any bait now and the boats will be here soon.'

'Couldna you have whelked wi Malcolm?'

Marion regarded the older girl as if she had two heads. 'Have you never been a-courting?'

Grizzel tilted her chin upwards. 'Aye—I be not short of lads in Lerwick.'

Marion continued to appraise her. 'Then you'll not be wanting a lad down here?'

Resisting the temptation to taunt her, Grizzel admitted to liking Angus Duncan, stating, 'There be a friend of my bridder's who's a fine lad,' in the hope that this inferred her lack of interest in the local Aitkens. 'We walk out on a Sunday.'

'There be many lads in Lerwick?'

'Aye, they come to wark on the docks.' Grizzel thought longingly of Gideon but she did not mention him. Knowledge of him was too precious to share with Marion Sinclair. 'And there be the troopers at the fort.'

A wistful expression replaced Marion's puzzled one as she considered this information. 'I canna think of having a choice.'

'You do have a choice,' pointed out Grizzel. 'There be two bridders.'

Marion's buckets were full so she stepped aside to allow Grizzel to reach the pump. The older girl positioned her first bucket and looked up. 'Ted Aitken is a canny lad. You could do worse.'

'I dunna want him.' The disparagement in her voice told Grizzel that there was no point in continuing to advocate Ted so she shrugged and returned her attention to the bucket.

Marion showed no sign of needing to hurry back. She tucked a stray strand of hair behind her ear, looked at her feet in studied concentration, and emitted a heartfelt sigh.

'Malcom Aitken be such a bonnie lad.'

'If you say so.'

Marion's eyes hardened as she lifted her head. 'A body would be blind not to see you liked him too.'

Grizzel was losing patience. She vigorously swapped over her buckets causing the water in the full one to slosh over the side. Irritated further, she exclaimed, 'I dunno why you think I be yer rival. We shouldna let a lad come betwixt us.'

'I ken,' agreed Marion reluctantly.

The memory of Malcolm's provocative behaviour hung between them. As the elder, Grizzel believed she should take control of the relationship as it would be a difficult summer without a cordial one, so she relented.

'I can never be interested in any lads here.'

'In Rerwick?'

'Aye—in Rerwick or Lerwick.' Grizzel watched Marion's eyes widen. 'Or in Shetland.'

'What do you mean?'

Grizzel stretched the truth, mentally crossing her fingers as she did so. 'I have a true love but he is far away.'

'Where?'

'That be me secret but you can see why you need not be faird of me taking Malcolm Aitken.'

The girls locked eyes and then Grizzel spoke slowly and clearly. 'To show me good faith, A'll give you some bait.'

Marion was still not convinced. 'What aboot yer bridder's friend if you be fond of this other laddie?'

Grizzel smiled conspiratorially, speaking as a girl on an island where women noticeably outnumbered men. 'A bird in the hand is worth two in the bush.'

Marion eyed her suspiciously. 'Where's that from?'

'I learnt it at school. It be a proverb. It means… '

'I ken what it means,' retorted Marion sharply.

'Well, then?'

'Well, then, what?' Marion began to smile in return.

'You ken what I mean.'

'I think that if you want two lads, why not three.'

'Marion Sinclair! You be not understanding me. A'm telling you I like two laddies so that you ken that I be nae interested in Malcolm Aitken.' Grizzel's words were uttered as forcefully as she could without raising her voice, yet, as she spoke an underlying uneasiness roiled in her gut. She may be totally disinterested in the elder Aitken brother but she was very aware of his interest in her.

Marion looked at Grizzel askance, only half convinced, but there was no time to continue the conversation. The sound of men's voices could be heard through the mist, coming from the direction of the beach.

Both girls picked up their buckets simultaneously and turned in the direction of their crofts. Joy made them fleet of foot: the men were home with the latest catch.

Grizzel rushed to top up the inside water barrel and poured the remaining water into the outside one. 'Me daa be hame,' she shouted at the top of her voice.

Her grandmother emerged from the barn, having just finished milking the cow, immediately followed by Adam. Grizzel watched Mary pause and knew that she would be offering a prayer of thanks, one which all women whispered when those they loved returned from the waves. The girl did not wait but turned and ran towards the beach, knowing that the cheerful voices meant all had returned.

Enveloped by the salty sharpness of the sea as she hugged her grandfather, Grizzel inhaled deeply and relaxed against his broad, barrel chest. William Petrie released her and took a step backwards.

'Let me look at you, bonnie lass. You be a sight for sore eyes.'

Grizzel preened herself, conscious of being a favoured grandchild, and declared, 'And you be too, Daa.'

He shook his head, tickled by her fetching manner, and said, 'Where be yer grannie?'

Grizzel nodded in the direction of the cottage just as a small figure came into view.

'It be the peerie laddie,' exclaimed William as his grandson bounded across the turf and slammed into him, temporarily winding the fisherman.

'What a greht welcome,' he said when he had recovered, his weary face diffused with affection. 'Come wi me. We need ta unload the catch.'

The sky was alive with wheeling gulls, their raucous screams masking the instructions of the fishermen as they clustered around the two yoals which had been used to transport the crofters' share of the fish from Scalloway. Grizzel eyed the glistening fish wriggling in the kishies. It was a copious catch and the fishermen's relief was tangible; despite being exhausted they unloaded quickly, maintaining a constant stream of banter.

Living under the system of fishing tenure, where the laird advanced his tenants the means to purchase their boats and tackle in return for them fishing for him, the fishermen were always at a disadvantage. If the expedition failed to meet the laird's target, the men were liable to a penalty and would fall into debt. The produce from the land they rented barely allowed them to subsist, and in no way, could be relied upon to make up for any shortfall so the fishing harvest was vital.

Guilt, that she had been mean to Marion over the bait collection, washed over Grizzel as she watched the men and she determined that she would share hers as soon as she returned to the croft. How could she have been so petty about such an important task when all the younger girl wanted was to walk out with her lad? Her grandfather and the other men would be out again in the morning, line fishing in the yoals, before they would return to Scalloway the following day to collect the laird's sixareen. Then the voyage would be dangerous, rowing out thirty or forty miles to the haaf fishing grounds, contending with summer storms which could strike without warning, regularly spelling disaster for the men in their open boats. Grizzel looked at her grandfather, his face etched by years of sea spray and wind, and felt a lurch of love. There was no time to slacken: the season was short, only two months, and it was almost half over.

While the men were fishing, Mary, Grizzel, and the other women and girls would salt the fish. Grizzel examined her hands and sighed. Rooin the sheep had done little damage but salting fish could have painful consequences. Even though she would bind her hands with rags, the salt would work its way under the cloth to find any cuts and scratches. She thought about her shawls with their delicate, intricate patterns and the emotion of the recollection, coupled with the signs of age on her grandfather's face, caused her eyes to fill.

She blinked once, twice, and then again before she turned in the direction of the voice. It was one which was unfamiliar. She glanced at the man walking with her grandfather, each holding a side of the heavy basket. He dwarfed the Shetlander so that the basket sat at a perilous angle. A pair of blue eyes, so pale as to be almost translucent, met Grizzel's.

Sven Thorvald repeated his question. 'Are you going to stand there all day, dreaming?'

Her grandfather chuckled. 'This be my lass, Janet's daughter—Grizzel.'

Sven acknowledged her with a tilt of his head, and at that moment, the thick cloud parted briefly and his hair, bleached by the sun, appeared almost white in the light.

Grizzel smiled her open, winning smile in return, as the mischievous thought flashed through her mind, 'I canna wait until Marion Sinclair sees you.'

Eighteen

The company was spellbound, gathered in a circle around the big Norwegian. Grizzel glanced at the rapt faces, those of her family, those of the Sinclairs, and of the third family of the toun, the Tullochs. It was late but light still glimmered pink behind the wisps of cloud left after the fret had cleared and nobody was inclined to move. Some of the younger children had succumbed to sleep and lay nestled on the springy turf or leant against their mothers but the novelty of the visitor had triumphed over any weariness in the adults. Sven Thorvald was holding court and enjoying every minute, so acutely conscious of his effect on the young women, whether married or not, that Grizzel adopted a pose of obvious disinterest.

He was describing a sighting of the Northern Lights, or the Mirrie Dancers as the Shetlanders named them, seen off Greenland when he was whaling. Grizzel was forced to concede the man's power to portray the beauty of the phenomenon but was mystified by the extent to which he could hold his audience. It was not as if her grandparents' neighbours had never seen the marvel themselves, as the curtains of crimson and green often flickered in the winter skies and she, herself, had seen them many times. While maintaining her apparent disregard, Grizzel was busy trying to ascertain why her grandfather's guest was so engaging, and decided that the way he used his hands to emphasise his words was potent.

Sven held his audience by looking them directly in the eye so that their attention never wavered from him, and if anyone's gaze dropped, his expressive gestures drew them back to his light, otherworldly eyes, made all the more striking by the contrast to his weather-beaten sailor's face. Grizzel observed that even Annie Tulloch's ancient great-aunt had managed to rouse herself from her usual stupor and was watching the young man, her milky half-blind eyes struggling to make out what little she could. Nobody asked questions nor challenged Sven's accounts and Grizzel looked to her grandfather, willing him to speak. William Petrie had been on the whaling boats in his youth, as had Grizzel's own father, and knew the Greenland waters well but he chose to remain silent. Frustrated, the girl made a show of rising to her feet. One or two heads turned in her direction but that was all. Sven had moved on to describe a particularly ferocious storm and his role in handling the boat and an uncharitable thought slipped into Grizzel's head. Taking a final sweep of Sven's audience, her eyes alighted on Marion Sinclair. The younger girl was transfixed, her mouth open, and looked, in Grizzel's mind, remarkably like one of the fish they had spent the day salting.

There was no escaping Sven Thorvald. He was to board with the Petries, sleeping in the lemm, the boarded loft space, in amongst the stored tackle and tools. Grizzel believed he would not be able to fit into the limited free space but she kept her opinion to herself. The croft would be very crowded when the men were home from fishing but it was as many neighbours lived. Widowed mothers, spinster sisters and aunts, and regularly the destitute and feeble of the parish were given a roof over their heads. Grizzel told herself she was fortunate. Her grandmother was small, as was she, and they fitted neatly into their box bed while Adam would sleep with his grandfather while they were staying. One very big Norseman would easily earn his keep, and more, so she held her peace, determined to be polite but distant.

The following morning, Sven followed her to the well. He watched her fill the buckets and then, without speaking, picked them up and started back towards the cottage. Pleased that he was walking slowly, as she would have had to adopt an undignified half-run to keep up with him otherwise, she fell into step next to him.

'It be a bonnie morn,' she commented, feeling the need to say something.

'Yes,' replied Sven in his distinctive accent.

Grizzel looked around expectantly, hoping Marion would see them but she was to be disappointed. There was nobody in sight.

'Thank you for yer help. It be a distance.'

He looked at her and then his eyes travelled towards the sea. 'This is much the same as my home.'

Here, was something that interested Grizzel. Unimpressed by his tales of valour on the seas, she was keen to know about Norway. 'In what way?'

'My family scrape by on land more infertile than here, always at the mercy of the landlord.'

'Is that why you are in Shetland?' Grizzel was used to seeing foreign sailors in Lerwick but it was more unusual in her grandparents' rural area.

'At the moment. I've been away from home for seven years.'

Grizzel digested this information; two years longer than Gideon had signed on for. 'Do you not miss yer hame?'

His eyes roamed over the sea which, on that morning, was a glorious deep blue tinged with turquoise, and he shook his head. Whether to indicate a negative answer or in despair, she did not know, but what she was aware of was a very different Sven Thorvald to the man she had seen the previous night.

Uncertain how to proceed, she said, softly, 'Norway be in the other direction. The German Sea be behind us.'

He seemed not to hear her. 'That,' she pointed out, 'be the Atlantic. You can sail all the way to Rupert's Land.'

She had his attention now. He laughed. 'Is that so!'

Embarrassed by her naivety, for of course he knew the Atlantic, Grizzel hastily added, 'If you go north from here the land becomes so narrow that you can see both seas from one point.'

He ignored her information and said, 'I thought I might go to Rupert's Land. There are great opportunities there. I'm tired of sailing in foreign ships.'

'Why don't you?'

'Times are changing.'

'In what way?'

'The British are freeing up their trade. The Navigation Acts were repealed last year.'

'What does that mean?'

'Ships from other nations can now carry imports into Britain.'

'And?'

'I'm thinking of returning home. Our ships are among the best. You, Shetlanders, import much of our boat-building skill and assemble it here as you have no timber of your own. There will be greater opportunities in Norway now.'

Grizzel mulled this over for the last few yards to the house. It was obvious that Sven Thorvald's visit was only transitory, but then again, so was hers. She would go back to Lerwick once the harvest was in and Sven would move on after the haaf fishing season. She would only need to tolerate his presence for a matter of weeks.

After breaking their fast, her grandfather, Adam, and Sven went line-fishing, while Grizzel and Mary set about the endless chores of everyday living. The day continued as it had begun, bright and sunny, and Grizzel was humming to herself as she was washing her grandfather's clothes in the stream. The slap of his shirt against the rock masked the voice at first and her brother, Will, was almost upon her before she registered his presence. Excitement bubbled inside her.

She stood up, shading her eyes against the sun.

Will grinned at her.

'Do you have a letter?'

'Aye.'

'Is that why you be here?'

'Among other things—A've come to collect some wool.'

Grizzel nodded. Her brother would not have sailed from Lerwick just to bring her a letter from Gideon Thompson. She carefully wrung out the shirt ready to place on the wall to dry and wiped her hands on her skirt ensuring every drop of moisture was removed.

'Have you been up to the hoose?'

'Nae. I saw you first and thought you'd like this.' Will handed her a parcel which obviously held more than a letter. She took it with a slightly shaking hand. He turned and left her, waving as he went.

Slowly, with a hammering heart, Grizzel prised open the package. There appeared to be four separate epistles and a wrapped object. She opened the letters in the order in which they were written, and making herself comfortable on the short, cropped grass, she began to read.

The first letter was begun when Gideon was still in Stromness and described his journey across the Atlantic and his arrival in Rupert's Land. She pored over his words, searching for the strength of his feelings for her but she soon became disheartened. In the second letter, written from Norway House, there were more details about the trials of travelling south, with only one line stating that he wished he was dancing with her instead of sitting alone, writing a letter to her. It was something to hold onto, she decided, but hardly a declaration of love from across the sea. She opened the third letter.

Norway House
December 1849
Dear Grizzel,

It is some time since I last writ to you and I do so now with a heavy heart. The world is a great expanse of white, the like of which I have never seen, and brings to mind the mighty distance betwixt Shetland and me. If I may be so bold, I should write betwixt you and me. At home, although we be poor, we have family. I think often of the plight of my grandparents and beg you, if you can, to include news of them in your letter, if any comes your way. Neither my grannie nor my daa know their letters like so many older folk.

You will be thinking of Christmas and the celebrations coming soon and I recall last Yule when I realised my admiration for you at the barrel race. It makes me smile to remember that day and how cold I thought the weather was. Here, there is cold beyond imagination. It numbs my face and is a great danger.

I have been told that, once winter is over, I will be going to the Saskatchewan District which stretches from here as far west as the Rocky Mountains. I was heartened to hear of this posting as many of this year's recruits are to go to the Athabasca District in the north. Think, Grizzel, I will see the great grasslands, the prairies, as well as the mountains.

I cannot deny though that I am somewhat downcast. Robbie Dunbar left Norway House at the end of September bound for the Red River Settlement and I miss him sorely, a link with home. I doubt I will see him again. It has been several weeks now and I still want to call out if I see a head of bright ginger hair in a group of men. Robbie, himself, was pleased to go as the two forts there are amongst the settlers and he believes there will be more opportunities for advancement.

Since I last writ, I have been working on the fishing boats due to me being a Shetlander, and therefore, something of an expert! But now, as winter tightens her grip, I have been assigned to help the blacksmith. Oh, the joy of the forge with its warmth and familiarity. If I close my eyes I can almost be on the dock in Lerwick looking forward to catching a glimpse of you at the end of the day, Grizzel.

Christmas and winter will be long gone by the time you read this. I am lost for words to convey how I feel so I will wish you good health, dear Grizzel.

Gideon Thompson

Grizzel placed the letter on her lap and rested her eyes on the horizon. She had looked at the Reverend Murray's globe: Gideon was thousands of miles away across a great expanse of sea and land. Yet, in her hands, she had his letters. He had touched the paper, folded it neatly and sent his words to her. Part of her marvelled at the wonder of it, while another part worried that there was none of the pretty language expected from an admirer, and in her eagerness to find such phrases, she missed the significance of his final sentence. She glanced down at the fourth letter which had the date, February 1850, written on the outside and decided to leave it until later. She studied his handwriting which was neat and well-formed, unlike hers, for some minutes, letting her mind roam over their previous encounters. Then, she took the object and carefully unwrapped it from its protective oilcloth. She picked it up gently and studied it, marvelling again, for there in her palm, lay a miniature carving, a tiny replica of the one Gideon had given her when he left for Rupert's Land.

Nineteen

It was Hairst, the time for bringing in the harvest and the men were home from the haaf to help. Once the oats had been gathered in, there would be one more excursion to the fishing grounds and then the shorter days would close in around the croft. Grizzel fingered the tiny wooden seal in her pocket as she straightened up from tying the sheaves and watched the men working together, sickles in hand. Sven Thorvald stood head and shoulders above most of them, his skill with the sickle equal to theirs despite his long years at sea, and he made a fine sight as he sliced through the oats. She encircled the carving in the palm of her hand reminding herself of Gideon's admiration, much more apparent in the final letter of his bundle. Now, some weeks after its receipt and its many perusals, Grizzel remembered her joy on first reading it.

Norway House
February 14th, 1850
Dear Grizzel,
I send you this gift as a token of my regard on this Valentine's Day. It is as near to the selkie I carved for you in Lerwick as I can remember, albeit much smaller. I recall your face that day, made all the more beautiful because I knew I would not see it again until five years had passed.

Think of me when you look at the selkie, as I have thought of you with each strike of my whittling knife. Yours is the face I see every night before I close my eyes, and every morning as I rise to greet the day. I make a promise to you, Grizzel, that each year on Valentine's Day I will wrap a gift for you, fashioned through the dark days of winter.

May God keep you safe.
Your humble admirer,
Gideon Thompson

Postscript: It may be of interest to you, Grizzel, that I leave for Carlton House in the Saskatchewan District shortly.

It was a glorious September day. The sunrise, flooding the sky with golden light, had fulfilled its promise. The chill of the early morning had rapidly disappeared, and now, as noon approached, the combination of warmth and labour demanded a brief respite. Grizzel looked to her left to see Marion Sinclair staring in the direction of the harvesters. With their relationship more cordial, Grizzel felt able to comment.

'It be a fine sight.'

Explanation was unnecessary. 'Aye,' replied Marion. 'Though he be not a man to settle in one place.'

Grizzel eyed her companion, unexpectedly aware of the younger girl's maturing perception. 'A'm pleased you ken it to be.'

Marion's lips curved in a ready smile. 'The likes of Sven Thorvald be not for us.'

Grizzel smiled in return. 'But we can look!'

Marion started to giggle. 'He be coming towards us.'

It was the case. The men had laid down their sickles and were gathering in small groups to eat their lunch. Mary could be seen weaving between them handing out bannocks, made from the almost depleted store of oatmeal, to her family and her neighbours. They had been fortunate this year, they had survived the hunger gap from the end of the previous harvest to the new one, but it was not always so. She reached the girls at the same time as Sven and silently thanked God for the big Norseman who was contributing more to the household than he took.

'You be sitting with Grizzel?' she asked, managing to intimate a warning into her question as she would have preferred him to keep his distance. The man was far too attractive. She glanced at Marion Sinclair, the flighty girl's cheeks were flushed a becoming pink, and then at her granddaughter who seemed impervious to the Norseman's charms. Perhaps she was worrying for no reason? Yet Mary had perceived a secrecy about Grizzel on this visit which she could not quite fathom.

'A'll be back once A've seen your daa and Adam,' she said, pointedly.

The three made themselves comfortable facing out to sea. Deep blue and calm, it stretched to a horizon of azure splendour over which arced a cloudless sky. At first, they ate in silence absorbing the heat of the sun, the memory of which would sustain them through the winter. Marion sneaked a glance at Sven but he was in no mood for flirting that day. Instead, he was staring moodily at the ocean with an intensity which began to unsettle the girls. Marion responded by being petulant.

'Why join us if you be so dimsket?'

Sven appeared not to hear her. Grizzel followed his line of sight, searching for a distant boat or seabird which had caught his attention, but she could only see the great expanse of sea and sky. She tried to shake off her feeling of unease, for it did no good for a sailor to contemplate the sea forlornly, and said brightly,

'It be because we be such good company.' She reached out and gently tapped his arm. He turned at her touch and his translucent eyes met hers. Her heart heaved. She glanced down, and when she looked up, his eyes were veiled. Nevertheless, she had seen it, clearly expressed in his eyes. Fear.

Sven shook his head and concentrated on finishing his lunch. Mary returned with some krappen, sharing it out again, and the progress of the harvest and the weather dominated the conversation.

By the end of two weeks, the harvest was in. The sheaves had been stacked in stooks, where the sunshine had dried them faster than usual, and then carried to the stack yard for storage until it was time for the thrashing to commence. The crop would have multiple uses: the oats, after thrashing, would be dried and ground into meal; the straw would be used to feed cattle, as thatching to patch the roofs and to make ropes. The women would weave it to make kishies and to stuff mattresses, refreshing the old lumpy bedding. However, for now, everyone deserved a day of rest.

Grizzel slipped away, on the pretext of collecting seaweed, in the search of some peace. Living together in such a small space made it difficult to find anywhere private to read Gideon's letters, and so, with a quick word to her grandfather, who watched her less closely than Mary, she grabbed a kishie and made for the beach.

It was deserted as most people were relaxing by the cottages. The men smoking their pipes, the women chatting while their busy hands knitted, and the younger children playing tig on the scattald. Grizzel had acted quickly, keen to avoid Adam who might have tagged along with her and sighed with relief at the empty beach. The tide was out, leaving her plenty of time to read her letters and then to collect the seaweed.

She found a comfortable, sheltered spot, and wrapping her shawl around herself, she began to read, the words of the final letter making all the previous ones more significant. Totally engrossed, she was defenceless against his strength. He came from behind her and pulled her back. Then, in one agile movement, he had swivelled and straddled her, crushing some of Gideon's precious letters while the others he tossed aside. He grabbed her flailing arms, forcing them back on either side of her head and clamped his mouth over hers, stifling any scream. She squeezed her eyes shut, determined to shut out his leering face, and drummed her legs as vigorously as she could.

'Just one kiss,' he rasped, his fishy, whisky breath making her retch.

He let go of her right arm, aiming to feel beneath her skirt, so she grabbed a handful of his hair. Her mouth free, she screamed. Furious, he slapped her hard on the side of her head, making her ear ring.

He sneered triumphantly. 'Nobody be here.'

Grizzel could hear the gulls wheeling and crying above her. His arm across her chest pressed her into the sand and he pinned her down with his weight as he started to pull at her blouse. She heard a rip and screamed again.

Later, Grizzel could never recall the details with certainty. She became aware of a shadow looming above them, and in one deft movement, Malcolm Aitken was torn from her and flung onto the nearby rocks. Sven Thorvald thundered towards him and she saw a boy cowering, rubbing his lower leg, badly bruised by his heavy landing. As the big Norwegian reached him, Malcolm covered his head with his arms, ready to fend off any blows, and it dawned on Grizzel that the youth was accustomed to violence.

'Leave him!' she exclaimed.

Startled, Sven stopped in his tracks and studied her face for affirmation. 'Leave him,' she repeated firmly.

He nodded and took a step back. Malcolm saw his chance, darted past them both, and raced across the sand towards his boat.

Sven walked back to her shaking his head. 'Why?'

'He be frightened enough. He won't force a kiss on me again.'

'What if he wanted more than kisses?'

'It won't happen again. You have seen him. He only dared to touch me because there was nae fok aboot. These are small communities. His greht fear is that you will talk.' As she was speaking, Grizzel stood up and inspected her ripped blouse. The tear was near the hem, and if she tucked her blouse more neatly into her skirt, it was invisible. She smiled at Sven shyly.

'Thank you.'

Then she stooped down and started collecting the letters together.

'Let me help you.' He walked towards the sheet that had travelled the farthest and picked it up, shaking off the sand.

'Dunna read it,' she ordered, believing he was about to.

He retorted, 'I can't read.'

'That's good,' she said, without thinking.

He could have been offended but he chose to laugh, his luminous pale eyes twinkling in his tanned face.

'You have a sweetheart,' he stated.

'Perhaps.'

'You have more than one letter there and you have kept them. That means a sweetheart.'

She reached out for the sheet he had retrieved. 'So where is he?' asked Sven, keeping a firm hold of the paper. 'I have been here half the summer and not seen him.'

'Rupert's Land.'

Sven whistled and passed her the letter. It was the one written on Valentine's Day. 'How long?'

'Five years.'

'How many so far?'

'One year.'

Sven whistled again. 'Do you want my advice?'

'Nae.'

'You are too bonnie a lassie to wait five years for a husband.'

'I havna thought of a husband. He just writs to me.'

'If he has wanderlust he'll not return.'

Grizzel shrugged, irritated by having the obvious pointed out. 'A'll see.'

'Is he your age?'

'Near enough.'

'He's not yet twenty-one?'

'Aye.'

'A man can change mightily from when he's young.'

'A'm tired of this conversation,' she announced as she folded the letters over and placed them in her pocket. She had managed to save all the pieces of the damaged ones.

'What does this young sweetheart of yours do in Rupert's Land?'

'He be a blacksmith.'

'What does your family think?'

'I said we be sending letters not a-courting.'

'They don't know, do they?'

'He's a friend of me bridder.'

'That's not an answer.'

'Me midder favours Angus Duncan. It be better if you dunna say anything to me grannie and daa.'

'I'll keep your secret, but listen to me. I left Norway when I was a very young man. I left a sweetheart who was going to wait for me but look where I am now.'

'Where be she?'

'In Norway—married with five children.'

'Not to you?' she asked, archly.

He laughed again. 'No—not to me!'

Grizzel grabbed the kishie. 'Will you help me get the kelp?'

'Aye.'

They gathered the seaweed in silence, each with their own thoughts. Soon, the basket was full and Sven swung it over his shoulder, leading the way from the beach.

As the croft came into view, he paused and waited for her to walk alongside him. 'Grizzel,' he said seriously, 'promise me that you will not close your heart to others.'

Then, he reached out and tucked some loose strands of hair behind her ear, but when he saw it was still reddened by Malcolm's blow, he very gently teased them back around her face.

'Not too bad,' he said. 'Does it hurt?'

'Not as much as me pride,' she replied honestly.

Grizzel patted her hair, avoiding his eyes. Where she had seen foreboding earlier in the month when he had watched the sea, now she could only read appreciation as he regarded her.

Twenty

Grizzel hurried back from the well, wishing she had worn her shawl. After the previous warm day, she had underestimated the morning bite in the autumn air and had grown increasingly chilled as she had dawdled by the pump in the hope of speaking to Marion Sinclair privately. She became aware of the beating of wings as a skein of geese passed overhead, the sound barely audible above the water sloshing perilously near her buckets' brims. She glanced up but the cloud was too dense for a sighting. In the distance, past the dyke, eerie shapes loomed out of the fog to reveal themselves as sheep nibbling the short grass on the scattald, and behind her, muffled voices came from the direction of the sea as some of the men prepared to go line-fishing.

It was four days since her encounter with Malcolm Aitken, and during every waking hour, Grizzel had wrestled with the dilemma of telling Marion about his behaviour. Although she had seen the girl several times over the period, Marion was never alone. Each night Grizzel went to bed, part of her glad that she had been unable to speak to the younger girl, and lay awake next to her gently snoring grandmother worrying about her quandary. She knew Marion's affection for the older Aitken brother appeared genuine yet she hoped to be able to persuade her of his unsuitability.

There was little time. At the end of the week, or the beginning of the next one at the latest, Grizzel was due to return to Lerwick. It had been decided that Adam, who had grown significantly over the summer, was to stay and live with his grandparents. For the foreseeable future, he would help on the croft, especially with the work William was finding more arduous and Grizzel found, to her surprise, that she was reluctant to leave. Despite the toll on her hands, she had enjoyed living in Dunrossness with its gently undulating land and spectacular coastline. The busy dock at Lerwick and her parents' house no longer beckoned as it had in the early days of the summer, and the more she examined her reluctance to leave, Grizzel found the imposing figure of Sven Thorvald came to mind.

He had left for the last haaf fishing expedition of the season, as had most of the men of the toun, and his participation had allowed William to stay at home and concentrate on the line-fishing with Adam. The incident with Malcolm Aitken was never mentioned after Sven had escorted Grizzel home that day and there had been few opportunities for conversation. He was still the extrovert who thrived on attention, but slowly, Grizzel had witnessed other facets of his character and she decided she had judged him too harshly. Also, she told herself, for a girl of eighteen years it was very agreeable for a handsome man in his prime to pay her attention and Grizzel determined that, when Sven returned, she would not appear so disinterested in his stories.

The cottage, although warmer than the outside, felt cool to Grizzel so she generously replenished the fire and then went in search of Mary in the barn. 'I be gyaan to the peat pile as we'll need some more soon.'

Mary looked up, surprised, but did not break the rhythm of milking. 'We have enough for cooking, hinny.'

Not wanting to admit to being cold, Grizzel replied cheerily, 'I wanna make sure you have plenty afore I leave.'

Mary smiled her thanks. 'You be a good lass,' she added, her words being lost in the flank of the cow as Grizzel was already running towards the peat banks.

She took her time filling the kishie with the amount of peat she could carry on her back, and when she had finished, Grizzel glanced out to sea from her vantage point. A wind had arisen, dispersing the sea fret, and she could hear the slap of waves on the beach. On the horizon, different clouds were now discernible, bubbling up as she watched, and she hoped her grandfather and Adam had decided to abort their fishing trip. She thought of Sven, perhaps some forty miles out on the treacherous sea, and a strong sense of menace gripped her heart.

The haaf fishermen were homeward bound when bitter winds, sweeping down from the Greenland ice, collided with the warmer air over the Gulf Stream. Gusts, increasingly more violent, began to perilously rock the sixareen as the fishermen fought to keep her steady. To the north west, they could see black-bellied clouds bearing down on them, their ominous billows reaching almost to the heavens, and moving so fast that the two open boats had no chance of escape. Sven studied his companions' faces and saw his own fear reflected there. Regretting that the crew included two young men relatively new to the deep sea, Sven's eyes briefly sought out one of them. It was Malcolm Aitken.

The youth, desperately ashamed of being caught by Thorvald, had kept his distance throughout the trip, neither speaking directly to Sven nor meeting his eye, and the Norwegian had made no reference to the incident. When the crews had assembled in Scalloway, Malcolm had been horrified to find himself in the same boat as Sven, but on reflection, he had decided it was an opportunity to redeem himself. He had pulled his weight on the trip, using the strength of his stocky build to keep up with the veterans, and more than once, he was rewarded by the favourable comment that it was good to see such aptitude and endurance in one so young.

Malcolm and Donald Fraser, the other youngster, stowed the sail while the remaining four fought to control the boat laden with the copious catch. The sea churned, and as the intimidating rumbling intensified and echoed around the defenceless boats, Sven could almost believe it was the unearthly sound of the pagan god, Thor, wielding his great hammer. A howling wind rendered all communication futile except by gesture, and then, that became impossible as the men bent their heads against the icy onslaught of hail. As fierce as in any winter storm, it lashed their faces and blinded their eyes. Some of the men started praying, while others, their lips clamped together in determination, concentrated on riding the seething sea. Flashes of lightning, crackling overhead and forking towards the water, lit up the sky repeatedly and allowed Sven to see that the other boat was nowhere in sight. It was as he expected but it was still a blow. If the boat had capsized, there would be no survivors as even the hardiest was no match for the raging sea, and if it was still afloat, the struggle had only just begun.

Between the bursts of lightning, darkness enveloped the sixareen and prevented any warning of the next deluge from the mountainous waves. Sven could feel the water swirling around his ankles; if the storm lasted all day, the boat would surely sink, even if they miraculously stayed upright. He gripped his oar, as did the others, desperately battling the elements and following the skipper Tom Anderson's orders as he reacted to the temperamental waves.

They lost track of time as they strove to control the boat, riding the waves, taking turns to keep her steady with the oars and to bail. The stinging hail gradually morphed into lashing sheets of rain, the thunder abated, and the lightning no longer rent the sky. Visibility improved as the sky began to lighten and the men felt a glimmer of hope. Yet it was too soon to believe that the danger had passed.

Tom Anderson assessed the calmer weather conditions and the mood of his crew. In the brightening light, he could see the exhaustion etched on their faces. Nobody questioned his order to hoist the sail in order for the boat to run with the wind and the crew took their positions with Tom at the helm. The sail strained on its sheets, the sound masking the groans of splintering wood as did the shriek of another squall. It was Sven who reacted first, springing from his taft with no heed of his own safety, as a stern shackle gave way and the stay whipped towards him.

The first fat drops of rain began to fall as Grizzel made her way back from the peat bank. She tried to hurry but the kishie was heavier than she anticipated, and after stumbling a couple of times, she decided to walk. If the top peats were soaked, so be it. They would dry eventually. The image of her grandmother carrying peats on her back while her hands were busy knitting came to mind and Grizzel felt very inadequate. At home, her brother Will usually saw to the peat, going out with Angus Duncan to the peat bogs, both of them with tushkars. When the peats were fully dried, the two young men would transport them most of the way by boat, docking almost at the Cattanachs' front door, ensuring a steady supply for cooking and warmth.

By the time she reached the cottage, Grizzel was relieved to see her grandfather and Adam had returned. They decreed that it was too unwise to go out on the sea; an unseasonable storm could be seen brewing in the northwest. Instead, they repaired to the barn to start thrashing the oats. Grizzel joined Mary who was spinning wool at the but end of the cottage. A kishie containing pieces of coarse cloth waiting to be worked was stored in the corner so Grizzel dragged the basket across the floor, earning a frown from her grandmother, and set to work, taating a new bed covering.

It was cosy inside. The fire burned brightly with the extra peat Grizzel had placed on it and the sound of the rain against the skin window was softer, more muffled, than at home. She decided she liked it. At home, when an easterly brought rain across the German Sea, it was flung against the glass, rattling the ill-fitting panes while the wind whistled in the chimney. Here, the cottage, snug under its thick turf and thatch roof, was so low that the wind passed over it and the hole cut in the roof, to let the smoke escape, without allowing too much rain to drip through.

They worked at their tasks as the day progressed, breaking off only briefly for some bannocks. As the afternoon wore on, Mary's eyes were repeatedly drawn to the door, and by early evening, the storm had passed and the sun shone weakly in a pale blue sky. She finished her spinning and packed the yarn away before storing her spinning wheel on the top of her box bed. Opening the door to allow the scent of wet earth to drift into the smoky room, Mary stood rigid.

'The luder,' was all she said, her eyes full of anguish. Grizzel joined her grandmother, and together, they stepped into the fresh, rain-washed air. William and Adam came running from the barn, William's eyes a mirror of Mary's.

They began to run towards the beach. There was no fog and there was no need to sound the foghorn, on a clear evening it should be carefully stowed in the boat, but now, someone was blowing the horn with all his might. Nothing had been said about the storm throughout the day, but everyone had thought of little else. Neighbours were streaming from their cottages, everyone making for the beach. Grizzel was well ahead, followed closely by Adam, while her grandparents became lost in the melee of people behind them.

The sixareen was rocking in the shallow water. Grizzel's heart raced, beating so fast she could scarcely breathe. She could see five men. She could only see five men. Where was Sven? Tom Anderson lowered the horn, his face said everything. Grizzel ran into the sea, the waves reaching her thighs and forcing her to stride against its weight. Others followed and they circled the brow of the boat. She found herself manoeuvred out of the way, as two of the crew jumped out and were joined by her grandfather and Marion's uncle. They held out their arms and received the big Norwegian.

Sven was dead. She could tell by the angle of his head. Tom Anderson spoke, his eyes moist in his weather-beaten face. 'The stern stay came away. It caught him on the neck, snapped it instantly.' Heads shook, disbelief was murmured, and a crocodile of stunned people followed Sven's body as it was ceremoniously carried to William Petrie's croft.

Grizzel stood at the side of the rectangle of newly dug earth and tried to marry the image of the makeshift coffin to the vibrant man. She had come to say goodbye in private, standing alone in the graveyard of the Dunrossness kirk, as she was leaving for Lerwick the following day. She glanced around at the gravestones, some with names eroded to illegibility by the elements, and contemplated the transient nature of life. she was not new to tragedy having experienced wracking grief on the loss of her father, but since then, death had not come so close. She wondered how Sven would have felt about being laid to rest so far from his native land, and about the sweetheart he had left behind who had given up waiting and had married another. Would she ever know of his fate?

William and Mary had sifted through the contents of Sven's kit bag, and the kist next to his bed in the lemm, in the hope of finding a clue to how they could contact his family. Sven could neither read nor write so there were no letters, nothing at all from his home except for a purse containing some coins. The people of the toun and the fishermen from up and down the coast were trying their best to recall what the big Norseman had said but everyone had to agree that his stories had been about his own adventures. William was sure that Sven had mentioned Bergen but that would probably be where he sailed from and not necessarily where his family lived. The best they could do, it was generally decided, was to spread the word in Lerwick and the larger ports in the hope that Norwegian sailors would take the news back home.

Grizzel crouched down and rested her hand on the damp earth, oblivious of the dew soaking the hem of her skirt. Then, with considered precision, she decorated the end of the grave, where she knew his head lay, with red campion and wild thyme. She laid her hand once more on the earth, left it there until her cramped legs forced her to move, and then slowly, she made her way back to the croft, a jumble of thoughts making a lie of her calm exterior.

Unsettled by the notion of Sven Thorvald buried so far from Norway, Grizzel's mind had leapt, once again, to Gideon Thompson. Life was so precarious, young men travelled far from their roots, and news of their demise would take months, maybe years to reach home, if ever. Grizzel's throat constricted: Gideon could already be dead. Although, eventually, in his case, news would arrive in Lerwick. He was literate. The Company men would find her letter and see her address. She started to hurry; she must write more letters. Soon, she was running, pictures of Sven's limp body being replaced by Gideon's, until she arrived at the cottage, breathless.

Ignoring Mary as she called to her from the byre, Grizzel hastily retrieved Gideon's letters from the bentwood box her grandmother had given her for storage. She feverishly found the last letter. Where will he be now? She scanned the page to confirm her memory and alighted on the words 'Carlton House in the Saskatchewan District.' Her heart gradually slowed as she made a plan. She would go to the Tolbooth the next time the Hudson's Bay Company's recruiting officer was in Lerwick and make herself known. For, how could she wait another four years with such uncertainty hanging over her?

Twenty-One

June 2019

Eve inhaled deeply and surveyed the expanse of grey water stretching ahead of her under an equally leaden sky. The air was alive with insects, some of an intimidating size, brushing against her face and tangling in her hair. She shook her head vigorously and then pulled her pashmina over it. Eve hugged the material closely; thankful she had had the foresight to bring the wrap with her after having seen a television travelogue which insisted it was the ideal accessory. It was surprisingly chilly after the warmth of Winnipeg.

They had left that morning, travelling north on Highway 6 before turning west to drive across the Narrows of Lake Manitoba. Joel had chosen the circuitous way so that she and Nate could see the Narrows, and even though the RV had a satnav, Eve had followed their progress on the map spread across her knees. She had found it in the glove compartment in front of her seat and had opened it with delight. Joel had teased her about being a dinosaur and she had retorted that he could expect nothing less from a lover of printed books and all things paper. Also, she announced, with some gravitas, that it was vital for her to see an overall view of their route in order for her to establish a sense of their whereabouts. The banter had set the tone of the journey and had dispelled any awkwardness Eve might have felt to be sitting next to a man she had not known a short while ago.

She found she enjoyed the view from the cab, being able to see more than if she was in a car, and knew she was travelling with a permanent smile on her face. The darkening sky, as they motored north, failed to suppress her excitement, as did the noise of the RV. She had not expected so many rattles and clangs which, coupled with the drone of the big diesel engine, made it necessary for her to raise her voice when speaking, especially when addressing Nate who was seated behind her. Every time they met a patch of uneven road, the gas rings on the hob clattered, and several times, the wardrobe door flew open, followed by the cutlery drawer. On each occasion, Joel had pulled over, and with Nate's help, had secured everything only for it to happen again.

Now, they were at the Narrows, and while Joel and Nate tidied away the debris from their picnic lunch of wafer-thin ham and cheese between chunks of freshly baked bread, Eve had wandered down to the shore. She stared at the water, the wind whipping it into waves, feeling very conscious of both the novelty and the finality of the view for her. It seemed impossible to believe that she would ever stand on this spot again and she determined to imprint all of the sensations on her mind. She had taken several photos but it was the sound of the water she wanted to remember, with the feel of moisture on her face and even the copious insects that doggedly flew in the strengthening wind.

'Are you ready to go?' Joel's voice startled her. 'Sorry—I thought you'd heard me approach.'

Eve looked up at him and then turned back for one last look.

Standing far enough away to watch her face, Joel followed her line of vision. 'Water attracts you?'

'Yes,' was the simple answer.

He studied the vista and shrugged. 'I prefer the land.'

'Of all things, I love the sea. But this is a good second!'

'Don't see much of that where I live.'

Eve gave him her full attention. 'You've seen the sea though?'

He laughed. 'Of course—I've been to Vancouver a couple of times.' He failed to mention that Colette had insisted that they honeymoon in the Caribbean. He had felt like a fish out of water, and with hindsight, it was the first sign of their incompatibility.

'I live next to the sea,' she said. 'When I went away to university, I missed it so much.'

She paused, taking a moment before she spoke, and when she did, her words were accompanied by an embarrassed chuckle. 'I believe the sea's in my blood. Do you think that is weird?

Now, totally earnest, she met his eyes squarely. He shifted his feet slightly, feeling uncomfortable and managed a single word as he struggled to ignore the mismatch of their views.

'Nope.'

'I'm ready now,' she said putting away her phone. She glanced towards the RV. 'I think Nate is champing at the bit,' she concluded, as she waved to the small boy gesturing for them to come.

They arrived at the town of Dauphin by mid-afternoon, to be greeted by persistent drizzle and a virtually empty campground. It was an attractive site on, what looked to Eve like, a communal park.

'Where is everyone?' she asked.

'Wait until early evening,' said Joel by way of an answer. 'Then we'll have company.'

'I'm hungry,' announced Nate, so, as soon as they had chosen their pitch and set up, they walked into town, stopping at the playground on the way.

Joel was proved correct as, by six o'clock, a few more rigs had arrived. Eve watched them with interest as their drivers manoeuvred them into their allocated site; some of them were almost as large as a British single-decker bus while others consisted of a cab with a trailer attached. Then, she turned her attention to father and son who were standing contemplating the tent and its pile of poles. Joel picked one up and studied it.

'How hard can it be?'

Eve had no answer. She had never camped, eschewing the Girl Guides and her school's Duke of Edinburgh Award Scheme in favour of lying on her bed and reading. She picked up a pole out of solidarity and hoped, unsuccessfully, for inspiration.

Nate looked from one adult to the other, a frown puckering his forehead, and said the most unhelpful words his father needed to hear,

'Jean-Claude has a tent which just pops up.'

Joel swore under his breath but kept his peace, and began to lay out the poles. He held his hand out for Eve's. She meekly handed it over and stood back to give him room. He laid out the tent next to them and then circled the arrangement. If Phil and Rach said it was easy to erect, it must be, but he could have kicked himself for not erecting the tent earlier when the campground was almost deserted.

'Howdy, neighbour.'

Joel's head shot up to see the owner of the rig nearest to them approaching. He swore again and plastered a welcoming expression on his face. Eve smiled genuinely while Nate took the opportunity to go inside the RV.

'Having trouble?'

Eve studied Joel's face and experienced a rush of affection for him. He was trying so hard for Nate and it was not going well. Nate, despite declaring his hunger, had picked at his food in the diner and had bordered on the morose on the way back to the campground. Colette's warning about their son's fear of insects rang in her ears. For some inexplicable reason, other than to save Joel answering, Eve found herself taking the initiative.

'No, we're fine. It's just been a while since we had the tent out.'

Joel's eyes visibly widened at the use of "we" but their visitor was looking at Eve.

'You're a Brit?'

'Guilty as charged.'

Lacking the interest to ask more, he turned to Joel. 'I wouldn't start with that one,' he said, pointing to the pole in Joel's hand, before crossing his arms and making himself comfortable in readiness to watch.

Eve noticed Joel's clenched hands. 'We're just checking everything is here,' she explained. 'The tent is a bit past its sell-by date. We've borrowed it from friends.'

'You're not putting it up?'

Joel had decided to keep quiet and enjoy the spectacle of Eve extricating herself. She sent him a sheepish smile, fortunately, unseen by their companion, and took the plunge. 'We're not putting it up just for one night, it's for when we reach Rosthern.'

'You're going to Rosthern?'

'Yes, I want to see Fort Carlton.'

This seemed of little interest, and now devoid of anything to watch, the camper moved on with a friendly, 'Have a good evening, folks.'

Joel and Eve watched him take stock of the newcomers filling the campground before he stopped to observe a couple having trouble backing into a site some distance from them.

'Do you think he'll help?'

'Nope,' replied Eve, mischievously.

He looked at her askance. 'Most people would,' he responded, as a neighbour of the new arrivals walked over to assist.

'But not him.'

'What makes you such a good judge of character, Miss Cummins?' he teased.

'Years of dealing with people,' she replied in the same light tone. 'How many people do you come into contact with during your working day?'

Joel pretended to give the question serious thought and then shook his head. 'Not many—usually cattle.'

'My days are full of people—you begin to be able to read them.'

'Like books?'

'Yes.'

'And how did you know our friend was a watcher and not a helper?'

She grinned. 'I just knew!'

Joel raised his eyebrows.

'Okay—I had seen him visit two sites, before he came to ours, while you were getting the tent out.'

At the mention of the tent, they both looked at it. 'Past its sell-by date?' queried Joel.

'Yes.'

'A bit like the RV.'

Eve nodded. 'Is it normal for everything to rattle so much and for the wardrobe door to fly open so often?'

'Rattle perhaps—but the clips are worn. The door and drawer should stay fastened. She's old.'

'Have you borrowed her before?'

'Nope.'

Eve gave him a smile of such warmth that his heart flipped. 'You did it for Nate?'

'I thought it would be an adventure—camping with Dad.'

'I'm sure it will be. I think Nate is a bit overwhelmed at the moment.' Eve thought of Colette's caution again and ploughed ahead. 'Perhaps we really should all sleep inside tonight?'

Joel considered her suggestion, the imagined fun night in the tent warring with reality. He looked at the sky, hoping to find a reason for his capitulation. It was there. The dark clouds were rolling over again and the first drops of drizzle, which had stopped earlier, could be felt on their faces. 'It looks like rain is setting in for the night.'

They gathered up the tent and poles. The former was already damp so Joel spread it across the front seats while Eve stashed the poles in a cupboard accessible from outside and then followed him inside. Nate greeted her enthusiastically and she noticed the frown had disappeared. 'We're not using the tent tonight?'

'Nope, bud. Eve is going to have to put up with the two of us.'

'Cool.'

Later that night as she lay listening to the rain drumming on the roof, Eve found that sleep eluded her. They had retired at the same time, slightly late for Nate but early for two adults. Through the gap in the curtains which covered her small window, she could see that it was not yet fully dark. She mulled over the day, picking at it, worrying that she had offended Joel in some way and that he was avoiding spending the evening with her. Then, she told herself not to be fanciful, they could hardly talk while Nate was trying to sleep and it was too wet to sit outside. She dissected every conversation, from the moment they had driven away from a widely grinning Phil and Rach to his brisk "goodnight" and could find no reason to explain his decision to go to bed early other than he was considering Nate and was very tired himself.

She punched the pillow to return some of its volume, thinking that it, too, was past its best and turned on her side facing the curtain which separated her bed from the living area. She tried not to think of Joel in physical terms, trying to block out the image of him in his T-shirt and boxers, lying above the cab with Nate. She strained her ears to see if she could hear anything to indicate that he was awake but the pattering rain on the roof masked all other sounds. Even when it ceased and she was still fretting, gusts of wind blew the rain from the trees and made her think that it had started again. Eventually, when it was quiet, and the deep breathing from the front of the RV told her that she was alone in her insomnia, Eve began to relax. Instead of thinking about Joel, she focused her mind on Gideon Thompson and the possibility that she might find evidence of him having been at Fort Carlton. She experienced a frisson of excitement; they would be there the day after tomorrow.

Twenty-Two

'What is so fascinating?' queried Joel, firmly holding the driving-wheel as yet another gust of wind rocked the vehicle. He had noticed her captivated expression while she stared through the windscreen, her seat belt straining as she leaned forward.

'Everything,' she replied, 'just everything! It's all so immense and the sky—I can't even begin to describe the sky.'

'You're in Saskatchewan!'

She heard the amusement in his voice. 'It may be everyday stuff to you but to me it is spectacular,' she said, somewhat defensively.

'I didn't mean to belittle you,' he replied quickly. 'I think it's spectacular too.'

'Me too!' piped up Nate from the back seat.

'Right on, bud,' commented Joel, pleased to have his son's endorsement. He reminded himself to be cautious and to rein in his delight in the woman who had fitted so easily into their lives. She would soon be gone as magically as she had appeared.

'The license plate says it all,' announced Nate. 'Watch out for them!'

Eve had been so preoccupied with the scenery that she had never thought to look at the other vehicles which had been few and far between on their route that day. Never interested in cars, she now found herself scanning the next truck to approach them. It had no plate.

'You only have to have them on the rear of the vehicle,' explained Nate, his pleasure at imparting the fact clear in his voice.

'Oh,' said Eve, disappointed. 'We haven't come up behind anyone for miles.'

'Don't worry, there's a gas station coming up soon,' said Joel. 'We can stop there.'

She glanced at the satnav and then down at the map on her knee. 'I could use a coffee.'

The fuel stop was at a crossroads where they were due to turn west towards Rosthern. Joel filled up the vehicle with diesel while Eve and Nate stretched their legs in the car park. There appeared to be nothing else there except the endless sky arcing above them and the prairie stretching to the horizon in every direction. The wind tore at Eve's hair and made dust devils on the unpaved road in front of her. Nate grabbed her arm, partly to help stay upright as a particularly ferocious gust battered his slight frame but mainly to point out the nearest license plate.

Brushing her loosened hair out of her eyes, Eve read out loud, 'Land of Living Skies.'

Nate gave her a triumphant grin, still hanging onto her arm.

Eve returned his smile, her eyes shining. 'That is so true.' They looked up in unison at the summer-blue sky and watched, entranced, the wispy cirrus clouds racing across it, dancing in the wind.

As Joel straightened up from retrieving his credit card from the pump, his eyes were drawn towards the two figures, arms locked, some twenty metres away. They were standing very still with their heads tilted at the same angle, although Eve's hair was being tossed this way and that, and Joel was bowled over by their togetherness. Anyone looking out of the café's large windows would probably assume the three of them were a family, and for a fleeting moment, he allowed himself to daydream before reality bit, making him curt.

'We haven't all day. Do you want a coffee or not?'

Eve turned around and walked back towards him, Nate now holding her hand. Her eyes had hardened taking on a purposeful aspect, their piercing colour boring into him.

'I'll get one to go,' she said haughtily and breezed past him. 'What would you like, Nate?'

Wrong-footed, Joel rubbed his hand over his cropped hair and watched them enter the café. Too stubborn to join them, he parked the RV and waited for what seemed a long time, fiddling with the radio for something to do.

The knock on the window made him look up. Eve held up a large coffee in each hand. He opened the window and she handed him one, a peace offering. She had no idea what she had done to cause his terseness, but being conciliatory was part of her nature, so she attributed his grouchiness to tiredness. After all, he was driving out of his way to take her to Fort Carlton so it was up to her to accommodate his moodiness; she was being unrealistic to expect their easy banter to last for the entire journey.

He thanked her politely noting that, although she had redone her hair, the wind was already tugging at the honey-coloured curls. Nate, who had been trailing behind her licking an ice cream, arrived at Eve's elbow.

Joel studied them both, annoyed with himself. 'You two had better get in,' he said gruffly, before softening his instruction. 'Mind as you go,' he added, reaching out to take Eve's coffee as she climbed up into the cab. She eased between their seats and opened the side door for Nate. He clambered up, the remains of the ice cream rammed in his mouth and flopped into his seat. 'Seat belt!' ordered his father. Nate pulled the belt across his chocolate-splattered T-shirt and gave Eve a thumbs-up.

The remaining journey began with the occasional comment made by Joel followed by a neutral response on Eve's part, as both of them tried to redeem the situation. Every now and then, she would steal a peak at him, but most of the time, he kept his eyes forward, resolutely on the empty road. She did likewise, except when she checked on Nate who was absorbed with a game on his console, and gradually, she began to relax. She became more animated, exclaiming every time she saw a grain elevator, and her enthusiasm eventually infected Joel. Eve noted the way he sank into his seat more comfortably while the tension eased from his shoulders and his hands loosened their grip on the wheel. She experienced the urge to reach out and touch him, preferably on his lower arm where he had rolled back his sleeve, and to rest her hand there.

He jumped at her touch but kept his eyes on the road. Instantly, she removed her hand and her mind scrambled for an explanation. 'Wow,' she said, as they were just approaching a bridge. Her head swivelled from side to side as they crossed the wide South Saskatchewan River flowing smoothly between its low banks.

'Do you want to stop?' Joel slowed down.

'No—it's fine. If we stop at everything we'll never get there. I noticed a sign to the "Batoche National Historic Site" a little way back but dismissed it as we are en route. I read about it in the guidebook. I would have liked to have stopped.'

'Why didn't you say?'

She shrugged. 'Like I said, we can't see everything. My plane at Calgary isn't going to wait for me!'

Joel pulled over and met her eyes. 'Next time?' he queried.

'Next time,' she answered softly, embarrassed by the warmth in his voice.

He turned off the engine. 'We might as well stretch our legs and you can take a photo of the river.'

Nate tugged at her arm. 'I can tell you all about the Métis and Batoche.'

'You can?'

'Yeah, we did it at school but I knew all about it already.'

Eve looked down into his earnest face. 'You did?'

'Yep! My mom has Métis blood.'

'Which means you do too.' In her romantic mind, Eve imagined Colette's forebears as a handsome French fur trader and a beautiful Cree maiden whose bloodline was clearly visible in Nate's engaging brown eyes.

'All they wanted was the same rights as other settlers so Louis Riel led a rebellion.'

'He was defeated at Batoche?' asked Eve, although she knew the answer, being an assiduous reader when it came to guidebooks.

Nate nodded.

'Not our proudest moment,' commented Joel. 'But as usual, neither side was blameless. Like much of history, it depends on your stance.'

'What's stance?' demanded Nate.

'Your view or opinion,' replied Joel. 'If you were a supporter of Riel, you would see him as a hero. However, if you were the government, you would see him as a rebel when he seized the trading post of Upper Fort Garry.'

All three of them stared at the river, reflecting on the past in their different ways and then Eve took out her phone.

'Stand together,' she instructed after she had taken a couple of photographs of the river. 'I'll take a shot of you two.' Nate moved towards his father immediately but Joel's whole demeanour shrieked reluctance so she pressed the camera icon quickly, not even checking the result.

Later that evening, while Joel and Eve were sitting by the campfire, lit for Nate's benefit as the evening was warm, Eve gathered her courage and asked,

'Have I done anything to upset you?'

He looked at her keenly. 'Nope.'

'That's your answer?'

'Yep.'

She studied him in the fading light as he turned away from her and stared into the flames. She took a sip from her mug of coffee and told herself to tread carefully.

'It sounds as if Nate is asleep,' she said, glancing at the tent with a feeling of satisfaction.

They had arrived at the provincial park in the late afternoon and had secured a quiet, secluded site. It was the perfect spot to wrangle with the tent, and eventually, after a considerable amount of frustration, it stood taut and solidly pegged out next to the RV. Nate's excitement had carried him through arranging the sleeping bags, undressing, doing his teeth, and having a story told by Eve. It was not until he was due to settle down that he remembered the insects. A narrow crease appeared between his brows and he had stood at the entrance while his father diligently checked inside and Eve watched, her fingers crossed behind her back.

Joel had wriggled back out, his face serious. 'I can announce that I have seen no insects.'

'None?'

His father nodded.

'Truly?'

'Truly—now, get into bed and I'll join you soon. Eve and I are just going to tidy up and dampen the fire.'

Against expectation, Nate had crawled into his sleeping bag and had apparently fallen asleep.

Joel lifted his eyes from the fire towards the tent. 'Do you think he's enjoying himself?'

'Yes,' affirmed Eve emphatically. 'I do.'

'Swell.'

'You don't sound so sure,' she said gently.

Joel sighed. 'He's grown so much since I last saw him at Christmas.'

Eve thought carefully about how to respond and decided to remain silent. What could she say? Something inane like children do grow quickly; a statement unlikely to reassure a father who saw his son so rarely.

He continued speaking, almost to himself. 'It all happened so gradually yet so quickly.' He turned then and looked at Eve. 'Does that make sense?'

'I'm not sure,' she replied, honestly.

'When Colette moved to Winnipeg, I believed it would be temporary. There was no talk of a separation—she just needed her mom to help with a new baby. My mom was still grief-stricken and she and Colette had never gotten along that well. I was working all hours of the day to get the ranch back on its feet. Colette was lonely, she had no friends nearby, and it made sense for her to go to Winnipeg. I expected her back in the spring but she didn't come. I went out to see them both but I couldn't stay long. Life went on like that for a while—I didn't like it but I couldn't abandon the ranch and Colette didn't want to come west to be with me. Then, out of the blue, along came Jean-Claude and he changed everything.'

The sadness in his voice was heart-wrenching. He lifted up both his hands, palms towards her, fingers splayed. 'My son is seven years old and I can count the number of occasions I have spent time with him on my fingers.'

Eve was aghast. 'Surely not?'

'Yep—I'm not counting flying visits but stretches of time when he begins to see me as his father once again.'

He laughed, a mirthless sound. 'Ignore me. I'm just feeling maudlin.'

They sat in silence watching the fire die down. Darkness descended so that Eve could no longer distinguish his features; he became an indistinct shape which made it easier for her to speak.

'I want to thank you for bringing me with you, Joel. It was an extremely unselfish act and I can't tell you how much I appreciate it.'

He made a sound which she thought was a cross between a chuckle and an intake of breath but it was difficult to determine without seeing his expression. 'That was very formal—very British.'

Eve decided to be light-hearted. 'I'll take that as a compliment!'

'Take it whichever way you want,' he said, flatly.

Eve paused, believing she had struck the wrong note. Uncertain again about her response and with no apparent encouragement to continue the conversation, she wished him a good night; adding, as a parting shot, that she hoped he would sleep well in the tent.

Joel sat for some time longer, with only his thoughts for company, before he stowed the folding chairs under the vehicle in case it rained in the night. Then, he walked slowly to the washrooms, the light of his torch picking out the occasional pair of eyes in the undergrowth as the nocturnal creatures took over the park. Once inside, he caught sight of himself in the mirror and pulled up short. He was evolving into his father. How had that happened so quickly?

Shaking his head, he moved to the sink, splashed his face with water, and addressed his image in the mirror. 'Why did you answer Eve like that, Joel Baxter? You know full well that asking her to come was the easiest decision you have ever made.'

He rubbed his face with the towel and raised his eyes to see the reflection of someone coming out of a stall behind him. The man eyed him warily and slid out of the washroom without a word. Joel smiled wryly at himself in the glass and then spoke under his breath just in case any of the other stalls had occupants. 'And it will be a whole lot harder to watch her go!'

Twenty-Three

The vehicle crunched to a stop on the gravelly surface and lurched as Joel parked. Eve turned towards him with shining eyes and a wide smile.

'I can't believe it,' she said, in a voice full of wonderment. 'We are actually here.'

Joel had already released his seatbelt, as had Nate. 'What are we waiting for?' he demanded, enthusiastically, all of his moroseness having disappeared after a good night's sleep and a breakfast to rival the best he had ever eaten.

They had risen early, woken by a cacophony of birdsong heralding the sunrise. Eve, on hearing voices outside, had emerged from the RV fully dressed and eager for the day to begin, her evident excitement lighting her face as she jumped down from the step. Nate had run to her, and catching her elation, he had taken her hands and the two of them had executed a wild jumping dance around the firepit, only stopping when Joel suggested that they drive into Rosthern for breakfast. They had been ready to go in record time, after packing a picnic for their day's excursion, and now, fortified by a stack of pancakes topped with maple syrup and crispy bacon, the reason for Eve's euphoria stood before them.

She knew she was looking at a reconstruction but it required little imagination to envisage Gideon's first sight of Carlton House. The trading post was surrounded by a high wooden stockade which stretched around the four sides of a rectangle. At each end of the side in front of them, there was a whitewashed watchtower while, behind the palisade, Eve could see a roof, consisting of wooden shingles with a central chimney. Next to it, a flagpole reached towards the sky, with the red Hudson's Bay Company flag flapping in the wind, silhouetted against a brilliant blue.

'We have chosen a good day to come,' commented Joel as he opened the door of the Visitor Centre and invited Eve and Nate to enter.

The Centre was a hive of activity with several Parks Canada staff making the most of the quiet time immediately after opening. Two were fiddling with a television screen at the end of the spacious foyer while a couple of others were in deep discussion near a diorama of the fort's history. All of them turned to greet the first visitors of the day, and as Joel paid at the desk, Eve and Nate walked over to the diorama.

It was colourful and eye-catching, being dominated by mannequins dressed in the costumes of the time. Eve studied the assortment of people: a Cree couple in their buckskins, a voyageur wearing the bright assumption belt, a Métis trader, and a trapper, who were standing in the foreground of a prairie scene dotted with tepees. Joel walked up behind her.

'What are you thinking?'

'I'm just wondering how Gideon Thompson felt when he arrived here.'

'Overwhelmed?' suggested Joel.

Eve nodded. 'He was so young and so far from home. He was from a small island and he is now living in this immense openness. I can't imagine how he adjusted.'

'People do,' stated Joel. 'They leave their homes, sometimes never to see them again, to search for a better life.'

Eve noticed he was speaking in the present tense. 'It's easier to keep in touch now. Remember that they told us at Lower Fort Garry that the mail only came once a year.'

'True,' replied Joel. He looked at the diorama briefly and then moved away to read the next section of information boards. 'Tell me when you are ready to take a tour. It looks like we'll be the only ones.'

Eve continued reading about the diorama, regaling to Nate the most fascinating points for a seven-year-old, until she became aware of another person behind her. She turned to see a young woman dressed in the Parks Canada uniform.

'Hi—just ask if you have any questions.'

'Hi,' replied Eve before she paused in order to find the correct words. 'I'm looking into one of my forebears—I think he could well have been stationed here.'

The woman's expression changed from professional politeness to genuine interest. 'When was this?'

'He left his home in the summer of 1849 so sometime after that. When I visited the Manitoba Archives, I found that he was assigned to the Saskatchewan District.'

'In what capacity?'

'He was a blacksmith.'

'We do have some records here. What was his name?'

'Gideon Thompson.'

'Nia,' she called over to another young woman. 'Would you like to do this tour while I check our archives?'

'Yes, Maddie.'

Maddie addressed Eve and Joel, who had come to join them. 'I'll see what I can find while you visit the fort.'

The fort was smaller than Eve expected although not all of the buildings had been reconstructed. She followed Nia as they walked around the ramparts, listening to her knowledgeable explanations, but lagging behind with half her attention drifting towards her own thoughts. As the walkway was narrow, Joel kept abreast with their guide while Nate was a couple of steps in front, continually turning to ask questions. He was pointing out the Red River cart on display below them before Nia had a chance to mention it and was all agog when she described the incessant noise they made, when travelling, because of their ungreased wheels. Eve stopped and studied the cart, imagining Gideon and his fellow occupants pricking up their ears when the carts were still a good distance from the fort, their hearts lifting with anticipation at the thought of company who would bring news and supplies.

Nate continued his quizzing in the trade store while Nia warmed to her enthusiastic visitor. Joel paced around, unable to keep still, all the while, watching Eve out of the corner of his eye. Her face wore a far-away expression which surprised him: he had expected Eve to take out her notebook and jot down what the guide was telling them as she had done at Lower Fort Garry. He addressed her, keen for her to fully participate in the experience.

'Look, Eve,' he demanded, drawing her attention to the ceiling where rows of animal traps were hanging.

Nia spoke before Eve could respond. 'The traps were shipped from England along with several other items. You'll see an iron stove in the living quarters which would have been imported as a flat pack.'

'But the fort would need a blacksmith to mend such things?'

'Sure,' agreed Nia.

'What else came from England?' asked Joel.

'Do you want to take a guess?' Nia looked at Nate before she included the adults in her invitation.

Nate took his time, his serious brown eyes weighing up every item. There was a wide selection from which to choose. The shelves behind the counter were stacked with tinned food; with jars of mustard which, Eve surprisingly noted, bore the name 'Durham' on the label, as well as with bolts of material. There were piles of the ubiquitous blankets with their characteristic colourful stripes and more of them were draped over a suspended hemp rope. An assortment of crockery, patterned in either pale blue or red, filled two shelves and strings of glass beads, in red, yellow, and blue, were hung so that they caught the light from the open door. Barrels and boxes containing tea, flour, salt, and sugar littered the floor while, on the counter, a rifle rested alongside a pile of lead shot.

'Cool,' uttered Nate as his eyes came to rest on the gun.

'Have you made a decision?' asked Nia.

Nate shrugged, not wanting to make a mistake and Eve came to his rescue. 'Most of the goods—I would say.'

'Yes—although the beads would have come from Italy and Bohemia.'

Eve had seen exhibits of beadwork in the museum in Winnipeg: exquisite, intricate patterns using the tiniest of beads. Nia took some strands from the hook so Eve could look more closely. 'Blue was the favourite colour.'

Nate butted in before Nia could say more about beadwork. 'How did the goods come from England?'

'They came across the sea to York Bay as soon as the ice had melted there. Then, they came by river and would arrive here in the fall. It was a hard journey as the crews had to row upstream. In the spring, the furs travelled in the opposite direction.'

Eve framed her thoughts as a question. 'Would the post arrive in the fall?'

'Yes—and any letters from Fort Carlton would travel north in the spring.'

'How isolated the men must have felt,' mused Eve. 'What if they couldn't read and write?'

'Not all the servants would have been able to. The officers would be literate and some of the craftsmen. Perhaps they helped by reading mail and penning an answer?'

'I think Gideon could. I have a valentine which I believe he wrote.' As she spoke, Eve became aware that Gideon had become increasingly real to her.

'From here?' The thrill in Nia's voice was unmistakable.

'I don't know,' admitted Eve. 'The valentine is only one part of a very big puzzle.'

Joel regarded her warmly. 'A puzzle Eve is determined to solve.'

'We are helping her,' piped up Nate. 'We are doing research.'

'In that case, young man, you need to see everything!' Nia glanced at her watch. 'I have another tour in fifteen minutes so I suggest you folks head on down to the river. You'll see the jetty where the boats used to dock, and then, make sure to come back to the Centre to check out what Maddie has found. Just keep alert as black bears love our wooded gullies.'

Eve looked alarmed. 'Don't worry,' said Nia, trying to reassure her. 'There hasn't been a sighting for several days but I would be remiss not to warn you.'

Once outside of the fort, Eve told herself to relax and enjoy the experience; bears were part of being in Canada. Nevertheless, she moved so close to the others that Joel suggested they hold hands, with Nate in the middle, as they crossed a stretch of prairie grass. She found it magical, the soft sough of the wind as it swayed the grass and the feel of Nate's small hand in hers. He looked up at her and grinned. Then, he began to pull on her arm forcing her, and his father, to swing him. They tried but their heights and reach were so different that, after much laughter, Eve had to admit defeat. Joel glanced down at them both, his eyes dancing.

'Any bears around here will be long gone!'

The approach to the river led them through dense woodland and Eve tensed as she walked. She had the strangest feeling of familiarity, and when they emerged from the trees, she caught her breath. In front of her, the mighty North Saskatchewan River flowed sedately by, with occasional ripples caused by the wind. A crude, wooden landing stage for boats jutted out into the water where the path stopped. She walked onto it, alone, leaving Joel and Nate at the water's edge. She looked in every direction. Upstream, she could see some low islands while, downstream, the river curved on its way to Hudson Bay. Opposite, was a narrow beach fringed with trees growing so closely together that a group of men could pass through them without being visible, let alone a bear. She stood for several minutes, Joel and Nate waiting patiently.

Her face, when she turned around, was luminous in a way Joel had never seen before. He had been attracted to her because her smiles were spontaneous, illuminating her face without artifice, but now, when she met his eyes, there was added amazement. He held out his hand to steady her as she stepped onto the bank.

'He was here. I can feel it. Gideon was here.'

Twenty-Four

Carlton House
November 1850
My dear Grizzel,

I received your letter today and I am determined to put pen to paper despite the hour being late.

It pains me to see that the date of your letter was April of this year, it having been writ two months after I had finished the second selkie for you. I hope my carving reached you with the summer post. I think of you cradling it in your hands, the wood growing warm from your touch, and I wish I were there with you.

It was good to hear news of home. You will have read in my letters that Robbie Dunbar is no longer with me. Please tell his mother, when you see her, that he was in good spirits as I bade him farewell on his leaving for the Red River Settlement.

As you can see, I am now at Carlton House, a trading post on the North Saskatchewan River. I am the only blacksmith here as most of the activity is dealing with provisions. We trade with the local tribes, mostly the Cree, who bring pemmican and buffalo robes. Once we have the hides, we press them into bales. You should see the press, Grizzel. It can turn ten hides into a two-foot bale ready for the boats to take upriver to York Bay. Each boat can take up to ninety bundles. There are also other furs. We barter for nutria, which is a type of water rat, and the much-desired silver fox. However, there is not much beaver as we are in the middle of magnificent prairie here which, strangely, appeals to me despite it being very different from home. For a start, there are plentiful woods, especially along the river banks, so unlike Shetland.

I am growing very fond of the York boats which are so familiar to me, being built along the same lines as our sixareens. They are better than the *local birchbark canoes for transporting the furs as they do not have as deep a keel. More and more are being built at Rocky Mountain House which is the most westerly fort on the North Saskatchewan. Your brother, Will, would be very welcome there as well as Angus Duncan. Do you see Angus often?*

Life is quiet here now winter has set in. As we are on the Carlton Trail, which runs from the Red River Colony to Fort Edmonton, there has been much traffic since I arrived here in the spring. Now, the weather, which I will tell you about later, has put a stop to that. I had half hoped to see Robbie Dunbar with one of the caravans of carts but it was not to be. It takes three weeks to reach here and then another ten days to travel to Fort Edmonton. As you can see, Grizzel, distances are great here. We are a depot for the winter express mail as we are well positioned as the place where men from the Athabasca and Upper Saskatchewan districts of the Company can meet those from Red River. I think I should have received your letter sooner, but apparently, it is not unusual for letters to go astray.

Although I be the only blacksmith here, I turn my hand to most things. I have just been mending one of our carts. Made entirely of wood, they travel over difficult terrain. The body is sturdy, made of hard maple, while the large wheels are oak and ash. We can tell when a caravan of carts is arriving, as the wheels are never greased due to the dust. They make an almighty screeching sound. Of course, now it is winter, we use the dogsleds.

Gideon stopped writing and re-read his last paragraph. What was he thinking of? It was so boring! Why did he think Grizzel would want to know about the Red River carts? What else should he mention? All he did was work, eat, and sleep.

He sighed and put his pen away. He picked up her letter, written six months ago, and studied it for words that would shine a light on her feelings. There were very few. It was a disappointingly short letter. She thought of him, which was promising, and valued the selkie and the spoon, keeping them by her bed. Though where else would she keep them? She said that he was missed by all but did not include herself specifically, and by signing herself as "Your friend", there was no real indication of the affection he craved. Gideon sighed again and rubbed his eyes. He was tired but knew he would not be able to sleep, so he gathered together the sheets of paper and then went in search of Jim Turnbull.

As an apprentice clerk, Jim shared an office with the other clerks so Gideon knew where to find him. The young man would still be at his desk, trying to make sense of the order book, even as the majority of the fort's inhabitants slept. Gideon enjoyed the clerk's company: they were the same age and shared the same interests. Both of them loved the sea and missed it with an intensity they had not expected. Jim hailed from Sunderland, a bustling, prosperous port on the northeast coast of England and adventure had brought him to Rupert's Land rather than necessity. His uncle was a Company man, as his grandfather had been, but it was Jim's own father who had eschewed the temptation to spread his wings, staying at home and gradually climbing the ladder of responsibility within the River Wear Commission.

Jim looked up, as Gideon pushed open the door, his expression wavering between welcome and frustration at being interrupted. It softened when he saw his friend was not empty-handed.

Gideon grinned. 'I come bearing gifts!' he exclaimed with a flourish, as he placed the two mugs of hot, black tea on the desk.

'Why are you not asleep?'

'I could ask you the same question.'

'You know what I'm doing. This account book is all over the place. I can hardly make out some of the entries.'

'They're not in your fair hand then?'

Jim totally missed Gideon's irony. 'No, the person who wrote these entries has the script of a demented spider.'

Gideon leant over his friend's shoulder. To him, the entries from the previous year looked to be very similar to Jim's. 'Definitely, a demented spider!'

Alerted, belatedly, to Gideon's tone, Jim eyed up his companion through spectacles which magnified his pale blue eyes, making them appear to swim behind the lenses.

'And what has kept you from your bed?' he asked, although he had a good idea.

Gideon took a sip of tea, hugging the mug to warm his hands. 'This and that.'

'And not a missive from a fair maid in Shetland?'

Gideon shook his head, amused at Jim's turn of phrase. 'Nothing at this fort gets past you!'

Jim nodded, acknowledging his own perception.

'Although, perhaps it was you who sorted the mail?'

'It was,' the clerk, admitted, thinking that Gideon's post was a thin envelope to have waited nearly eighteen months for. Jim had received a thick bundle of letters written by several members of his family as well as a couple of sketches from his younger sister and Gideon's post had looked paltry by comparison.

'She's not used to writing,' stated Gideon, defensively, pre-empting any further comment from his friend.

A blast of wind, bringing hail from the north, battered the rawhide window and howled around the chimney. Jim put down his mug and fed the stove with another log.

'Are you nearly finished?' asked Gideon with a nod towards the desk.

'No, I feel I'll never be finished.'

Reluctant to leave, as the smallness of the room made the clerks' office one of the warmest in the fort, Gideon found himself saying, 'Can I help?'

Jim regarded the Shetlander for a good minute, trying to determine his purpose. Like all Company officers, Jim Turnbull was aware of the islanders' reputation as the hardiest of recruits, who could withstand the harsh conditions in Rupert's Land, but they were not usually renowned for their literacy. He had been surprised when he first met Gideon Thompson who spoke English like an educated man, the words delivered in the soft accent of the Northern Isles. He had come across the young blacksmith examining the books in the fort's library. Replaced annually, the books were accessible to all but Jim had not expected the blacksmith to lift "Ivanhoe" from the shelf just as he was about to make it his own choice. Fortunately, the clerk had managed to mask his surprise and the resultant caustic comment remained unsaid. It had been a fortunate decision as the two young men had bonded over books and they now amicably discussed each other's choice.

The clerk looked back down at the ledger on his desk. 'I've been checking the accounts for the last two years and the fort seemed to be living from hand-to-mouth. I'm worried it will be the same this winter.'

Without waiting for Jim's answer, Gideon moved so that he could make sense of the entries. 'Explain to me how everything is set out.'

Half-an-hour later, both men had come to the same conclusion. The fort would not have enough provisions for itself to last the winter, let alone provide for other posts, unless the Cree arrived quickly laden with pemmican. Jim's eyes widened as the enormity of the situation manifested itself. It would be a hard winter living on the food stock in the root cellar and what they could hunt themselves. His sloping shoulders slumped further and Gideon placed a reassuring hand on his back.

'I'm sure they will arrive soon. Perhaps as soon as the end of the week.'

For once, Jim found his friend's optimism irritating and then he chided himself. Gideon could not change his nature any more than Jim could change his. The clerk removed his spectacles and the columns of entries were transformed into grey blurs.

'I've had enough for one day,' he announced abruptly, closing the ledger with a thud. He pushed back from the desk and sent his chair flying backwards, knocking his mug of cold tea with his elbow.

Gideon followed its trajectory towards the floor and caught it one-handed just before it hit the boards. He laughed at Jim's scowl.

'At least the tea was cold. You wouldn't have drunk it anyway!'

Jim pulled himself up to his full height. He was tall, very thin, and gangly in an awkward way; knocking objects over was a regular occurrence. He ran his hand over his fine hair which was receding despite him being only twenty and fixed his eyes on his friend.

'I suppose you've never sent a mug tumbling to the floor!'

'Can't say I have. Or, if I have, it wasn't worth remembering.' Gideon looked at him affectionately. 'Go to bed, Jim. You're just tired.'

He walked towards the door and then waited.

'What are you waiting for?' asked Jim.

'I'm waiting for you to pick up that lantern and follow me out of the room. You are not sitting back down again.'

Jim did as he was told but could not resist a parting shot. 'Make sure you get to bed too. Don't sit up writing to the fair maid from Shetland.' Then, he turned towards the officers' quarters.

Once back in his room at the end of the servants' quarters, Gideon took out Grizzel's letter again but it was too dark in the room to re-read it without lighting the paraffin lamp. Conscious of the need to make himself go to bed, he placed her letter carefully next to his unfinished one. However, instead of retiring, he reached under his bunk and retrieved the box where he kept his possessions.

Using the glow from the stove in the men's room, Gideon unwrapped his carving and ran his fingers over its smooth lines. It was almost finished, needing only the final details of the fur to bring the wood to life. He smiled into the dark room and imagined Grizzel's face when she beheld it. She would wonder at the bear, a miniature replica of the one Gideon had spotted making its way along the riverbank, and know how much he cared for her. She would add it to the two selkies, a tangible marker of the passing years, and feel gladdened that the time was passing. He sat for some time, holding the bear in his hands, until the cold drove him to his bed.

Twenty-Five

July 2019

Eve stretched out her legs, wriggling her toes nearer to the fire. The warmth was inviting as the temperature had dropped when the last of the light had faded from the sky, and now, it was fully dark. She felt absurdly happy: in front of her, the logs shifted and sighed in the fire-pit, above her, ice-white stars sparkled in an expanse of breath-taking clarity, and beside her, Joel sat in companionable silence nursing a beer. If she moved to fetch her cardigan the spell would be broken and Eve wanted to cherish every second of the late evening.

The visit to Fort Carlton had been a success. She had learnt so much about everyday life in the Saskatchewan District, Nate had not stopped talking about the fort all the way back to the campsite, and Joel appeared to have shed his moodiness. The only disappointment was that Maddie had been unable to find any evidence of Gideon Thompson being there. However, she had reassured Eve that it was not unusual to find no record of the servants and craftsmen. She had managed to locate a list of the officers stationed at the fort in 1851, and as Eve read down the list of names, many of whom sounded Scottish, she imagined them knowing Gideon. Also, there was no denying her certainty that the young blacksmith had been there. Not normally given to flights of fancy, Eve had definitely experienced something, and as she mulled it over, a quote from Hamlet, as the prince spoke to Horatio, came to mind.

She glanced up at the inky sky, populated by billions of pricks of brightness, and said to herself, 'There is so much we don't understand, we don't know.'

'Pardon?' Joel's voice startled her.

'Did I speak out loud?'

'You mumbled something.'

'I didn't mumble. I was musing!' Eve retorted archly.

'Anything interesting?'

Eve took her time answering. 'I was thinking that there is a lot we don't understand.'

Joel nodded in response and took a swig of his beer.

'Although we didn't find any evidence of Gideon Thompson being at Fort Carlton, I feel sure he was there. When I was standing on the jetty I had a moment.'

'A moment?'

'I felt a presence.'

Joel's silence spoke volumes. He was out of his depth. After a break in conversation long enough for Eve to feel uncomfortable, he turned to the pragmatic.

'There is a good chance he was there at some time. The archives state he was in the Saskatchewan District.'

'You believe I want my research to be so successful that I imagined it?'

'Nope,' he said slowly. 'You experienced something out there on the river today. I saw your face.'

Eve felt a wave of affection for him. Joel was trying so hard, just as he did with Nate, but it was obvious he was floundering. Where was the man she had first met; the one so comfortable in his own skin? She reached across to him and took his hand. She would make it easy for him.

'You think it was the wind,' she stated, her voice soft in the darkness.

He rotated his palm and entwined his fingers with hers. 'What would I know?' he asked with a hint of irony. 'I'm just a simple cowboy!'

Eve squeezed his hand hoping he would understand her gesture and then she wriggled free, astonished at her boldness. She sensed Joel stiffen and willed him to take hold of her hand again, without success.

The remaining logs in the firepit collapsed into embers as Eve struggled to retrieve their companionship. She glanced sideways at him but there was not enough light to make out his features.

'Shall I put another log on?'

In answer, Joel stretched forward and replenished the fire. 'That's better,' he commented as he leaned back in the chair. 'You warm enough?'

'Yes, thanks,' she lied.

They sat and watched the flickering flames as they licked across the logs, both conscious of a shift in their relationship. Joel reminded himself that, although they had had an immediate rapport which he had instinctively reacted to, there was no future for them, and he thought too highly of Eve to have a casual liaison with her. Eve, on her part, realised that she was halfway to being in love, but with just over a week left of her trip, an unfamiliar feeling of panic constricted her chest.

Eve's phone pinged in the pocket of her jeans, piercing the enveloping silence. 'Sorry,' she said, as she pulled it out and checked the sender, although she suspected who it would be. It was late afternoon in England, time for Aidan's tea break.

'Answer it,' invited Joel.

'No, it'll wait. It's just Aidan.' She would reply later once she was inside the RV.

Joel had noticed the frequency of texts which had increased as they had travelled west, but he had held his peace, not wanting to pry. Now, however, he found himself saying,

'You sure get a lot of messages.'

Eve smiled into the darkness at his tone, and for a moment she was tempted to be mischievous, as she had been in the souvenir shop at Lower Fort Garry.

'Most of them are from Aidan and Lara, my niece.'

'Aidan?'

'My friend from work.'

'Not your boyfriend?'

'I don't have a boyfriend.'

There was a sadness in Eve's voice which stopped Joel from making a flippant comment about pretty girls always having boyfriends, and when she began to speak, he was thankful he had followed his instinct.

'I had a boyfriend when I was at university. We met in the first week at a Freshers' Fair, and after that, we became inseparable. Looking back now, we were so young but I knew I wanted to spend the rest of my life with him. Although we were never officially engaged, we always talked about our future, what we would do together, and how lucky we were to have met each other.'

Joel could feel the desolation emanating from her as she recalled the past and he was almost afraid to ask, 'What happened?'

'In the January of our second year, he skidded on black ice and slammed into a tree.'

Somewhere in the distance an owl hooted, a melancholy sound under the circumstances, a herald of death as he hunted. Eve shivered and Joel threw another log on the fire. He gave her the time to collect herself, before he said,

'Life can be cruel.'

She nodded. 'After the accident, I threw myself into my studies. I had a small circle of friends who tried to help but everything paled into insignificance compared to my loss. I couldn't bear to socialise. There were memories everywhere I went; going out and enjoying myself seemed like a betrayal. My hard work was rewarded, I did my MA, and as I told you, my father died just before I was going to take my studies further. I came back home.'

Eve glanced up at Joel, a shadowy figure in the firelight, and almost whispered, 'Once you stop doing something it is very difficult to start again.'

'I understand, Eve.'

'All the grief I had felt came back again on my father's death. It was suffocating to be in the house with my mother. I would walk for hours along the coast, the sea my comforting constant. In all my turmoil, I experienced a sense of calm in knowing that, whatever happens, every day the tide will come in and the tide will go out.'

'You couldn't continue with your studies?'

'I tried but I didn't have the discipline. Doing a doctorate is a lonely business and I couldn't summon up enough motivation. I regret it now, but at the time, I was pleased to find a job as a librarian.'

'You'd have friends back home?'

'I did—a few I'd been at school with but we'd already begun to drift apart when I was at university. Before long, they settled down, started families, and I found myself increasingly isolated from friends my own age. Aidan was a godsend when he started to work at the library. Technically, he's my boss as he is a fully qualified librarian although he's not so experienced.' Eve turned to Joel and said, with complete honesty, 'I keep him right.'

'No romance there?'

Eve chuckled. 'No—I believe you need the spark,' she stated, pushing away the memory of an attempted goodnight kiss early in their friendship, which she had turned into an amicable hug.

'The spark?'

'Yes—if you have ever read any romance novels you would know what I mean.'

'Can't say I'm acquainted with those, ma'am.'

'They're my guilty pleasure.'

'How come?'

'I flick through them when I'm working in the evenings and the library is quiet.' The frankness of her admission startled Eve so she gabbled the rest of it. 'But I feel they are pure escapism.'

'How so?'

'Boy meets girl, they fall madly in love, there's a big crisis, and then everything is fine. Or girl meets boy, they loathe each other, there's a big crisis, and then they realise they are madly in love and everything is fine. Often in a very short space of time.'

'A bit like Christmas movies,' he confirmed.

'I don't know—what do you know about them?'

'Not much, but my sisters used to watch them when they were younger. Canada has a very thriving movie industry.'

'The romances happen at Christmas?'

'Well, that's the only time I saw them.'

'I expect it was very irritating for your sisters to have you poking fun while they were watching.'

Joel laughed, deep and throaty. 'How did you know?'

'It doesn't take much to work that out!'

'Now, that's what I enjoy—a good detective story.'

'A mystery?'

'Yes—like your mystery, Eve.'

'I don't seem to be getting very far with that.'

'But you are enjoying yourself?'

'Immensely,' Eve replied, with so much enthusiasm that she felt her cheeks redden. She was aware of Joel shifting in his seat, and when he spoke, she could hear the tease in his voice.

'I think you are a romantic, Eve Cummins. I believe you really enjoy those novels.'

'How so, Joel?'

'The valentine you found was a token of somebody's relationship and it has stirred you to action.'

'That's true but it is the research I cherish. In fact, this trip has acted as a wake-up call for me.'

'In what way?'

'I'm going to explore possibilities of continuing with my doctorate.'

By articulating her recent thoughts, Eve had surprised herself. 'Yes—that is exactly what I'm going to do.'

Joel's response was interrupted by a sleepy wail followed by the unmistakable sound of a tent zip.

'What's up, bud?'

'It's wet!'

'Let's see.'

Eve watched Joel crawl into the tent and then retreat, followed by a very drowsy Nate. 'I'll get the bedding,' she offered as Joel scooped up his son.

'Thanks.'

It was noticeably warmer inside the RV, and after he had changed his pyjamas, Eve noticed Nate looking longingly at the bed above the cab. The conversation with Colette came to mind. She turned to Joel trusting he would not be offended by her making suggestions.

'Nate's sleeping bag needs a wash. Is there a spare duvet in the wardrobe?'

'What's a duvet?' Nate was now fully awake.

'A comforter,' explained his father. 'There is an old spare one but it's very thin.'

'Perhaps Nate could sleep inside with me tonight?'

'What do you think, bud?'

'Well, just for tonight,' replied Nate diplomatically, trying to hide his delight.

'After tonight, we will only be having one night stops so we might not get the tent up until we reach Rocky Mountain House.'

Nate's large brown eyes swivelled from his father back to Eve, alighting on the bathroom door behind her. 'That's okay, Dad. The tent was cool but I don't mind sleeping in here.'

Joel studied them both, quashing the feeling he was missing something, before he picked up the torch with studied deliberation. 'Sure you don't want to come back to the tent? We could work something out.'

Nate looked to Eve who experienced a brief surge of exasperation before she firmly suppressed it. It was late, it had been a long day, and suddenly, all Eve wanted to do was go to bed.

Joel shrugged, his disappointment obvious, and wished them a wistful goodnight.

'You might as well sleep above the cab,' suggested Eve, as he was halfway out of the door.

Tempted, he hesitated for a second and then he turned back around. 'The tent's fine for me. Shut this door quickly. You're letting in the bugs.'

Fighting the urge to keep Joel talking despite feeling exhausted, Eve shut the door firmly and then she prepared for bed. However, if she was expecting to settle down immediately she was mistaken. Nate was hungry, he needed a snack, then he needed to clean his teeth again, and finally, as he was settled under the old duvet, he decided he was thirsty.

'Just water,' instructed Eve. 'You've already done your teeth.' She filled his bottle and left it with him. 'Be careful to close the lid securely.'

Her head just touched the pillow, when a small voice said, 'Eve.'

'Yes.'

'Is Rocky Mountain House the last fort we'll visit?'

'I believe so.'

'And then you're going back to England?'

'Yes but there are some interesting things we'll do before then. Your Dad is planning to take us to Elk Island to see the wildlife. I've never seen bison,' Eve replied, sitting up and trying to sound bright and positive.

There was a pause, long enough for Eve to think about lying down again before Nate announced, 'I wish you were coming to Grandma's.'

'I would have liked that too, but I only have three weeks in Canada.'

'Why don't you change your flight?'

'I wish I could,' replied Eve, wholeheartedly, 'but I have to go back to work.'

'It would be so much better if you came.'

There was another long pause and a big sigh. 'Grandma is scary.'

Eve took care with her answer. 'Sometimes we think people or things are scary because we aren't used to them.'

Nate was quiet while he thought about this. 'No, Grandma is just scary.'

'In that case, you need to have a plan.'

'A plan?'

'Yes, a plan of action—what you will do so you don't find her scary.'

'How?'

'You could talk to her. Ask her about something she likes doing. What does she like?'

'She likes riding horses.'

'There you go.'

'That's no good.'

'Why?'

'I don't want to ride. Grandma gets cross when I refuse.'

'What else does Grandma enjoy?'

'She cooks a lot.'

'You could ask her to let you help with the cooking?'

Nate's response was hardly a whisper. 'I'm too scared to ask.'

'Why is that?' Eve asked, gently.

'There's lots of meat.'

It was not an answer Eve was anticipating. 'Is that a problem?'

'Jean-Claude says we shouldn't eat animals.'

'Ah!'

Totally stumped, Eve chose to procrastinate. 'It's late, Nate. Let's talk about this in the morning. Snuggle down.'

She waited, hoping to hear the soft sound of a sleeping child, and soon, all was quiet. She turned her thoughts to Gideon Thompson. Her experience at Carlton House had given her a thirst to find out more and the evocative name of Rocky Mountain House played in her mind as she attempted to sleep. An owl hooted again in the distance as she felt drowsiness descend and it took some time for the small voice to penetrate her consciousness.

'Eve! I need to pee.'

Twenty-Six

December 1850

Gideon sat at the small table in his living quarters and stared at the letter. It had been more than a week since he had abandoned his writing; a week of relentless monotony. He tried to shut out the sound of the wind, a continuous nerve-wracking wail, as it groaned around the cabin, clamouring for entry, and to concentrate on what he would tell Grizzel. Bowed down by negativity, there was precious little he could write about, so he picked up his pen only to lay it back down.

He was hungry, hungrier than he had ever been in Lerwick. He thought of his grandmother, how thin she had become, and experienced a deep visceral longing to see her and his grandfather. His yearning was matched by that of being home, to be in Shetland, and to see the sea. In his imagination, Gideon stood at the point above John Gray's croft where he could look out over the North Sea and then turn around to see the Atlantic. He could smell the saltiness underlaid with the tang of seaweed, the unmistakable redolence of the sea which, to him, was perfect. The bay where the sea otters played was below him. In his mind's eye, he saw them emerging from the water, sleek and wet, before they settled down to preen, just as they did when he and John had watched them.

Lost in his thoughts, Gideon inhaled deeply and was rudely awakened from his reverie by a lungful of stale air. His stomach growled, yet the greasy taste of pemmican was still in his mouth from supper. He tried to ignore both the fetid air and the rancid taste in favour of concentrating on the letter in front of him. What did people normally write in letters? News of what they had done and the people they had met? He doubted Grizzel would want to hear about a recruit from Orkney who, a couple of years ago, had accompanied a band of Cree and had married one of the chief's daughters. They now had a son who lived with his Cree grandparents, as was the custom of the tribe.

Gideon picked up his pen again, hoping the feel of it in his hand might spark some inspiration, and dipped it in the ink. He would write about what he had done since he had last put pen to paper, the previous month.

Carlton House
December 1850
My dear Grizzel,

I hope this letter finds you in good health. I think of you often, never more so than in these, the darkest days of winter. It is now my second winter in Rupert's Land and this one is already worse than the last. The cold is the same but here we live much more hand-to-mouth than at Norway House. Also, the company is not so varied here, although I have met a clerk, Jim Turnbull, whose conversation I welcome. We both avail ourselves of the fort's library at every opportunity and I am learning something of the account-keeping from him.

I do not have many experiences to recount for you as life follows a dreary pattern. One, though, I believe, is worthy of sharing. It is an account of my latest foray to replenish the fort's food stocks. We rely heavily on the Indians to provide us with meat and pemmican, and when they fail to arrive, we need to hunt ourselves. My life in Shetland did not prepare me for this. I can tackle any smithing task asked of me but controlling a dog sled is very different.

We set off in search of game, hoping to find buffalo sheltering in the coolies. Although the prairies are thought of as flat, there are undulating hills and it was these which caused me some difficulty with the sled. Three teams set out. I accompanied, Joe Kennedy, a Métis, who was invaluable to a greenhand like me, and the other member of the party, Alec Fraser, was also a seasoned hunter who had learnt much from his mother's people, the Cree.

One of the things I must mention to you, Grizzel, is that I have permanently changed my boots for moccasins this winter and my feet fare much better. They can move more freely and are warmer than when constricted inside my boots.

Our search for game drove us towards the west, as there has been a shortage of buffalo around Carlton House this year. This can be dangerous as we come nearer to the area where the Blackfoot tribe roams and there is animosity between them and the Cree. A couple of years ago, a large group of the Blackfoot federation marched as far as this fort and attacked a Cree encampment. The Cree retaliated earlier this year, killing a renowned Blackfoot warrior. I was glad we were well-armed.

On our outward journey, we were hit by a blistering blizzard, the like of which I had never experienced. It is one thing to be inside a sturdy wooden cabin, Grizzel, when the killing wind blows but it is an entirely different situation being out on the prairie. I had been schooled in what to do but I was still filled with trepidation as Joe and I scooped a hole in the snow. We lined it with the buffalo robes we carried, and then, we all three crawled in and lay down, pulling more robes and blankets over us. We stayed like this, with the dogs sheltering beside us, until the storm passed.

Being in a sheltered spot, we only moved a short distance to dig under the snow in order to find dried buffalo dung for our fire. Once it was lit, we boiled the kettle for tea and ate some pemmican. You have to drink the tea quickly, Grizzel, before it freezes. Joe told me that he had once spent two days and two nights in a snow hole, which you can imagine was not too agreeable other than one survived the snowstorm. I was pleased to be with two old hands.

Joe led the way and one of the fears I had was that, if a storm blew up quickly, I would lose sight of him. Alec brought up the rear so I was protected between them. Very early on our journey, I became aware of wolves following us. They kept their distance but it was as if they knew there would be pickings if we made a kill. Alec assured me that they were more frightened of us than we were of them but I felt unsettled the entire trip.

I had been given the most amenable dog as the leader of my team, a veteran of many trips, and I must admit that I enjoyed the sensation of skimming across the snow. The problem came when we needed to cross a slope and my lack of experience came to light in a spectacular fashion. The sled overturned and I was thrown out to be rescued by Alec, as were the dogs who were tangled in the harness. Fortunately, we had not yet come across the buffalo so no damage was done to valuable cargo.

On the second day, we did come across a small group of animals. Joe and I stayed back with the dogs while Alec crept ahead on his snow shoes. He managed to hit one young bull, before the others scattered, which was most welcome when we returned to the fort. In all, we were successful on our trip as, later that day, Joe shot a second older bull, whose meat would not be so good although still palatable.

I think of you, Grizzel, at home in Lerwick and send you my warmest wishes. The Christmas season will soon be upon us, but here, it is marked very poorly. I will tell you about it in my next letter.

Your friend,
Gideon

He leant back in his chair and rested the pen in the inkwell. He had intended to write more and to be more effusive with his words concerning Grizzel but a worm of uncertainty had prevented him. He had had one letter from her, and as he analysed the situation objectively, he was crushed with the futility of his dream of returning home to find her unwed and waiting for him. If he declared himself and laid his soul bare in his letters, how difficult would it be if she thought differently? He lifted up the letter now the ink was dry, and fingered the paper. It would travel north to York Factory in the spring, accompanying the furs, once the ice had melted on the Saskatchewan. Then, it would cross the Atlantic, and if the stars were aligned, Grizzel might receive it by June. What had she been doing since she had written to him? Fifteen months would have passed, and in his melancholy mood, he could not imagine her giving him much thought.

'What ails you?' asked a bright voice.

Gideon glanced up from the letter at the same time as he laid it aside.

'I did not mean to disturb you,' explained Jim, with a half-apologetic smile on his face.

'I've finished and would be glad of some company.'

There was only one chair in the room so Jim sat on the bed and eased his long legs out in front of him. 'Look!' he announced as he held up the book.

Gideon's eyes lit up. As the number of books in the travelling library was limited, the competition for some volumes was intense, especially as it was six months since they had arrived. He grinned at his friend.

Jim was so pleased with himself that he waved the copy of "Rob Roy" with a flourish.

'I look forward to reading it when you've finished with it.'

'You can read it now!' declared Jim. 'I've read it before—at home.'

Gideon took the book and studied it reverently, momentarily envious of Jim's home life where books had been a natural part of an educated household. Jim watched him briefly and then transferred his attention to the letter on the table.

'Busy with your correspondence, I see. No doubt to the fair maid in Shetland?'

'Are you ever at a loss on what to write home, Jim?'

Jim sobered slightly. It was not a question he was expecting. In all their conversations, Gideon Thompson had never veered towards anything of a personal nature. He batted away any questions about the recipient of his letters and Jim knew nothing of him other than he had been a blacksmith in his native Shetland and that he had acquired his seaman's ticket before he had been recruited to serve in Rupert's Land. The apprentice clerk had soon discovered that the islander was quick of wit and industrious but of his education, Gideon had revealed little.

Jim's reply was unsatisfactory as he explained that he responded to the news from home. The letters he received from his mother and sisters were full of details of their busy lives; their charity work, the social circle within which they moved, drawing lessons and pianoforte lessons, and always, what books were of interest. He diligently commented on every snippet in his return letters, but as he only briefly mentioned his work as a clerk, he was unable to help Gideon.

'What news do you have of home?'

Gideon shrugged and then met his friend's eyes keenly, defying him to be censorious. 'My grandparents are illiterate.' The use of his final word caused him to pause, remembering the first time he had heard it when the Reverend Murray had explained its meaning. 'Grizzel has no need of her letters but she has had schooling and wrote me a fine letter.' He thought of the cobweb-fine knitting she produced without the need to read a pattern and his heart swelled with pride for her.

Jim's pale blue eyes were fixed on him. Gideon responded to the genuine warmth they radiated. 'And my parents are dead.'

Uncertain how to proceed, as any reference to his lack of parents would not help Gideon's quandary about what to write home, Jim suddenly had an idea. He mulled it over briefly and then pronounced his solution.

'Why don't you compose a poem?'

'A poem?' spluttered Gideon in disbelief. 'I know nothing of poetry.'

'There are some volumes in the library. You could always copy some lines down.'

'Perhaps,' said Gideon, unconvinced.

'Only that would be cheating,' announced Jim. 'What you write should come from your heart.'

'I only asked you what you wrote in your letters.'

'True—but I'm not trying to woo a fair damsel.'

'There's nobody at home, besides your family, who you think about?'

Jim, jokingly, mimed the pose of a great thinker, followed by a dramatic pause.

'No.'

Gideon laughed, but later, when he was next writing to Grizzel, he remembered Jim's suggestion.

Carlton House
February 1851
Dearest Grizzel,

I have returned to my letters to you to find that I have neglected to write since before Christmas. Do not take this as any reduction in my regard for you as I can assure you that my admiration of you has continued to grow.

My lapse can only be credited to the routine of the fort which lulls oneself into a weariness born of boredom. There are long stretches when we are confined like prisoners within the exterior walls with the weather our gaoler. The monotony is only broken by the arrival of the Indians to trade, when the weather permits, or for us to venture out ourselves during those opportune times, to hunt.

Christmas Day came and went with very little to cheer it. We were still very short of rations, but after the Christmas service had been read by the Chief Factor, we did enjoy some buffalo tongue and some chocolate which had been kept specifically to raise our spirits on that significant day.

We fared much better on New Year's Day. On the twenty-seventh of December, a band of Stonies came to trade. They had buffalo robes, furs, and leather, but best of all, they had provisions. We were able to replenish our dried meat and pemmican stocks so our dinner to celebrate the arrival of 1851 was more copious than that at Christmas. We were also given tobacco and rum to mark the day. I did think of home and of you, Grizzel, with great affection as we welcomed the new year.

As today is St Valentine's Day, the timing of which has prompted me to write, I am sending you a token of my regard. It is a carving of a black bear modelled on those I see often. I hope you will keep it with the two selkies. I am sorry that I do not have a card to send you, the like of which you deserve. I am sure Kitty will be receiving one from Will. Please remember me to them and I ask, if possible, would you be able to send news of my grandparents in your next letter?

Before he finished the letter, Gideon took a piece of card that Jim, on hearing his friend's intention, had found at the back of the stationery cupboard in the clerk's office. Already somewhat crumpled, Gideon had smoothed out the worst wrinkles by sandwiching the card between two weights in the forge. Now, he folded it carefully. He studied the cover for a moment and wrote 'My Dearest Love' in his best script before he turned his attention to the inside. There he drew a large heart and inscribed within it the thought always at the forefront of his mind.

Though I be beyond the Shetland Sea, my heart will always be with thee.

He felt his cheeks wash with embarrassment but he forced himself to continue. Grizzel must understand what she had come to mean to him. The thought of Angus Duncan wooing her spurred him on. Moving the lamp to allow better illumination, Gideon began to surround the heart with meticulously decorated bears. When he had finished, he leant back and admired it before deciding to leave it unsigned. It was, after all, a valentine.

After several reflective minutes, Gideon picked up his pen once more. He re-read his request for news of his grandparents and wondered whether he had emphasised his need strongly enough. He could only trust Grizzel to try her best. Perhaps the merchant, Laing, would give her news of his grandmother; surely Margaret would have been to Lerwick to sell her shawls? Gideon glanced up from the paper and watched the lantern flame flicker, casting shadows into the dark room. Suddenly, he wanted to stand up and howl with frustration. The ambition of returning home with money for his grandparents had faded more than his dream of making Grizzel his own. He had ceased to think about his wages, which he would receive when his five years had been served, and as he placed his head in his hands, he felt that his world had shrunk to a fort on the North Saskatchewan River, from which he would never escape.

Twenty-Seven

That night, following the visit to Fort Carlton, Nate finally settled down and slept after he had made two further trips to the bathroom. Eve lay still, pretending to be asleep, until she heard his even breathing and allowed herself to relax into a deep sleep only to be woken in the morning by Joel's voice raised in frustrated exclamation.

'What is it?' she asked, hastily pulling her sweatshirt over her pyjamas and thrusting her feet into her flip-flops.

She emerged into early morning sunlight to find Joel staring at his phone in disbelief. 'Look!' he said passing it to her so that she could read the screen.

'Fort Edmonton is closed? 'she questioned, although the text was unambiguous.

'Yes,' replied Joel. 'It's closed for renovations for the whole of the season.'

'Oh, no! I really wanted to visit it. I'd read that it was the headquarters of the Saskatchewan District and that, in the mid-nineteenth century, it had started to attract visitors. Curious travellers found their way there, as did artists like Paul Kane. Apparently, it has been authentically restored and you can see the Chief Factor's House and all the servants' quarters. It would have been great to see it—especially as Gideon might have served there.'

Nate, still sleepily rubbing his eyes, had joined them while Eve was speaking. He plonked himself down on the nearest of the chairs which Joel had arranged around the firepit. The boy noticed that the tent had been taken down and was neatly rolled up, ready to be stowed away in one of the outside lockers, while his father's sleeping bag was draped over the hedge to air. They were obviously having a prompt start.

'What are we going to do instead?' he asked, a fledgling idea taking hold as he fully woke up.

'I'm not sure. What do you think, Eve?'

She glanced from father to son. 'What else is there to see around Edmonton?'

'Depends on what you want to see, Eve, and you too, Nate.'

'It's a big city, isn't it?'

'Yep.'

'I think, on balance, I'd rather see more of the countryside.'

'How long were we going to stay at Edmonton?' Nate asked his father.

'A couple of nights at least.'

Nate appeared to mull over this information and then he suggested, nonchalantly, 'Why don't we invite Eve to Grandma's if we have two spare days?'

His ingenuous tone failed to fool Eve although Joel appeared to consider the proposal. She jumped in before he could answer. 'I'd still like to go to Rocky Mountain House and visit Elk Island on the way.'

'Couldn't we do both, Dad?'

'It's a lot to fit in.'

'We could miss out Elk Island. That would give us another day as well,' recommended Nate.

'I thought you wanted to go to Elk Island?'

'It'll be there next year,' replied Nate, trying to sound worldly-wise.

'What about me?' asked Eve. 'I might want to see the buffalo.'

Nate stood up and crossed his arms. 'Eve,' he said with great emphasis. 'Last time we went, I saw only two bison and there were so many people making a noise on the lake, kayaking, that there was no chance of seeing any beavers.'

'When did you go?' asked Joel, taken aback.

Nate flinched slightly at the sharpness in his father's voice. 'I went with Mom and Jean-Claude.'

'When?'

'Last year—we were staying with Nicole, Jean-Claude's sister,' Nate retorted somewhat belligerently.

Eve watched Joel closely sensing another treat he had planned for Nate had lost its gloss. She spoke quietly, hoping to diffuse the tension. 'Perhaps if we got there very early we would see more animals? Before most people arrive.'

Neither of them answered. Sensing an impasse, she gave both of them her warmest smile and said, 'Breakfast, anyone?'

After they had eaten, everyone felt better, so Joel and Eve planned out the rest of the trip. They would drive straight to Rocky Mountain House, dropping south at Battleford and then they would drive due west. They would need one overnight stop and then a couple of days at Rocky Mountain House. From there to the ranch was a little over four hundred kilometres, so it was doable. The key question was fitting in Eve's return visit to the Lennons.

'When are they expecting you?' asked Nate, now determined that Eve would stay with them as long as possible.

'I haven't arranged it with them yet.' Eve was quickly calculating the latest time she could arrive in Calgary without seeming to be impolite.

'What time is your flight?'

'It's an overnight flight. I seem to remember we take off at ten-thirty p.m.'

'Dad!' exclaimed Nate. 'Eve could get to the airport from the ranch.'

'No, I couldn't do that,' replied Eve.

'Why not?' Nate was still standing with his arms folded, his brow wrinkled with resolve.

'The Lennons have been very kind to me, inviting me to stay. It would be rude not to see them before I left.'

'We have been very kind to you, bringing you with us.'

Eve was stumped. She assessed the small fierce figure, trying to find the correct words to resolve the situation. 'That is so true, Nate, and I am having a wonderful time but I need to think about the end of my holiday.' She spoke with composure but not so slowly that he would be offended. 'How would I get from your ranch back to Calgary? I don't have my own car and I'm sure it would not be an easy journey by public transport. I can't miss my flight.'

'We'll drive you there, won't we, Dad?'

Eve risked a glance at Joel. Throughout the exchange, he had been standing, totally silent and exuding an aura of calm, just as he had when she had first met him at the airport. His eyes were twinkling. She raised her eyebrows, asking for help. None came.

'Let's pack up,' she suggested by way of a compromise, 'and then we can discuss the next few days as we're travelling.'

They collected up the breakfast dishes and Nate followed Eve inside while Joel lifted the hood and checked the engine.

'I did what you said,' announced Nate as Eve passed him the tea towel.

'What do you mean?' she asked, turning her head to see him fully.

'I made a plan,' he replied, triumph shining in his eyes. He reached out and touched her soapy hand. 'You will come, won't you?'

It would have taken a harder heart than Eve's to refuse, but as she replied, 'Of course,' a twinge of doubt crept in. Joel had not officially invited her.

It was too late for her to speak to him as Nate was out of the door in a flash, the tea towel still in his hand. Eve watched him, through the front window, disappear from view behind the open hood. She waited, holding her breath, as the hood was carefully lowered and she could clearly see Joel and Nate. The latter was jumping up and down giving her the thumbs up with both hands, while Joel looked at her with such intensity that she avoided his eyes.

Fighting the rising tide of emotions, Eve plunged her hands back into the soapy water and vigorously began to sponge the coffee mug. Nate flung back the door, making the insect screen rattle.

'Whoah!' shouted his father. 'Don't break it.'

Eve heard Joel enter but kept her eyes firmly on the mug.

He watched her for, what seemed to Eve, too long. 'Are you aiming to scrub off the pattern?' he teased.

She put the sponge down and rinsed the mug under the tap. Watching the running water, she said, 'Please don't feel pressurised into taking me home with you.'

Joel leaned over her and flicked off the tap. 'I'll have to fill up the tank if you're going at it like that.'

'Sorry.'

'Don't apologise! And nobody is pressurising me, ma'am.'

She responded with a smile in her voice. 'Okay! But don't call me ma'am!'

Joel waited for her to turn and look at him but she remained resolutely focused on wiping down the sink. He shrugged and addressed Nate instead. What he truly wanted to say could wait.

'C'mon—let's get this old girl on the road. We've a day of driving ahead of us.'

After the two of them had clattered down the steps, Eve began to tidy away the bedding and to secure the catches on the cupboards. As her head buzzed with feelings for Joel, entwined with excitement about travelling west, her thoughts roamed to Gideon. She was convinced he had been at Fort Carlton. Would she feel the same when she visited Rocky Mountain House? Had the blacksmith made the same journey they were about to make, albeit under very different circumstances? The anticipation and thrill of discovery sang in her blood. Could she find some concrete evidence in the most westerly fort of the Saskatchewan District?

Once they set off, Eve was not alone in her excitement. Nate bounced up and down on his seat, adding creaks to the usual rattles and clangs, as the RV bowled along the highway, while Joel turned on the radio and sang along, his deep bass joining the cacophony of sounds. Eve watched the sky, as high cumulus clouds drifted across a sweep of azure, so perfect that she tried to imprint it in her mind forever. She could feel the involuntary upturning of her lips until she could no longer stop herself from exclaiming in joy. It was loud enough to temporarily halt both the bouncing and the singing.

'What's up?' Joel eyed her quizzically, coping as he was with his own seesaw of emotions. He was taking Eve home, the first woman since Colette had left him, and she was leaving Canada within the week. Fluctuating between wanting to acknowledge his attraction to her; being glad that circumstances put paid to any possibility of developing a relationship and fighting the fear of being hurt again, Joel knew that he had been uncharacteristically moody. Yet, as he settled into the rhythm of the journey, he had become aware of a dominant emotion; one he had not experienced for some time. It was hope.

Eve dragged herself away from the sky, bestowed on him a captivating smile which made his stomach flip and announced, 'It's so magnificent.'

He managed one word. 'Happy?'

'Yes,' she replied emphatically. 'In fact, so happy that I want to bottle it!'

He laughed. 'It doesn't take much to make you happy.'

'True,' she said, 'but I am a bit worried about something.'

'What?'

She paused for a moment and fiddled with the map on her knee, avoiding his gaze. 'Won't your mother think it odd you bringing me home? Some strange girl from England.'

'Nope! She's used to it.'

'Used to it?'

'Yep! I'm always bringing strange girls home.'

Then, she did look at him and the warmth in his eyes made a lie of his words. 'Shouldn't you keep your eyes on the road,' she advised, turning back so she could seal the view in her memory.

'Yes, ma'am!'

She chose to ignore him, instead concentrating on the prairie grass rippled into mesmerising waves by the wind, but he had noticed the faint colour blushing her pale cheeks and the secret smile before she turned her head.

Twenty-Eight

Rocky Mountain House, July 2019

Eve was in a small museum adjacent to the Visitor Services Centre in the town of Rocky Mountain House, studying a display of two hundred different types of barbed wire. However, it was not the exhibit, which would have been beyond her imagination earlier in the year, but the brand names which had caught her eye. Fortunately, the room was empty except for the three of them.

'Oh, my goodness,' exclaimed Eve. 'Look at that!'

Each of the examples was labelled and Nate, who was at her side, read the one at the end of her finger. He sounded out the syllables, 'Sun—der—land.'

Joel, who had been glancing at an exhibition of articles from pioneer life, some of which he recognised from his home, strolled over. 'What is it?'

'Look at the name of that wire. It's called Sunderland.'

'And?'

'That's where I come from. Isn't it a coincidence?'

Eve sensed Joel's shrug rather than witnessed it. 'Don't you think it comes from there?' As soon as she asked the question, Eve looked up at him and saw the amusement on his face. She frantically tried to recall whether it could be a possibility. Her father had had a map of Sunderland, dated 1870, framed and it still hung in their hall in Roker. He had loved maps, as did she, and from the recesses of her mind, came a childhood memory. She could see the words clearly on the map, near to where her aunt had lived just south of the river. It made sense. Sunderland was, after all, a leading shipbuilding port at that time.

'It could have been—we did have ironworks then.' She pointed to the date on the label, '1884'.

Joel continued to watch her, delighting in her enthusiasm. 'Did the works make barbed wire?'

'I have no idea,' she admitted as she bent closer to the display case. 'It looks particularly vicious.'

Nate joined her so that their heads were level, almost bumping. 'I can't believe there are so many types of barbed wire.'

Eve ran her eyes down the selection. Each one was unique with the "Sunderland" having a long double hook on a single strand of wire. Many others had double strands. She gazed up at Joel. 'I suppose you know a lot about barbed wire.'

'Some, but I've never seen an antique collection like this.'

'Why do you think it's called "Sunderland", then?

'Perhaps because a man called Leslie E. Sunderland patented it?'

'Oh.'

'Yep.'

'In 1884?'

'I believe so.'

'Well, that sorts that out.'

'Yep, are you ready to go yet?' Museums were not Joel's favourite places.

'I just want to have another look at the Hudson's Bay Company section upstairs.'

'Come on then, we need to get a move on if we are having lunch before we go to the fort.'

Eve tried to organise the information sheets on her knee as the RV rattled along the road. She had managed a quick scan of their contents over lunch but Joel had insisted that they enjoy a meal free of conversation about the HBC. He wanted her to enjoy the here and now of Rocky Mountain House, and so far, she had been happy to comply. They had arrived the previous evening and set up camp at a site on the North Saskatchewan River, the same river on which Fort Carlton was situated. The decision to abandon the tent had been easily made, giving them more time to enjoy a leisurely supper and then a stroll along the riverbank in the evening sunlight. However, as she had watched the dipping sun burnishing the water, Eve had to stop herself imagining Gideon and a brigade of York

Boats rowing past in favour of concentrating on Joel and Nate's conversation. Now that it had been established that she was coming to the ranch with them, both father and son demonstrated a keenness to be on their way, and especially in Nate's case, a lack of enthusiasm about visiting yet another fort and doing more research on the HBC.

Nate was whingeing in the back seat. 'I don't know why we are going—the lady in the Visitors' Centre said there was nothing there but two old chimneys. Everything else has gone.'

'True,' replied his father. 'But Eve wants to see the site.'

'Why—there's nothing there?'

Eve had some sympathy for Nate. How could she explain to a seven-year-old her need to see where Gideon might have been? Her hopes had been raised by one of the museum staff who had explained how York Boats had been made at Rocky Mountain House. Using the plentiful supply of local timber, boatbuilders constructed up to seven boats over the winter months. In the spring, once the ice had melted, the boats were taken downstream to Fort Edmonton, either packed with furs and robes or floated empty. From there, the hardy boats, all now laden, would start the long journey to York Factory on Hudson Bay. The Orkney men, which Eve had remembered was a generic term for men from both Orkney and Shetland, were prized for their skill with boats, and when she read in one of the leaflets about the blacksmiths, Gideon's presence became a strong possibility.

'Had he worked on the docks at Lerwick? If so, he would be an ideal recruit to send to Rocky Mountain House.'

'Pardon?'

'Did I speak?'

'Yes, but you spoke so quietly I couldn't hear.'

'Sorry, Joel, I was talking to myself.'

'Are you following on the map? I'm sure we should have reached the turn-off by now.'

Eve guiltily shuffled the leaflets and retrieved the map which had fallen in the footwell. She peered out of the window to see if she could recognise a landmark. 'We do seem to have been driving too long but I haven't seen a sign.'

'How could you see a sign?' demanded a disgruntled Nate. 'You've been looking at your lap for most of the journey, reading those sheets of paper.'

'I'd have seen a sign,' retorted Eve, firmly. 'And so would your father!' She glanced at Joel and was rewarded with a conspirative wink.

'Did you see anything, bud?'

'No,' replied Nate, drawing out the word in a long breath.

'Well, then, we'll just keep on going for a bit.'

They continued driving with their eyes peeled on the roadside until the road forced a decision. Without warning, it narrowed and changed into a rough track.

'This can't be right,' announced Joel as he executed a three-point turn. 'We must have missed the sign.'

Accompanied by sighs from the backseat, they retraced their journey, now travelling towards the town.

'Look,' shouted Nate triumphantly as they approached a road joining the highway on the right. A large sign indicated that they take it, and as they turned, Eve noticed a much smaller sign on the opposite side of the road which they had missed. Choosing not to mention it, she congratulated Nate on finding the way.

It was a short distance to the historic site, and as they covered the last couple of kilometres, Eve started to summarise some information from the sheets for everyone's benefit.

'There have been several forts built on this site. At first, there was the Hudson's Bay Company one, which was called Acton House, and the North Western Company one, called Rocky Mountain House.'

'When was that?' asked Joel.

'1799.'

'A bit before Gideon Thompson's time.'

'Yes—but after the two companies merged, it was called Rocky Mountain House as the French had called it.'

'That was in?'

'The 1820s.'

'What else does it say?'

'That the forts were small. When they merged, there were eleven people at Acton House and twenty-seven at the French fort.'

'French Canadians mainly?'

'Yes.'

'The chimneys are from the Hudson's Bay Fort of 1799,' declared Nate as he leant over Eve's seat and waved a postcard towards the two adults. 'It says here.'

Eve took the postcard and read the back, although she had already seen it in the museum shop the previous day. 'You're correct, Nate. They look quite big. I'll think it'll be fun to find them. There are four different sites of forts on the map. As a trading post, Rocky Mountain House lasted for seventy-six years and the fort was abandoned and rebuilt several times.'

'It's quite a big site then?' asked Joel.

'Yes, I think so.'

'Good—plenty of room to stretch our legs and explore.'

Fortunately, there was a great deal more to see than Nate expected. The Visitor Centre had fascinating displays of fur trade artefacts and there was a replica of the fur trading room. There was also a Trading Post gift shop stocked with the famous blankets, books, crafts, and objects a small boy was itching to fiddle with. Joel led them straight through everything, having decided some fresh air was needed, with the promise that they could check out everything after they had seen the site.

The early fur traders had chosen well. Situated near the confluence of the North Saskatchewan and the Clearwater Rivers, the two original forts were only half a mile apart and were built in Blackfoot territory. Hoping to take advantage of the proximity to the Rocky Mountains, both companies had hoped to be able to trade with the Kootenay tribe whose territory was across the mountains where there was a plentiful supply of beaver. However, as the Blackfoot were hostile to this, as well as to the HBC trading with the Cree who rarely ventured so far west, it was vital that the site was well-protected. The Blackfoot could attack if they felt they were being undermined by their traditional enemies.

Joel and Eve stood on the site of the earliest fort and tried to work out the defences, with Eve referring to one of the information sheets. 'The Blackfoot would come from the south to trade as the North Saskatchewan River marked the northern limit of their territory. They would follow an old trail along the Clearwater River and approach the fort from the east, where the North Saskatchewan would need to be crossed. The fort itself was obviously constructed for protection, consisting of a rectangular wooden stockade with bastions at each corner, which surrounded the living quarters, the storerooms, the trading quarters and the blacksmith shops. The boats' shed would be outside of the stockade next to the river.'

'Come over here!' shouted Nate who was dancing in front of the two chimneys. Joel wandered over and called over his shoulder to Eve, 'There were obviously some stone structures.'

She crossed the grass towards him. 'They're pretty impressive,' she said, allowing her eyes to travel up the rough stone. What's left must be at least three metres high.'

'At least the fort's occupants could keep warm. Your Gideon would be okay in his forge.'

'True,' said Eve, 'but it says here that Rocky Mountain House was a precarious post for the recruits. It was only opened in the autumn for the trading season, so no reserves of food could be accumulated. If the men couldn't hunt, they would starve. They even had to eat dogs and horses to stay alive!'

'Ugh!'

'Yes, it's awful, Nate,'

'Yet Gideon Thompson did survive,' stated Joel

'Apparently so—his service ended in 1854 so he completed his five years. What I don't know, is did he go home to Shetland?'

'Rach said that most of the recruits stayed because they were granted land.'

'I remember, Joel. What an incentive.'

They wandered back along the river to the sites of the later forts and then decided to go and see the small herd of bison grazing on the surrounding parkland. The wind lightly touched the tips of the grass, the sun streamed through a break in the clouds and the air was alive with the sound of summer. Eve closed her eyes and breathed deeply, enjoying a moment of pure serenity.

Joel was watching her. 'Any vibes from across the years?'

Eve's eyes snapped open. 'Pardon?'

'At Fort Carlton, you felt certain Gideon had been there. What about here?'

Eve chuckled. 'Don't go thinking I'm psychic! All I'm feeling here is contentment.'

'Now I'm disappointed!'

She grinned at him. 'I'm sure you'll cope.'

Joel was about to respond when Nate bounded towards them, his good humour restored. 'Hi, bud—what do you want to do next?'

'Go to the shop, Dad.'

'You okay with that, Eve? Joel was studying her, his hat tipped low making it difficult to read his eyes.

She nodded and set off, following Nate who was walking with determination towards the Visitor Centre.

Joel came alongside her, his leisurely gait matching her quick steps, and as they walked in companionable silence, she realised with depressing certainty that her heart was truly lost. Later, when she analysed her feelings, Eve would ponder on the absurdity of the circumstances. There had been no longing looks or declaration of love, nothing to mark the significance of the moment yet, for her, it was a revelation of seismic clarity. Without doubt, Eve knew that she wanted Joel in her life despite the obstacle of thousands of kilometres and the fact that she was leaving in three days.

They were back at the campsite watching the dying embers of the fire. Darkness had descended, it was very late for Nate to still be up, yet nobody made a move to leave the comforting glow. He articulated what Eve and Joel were thinking.

'This is our last night in the RV. I don't want it to be over.'

'Neither do I, bud. Have you enjoyed the trip?'

Nate nodded. 'It's been cool.'

'Despite too many forts?' teased Eve.

'They were cool—even the last one.'

'The one where there was nothing to see?'

'But there was in the end. Did you see all the things you could do? You can camp there in tipis or cabins and you can do different activities. Can we go next year, Dad?'

'I don't see why not, bud.'

There was a significant pause. Eve shifted in her seat hoping Nate would ask if she would come. Instead, he said, with deliberation, 'That is not a yes.'

Joel laughed. 'I thought you didn't like sleeping in a tent.'

'A tipi isn't just like a tent. For a start, you can stand up in them.'

'That makes all the difference?'

Nate thought about this and changed tack. 'We'd be better in a cabin.'
'I'll think about it for next year.'
'That's still not a yes.'
'It'll have to do.'
'Eve can come,' he said artfully, looking at her. 'Can't you?'

Having achieved her desire, Eve was now stumped for an answer. She wanted to shout out that she would join them but pragmatism triumphed. 'Next year is a long way away to make plans,' she said gently.

She sensed the small figure slump in the canvas chair. He crossed his arms ready for recalcitrance but Joel was too swift.

'C'mon, bud,' he encouraged, scooping up the boy and flinging him across his shoulder in a fireman's lift. 'It's time for bed.' Nate went floppy, his arms dangling down Joel's back, and he lifted his head to give Eve a wide grin as Joel carried him into the RV.

Eve leaned forward, threw a couple logs onto the embers, and waited for Joel with her heart hammering in her chest. A voice inside her head told her to calm down, to hide the desperation she felt at leaving him, and to let him take the lead in the conversation. Her intention to be bold, to declare her feelings which had crystalised that afternoon, evaporated, as she watched him casually approach the fire and ease himself into the chair opposite hers. She had hoped that he would have taken the adjacent one so that her face would have been more difficult to read, rather than to sit directly in front of her across the fire.

Joel leant back in the chair, his right leg resting on his left thigh, and she noticed his boots as she had done that first meeting in the airport. Reality hit her: how could she even contemplate a relationship with him? He came from another world, one she could not imagine; although, she acknowledged with a frisson of excitement, one which she would glimpse the following day. She studied the fire, trying to collect herself, afraid he would see the hopelessness in her eyes.

'Found what you're looking for?'
'Pardon?' She glanced up, bewildered.
'There must be something mighty interesting in that fire, ma'am.'
'I like watching the flames.'
'I can put another log on.'
'No—I'm tired. I'll go to bed soon.'

'Why didn't you go when Nate did?' His intense gaze unnerved her.

'Be brave, be brave,' she told herself. 'I wanted to speak to you.'

Joel slowly uncrossed his legs and leant forward, an elbow resting on each knee, his eyes never leaving her. 'What would you like to say, Eve Cummins?'

In that moment, her resolve faltered. He was a man she had only known for two weeks, a man who lived an ocean away from her, a man who spent his days outdoors, and she was a librarian who had hidden from life for the last decade. She found herself mumbling,

'I just wanted to thank you for bringing me.'

Flustered, she returned to contemplating the fire and missed the fleeting regret in his eyes which shaped his trite answer. 'You're welcome.'

He waited for more. It did not come. 'Do you think you'll come back to Canada?' he asked conversationally, with no hint of the intensity he was feeling.

'Oh, I think so. It's a lovely country.'

'You've only seen a tiny part of it.'

'True,' she agreed. 'But perhaps it is the best bit?'

He laughed at that, his eyes twinkling again. Eve lifted her head and returned his smile as he said, 'Wait until tomorrow.'

Twenty-Nine

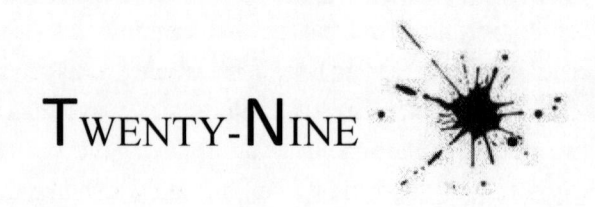

Joel swung the RV off the highway and steered between the posts of an imposing entrance with a confidence honed by familiarity.

'Wow!' The exclamation had escaped Eve's lips before she could stop herself. 'Could you have found a bigger set of horns?'

'Nope,' he replied good-naturedly. 'They're there to impress.'

The sign overhead was a large plank of wood with 'BAXTER RANCH' scorched into it, both words eclipsed by the magnificent horns which hung between them, unequivocally announcing to Eve that she was in ranching country. They had arrived and the knot of nerves in her stomach tightened as they bounced along the uneven track, setting everything clanging and clattering in the van.

They drove for, what seemed to Eve, a very long time, through rolling grassland which stretched as far as she could see, and then, suddenly, the ranch was in front of them. She felt that she should be used to the vastness of the scenery with its far horizons and seemingly unlimited space yet, the size of the house and the number of barns still took her by surprise. Through the open window, her senses were assaulted by the greenness of the nearest pasture, neatly fenced and lazily grazed by half a dozen horses, and the whispering of the trees which protected the buildings from the prevailing wind. For a moment, Eve was mesmerised by the horses' tails swishing away the flies and she almost missed the figure emerging from the stables.

Rose Baxter was exactly as Eve had imagined. Bearing a striking resemblance to her son; she was tall and rangy with chestnut hair streaked with grey. Eve could see the same square face and straight nose, although the eyes, which candidly appraised her, were hazel, unlike the chameleon colour of Joel's. As Rose came towards her, the older woman's expression changed from one of polite curiosity to marked interest.

Eve, on the other hand, was totally different to Rose Baxter's expectation. Intrigued, she watched her son and grandson climb out of the old RV and walk around to the passenger door. Joel opened it and a small, untidy-looking woman stepped down and looked around with evident delight. Nate took her hand and pulled her forward while Joel flanked her on the opposite side.

'This is Eve,' announced Nate, before anyone had the chance to speak.

Joel chided him gently. 'What about saying hello to Grandma first?'

'Hi, Grandma—this is Eve.'

'So it is!' replied Rose, having already decided that she would like Eve. The woman her son had brought home was so different to his ex-wife and to the other women he had occasionally dated before he met Colette, that Rose was briefly taken aback. They had had a tendency to be slender and elegant, and in Rose's opinion, when they had arrived at the ranch in their white jeans and fancy footwear, they had concentrated too much on their own poise. The young woman who was smiling at her was entirely different; all of her attention was taken by her surroundings.

'What a wonderful home you have, Mrs Baxter,' she said sincerely. 'Thank you so much for letting me stay.'

'You're welcome,' replied Rose with equal sincerity, highly approving of Eve's total disregard for looking fashionable but slightly wary of her affability. Her jeans were serviceable and loose-fitting, as was her shirt which appeared a couple of sizes too big. A phrase Rose's grandmother had been particularly fond of popped into her head, as the evening sun gilded Eve's mass of curls and intensified the blue of her irises, "She'd scrub up well if she'd a mind to." The older woman was heartened to see that, despite Eve's tendency to look dishevelled, her clothes were of good quality and remarkably clean after a week on the road; the young woman clearly had standards.

The interior of the house also fitted Eve's imagination perfectly. After using the back entrance and passing through a mudroom which was full of enough boots, coats, and hats for a much larger household, followed by a utility space, Eve found herself in the largest kitchen she had ever seen. It accommodated an enormous scrubbed wooden table with seating for at least a dozen people, an array of cupboards, again of wood, and a large modern stove from which came a delicious aroma.

'Lasagne,' explained Rose. 'Joel told me you liked pasta.'

'I do,' replied Eve, conscious that her knotted stomach had returned. She wished Nate had not confided in her and had said, 'Grandma is scary,' making her analyse every nuance of Rose's speech. Eve's effusive greeting had been an attempt to cover her nervousness, and now, she told herself not to be so stupid as to read anything into Rose's simple sentence.

'Wash up quickly,' instructed her hostess. 'I didn't expect you so late. I don't want supper drying out.'

'Of course, Mom. We'll be at the table in five minutes,' said Joel, placatively.

The lasagne was tasty with a rich sauce and Rose had made a crisp salad to accompany it. The conversation turned to their trip, Eve's research, and the forthcoming Stampede. Nate remained unnaturally quiet, and instantly, the tenor of the meal changed due to Rose's forthrightness.

'Why are you picking at your food, Nate?'

Nate shrugged. 'Don't know.'

'What do you mean you don't know?'

'Just that.'

'You must know,' demanded his grandmother.

'Mom—let him be,' suggested Joel.

'No—you can't sit there playing with good food.'

Nate looked up from his plate and Eve saw the defiance in his eyes. 'I don't like it.'

'Why ever not?'

'There's too much meat.'

'Too much meat,' echoed Rose in disbelief.

'Yes, we shouldn't eat so much meat.'

Rose raised her voice. 'Who says?'

Eve glanced at Joel who was sitting rigidly, poised between mouthfuls.

'Jean-Claude,' announced Nate.

'And what does he know?'

Nate giggled like the seven-year-old he was, trying to decide on how far he could needle his grandmother. Joel's eyes flashed a warning. Thinking better of it, the little boy said,

'They emit gas, Grandma,' and finished the sentence with a snigger.

Rose eyed her grandson, her heart swelling with love and the unfairness of the situation. 'How can you be a cattle rancher if you don't like meat?'

'I didn't say I didn't like meat but that we shouldn't eat so much. Mom sometimes gives us chicken although Jean-Claude says we should be totally vegetarian.'

'God would not have given us incisors to eat meat if it is off the menu,' retorted his grandmother with a hint of triumph in her voice.

Joel had had enough. 'Stop, Nate!' he ordered as he looked from his son to his mother. 'And Mom—we have talked about this before. There must be no pressure on Nate to be a rancher.'

To Eve's surprise, Rose's eyes moistened before she quickly recovered and sat in silence, po-faced. She fiddled with her napkin, folding and then refolding it.

Joel lowered his voice and locked eyes with his indignant son. 'You are correct to be concerned about global warming and there is a problem when cattle are intensively reared and fed artificially, but our cattle are pasture-fed and roam across our open range. There are arguments on both sides but we must always respect each other's opinions.' He glanced quickly at his mother but she was still fiddling with the napkin. The tension in the room was palpable. 'There are problems with growing soya as well. It is not as green as the marketing people want us to believe. We must keep everything in balance.'

The room went quiet until Rose sniffed, deliberately, and said, 'If everyone has had enough, I'd best bring out the pie.'

'Thanks, Mom. Hope it's my favourite.' Joel gave Eve an apologetic, rueful smile.

With token harmony restored, Eve tucked into the most scrumptious-looking pie she had ever seen. The short, buttery pastry broke under the pressure of her spoon to reveal a thick layer of bright red cherries. The juice ran into the dollop of creamy, dairy ice cream which Rose had plonked on top and which had now slid into the bowl.

Eve felt her face grinning in pure pleasure. 'Is it your favourite?'

'Yep—the best pie in the province.'

Nate, not to be outdone, added his own accolade. 'The best pie in the whole world, Grandma.'

Eve witnessed the family dynamics change with a sense of relief. Rose accepted Nate's compliment with good grace, simultaneously dismissing her baking skill as negligible while her face told a different story. Eve relaxed further and concentrated on the pie.

However, once Joel had taken Nate up for a bath and Eve was alone with Rose, the questions began. On the latter's insistence, Eve was to remain seated at the table while the remnants of the meal were tidied away and then Rose would make some coffee.

The pasta bowls were not even stacked in the dishwasher when Rose asked, 'You're just here for a holiday, Eve?'

'Yes, in a way, although I am looking into one of my forebears.'

'A lot of folks are doing that nowadays,' responded Rose, dismissively.

Eve felt a slight prickle of resentment and then squashed it. She countered Rose's tone by saying brightly, 'I've found it very exciting.'

'Some folks know exactly where they have come from.'

Eve chose not to comment, having learnt from Anne Lennon of the five generations of Baxters. Also, she experienced a reluctance to share too much information about Gideon. She was searching for another topic of conversation when Rose returned to the table and picked up the dessert dishes. Pausing with the pile in mid-air, she asked,

'How did you meet Joel and Nate?'

'Joel helped me at Calgary Airport. I wasn't used to the self-service check-in system.'

'When was that?'

'A couple of weeks ago.'

Rose's eyes widened. She placed the dishes back on the table and sat down. Eve, feeling that some difficult questions were on their way, chose to deflect her. It would be too embarrassing to admit to the Lennons checking up on Joel or to allow his mother to speculate about her own intentions in travelling with a virtual stranger.

Eve launched into a hurried explanation. 'My mother died last year after many years of ill health. I haven't travelled by myself since I was at university and then I came home to be with Mum. After that, if we managed a short break, we were lucky. Coming to Canada was a big adventure and I had a purpose in doing some research. Joel was very helpful. I had stayed with a friend of my mum's in Calgary, but when she dropped me off at the airport, I was a bit flummoxed.'

Recalling how overwhelmed she had felt at the airport, all alone in the bustling Departures Hall struggling with the machine, Eve had little memory of what Joel had actually said but she would always remember his aura of calm. Now that she had started to explain to Rose, Eve found the words tumbling out.

'I saw Joel again while we were waiting to board and bumped into him in Winnipeg. He was gracious enough to show me around. I find everybody very pleasant here. He introduced me to his friend, Rach, who helped me with my research.'

Eve took a deep breath, mortified that the mention of research and the association with Hannah's box triggered a sensation of immense grief. It came in a wave encompassing the loss of Hannah and her mother, before widening to include her father and her boyfriend, Jon. She lifted her eyes to Rose, ignoring the tears tracking her face, and experienced total understanding. Rose reached out and placed her large, work-worn hand over Eve's.

'We carry it with us always.'

They sat together, two women remembering their loss, and watched the sun dipping towards the horizon through the kitchen window. It cast long shadows across the pasture until, eventually, the colours were leached to the monochrome of dusk. Rose gave Eve's hand a final pat and cleared the table.

She spoke gently to Eve, 'If you're okay, I'll go and see what's happening upstairs.'

A few minutes later Joel appeared. 'Mom is reading Nate a story.' He looked at Eve keenly, saw her reddened eyes, and was about to comment when she shook her head.

'I'm fine—just a bit emotional.'

'End of holiday blues?' he queried, without much conviction.

'Perhaps,' she responded jokingly, determined to keep the conversation light.

'Then we'd better make tomorrow a day to remember.'

'Good.'

'What would you like to do?'

'I'd like to see the ranch.'

'It's seen best on horseback.'

'That would be great,' said Eve enthusiastically.

'You can ride?'

'I used to ride every chance I had when I was younger. I don't know why I stopped but I have been thinking that, once I'm home again, I'll pay the riding school a visit. They always want help with the horses.' Now she had articulated her plan, Eve realised it was not a spontaneous thought. When she had visited Ada in Saltburn earlier in the year, she had experienced a moment of envy as she watched the riders and horses trotting along the shoreline.

'Another thing to restart, like your PhD. You must make sure that you do.'

'I will.'

'Promise?'

'Yes, bossy,' replied Eve, with a chuckle in her voice, as she watched Joel walk over to the fridge. He took out a can of beer and offered it to her. 'No, thanks. Your mom has put some coffee on.'

Joel eased onto the chair opposite her and placed his beer very carefully on the table. He studied it, as if it was the most interesting object, and then leant back and gave Eve the same attention. Her stomach flipped.

'Stop it!'

'Stop what?'

She was almost too reserved to respond, but in a moment of brilliant clarity, she appreciated that she had nothing to lose. 'Looking at me,' she said in a small voice.

'The Eve I have come to know would be more assertive.'

'Are you criticising me?' she demanded more forcibly.

Joel's eyes twinkled, he leant forward and rested his elbows on the table. 'No.'

Eve did likewise. He was so close she imagined closing her eyes and waiting for his kiss. Instead, she kept them wide open and said, 'Two can play at this game.'

'What game is that?'

'You tell me.'

'Have you enjoyed your trip, Eve?'

They were on more even ground now. 'Yes, immensely—did you?'

Joel took a swig of his beer. Eve waited, nervous about his response, and forced herself to relax back into the chair.

Both of them jumped when the phone rang. It was the house phone, an old-fashioned slim line attached to the wall. Joel's chair scraped the floor, reflecting his annoyance, as he rose to answer it. Eve could not avoid listening to the one-sided conversation but something closed inside of her as he turned his back and looked out into the night.

'Hi, Amy.'

'Yes, I'm back.'

'Tomorrow?' There was a pause. 'Tomorrow isn't good.'

'I've a friend staying. We'll be out most of the day.'

'I thought we'd agreed at the beginning of next week.'

'I know I'm back a bit earlier than expected. How did you know?'

'I didn't know you'd bumped into Mom.'

'Well, if you're going to Lethbridge, of course, you can come visit.'

Joel replaced the receiver and turned around. He searched Eve's face but his opportunity had gone.

Thirty

Dawn had broken, although the sun was yet to rise when Joel pushed open the kitchen door. Rose was already preparing pancakes, bacon and eggs and tomatoes. A large loaf of bread rested on the counter alongside a dish of yellow butter, the coffee was already made, with the industrial-size jug keeping warm on the hot-plate, and the crockery and cutlery were neatly stacked at the end of the long table. There were pots of jam and marmalade and a jar of local honey, already arranged along its length.

'Morning, Mom,' greeted Joel, as he walked towards the coffee machine.

'Morning, son,' replied Rose, pleased that he was the first to arrive. 'Ready to eat?'

Joel glanced at the kitchen clock. 'I'll wait until Jed and the boys arrive.'

'Pour me a coffee then, and I'll keep you company. We've a few minutes.'

Joel leaned against the kitchen counter while Rose took the weight off her feet by sitting at the table. She took a sip of coffee and scanned Joel. 'Everything about you says you like this girl.'

'Am I that obvious?'

'To me you are.'

'Nate really likes her too. Eve has a great way with kids.'

'You've had a good couple of weeks?'

'The best—how did you know it was only a couple of weeks?'

'Eve told me last night when you were with Nate.'

Joel drained his mug and then slowly refilled it, trying to give himself time to think.

Rose interrupted his train of thought. 'You can't know a person after two weeks, however attractive you find them.'

'I know, Mom.'

'Doesn't she go home soon?'

'The day after tomorrow.'

'Well, then. There's not much chance of taking things further.'

'Don't you think I don't know that!'

Rose had hit a nerve. It was so unusual for Joel to raise his voice that she flinched. 'I'm sorry, Joel. There's nothing more I'd like than for you to settle down, but you need to be realistic. Think of Colette—that didn't work. You need a girl who is used to this life. One who will take my place here, in the kitchen. I'm not going to go on forever.'

'Mom—you're sixty-three! I don't think you will be hanging up your apron quite yet.'

Rose laughed, hoping to relieve some of the tension. 'You know what I mean.'

'I'm going to show Eve the spread today.' It was a simple statement, loaded with meaning. Rose chose to ignore the message.

'You can't be out. Amy is calling in.'

'We may be back but I'm not hurrying. I plan on taking a picnic,' said Joel firmly. 'And Mom, please get the idea that Amy Grey would make me a good wife out of your head.'

'It would be rude to be out.'

'No, it wouldn't. I didn't invite her and I can't understand how she knew I was back,' he retorted pointedly.

Rose feigned innocence. 'I thought you'd invited her over?'

'No, I had an arrangement for her to come next week. She's recently bought a Morgan mare.'

'Do you think she has a notion to breed from her?'

'Not necessarily, I hadn't given it much thought. She just asked to come and see Samson.'

'Why now?' asked Rose. 'We've had him long enough.'

'Exactly! She can come next week if she's really interested.'

Rose glanced at the clock; the boys would be in soon, expecting their breakfast. She rose from the table and began to fry the bacon, ready to keep warm while she did the pancakes. Thwarted in her strategy, she contemplated other possible candidates as the bacon crackled on the griddle. There were depressingly few, Amy Grey had been her last hope. Joel studied his mother over the rim of his mug and felt a surge of filial affection. For the last five years, she had tried to match him with every eligible woman in the district with zero success, firm in the belief that a local girl would be the key to his happiness. He was not averse to her efforts in principle, but he refused to pursue a relationship with the sole purpose of finding a wife, and consequently, most of his mother's matches had floundered after a couple of dates. Some friendships had developed, which he enjoyed, but he had never met anyone who had added sparkle to his life. Until now.

When Eve entered the kitchen, half an hour later, she was met by the delicious aroma of breakfast and the low murmur of voices. Three strangers were sitting at the table with Rose, Joel, and Nate. All of them turned towards her as the door clicked shut. Joel stood up, much to her relief, as shyness engulfed her at the unfamiliar scene and led her towards the table. The introductions were brief, although curiosity was thinly masked on the men's part before they turned their attention to the serious task of eating. Eve repeated their names back to herself as Joel automatically piled her plate; Jed Novak, the foreman, Dan Hoffman and Eddie Pine. Jed was a thin wiry man in his early fifties, Dan was probably a decade younger, while Eddie was little more than a youth. They would be easy to distinguish because of their ages, she thought, before reality struck. She would be gone tomorrow so the likelihood of needing to remember their names was negligible.

She eyed the enormous plateful of pancakes, bacon, and tomatoes, pleased that Joel had remembered her dislike of eggs early in the day, but mindful of offending Rose by leaving some. She began to eat slowly, anxious that her knotted stomach would betray her, and told herself to enjoy her last day with the Baxters. Nate was quiet too, watching everyone in turn with his dark, serious eyes.

'Want to go riding, bud?'

Nate jumped at his father's voice, panic flaring at the thought.

Eve, remembering the boy's confidences in the RV, waited for his answer with conflicting emotions. Torn between helping him overcome his reluctance to ride and her own desire to have an opportunity to be alone with Joel, she decided to let fate take its course.

'Is Eve going to ride?'

'Yes.'

'Then I will.'

Rose's face lit with pleasure. 'Good lad,' she said, before turning to Eve. 'What size shoes do you wear?'

Nonplussed, Eve replied, 'Four.'

'What's that here?'

Everyone shrugged. Jed suggested, 'Small.'

'I know it's thirty-seven in European sizes,' added Eve.

Rose thought for a moment. 'The nearest we'll have would be a pair of Ruth's. We can give you some thick socks.'

'Can't I wear my trainers? I know they're not ideal.'

'You'd be better with heeled boots—they're safer with a western stirrup,' replied Rose categorically, leaving Eve little room to negotiate.

'Will your daughter mind me using her boots?'

'Goodness—no!'

It was obviously settled. The next hurdle, Eve thought, would be the horse.

They stepped into the freshness of an early morning which promised a perfect summer's day. High above them, wisps of white cloud were rapidly dispersing to reveal a flawless cerulean sky. Dan had used the time after breakfast, while Joel and Eve had packed a picnic lunch, to saddle a horse for Eve and a pony for Nate, and he was waiting by the corral with them while Joel saddled his own horse. Normally taciturn at best, Dan had no choice but to respond to Eve's infectious enthusiasm. He answered her questions, watching Eve's delight as she talked to the mare.

'What's her name?'

'Luna.'

It was an apt name as Luna was silver dappled, the colour of the moon. She was a heavier build than the two inquisitive horses who soon came over to the fence, one of which was a magnificent stallion. 'Who is this,' asked Eve as the horse nudged Dan with his expressive head.

'Samson—he's the boss's horse.'

'He's Joel's,' she stated, misunderstanding.

Dan shifted from foot to foot in embarrassment. 'Samson was only a youngster when the boss died.'

'I see,' she replied, as she watched Dan stroke Samson's nose. 'He belonged to Joel's father.'

'Yup,' he said, with a finality that discouraged further conversation.

Eve turned to Nate who was standing to attention by the pony and looking very uncomfortable. 'I wonder what's keeping your dad?'

'This,' said a voice behind her and she swung around to see Joel leading an impressive horse and waving a smaller version of his hat. 'This is for you.'

He leaned towards her and placed the hat on her head. 'A real cowgirl,' he teased, his eyes dancing.

'You look cool,' announced Nate.

She felt her cheeks burning, which was disconcerting, so she turned everyone's attention to Joel's horse by saying the first thing that came into her head. 'He looks very solid and trustworthy.'

'He certainly is,' said Joel. 'This is Rocky.'

'After the boxer?'

'No, because he's a Rocky Mountain.'

Nate saw the puzzlement on her face. 'It's a breed, Eve.'

'Oh—very original name, then!'

'I think so!' countered Joel.

Dan found his voice. 'Rocky Mountains are suited to ranch work. They're hardy and can cover the range all day, they're sure-footed, good-natured, and gentle.'

'So, just about perfect?'

'Yes, ma'am. In my opinion, they are.'

'And they're local to these mountains?' she queried, pointing westwards.

Dan corrected her. 'No, ma'am. They originate from the Appalachians.' A slow smile spread across his face and he pointed vaguely south-eastwards. 'In the US,' he added, for her benefit. He was warming towards his subject now. 'Your Rocky Mountain is about the best horse a man working cattle can have. The more you ask of him, the more he gives. He wants to be the best and for sure, ma'am, he is.'

Eve stroked Rocky's brown nose and whispered softly, 'You hear that. We're talking about you.'

Joel glanced from Eve to Dan. 'Are we going to stand here all day and sing the praises of this horse or are we ready to go?' he asked in mock exasperation, secretly pleased that Eve was making headway with the notoriously laconic Dan.

Full of high spirits, Joel and Eve set off at an ambling pace allowing Nate to settle into the gait of his mount, Daisy, named by his cousin, Ellie. Eve, finding Luna's four-beat single-foot gait a comfortable ride, was reminded of how much she had enjoyed riding. She felt on top of the world as Joel led them across open undulating grassland, through stands of lodgepole pine, and along a creek winding lazily between some old cottonwoods. He reined up in a shady glade, dappled with sunlight, and suggested they have a break. The ground was soft and tussocky, the perfect place to relax. Nate immediately started playing in the water, at first throwing stones and then using them to build a dam.

Joel stretched out, his hands behind his head, and watched his son splashing around in the creek. His hat was low over his forehead making it impossible for Eve to read his eyes when she turned to face him. She was sitting upright, leaning forwards slightly with her arms wrapped around her legs.

'What are you thinking about?' he asked.

Eve sighed. 'I was thinking that today is Monday and that on Thursday I will be back home.'

'You could stay longer?'

She tried to read his tone but failed. Was it an idle suggestion or one from the heart? She decided not to respond. She waited, apparently studying Nate's dam construction with interest.

Eventually, Joel spoke. 'It would be great if you could stay a while. My sister, Ruth, and her family and my other sister, Fiona, and hers will be coming for the Stampede. The house will be full of kids—six, including Nate. Then, for the last week, remember that Phil and Rach are flying in. They'll sleep in the RV. They'd all like to see you.'

'With all those people, there wouldn't be room for me then?'

A smile played around Joel's lips. 'I'm sure I could squeeze you in somewhere.'

Eve chuckled. 'In the stable with Luna?'

'I'm thinking of a much more comfortable place.'

Conscious of the subtext, she was unsure about how to reply. She stared straight ahead, firmly suppressing the image of sharing his bed, and heard him shift into a sitting position, mirroring her. He was so close their elbows brushed.

She leaned into him, resting her head on his shoulder. 'It's so beautiful here.'

'There's no sea,' he murmured.

'There's a sea of grass just as magnificent.'

Joel told himself that he needed to be honest if there was any chance of a relationship. 'It's not like this in the winter. There are regularly winds of fifty miles an hour—the Chinook blows a mighty blast.'

Eve had seen some grazing stock in the distance as they rode. 'Do the cattle stay out all winter?'

'Yes. We have over thirty thousand acres—that's enough grassland for more beasts than I could house in a barn.'

'Poor things!'

'They're fine—they are bred for the conditions. If need be, we spread hay and oats in the winter.'

'Don't the cattle get buried in the snow?'

'Not generally, as we have some sheltered valleys and the Chinook keeps the foothills clear.'

Eve breathed in deeply and closed her eyes, enjoying the sensation of clean summer air reaching the very bottom of her lungs. Then, she exhaled slowly and looked around, taking in the perfection of the moment; the sough of the breeze in the trees, the dappled sunlight alive with tiny dancing insects, and the tinkling of the creek as it parted around Nate's sun-bronzed legs. She spoke quietly so that the boy would not hear. 'Your mom is very keen for Nate to continue the Baxter line of ranchers.'

Joel glanced over to his son. 'She finds it hard to accept that he probably won't.'

'What will happen to the ranch eventually?' Having seen it, Eve could understand the enormity of loss involved.

'There are other grandchildren to take over although, what the future holds—I don't know. The concerns about animal methane have meant there's been a fall in demand recently. Ruth and Fiona both have sons but my money is on Fi's daughter, Madison. I think she was born in the saddle and she loves it out here.'

'How old is she?'

'Thirteen,' he replied, without hesitation, and then added, 'or thereabouts.'

'You're not sure?'

'You know what it's like. They grow up so fast.'

'All is not lost then?'

'No—but Mom can't let it be.'

'Is that where Amy comes in?'

Joel narrowed his eyes. 'What do you know about Amy?'

'Not a thing except that she's calling in today.'

'Mom will have invited her, although she pretends she hasn't. She's keen for me to marry again.'

'Is Amy a strong contender?'

His gaze was intense but she forced herself to keep eye contact as he said to test her, 'She might be.'

'I'll be sure to check her out then,' promised Eve, pleased to see she had wrong-footed him.

He threw back his head and laughed, a deep throaty laugh which was contagious. She began to laugh, lightly at first, until tears rolled down her cheeks and she did not know whether she was crying for joy or for missed chances.

Nate, distracted by the noise, looked up from his consuming task of converting the course of the creek to see what was happening. Joel and Eve were several feet away but Nate could hear clearly as his father was now making no attempt to lower his voice. The laughter petered out and Nate watched, intrigued, as his father wrapped his arms around Eve and demanded,

'Eve Cummins, what am I going to do about you?'

THIRTY-ONE

Eve braced herself against the back of her seat, as the aircraft hurtled down the runway, waiting for the instant when the thrust of its engines lifted it from the ground. She registered the clunk of the wheels being retracted and the reverberating roar as they gathered height, both through a mist of misery. In no time, the lights of Calgary had receded and she was confronted with an oval of total blackness reflecting her own despondency. The plane levelled out, the engine note changed, and the cabin was, once again, illuminated. The click of seatbelts being released joined the general hum, the stewards started moving around instilling an air of normal efficiency, but Eve remained resolutely facing the window in the hope that her neighbour, a woman in late middle age who had been visiting her daughter, would leave her alone.

She wanted to think about, to pick over and dissect, every word, every gesture, and every nuance of Joel's since he had embraced her by the creek. She had wanted him to kiss her, she was sure he would have done so if they had been alone, but Nate had chosen that moment to announce he was hungry. He had abandoned his dam and come and flopped down next to them. To his credit, Joel had kept his arms around her until she had given him a rueful smile and pulled away. Then, he had leant over and ruffled Nate's hair before he had pushed himself up and retrieved the picnic from the saddlebags.

For the rest of the day, Eve had been enveloped in a warm glow, enjoying the ride with a strange sense of detachment as if she were watching herself instead of being herself. She listened to Joel, responded when he teased her or pointed out something of interest, and congratulated Nate on his riding, yet part of her was strangely absent. Later, she wondered if she had actually experienced the sensation known as walking on air.

Her state of heightened emotion lasted until they returned to the ranch. The late afternoon sun was casting long shadows as it had done the previous day and the wind was whispering through the trees, a constant reminder of the open countryside. Her heart had lurched at the knowledge that the following evening would come and she would be gone. As they approached, two figures had come into view, relaxing on the veranda which wrapped itself around the ground floor, one sitting in the old glider while the other was leaning on the rail waiting for them. As the weary riders reined up, Eddie appeared from the stables, looking very neat and presentable for such a late time in the day, and Rose and Amy Grey slowly descended the wooden steps of the veranda.

Amy Grey had been a revelation to Eve. Coming towards them with a broad smile lighting her amiable face, the girl looked hardly out of her teens. It soon became apparent that her interest lay with Samson and not with Joel, as immediately after her warm greeting, Amy had asked him to take her to see the stallion whilst, simultaneously, sliding her eyes in Eddie's direction. Eve, with all her focus on Joel, had registered the disappointment in his eyes as he communicated a silent apology to her, before he acquiesced and walked away with Amy. Eddie followed, leading Luna and Daisy as Rose had insisted that Eve and Nate stay with her, waving aside her grandson's observation that she usually insisted that he stable the pony himself. Eve had smiled to herself at the older woman's misguided blatantness; her son would appear middle-aged to Amy, and by the expression on Eddie's face, it was definitely not Joel who was the reason for her visit.

The thought was of little comfort to Eve as Amy's visit still meant it was suppertime before she saw Joel again. After sitting on the veranda with Rose for a while, she excused herself and retired to her room. There, she had paced backwards and forwards, trying to compose herself, tracking across the floorboards worn by countless pairs of Baxter feet, but to no avail. In the end, after deciding that she had no alternative but to return home, she flung the case onto the bed and packed, ready for the following morning. She could not abandon her job on a romantic whim and stay longer, nor did she have the means to fly regularly to Canada in order to maintain a long-distance relationship. The object of her affection was so tied to the land it was unlikely he would have time to come and see her even if he could afford it. She convinced herself it was a doomed attraction and threw her clothes into the case with an uncharacteristic ferocity, slamming the lid shut with a rewarding thud. She swung around and then stopped abruptly.

There, in the full-length mirror a small angry figure stood framed, but as Eve studied her image, a surprising awareness crept upon her. She looked good, in fact, she looked amazingly good, for her. It was the first time she had noticed her reflection since the early days in Winnipeg when she had bought the turquoise dress. What was it that made her so different? Eve tried to put her finger on it but it took a whole minute for realisation to dawn. She glowed; her pale face was sun-kissed to a light tan while her mass of honey-coloured curls was threaded with buttery highlights. Eve could feel her frustration fall away. Her sapphire eyes shone, more striking than ever, staring back at her, sparkling with the knowledge that Joel had embraced her. She had crept under his skin as surely as he had crept under hers. Optimism had reasserted itself and Eve made her way down to supper with a renewed spring in her step.

The rattle of the trolley broke into Eve's recollections. The steward was methodically making his way down the aisle, distributing snacks to fill the time before dinner was served and Eve briefly tore her eyes away from the window to thank him. Her neighbour, seeing an opportunity for conversation, glanced at her hopefully but Eve gave her a tepid smile and turned back to studying the night sky.

Looking back over the previous thirty-six hours, Eve now wondered how she had remained so calm, presenting a relaxed aura while all the time she wanted to scream. It had been impossible to find time to be alone with Joel. Their relationship had not progressed enough for him to creep along the corridor and visit her during the night, and although the possibility of her knocking on his door kept surfacing as she tossed and turned, she stayed firmly where she was until she woke, groggy and irritable, as the early morning light flooded the room. Breakfast had followed, with everyone gathered around the long table, and then Joel had driven her to the Lennons. Nate had insisted on coming, ignoring his father's suggestion that he would enjoy a day with Grandma, and when they reached Calgary, the Lennons, in Eve's view, had shown an unforgivable lack of tact.

Anne and Andrew had welcomed them warmly and they had shared a delicious lunch with lively conversation, but when it was time for Joel and

Nate to leave, the couple politely accompanied them to the door and remained there. Eve wondered whether they were behaving in such a way on purpose and then dismissed the thought as uncharitable. She was convinced that they would drift back into the house and leave her and Joel to say their goodbyes. Yet why should they? They had no comprehension of how she felt and Joel, himself, was uncharacteristically reserved once lunch had finished. Nate had flung himself at her and she had squeezed him tight, accompanied by an equivocal response to his request that she would return the next year, while Joel, under the scrutiny of Anne and Andrew, had stood rigid.

In the end, Eve made the first move. She stood on tiptoe ready to plant a friendly kiss on his cheek and was mortified when he held out his hand. Embarrassed, she dropped back onto her heels and missed the confusion clear in his eyes. Trying to rescue the situation, Joel gave her a quick air hug, which made her feel worse, and stated that she would be welcome at the ranch anytime. Then he was gone.

Somehow, she had managed to fix a happy expression on her face throughout the rest of the day and to show her appreciation of the Lennons' hospitality. She rose on her final morning in Canada with a heavy heart, a pounding headache, and a sore jaw from her false smile. Anne, diagnosing exhaustion from the long drive, recommended a quiet day in the garden until it was time to go to the airport. Eve readily agreed and spent most of the day on the lounger flicking between Anne's magazines and her phone. She scrolled through her photos to find that there were depressingly few of Joel and none of them together. How had that happened? Had she been so much in the moment that she had forgotten to record her trip? However, there were several shots of the forts they had visited and a few of Nate, but the only one where Joel was looking at the camera was the one she had taken on the bank of the North Saskatchewan River. She enlarged the image to try and read his expression and saw that he appeared decidedly out of sorts. In the other photos, he was always doing something and was mainly in the background. She wondered if he would message her but her phone remained disappointingly silent.

When Eve sat all alone in the cavernous International Departure Hall of Calgary Airport that evening, an imaginary scenario had played through her mind. She would be reading, as she was in reality, lost in her book until the rapid pad of feet alerted her to the fact that someone was approaching. She would look up and he would be there, trying to catch his breath. He would not need to speak as his very presence spoke volumes. She would slowly close her book and place it carefully on the seat, prolonging the anticipation before she met his eyes. He would reach out to her and she would rise, calmly and elegantly, ready to receive his assertion of love.

Eve had glanced up, her eyes sweeping the quiet hall, and found it impossible not to be drawn to the entrance, but all was quiet. A few people were checking in but her flight's desk had not yet opened. She had enquired when she had arrived as there was no desk labelled British Airways and had been assured that, when it was time, one would open. There was no alternative but to remain where she was until then, so she sat on the hard metal seat for a couple of hours trying to concentrate on her book and quell her sadness.

Eventually, she checked in, dropped off her luggage, and went through customs feeling absolutely desolate. The contrast to her outward journey could not have been more different. Three weeks previously, she had boarded the plane at Heathrow, full of expectation tinged with trepidation. Now, she wanted to turn tail and run out of the airport. She told herself to be thankful for her wonderful trip and not to wallow in self-pity. She began to daydream again. There was still a chance and she re-enacted a scene she had seen in a film. She would be in the queue for boarding and Joel would run down the corridor towards her departure gate, his boots echoing on the polished floor. She would see him in the distance weaving between the crowds, as there were always many people milling around in films, and he would reach her just in time. Or, miraculously, he would have managed, as well as dodging security, to board the plane. He would frantically make his way down the aisle until his eyes alighted on her. He would pull her out of her seat and beg her to stay.

Once again, Eve dragged her eyes from the window in response to the steward who was offering her some dinner. She ate it mechanically while her travel companion tried to engage her in conversation. Under normal circumstances, she would have been happy to chat but all she could manage were brief replies, and as she never initiated any dialogue, she was soon left in peace. It was a relief when dinner was over and the stewards dimmed the lights ready for everyone to sleep.

It was well after midnight but sleep was elusive. She had always found it difficult to relax on planes so Eve reached into her handbag and found her notebook. She switched on her individual light and received a glare from her neighbour who turned her face the other way with a meaningful sigh. Eve adjusted the light so that it would be as unobtrusive as possible, and turning to the first page, she started to read.

It surprised her how much she had found out in one way, yet, she had made little progress in discovering anything about Gideon Thompson and the significance of the valentine. She knew a great deal more about the Hudson's Bay Company and its workings but virtually nothing about Gideon the person. She set her mind to the means by which she could progress. For a start, she was still uncertain of her exact relationship to him so that was a good place to begin. Perhaps Ada had made contact with distant members of the family as she had been interested when Eve and Lara had visited her in Saltburn. Eve made a note to contact her in a list under the heading "To do", and as she finished the last word, inspiration flared. On the website where her DNA had been tested, there had been a section of familial matches. Most of them had been fourth or fifth cousins and she had dismissed their significance after googling that a person has thousands of these. If she remembered correctly it was about fifteen hundred fourth cousins, and fifth cousins numbered over seventeen thousand. Nevertheless, Eve jotted down on her new list that she would start to make contact; after all, on the website, there were fewer than thirty names in her familial matches.

She shuffled in her seat trying to get comfortable. Her thighs hurt from riding. She had always found that it was never the day following unaccustomed exercise when her muscles ached, but the next one, and she longed to get up and stretch her legs. She studied her slumbering neighbour and decided it would be unfair to wake her. Why had she chosen a window seat? It was not as if she would see the view as she had done on the way over. Then she remembered. They were due to land at Heathrow mid-afternoon which meant that, soon, she would see the dawn. Perhaps her neighbour would need to visit the toilet before too long? Eve wriggled more vigorously and was heartened to see a pair of sleepy eyes reluctantly flicker open.

With the help of the tailwind, the plane made excellent time and arrived at Heathrow nearly half-an-hour earlier than scheduled. Facing a three-hour wait for her connection, Eve bought a strong cup of coffee and settled down to drink it as she surveyed the attractions of Terminal Five. She knew that, once fortified by caffeine, she would be able to look at handbags she could never afford, sample perfumes until she was too confused to remember which one was which, and browse the bookstands, probably settling for a romcom where she was certain that the hero would actually turn up at the last minute. She took a sip of the hot, black liquid and turned on her phone. It pinged immediately. Expecting it to be Aidan who was picking her up at Newcastle, she took her time.

Bored with waiting and reading, the old couple seated opposite Eve were people-watching to pass the time. Attracted by the noise of her phone, their eyes fixed on Eve. They watched entranced as the young woman's face lit up with absolute delight.

They could not stop themselves from asking, 'Good news?'

Eve nodded and looked back at the screen. Joel's message was short, stating that he hoped she had had a good journey. It warmed her heart. It would be early morning at the ranch and his thoughts on waking had turned to her. However, it was the second message which immediately followed the first which misted her eyes. It simply said, 'Calgary University has a Classics Department', in an enigmatically tempting way.

Thirty-Two

Lerwick, April 1852

Grizzel Cattanach smoothed down her skirt and pulled her shawl more tightly around her shoulders, ready to face the wearied annoyance of the merchant, George Laing, for the second time that week. She pushed open the shop door and the accompanying tinkle of the overhead bell brought him scuttling from the back room. In one quick glance, he registered her empty hands and her hesitant expression.

He pre-empted her question. 'No, Margaret Thompson has not been in with her shawls. I haven't seen her since last autumn.'

'Since hairst? You didna say that last time and she should have brought her haps by now.'

George Laing, who saw no reason why he should be bothered by the young woman's concern, replied, somewhat shortly, 'Do I have time to worry about the comings and goings of folks? She'll probably be in by the end of the month.'

'You said that last month.'

Laing sighed. 'I'll check in the book to be sure.'

Grizzel watched him reach under the counter and bring out the thick ledger. He spent some time trailing a fleshy finger down several pages, his brows beginning to pucker as he progressed. Eventually, he looked up and peered at Grizzel over his spectacles.

'I have been mistook. Margaret Thompson has not been in for a full year—not since she bought wool last May.'

'She would have knit her haps by now,' stated Grizzel, needlessly.

'Aye,' the merchant replied, realising that perhaps something was amiss. How could he have missed not receiving the finished articles? 'I think you should go and see her.'

Grizzel did not reply. She was fighting the sinking sensation deep in the pit of her stomach. Gideon had asked her to tell him news of his grandparents and she desperately wanted to be able to do so. It was almost three years since she had seen him and he was becoming increasingly distanced from her. He had declared his love with the valentine she had received the previous year, part of a parcel which included several letters and a beautifully carved bear. The euphoria had been intoxicating when she had read the valentine, but gradually, as she read his letters it had died. She could no longer hear his voice, the letters had been written in such formal English as to be alien to her, and it became increasingly difficult to marry his words to the young blacksmith who had admired her so awkwardly.

She was very conscious of her own unsophisticated prose and had procrastinated throughout the winter in penning a reply. However, now she was running out of time and it became imperative that she should be able to tell Gideon news of his grandparents. She would be giving him a gift which negated all the shortcomings of her letter writing and fill his heart with warmth towards her. She glanced back through the window to see Kitty gesticulating for her to leave but Grizzel focused her attention on the merchant who was now flipping the pages of the ledger backwards and forwards as if seeking illumination. Grizzel wondered what other information could be found among the neat writing and numerals.

'Do you ken where she bides?'

Laing shrugged his shoulders and pushed his spectacles back up his nose. 'Nae.' He registered Grizzel's dejected demeanour and was moved to be more helpful. 'I can tell you she stays with a cousin when she's in Lerwick.'

Grizzel brightened. 'Who?'

'Ann Hardie—she has a boarding house on Hangcliff Lane.' Laing tutted at Grizzel's blank expression. 'Steep Closs,' he clarified, 'at the top, on the righthand side.'

'I ken its name,' retorted Grizzel, although she was puzzled, not by the new name given to the closs by the Police Commissioners but by its location. To her knowledge, she had never walked up that lane. She said as much.

'How do you get to Hillhead from the harbour then?'

'Up the closs I'm nearest to,' she replied, a touch too saucily for the merchant.

'Be away with you, Grizzel Cattanach. I am a busy man.'

She bestowed on him her winning smile, which usually had the desired effect, and was pleased to see Laing disconcerted. 'Thank you, Mister Laing, for yer help.'

'Well,' said Kitty as Grizzel emerged from the shop. It was neither a question nor was it a statement, and if Grizzel had chosen to identify her friend's greeting, she would have called it a long-suffering utterance.

'You didna have ta come,' she retorted.

Kitty pouted and looked around to see if there was anyone of interest on Commercial Street. There was nobody, just the usual assortment of seafarers talking loudly in their own language. One of them gave her an appreciative glance as he passed and commented in Dutch which triggered a series of sniggers from his two companions. Kitty turned her back and ignored them, theatrically pulling her handkerchief from her sleeve and lifting it to her nose. The smell of fish, which often hung in the air, was particularly rank as they passed.

'Laing hasna seen Margaret Thompson for a year. I must find out how she be.'

'How can you do that?'

'She has a cousin where she stays when she's in Lerwick.'

'I remember—we did walk with her when she was at Gideon's.'

Grizzel, who had forgotten this, brightened. 'You ken which lodging in Hangcliff Lane?'

'Aye—but I canna remember the cousin's name.'

'Ann Hardie.'

'Then, betwixt us, we'll find her.'

It was a fine blustery day and the wind, funnelled between the grey stone houses, teased the girls' skirts and shawls as they made their way up Hangcliff Lane. Kitty, pleased to be taking the lead, found Ann's door immediately and loudly knocked several times before a small figure peered out into the closs and eyed them suspiciously. Grizzel was just about to explain the reason for their visit when, much to her annoyance, Kitty spoke for her. She shot her friend a cautionary glance but Kitty was oblivious. Ever since her relationship with William Cattanach had been formalised by the setting of a wedding date, Kitty had been cultivating a superior air based on her forthcoming status as a married woman. It had become so marked in the previous few weeks that Grizzel had started to avoid her and it was only a chance meeting on the way to Laing's which had brought the girls together.

Kitty had already harangued Grizzel many times about the futility of waiting for Gideon Thompson and was only accompanying her to Ann Hardie's out of curiosity. Fortunately, the boarder who had opened the door, announced that the mistress was out retrieving the bed linen from the communal drying green. It was some way to North Hillhead where Ann would be and Grizzel hoped that Kitty would have better things to do than tag along with her. She pointed this out but Kitty was not to be deterred.

The girls walked in silence for a while with Grizzel slightly ahead. Kitty watched her friend's small, determined figure increase the distance between them and decided to play her trump card. She had been waiting for an opportune time and this was it.

'Grizzel, slow down,' she ordered.

'You dunna have to come wi me,' Grizzel retorted, increasing her pace.

'Please, Grizzel,' panted Kitty, holding her side.

Grizzel turned, saw her friend's flushed cheeks, softened, and waited until she caught up. Kitty paused while she collected herself and her face gradually lost its high colour only to be replaced by a benign expression similar to one bestowed on a naïve child. Grizzel knew what was coming, expecting another lecture about wasting her time with Gideon Thompson, and was completely taken aback by Kitty's question.

'Do you want to come to London?'

'London? Why would I want to geng there?' To Grizzel, London was a den of iniquity, a place which lured young Shetlanders with its charms, preventing them from returning home on their way back from Rupert's Land. Since Gideon had left, she had heard of several recruits who had decided to stay in the capital and chance their luck.

'Dunna you want to see the Crystal Palace?' Kitty had been full of news of the Great Exhibition the previous autumn, gleaned from the magazines her aunt passed on. By the time Kitty had read about the Exhibition, it had already closed but the magnificent glass building, built especially to house it, could still be seen in Hyde Park. For weeks, it was all she wanted to talk about, continually telling Grizzel about how the building had three hundred thousand identical plates of glass and how it was one-third of a mile long. At first, Grizzel's interest had been piqued, but by the time winter came, it had waned. She had listened more carefully when Kitty had described some of the metal working exhibits, fearful that opportunity might attract Gideon to disembark and remain in the capital, but as the months dragged on, she had quashed that worry. Now Kitty had resurrected it, spurring Grizzel on to be able to include news of Margaret Thompson in her letter.

Grizzel, eyed her friend, ignoring her question. 'Hurry up, I dunna have all day.'

'It's a long way,' grumbled Kitty.

'Aye,' replied Grizzel walking on ahead, passing the newer houses which were more openly spaced than those in the overcrowded steep lanes, whose inhabitants needed the communal drying greens and bleach fields. As she walked, Kitty's reference to the Crystal Palace brought to mind her own knitting and she remembered the pride she had felt when Kitty had told her that examples of Shetland lace had been shown at the Exhibition. That was some news she could tell Gideon. She began to daydream that it was her actual work and then chided herself for her flight of fancy. Although, she told herself, some of the visitors, especially those who could afford the five shilling entry fee on the days allocated to them rather than the standard one shilling entry, could well be wearing one of her shawls. Kitty had announced that the day Queen Victoria opened the exhibition was a fine spring day. She was basking in her reverie when Kitty's voice cut through her thoughts.

'Will and I be thinking of London.'

Grizzel stopped abruptly, a feeling of dread enveloping her. All images of elegant ladies wearing her cobweb-fine work vanished in the face of harsh reality. If her brother and Kitty left for London once they were married, she would be left behind. A vision of the future unfurled before her. There was no certainty that Gideon would return, and even if he did, he had made no promise yet. She could be destined to be the unmarried daughter, then the unmarried sister, perhaps beholden to Adam for a home, like so many women on the island. She had been so proud of her independence, of earning her own money by her fine lacework, an occupation made official by her entry in the census of the previous year, but now, she could see it was a falsehood. Her work would never enable her to survive alone.

Kitty Hart watched her friend's stricken face and experienced a curious combination of sympathy and victory. Determined to be a wife herself, the girl could understand Grizzel's reaction to the news but what she could not understand was her friend's fixation on Gideon Thompson. Pushing aside her genuine empathy, Kitty delivered her triumphant blow.

'Angus Duncan has said that he be interested in London. He and Will make a fine team, and once they be master boatbuilders, they'll be in greht demand. You ken Angus has always liked you. Marry him and we can all geng together.'

Panic rose in Grizzel's chest. She must definitely find out what had happened to Gideon's grandparents, she must write to him soon and be braver in declaring her affection, and then she would need to wait another full year for his answer. Tears threatened at the thought but she steeled herself as she turned to face Kitty.

'When are you gyaan as you be not yet wed?'

Kitty floundered slightly. No timescale had been agreed as the idea had only just been floated, but she had promised Angus that she would sow the seed of possibility in Grizzel's mind. She shrugged and replied,

'As soon as we can.'

Thirty-Three

Dunrossness, May 1852

Two weeks later, Grizzel Cattanach was implementing her plan as she acted on Ann Hardie's news. Sadly, Matthew Thompson, Gideon's grandfather had died the previous autumn and Ann had had no news of Margaret since. Grizzel, reluctant to tell her mother the true reason for wanting to travel to Dunrossness, had alighted on the idea of helping her grandmother, Mary, plant out the kale. At first, Janet Cattanach had been suspicious of Grizzel's enthusiasm to help on the croft but she gradually came around to the advantage of her daughter checking up on her parents. It would save Janet, who disliked sailing, from making the journey south later in the month. Grizzel had surprised her grandmother too by arriving with such a willingness to help that she had made no comment about her hands suffering as she set to work.

Now, it was only her second day at her grandparents' croft, and already, Grizzel had impressed Mary. They had worked together since early morning, transplanting the kale seedlings from the planticrubs, where they had been safe all winter from the sheep and the rabbits as well as from the wind, to the prepared kale yards. The time had passed quickly, with the women of the toun chatting as they bent over the earth enjoying the May sunshine, and soon, it was approaching noon. Grizzel stood up straight, and stretched her back, catching Marion Sinclair's eye as the younger girl leant against the stone wall of the planticrub. She was the one person Grizzel was keen to see, although a shyness washed over the older girl as she remembered her encounter with Marion the previous summer.

Marion had come across Grizzel in deep conversation with Malcolm Aitken while she was fetching water, and still harbouring her jealousy, the younger girl had immediately misread the situation. It had been Malcolm who had sought out Grizzel, his expression very different from the usual leer he had sported when he talked to her. He had asked to speak to her, his eyes resting on the bucket at her feet, and begged her forgiveness for forcing a kiss when he had seen her that time on the beach. Grizzel had been of a mind to turn around and walk away but his stance had been so apologetic that she had stayed at the well. Still, with his eyes downcast and twisting his fisherman's hat in his hands, Malcolm had explained that he had been taking nips of his father's liquor and that it had made him bold in a way totally against his normal nature. Grizzel had waited expectantly, interested to see what he would say next for she doubted his sincerity, but as she was about to demand why it had taken him so long to apologise, it being a full twelve months since the incident, Marion had arrived in high dudgeon and had pulled him away.

Grizzel had been left by the pump, with only one bucket filled, and had watched Marion drag Malcolm towards the Sinclairs' cottage, every movement screaming possession. It was not long before she had learnt the reason for Malcolm's contriteness. He had asked Marion Sinclair to marry him and she had accepted. Grizzel had lost her chance to warn Marion about her intended's behaviour when it had happened, and now, it would have looked like sour grapes if she had mentioned it. Grizzel had reasoned with herself, perhaps it had been the drink? She remembered the stench of his fishy breath laced with alcohol, and then, she thought of Sven Thorvald and how he had grabbed the boy and yanked him off her, and how frightened Malcolm had been. She had made a decision, she would keep her peace but continue to watch the elder Aitken with a wary eye.

Now, Marion pushed herself away from the wall and walked towards Grizzel. 'I didna expect ta see you,' she announced, although she had heard of Grizzel's arrival from a neighbour.

'A've come ta help me grannie,' replied Grizzel, unable to stop herself from glancing at Marion's hands. There was no wedding ring.

Marion bristled at the action and Grizzel hastened to smooth over the perceived offence. 'I didna think you'd be married yet—you and Malcolm being so young.'

'Aye,' acknowledged the younger girl. 'We'll be wed next year. Malcolm gave me a pretty ring but I never wear it when A'm working. A'll show it ta you, if you wish.'

Grizzel gave a polite affirmative, despite her disinterest and immediately asked, 'Are Malcolm and Ted away for the haaf?'

'Malcolm is but Ted isna a haaf-man yet.' Marion was squinting into the sun but she clearly registered her companion's reaction. 'Why be you smiling?'

'I want to see Ted,' replied Grizzel, her pleasure still clear on her face. If Ted was coastal fishing her plan could actually work.

'Why do you want to see Ted?'

Grizzel was cautious. It was impossible to share a confidence with Marion Sinclair and explain about her need to visit Margaret Thompson, yet, she wanted Ted Aitken to take her down the coast in his yoal. She decided to tell a half-truth.

'A've a friend in Lerwick who's asked me to look in on her grannie.'

Marion accepted such a normal explanation without a flicker of interest. William Petrie was unable to row his granddaughter himself as he was away for the haaf, and although many women could handle a boat as well as the men, Marion doubted that Grizzel Cattanach was one of them.

'You're in luck, Ted is due on Sunday. He has his eyes on Agnes Tulloch.'

'She be but a bairn!' exclaimed Grizzel, in the heat of hearing about another pairing.

'Fourteen,' said Marion matter-of-factly, 'is not too young to start to court.' Then she giggled. 'They're not gyaan in front of the minister yet.'

'Aye,' agreed Grizzel, feeling old at nearly twenty with the spectre of spinsterhood raising its head once again.

Ted Aitken had readily agreed to her proposal. He would row Grizzel to the Thompson's croft, drop her off, and then pick her up and be back home by nightfall. He would fish while she was visiting Margaret and he assured her that her plan was feasible. All that was needed were favourable conditions which would make the rowing easier and an explanation that would satisfy Mary Petrie. Unable to mislead her grandmother, Grizzel decided to tell the truth and waited for an opportune moment. To her relief, Mary had proved very understanding and had passed no comment on the futility of her granddaughter pinning her hopes on a young man in Rupert's

Land, mainly because she thoroughly approved of Grizzel seeking news of Margaret.

Thus, four days after she had arrived in Dunrossness, Grizzel was sitting in Ted's yoal, surrounded by fishing tackle and bait with a basket of food for the journey and one for Margaret tucked away by her feet. Ted had confidently pinpointed where to land from Ann Hardie's instructions claiming, as he had done many times previously, that he knew every bit of sand and rock from Rerwick south. They had left early, setting out under a thin blanket of dove-grey cloud, and the voyage passed without incident under Ted's steady seamanship as he rowed down the coast and across Quendale Bay, until they reached their destination.

The overcast day brightened as Grizzel disembarked just north of the Thompsons' croft, and remembering Ann's directions, it was but a short walk from the beach. She refused Ted's offer to accompany her but she made certain that he understood where she was going. They made arrangements to meet back up for the return journey and Ted watched her walk purposely away. He rested for a moment before he was ready to leave and scanned the beach. As his eyes travelled along the shoreline, taking in the noosts secure above the waterline, a feeling of disquiet descended on the young fisherman. Two yoals, lilting at an unusual angle, appeared in a state of ill repair with the timbers showing clear signs of rot. Ted dragged his own yoal up the beach, made it safe, and approached the noosts, his unease increasing with each step. No fisherman could afford to allow his boat to deteriorate in such a way; there was only one reason why he would.

Ted crested the shallow embankment, fringing the beach, in three long strides and breathed a sigh of relief when he spotted the unmistakable figure of Grizzel. He called after her but the buffeting wind, which had frayed the clouds to reveal a summer-blue sky, whipped away his words. He increased his pace and caught up with her just as the first croft came into view. She grabbed his arm to steady herself, and her stricken face when she turned to him spoke volumes, but no words, to break the eerie silence, escaped her lips. There was not a person in sight; no kaleyard ready to be planted, no shoots of oats or barley swaying in the breeze and definitely no sign of any potatoes. The only sound to be heard, except for the occasional call of a gull, was the sound of sheep nibbling the grass. There were more sheep together than Grizzel had ever seen and not all of them were the easily recognisable Shetland breed.

They walked towards the buildings which showed obvious signs of abandonment. The door to the byre was swinging loose on its hinges, the skin window of the but end of the cottage had perished, and when Grizzel and Ted peered in, they could see the remnants of a home scattered around. Anything of use had been taken, like the gridiron and the utensils, but a couple of rickety chairs stood forlornly on either side of the cold and still-scorched hearth. Ted lifted the door latch and led Grizzel through to the ben end, both anxious about what they might find there. It was surprisingly empty, with only the scuff marks on the floor to indicate where two box beds had stood.

She exhaled, expelling the breath she had been instinctively holding, and announced, 'It may be that Margaret has taken them?'

'Aye,' agreed Ted without conviction, as he glanced around the room looking for any evidence of where Margaret might have gone. 'Let's geng and find a neebour.'

He held out his hand and she took it, primarily for comfort as the despair in the room was tangible, and followed closely on his heels back into the light. They stood for some time deciding on the direction to take until Ted spotted a plume of smoke in the far distance. Keeping it in sight, they eventually found themselves at another croft, surrounded by cultivated land well-protected from the sheep on the scattald, where a clutch of scrawny hens pecked around the byre door. Ted called out when they were still some yards away and a woman appeared from the back of the cottage. She regarded the two strangers suspiciously and waited immobile until they reached her.

Grizzel stepped forward, leaving Ted a couple of paces behind her, and greeted the woman, before stating, 'A'm looking for Margaret Thompson.'

'How do you ken Margaret?' asked the woman continuing to assess her two visitors. The lad appeared to be what she expected, a fisherman, but the lass was different so she addressed her directly.

Grizzel, worried about how it would seem, wished she had stopped holding Ted's hand earlier, and rushed her explanation. 'I seek news of Margaret for her grandson, Gideon. A'm a friend of his.'

'He's been in Rupert's Land these last three years.'

'I ken.'

'You're from Lerwick,' the woman announced emphatically as if everything now slotted into place. She glanced at Grizzel's hands, so obviously those of a lace-knitter, and then stated, 'You've come a long way.'

'Me daa and grannie bide at Rerwick.'

'You'd best come in then. Yer lad can wait here.'

'He's not me lad,' retorted Grizzel, somewhat more shortly than she had meant to, horrified that somehow news of her being with Ted would reach Gideon.

'Aye,' replied the woman with obvious reservation.

'Ted be a friend who has brought me here.'

'You be a popular lass—all these friends.' The woman continued to study Grizzel dourly. 'A'm Eliza Moir.'

Grizzel followed Eliza into the byre and then through to the ben end of her cottage. It was only then that she realised how rude she had been, leaving Ted outside without a word of thanks or any acknowledgement, and she turned to retrace her steps and apologise. As she did so, Grizzel caught sight of the woman lying in a box bed squeezed into the corner, her emaciated shape covered by a threadbare blanket, and all thoughts of Ted flew from her mind.

Thirty-Four

The atmosphere in the room was heavy with smouldering peat under which lurked the unmistakable odour of decay. The culprit was not the shrunken woman curled up in the corner while her life ebbed away but the general malaise of the building which had lost its battle against the damp. The smell caught at the back of Grizzel's throat as she took a step towards Margaret Thompson. It was hard to move, as the extra bed filled the only available space, and as she reached the bedside, Grizzel turned and met Eliza Moir's eyes only to witness the expressive shake of her head. The latter moved closer to Grizzel, bringing with her the sour stench of the unkempt, and stated in a loud voice, 'Margaret, here be Grizzel Cattanach to see you.'

The shape in the bed did not stir and Grizzel feared she was too late to speak to Gideon's grandmother. All she would be able to do was to send him news of her parlous state. She remained rooted to the spot for what seemed to her an eternity, when Margaret uttered an unintelligible sound. Grizzel moved nearer until she was leaning close to the dying woman's face and watched as Margaret appeared to force open her eyes, faded now, but with an echo of the once arresting blue. Startled, Grizzel felt herself directly meeting Gideon's gaze. An emaciated hand plucked at the worn blanket and painstakingly made its way towards her.

Grizzel gently wrapped her fingers over Margaret's and simply said, 'A'm a friend of Gideon's.'

The girl read Margaret's lips rather than heard the sound. 'I ken.'

'He asked me to send news of you.'

Margaret's fingers shifted slightly and she led Grizzel's hand to the pillow, all the while keeping eye contact. It took a moment for the girl to work out what the woman wanted her to do, but eventually, Grizzel slid her free hand underneath Margaret's head and felt the paper. Pulling it out tentatively, while Margaret laboriously lifted herself, Grizzel had to stifle a gasp as she saw Gideon's handwriting. She carefully released his grandmother's hand and found her own shaking as she unfolded the single page. The letter was dated the same as that of the last letter she had received the previous summer. She looked up at Margaret who mouthed, 'Read it,' and slowly and haltingly Grizzel obeyed.

> Carlton House
> February 1851
>
> Dear Grannie and Daa,
>
> I trust that you received my letters from York Factory and from Norway House so that you know I am faring well. Perhaps the minister read them to you? I think of you both often.
>
> I hope this letter finds you both in good spirits and I truly wish for Daa's chest to be less troublesome. You will be glad, no doubt, when the winter is over.
>
> I am working hard and there are many opportunities for advancement. I have my smithing but I have also been learning how to keep accounts from a friend, Jim Turnbull, who is a clerk here at Fort Carlton. He believes that bookkeeping is a necessary skill for me to acquire for when I return home and set up my own blacksmith's shop. He says that a man must be in control of all transactions and of the means to record them. You would like Jim, for he is an honourable man completely without malice, although he can become despondent.
>
> The winter has been long and the cold unlike anything we experience at home. You would not recognise me all dressed up in my buffalo robe. I have learnt to handle a dog sled, although I am still in need of some polish, and I am becoming an able hunter. I am looking forward to spring and the Saskatchewan River thawing so that I can travel. There is talk that I might be sent to Rocky Mountain House eventually, as there is a shortage of blacksmiths and our skill is sorely needed in helping to build the York boats.
>
> Daa, you would be interested in the design of the boats as it is based on our sixareens, many of which you have sailed in for the haaf. Shetland boatbuilders are also in demand so I feel that if any smith is sent to Rocky Mountain House, it will be me. If I am fortunate, I will have another year at Carlton House, with perhaps a temporary season at Edmonton House, as I am learning so much from Jim. We have much to discuss as we can

avail ourselves of the books in the fort's library and Jim and I are often rivals to read a book first. You would be proud to see what I can now read.

You do not need to worry about the croft when I return. So far, I have accrued over £40. It is a shame that I will not receive the final sum until the end of my service but I trust that my advance payment of half a year's service has helped you through the last two years. I wish I could do more but that is how it is.

Grannie, please will you do me a favour when you are next in Lerwick selling your haps. You might remember a lass, Grizzel Cattanach, who you met the year before last when you came. She has been kind enough to write to me and I hold her in high esteem. Could you make enquiries about her when you visit the merchant, George Laing, as I know she sells her knitting to him too? She lives by the dock in Roadside. I am also keen to receive news about her brother, Will, and his friend, Angus Duncan. They are both boatbuilders at Hay's Dock. I would be very disappointed if I returned to Shetland to find Grizzel married to Angus Duncan. Again, perhaps the minister could pen your reply. I would truly appreciate news of Grizzel.

Remember me in your prayers, as I do you.

Your loving grandson, Gideon.

Grizzel placed the letter on her lap and clasped her hands to stop them from trembling. Glee gathered in her heart at Gideon's words, to be immediately replaced by doubt. Had she read the letter correctly and had she understood the significance of his feelings when he wrote about her? The letter had been so hard to read that she had missed out some of the longer words. Also, the language was so formal, so stilted, that she wondered if Margaret had fully comprehended. If she had had more time, Grizzel would have studied the letter and summarised it for the old woman, but as it was, she had read it out nervously, often pronouncing each syllable of a word. As she continued to stare at the letter, Margaret reached out towards her and motioned for Grizzel to read out the letter again.

This time, as she read, Grizzel made an effort to take particular notice of any reference to herself and she experienced such overwhelming elation on grasping the obvious depth of Gideon's concern that she missed the tragedy elsewhere in the letter. Realisation followed swiftly on the heels of her euphoria: Gideon was working so hard in Rupert's Land to help his grandparents yet his grandfather had already died and Margaret would follow soon. Shame at her selfishness burned her cheeks and she was glad of the peaty fug which masked her blush as she reached out and grasped the dying woman's hand. It must have startled Margaret but she made no sound.

'Not long now,' announced Eliza Moir, her arms crossed against her drooping breasts. 'Joannie Piper casted the heart.'

Grizzel turned and looked up at her, her eyes full of anguish. She noticed the loose jowls, now devoid of flesh, testament that Eliza had once been a sturdy woman, and her threadbare clothes. Her brow puckered in a frown, demonstrating her disapproval at Eliza's lack of tact. Grizzel knew of the old practice of casting the heart if a person was ailing but she had never heard of an instance when it had occurred. A wise woman was called upon to carry out the procedure of melting lead and passing it through a sieve. If the lead hardened into the shape of a heart when it made contact with the cold water under the sieve, the patient was to wear it around the neck as a sign that the charm was working. Grizzel swivelled back to face Margaret and gently lifted her nightdress away from her neck. There was no amulet, a potent sign that her heart would not mend.

Eliza bristled. What right had a young lass, who obviously had enough to eat, to judge her? She glared at Grizzel and demanded, 'What do you have there?'

The basket of food she had brought stood forgotten next to the bed. In it was some krappen. Mary had used a portion of their dwindling supply of oatmeal, mixed it with chopped liver and then stuffed enough fish heads to feed themselves and Margaret. Grizzel passed it wordlessly to Eliza who pulled back the cloth cover.

'She hasna eaten for days,' she said nodding towards the bed. 'But I thank you for it.'

Grizzel stood up slowly, an unusual weariness enveloping her. She leant over Margaret and spoke directly into her ear. 'A'll writ ta Gideon and tell him how prood you be of him.' Then she paused but Margaret's eyes remained firmly closed. 'And A'll tell him there's nae wedding for me until he's hame.' Grizzel waited for a few minutes next to the bed hoping for a response, and when none came, she whispered a prayer. Then, she collected the now empty basket from Eliza Moir and walked out of the gloomy cottage and into the softness of a summer evening.

Ted was sitting on a small mound, sucking a piece of grass, not far from the cottage. He was alone with nobody in sight, the scrawny hens having soon abandoned him when it was obvious he had no food, except for a distant figure from the neighbouring croft who was hoeing. Ted stood up when he saw her and beamed a smile which immediately faded when he noticed her expression. Any expectation that Grizzel would thank him for waiting dissolved in the face of her obvious distress. In answer to his enquiry, she just shook her head, too emotional to speak, her eyes glistening with tears. He contemplated offering her his arm but Grizzel's demeanour made him hesitate, and instead, they fell into step side by side.

Later, along the track, when she recalled her last words to Margaret, Grizzel was convinced that the old woman had responded with a flicker of her eyelids, and as she walked back to the yoal with Ted, she comforted herself with the knowledge that her visit had not been in vain. Margaret Thompson would leave her earthly life gladdened by the knowledge that her grandson was well and working hard for his family in Rupert's Land, and that a bride-to-be waited for him at home. Ted, his hopes briefly raised by their handholding earlier in the day, sneaked several sideways glances at Grizzel but he kept his peace. Despite Marion Sinclair's belief that he had his eyes on Agnes Tulloch, Ted had harboured an admiration for Grizzel since their first encounter on the beach. 'Why else would I abandon a day's precious fishing to bring her sooth?' he thought as he caught her staring at the horizon.

'What is it?' he asked.

Grizzel showed no indication of having heard. She was looking out across the sea, silvered by the sinking sun, towards Rupert's Land and willing Gideon Thompson, with every fibre of her being, to come home. She was making plans to return to Lerwick immediately and to write to him. She would tell him the heart-breaking news about his grandparents and then she would temper his sadness by declaring her affection. She would not be shy nor would she be tempted to abandon her dream. She would continue to ignore her mother and Kitty, who both favoured Angus Duncan, and all those who felt she was foolish to wait.

Thirty-Five

Rupert's Land 1852

Gideon Thompson did not receive Grizzel's letter of May 1852 until the late summer of the following year. The letter was dispatched on time, with Grizzel hurrying to catch the outward mail which reached York Factory three months later, but she was not to know that her considered words languished for several months at Carlton House, as an early winter closed in, making travel impossible. It had missed Gideon by a matter of days as he had already departed for Rocky Mountain House. At first, Jim Turnbull would finger the letter thoughtfully before laying it to one side, but as time passed and the thick snow blanketed the fort, it was forgotten as the need for survival dominated every hour of the day. However, if circumstances became difficult for Jim, the problems paled into insignificance compared to Gideon's experience further west.

The sun hung low over the horizon as Gideon and his companions rowed the last mile towards the fort. Not used to rowing so far, his back and arms ached from the effort of fighting against the current as it flowed downstream from the Rocky Mountains on its way north, its waters still swollen with snow melt. Hunger gnawed at his stomach as he pulled on the oars, oblivious to the beauty of his surroundings as the setting sun gilded the wake of the boat in front of him, while the verdant banks overgrown with an abundance of grasses and trees increased his despondency further. The brigade was late, having spent too much time at Edmonton House, and no welcome awaited them at Rocky Mountain House. Jim had warned Gideon several times about the hardship at the Saskatchewan District's most westerly post; it was routinely abandoned over the summer months only to be occupied for the winter trading season, and the main tribes who traded there, the Blackfoot-speaking peoples, were renowned among the Company's men for their mercurial, and at times, antagonistic behaviour.

The weary men disembarked just south of the confluence of the North Saskatchewan and Clearwater Rivers to be faced by a desolate sight. The timber palisades and bastions were standing but appeared in disrepair due to the encroachment of the wild grass. It brushed the men's thighs as they pushed their way through it in single file, the supplies they could carry balanced on their shoulders. Once inside the defences, the fort was smaller than Gideon had imagined, although Jim had also informed him that usually a skeleton workforce would be stationed there, and the wooden buildings inside the stockade appeared to consist of living quarters, some storerooms, the trading shop, and furthest away from them, Gideon identified the anticipated blacksmith shops. Hamish McGregor, a tall Highlander, stopped abruptly, nearly causing Gideon to bump into him.

'What is it?'

Hamish inhaled deeply, a sigh which spoke of uncertainty, and uttered, 'I canna see it.'

'Canna see what?'

'The marker for the hole.'

Gideon scanned the sea of swaying grass with a sinking heart. At the end of the trading season, when the fort was to be closed for the summer, all goods which could be stored were hidden in a cache to avoid being stolen. The men would need to dig to recover tools and cooking utensils as well as, hopefully, some tobacco and dried meat.

'You ken where it is—more or less?'

Hamish was exhausted, as were all of the men, and pointed vaguely in the direction of the blacksmith shed. 'By the smiddy,' he announced, with more authority than he felt, and looked back along the line for Duncan Mackenzie who had also been at Rocky Mountain House the previous season.

Duncan shuffled towards them, bent almost double by the barrel he was struggling with, and eyed the area in front of the forge. The two Highlanders had a brief exchange in Gaelic which did not go unmarked by Gideon, and if the Shetlander had been of a different disposition, he might have enjoyed the discomfort so evident in their glances. However, the superiority and the clan mentality of the Highlanders, which they had exhibited at Norway House, had long ameliorated in the face of endurance in the wilderness.

There was no one to match the hardiness of the Orcadians and the Shetlanders. Duncan, aware that it was unwise to antagonise them as the brigade included several men from the northern isles, turned to the group gathering behind him and spoke in English, the language used by all in place of their dialects.

'We must store what we've brought first, and tomorrow, we can retrieve what's been left. We can camp tonight and sort out in the morning.'

Murmurings rippled down the line, a combination of agreement and disagreement as varied as the men who had been assigned to the post. They would have a few days before Harriott, the Chief Factor, would arrive and everyone needed to pull together until then under the leadership of the Chief Clerk, Donald Miller. The group consisted mainly of craftsmen who would build the boats over the winter, ready to carry the season's furs and provisions downriver when the spring thaw came, and those involved in trading including Miller himself, his apprentice clerk, and an interpreter and his apprentice. Everybody had their own view about what to do and turned their attention from the Highlanders to the Chief Clerk, who was the last to arrive, having overseen the disembarkation. The interpreter, James Stewart, who was a renowned hunter and a seasoned employee of the Company, eyed the younger man expectantly and said, looking at the sky,

'Aye, we canna find the cache in the dimming light.' He carefully lowered the barrel he had been carrying and added, 'We'd best get all this inside. The Blackfoot will know we have arrived by now.'

Gideon woke the following morning, stiff and aching from the journey, and watched the dawn light from the ill-fitting shutters drift across the faces of his sleeping companions. The luxury of his own room, which had sometimes occurred in the permanent forts, was impossible at Rocky Mountain House. As he made his way outside, weaving through the makeshift cots, Gideon chided himself over his disappointment for he had never slept alone back in Shetland. He was changing, a process he recognised in himself, and his expectations had shifted. In his darkest hours, he questioned whether he would ever return home, and during those unsettling times, he would try to bring Grizzel to mind but even she was beginning to fade. The disappointment of not receiving a letter from her that year with her news, and hopefully, word about his grandparents, was akin to a physical blow and he had thought long and hard on the reasons for such circumstances.

As he left the living quarters, Gideon could see a light in the trading shop so he made his way towards it; he was obviously not the first to rise that morning. A track had already been trodden through the enveloping grass the previous evening, yet more signs of movement could be easily seen. Barrels, being rolled, had flattened the path wider, and when Gideon pushed the sturdy door open, he saw a hive of activity being organised by Donald Miller. He recognised Miller's apprentice, Jamie McTavish, a young man in his early twenties like himself, the interpreter, James Stewart, and his apprentice, Andrew Ross, as well as a couple of labourers who had joined the brigade at Edmonton House. Miller looked up as he heard the door creak and waved Gideon over.

Rather than breaking his fast, which was what he had hoped for, Gideon found himself unpacking bundles of the Hudson's Bay Company blankets which had made the long journey from Witney, England, and stacking them neatly on shelves. That completed, there were boxes of knives, hatchets, multicoloured glass beads and tinkling metal bells, all to be neatly stored. Miller was overseeing some barrels of gunpowder which would remain in the shop, ensuring no fire could be lit to give comfort once the bitter winter arrived, while Stewart was carefully unpacking the guns which were prized by the Blackfoot who would shorten the barrels to suit their hunting on horseback. Jamie McTavish was checking the inventory, perched on the shop's counter with his long, thin legs crossed and a look of studied concentration on his face. Gideon, having unpacked the beads and bells, wandered over to him.

'Can I help?'

Jamie's head shot up, surprised at the unexpected offer. He eyed the blacksmith warily, uncertain how he could offer any help and shook his head.

'It would be faster with two. I could count while you tick the items off or vice-versa.'

The apprentice clerk's eyes widened with interest at his companion's turn of phrase and swept the man before him from head-to-toe. The blacksmith was of medium height and wiry, with the strong arms characteristic of his trade. He met the scrutiny with amusement, a faint smile which threatened to turn into a grin curved his lips, and a direct gaze which contained a challenge. As Jamie McTavish eased himself off the counter without acknowledging him, Gideon took a step back and followed the clerk's line of vision.

'What are you checking?' he asked.

Jamie, reluctant to appear rude, replied, 'The blankets.'

'There are five dozen on the shelves there.'

'How do you know?'

'I've just unpacked them.'

'You count everything you unpack?'

'No,' responded Gideon, stretching out the word. 'But I stacked them in piles of six and you can see, from here, that there are ten piles in a row.'

Jamie thought for a moment and looked down at the thick sheaf of paper in his hands.

Gideon laughed. 'A'm literate too.'

Whether it was the enormity of the task he faced or Gideon's lapse from the English he was trying to perfect, was uncertain, but Jamie decided to accept his offer. He passed the inventory to Gideon, conscious that he needed to do the counting, and glanced over to see what Miller was doing. His superior had been encouraging him to use his initiative, still underused after three years in the Company's service, and there was no harm in having help. He could always check Thompson's work if need be.

'You're an Orkneyman?' he asked.

'Aye,' replied Gideon. 'Shetland.' He did not ask Jamie about his origins preferring to wait for the young man to open up. Snippets about the apprentice clerk had been exchanged between the boat's crew as they journeyed towards the fort but Gideon had chosen to ignore the idle gossip and innuendo. He would, as he always did, take each man he met with an open mind. He believed that Jamie McTavish was the son of a Company man and was native to Rupert's Land as were many of the apprentice officers but his name told of his Scottish roots.

'When did you come out?' asked Jamie as they both walked towards the crates which held tools.

'In the summer of '49.'

'Same as me.'

'I thought you hailed from here.'

'What made you think that?'

Gideon shrugged. If the gossip about Jamie's origins was incorrect perhaps the sniggers about his smooth, fine-boned face were misplaced? Either way, he did not care as McTavish, now he had accepted Gideon's help, was politely making conversation instead of ordering him about.

'Where do you hail from?' he asked, hoping to divert the clerk.

'Perth—my father thought it a good idea to experience some adventure.' Jamie, his eyes briefly flicking from the box in front of him and seeking Gideon's, laughed sardonically and said, 'To make a man out of me.'

'Have you found it?'

'What?' asked the clerk, reading the contents of the box with studied concentration.

'Adventure.'

Before Jamie could respond, Jon Ferguson, a craftsman like Gideon, interrupted. 'Adventure—all you get here is monotony.'

Gideon turned his attention to the older man and raised his eyebrows, 'It was definitely an adventure sailing across the North Atlantic and into Hudson Bay,' he said, trying to be positive.

Jamie nodded in agreement while Ferguson, who was born in the Red River Settlement, announced, 'I missed out on that, coming from the east.'

'When did you come?'

'This is my fourth winter here and I can tell you that the only excitement here is when the Blackfoot come to trade.'

'Like most forts,' agreed Jamie, 'all there is to do is work and sleep with the added luxury of buffalo meat.'

Jon chuckled, 'Don't you just love pemmican?'

'Especially the hairs!' added Gideon.

The three men looked at each other, united by circumstance, and Gideon experienced the warmth of companionship. He was missing Jim Turnbull's company, and thinking of the library at Fort Carlton, he said,

'At least we'll have the books.'

A look of puzzlement appeared on Jon Ferguson's face. 'What books?'

Gideon's heart sank. 'The library books.'

'There's nae books here, laddie,' clarified Jamie, imitating the Chief Clerk's speech. He laughed at himself, a deep laugh which seemed to belong to a much sturdier man, and glanced guiltily towards Miller, as did

Gideon whose mouth curled into a smile. Fortunately, Miller was too preoccupied to notice the group, and as their acquaintance progressed, Gideon would learn what an excellent mimic Jamie was.

Thirty-Six

Against all expectation, the first two months of Gideon's employment at Rocky Mountain House were not monotonous. The days passed swiftly, filled with the need to be ready for winter. The first flurries of snow came, intermittent at first but an ominous harbinger of what was to come, and briefly dusted the glorious autumn colours white. The cache was found with a good amount of tobacco, enough to satisfy all the men who smoked, which lifted their spirits, as did the arrival of a second brigade laden with more provisions. Best of all, a new iron stove for the men's quarters was among the supplies. Packed in its various pieces, it was Gideon's task to assemble it and fire it up, an activity he enjoyed immensely.

He knew he was privileged to work in the forge, predominantly making the iron parts for the boats, but there were also other necessary jobs to attend to. One of the first, was to make a new steam box ready for when the boat ribs required bending and to provide enough extra nails to store in the boats as spares in case any repairs were required en route. The latter would be stowed away with a hammer, a saw, a chisel and some oakum for padding. A detail was sent out to cut new timber, before the snow came in earnest, to replenish the stocks which would be used over the season; Gideon felt a fleeting yearning to accompany it, to feel the freedom of being away from the fort, but it was only momentary as the claustrophobic days of winter were yet to come. The pinery which provided the ribs was a day's journey downstream, and when Jon Ferguson returned from the felling, he regaled Gideon and Jamie with tales about sightings of Blackfoot riders obviously monitoring the task force, and of buffalo and bears.

One evening, they were sitting on Jon's bunk in the men's quarters, as it was closest to the stove, listening to his account of the felling expedition for the third time. Gideon had planned to start a letter to Grizzel but the lack of privacy made him reluctant to take out his pen and paper. It was easier to join the other two by the warmth rather than sit, silhouetted in the shadow of the paraffin lamp, struggling to write to a girl who might never read his words. The absence of a letter from her that year had undermined his hope that they would have a future together, and although he knew that post did go astray, he was unprepared for the resulting hollowness he felt. Gideon had glanced across to his companions and registered Jamie's expression of fostered interest, the stories became more colourful with each telling, and had decided to rescue him. Jon had stopped talking long enough to ask Gideon a question.

'What's that you've got there?'

Gideon carefully placed the lamp down and held out his carving which would be his gift to Grizzel the following spring. In the yellow glow, Jon could just discern the outline of a buffalo, the animal's heavy shoulders providing the clue.

'Who's it for?'

Gideon chose his words carefully. It was all well and good sharing his private life with Jim Turnbull, but in this new fort, with different companions, Gideon chose to dissemble.

'A'm undecided.'

For a moment, Jon eyed him keenly, sliding his gaze towards Jamie and back, which made the latter blush. 'A wee gift for a sweetheart?'

Gideon chose to ignore the inference which, he had quickly learnt, was the best way to cope with the carpenter's occasional malice. Generally, so far, he found much to like in Jon's character; his joie de vivre and optimism and his willingness to pitch in and help without being asked. There was also his story-telling, a welcome means of passing a companionable hour or two, but there was no denying that his barbed comments were usually targeted at Jamie McTavish. When Gideon pondered on this, which he had begun to do as he methodically hammered the iron, he was reminded of an adage that his grandmother used to say; something about two people rather than three. The words, company and crowd, were there somewhere, he thought, but he could not recall the saying accurately. He had tried to recollect Margaret Thompson's voice, and on failing to do so, he had panicked and he found his hand was shaking as he plunged the red hot iron into the water tub. It was the same with Grizzel, this gradual fading, but as the steam rose, he concentrated on her face and felt relief flooding through him as she appeared in his mind, with her winning smile and luminous grey eyes. He had cautioned himself then. A blacksmith's shop was no place for daydreaming; he had seen too many accidents on Shetland when a man had not paid full attention. He must live in the present, making the most of his time in Rupert's Land, yet all the while planning for the future.

He had already made himself useful, helping Jamie as he had done Jim Turnbull, and he had now developed a good grasp of a clerk's responsibility to keep records whether they be account books, inventories, or journals. He was even quite proud of his neat hand, holding the quill with confidence when Jim had allowed him to make entries, and when he had last penned his correspondence to Grizzel, he had practised further, taking great care with the formation of his letters.

'Surely, you have a sweetheart?' asked Jon, when Gideon had not responded. 'A strapping lad like you!' He reached out extending his hand to receive the buffalo. Gideon paused for a moment and then handed it to him.

'A man of many talents,' said the carpenter lovingly running his hand over the wood.

'It's just a bit of whittling.'

'I'd call it more than that.'

'Call it what you like,' replied Gideon, falling short of his customary geniality.

'I think I'll keep it.'

'Nae—it be not for you.'

'But if you have no sweetheart.'

'Hand it back.'

Jon was enjoying himself, needling the blacksmith while the clerk looked on, a wary look on his face. What on earth was that young man doing out in the wilderness? The older man glanced at Jamie's hands, they were long and slender, like his face, without a callous as evidence of honest hard labour. What hair grew on his face was very fine, blond, and wispy, totally unlike the Shetlander's who was the same age. His was a striking dark auburn, noticeable, because of its contrast to his lighter hair and the fact that it was neatly trimmed. The blacksmith refused to back down, his eyes eerily dark in the dim light of the room.

'Hand it back,' he repeated, the quietness of his voice brooking no resistance. 'A'm a patient man,' he continued, 'but dunna test me.'

Although Gideon had spoken softly, his tone had caused the nearest group of men to pause. The two with their backs towards him swivelled round to watch, the hand of cards they were clutching forgotten, their faces, illuminated by the lamp, hungry for a diversion.

One of them, who had served with Jon Ferguson for a couple of years, stood up and wandered over on the pretext of warming his hands, leaving his cards face down on his bunk. Now that he had an audience, the carpenter began to toss Gideon's carving from hand to hand, confident that he was increasingly becoming the centre of attention, determined to milk the situation to his advantage. Jon wanted to turn his head, to check that all eyes were on him, but he had witnessed the blacksmith's dexterity several times in the preceding few weeks. He continued to stare at Gideon, egging him on with a slight sneer on his face, but the younger man sat perfectly still, his hands resting on his thighs. One of the cardplayers sniggered and Jon turned briefly to acknowledge the attention. Nothing happened which surprised Ferguson and he grew careless, alternatively staring at Gideon and then throwing a knowing look towards the cardplayers. Gideon watched his adversary, paying no heed to the onlookers, and bided his time. When he struck, and caught the buffalo in mid-air, it was when the carpenter's eyes were locked on his. The room erupted with cheers, from not just Jamie and the cardplayers but also from the bunks in the far reaches of the room.

Once Gideon had the carving, Jon's expression changed to a darker one, and what had started as a convivial evening, had morphed into something quite different, intangible to Gideon, yet threatening. On the surface, the carpenter's acknowledgement of the younger man's victory appeared friendly, but beneath the geniality, Gideon experienced his first sense of unease. He glanced around the room, filled with men of whom he knew very little, and decided to distance himself from them. As he finished his sweep of the room, he saw Jamie quietly leaving for the officers' quarters and envied him. He wished he had his own quarters where he could retreat to read, but he had neither solitude nor books.

The following night, Gideon asked the Chief Clerk if he could use a desk in the office to write a letter. Surprised at the request, Donald Miller paused and then acquiesced when he saw the paper and quill in the blacksmith's hand. The Chief Clerk had pressing matters to attend to in the trade shop, as messengers had arrived earlier in the day to announce that a large Blackfoot band was approaching, and he needed to check that all was in order. Gideon watched him go and then sat at a desk, with nothing to distract him except the hum of the wind.

Rocky Mountain House,
September 1852
My Dearest Grizzel,

I trust this letter will find you in good health and spirit. It is with sadness that I confess I have not received a letter from you this year and I pray that this is the result of the vagaries of the postal service and not of your disinterest in writing to me. Or more worrying, the notion that ill has befallen you, for I hold you so dear in my heart.

For myself, I fare well and I am now stationed at Rocky Mountain House which feels more isolated than Carlton House. Here, we are small in numbers, concentrating on trading and the building of boats. I fear I have already told you of such things but I trust what happened today will be of interest of you. The Blackfoot have arrived.

The first men to arrive were messengers, whose mission was to inform us that a band of Peigan was coming to trade. The Peigan are one of the Blackfoot nations and they had travelled to us by way of the trail along the Clearwater River. The chief trader went out to meet them and presented a gift of tobacco. One of our scouts had informed us that the main band was already pitching camp alongside the Clearwater. Our fort is well-protected by its palisades and bastions, but after the messengers were seen approaching, we men were armed and told to stay vigilant as the Blackfoot peoples have a reputation for aggression.

Jon Ferguson, a carpenter who has worked at Rocky Mountain House for several seasons, was surprised to see the Peigan, as much of the trade with them has been lost to American traders in the south. He says that, probably tomorrow, the band will parade to the fort, and after the ceremony, trading will begin. Although I have seen this at Carlton House, Ferguson says that there is nothing to compare to the Blackfoot decked out in all their finery. The hides they wear are bleached white and are highly decorated with painted symbols, porcupine quills, shells, and also glass beads which are purchased by the Blackfoot in return for their pelts.

Grizzel, I believe the porcupine will be an animal unknown to you, as it was to me before I came to Rupert's Land. It is a rodent of considerable size, up to a yard long with a tail well over half-a-foot, and is covered with sharp quills. These quills are used in the elaborate headdresses, along with large feathers, which are worn by the men who are excellent riders. The horses are impressive and the Blackfoot are renowned riders and skilled horse handlers. Their tipis and luggage travel by travois pulled by horses that are very different from our Shetland ponies.

I am looking forward to such a spectacle. I will be able to see if Ferguson has exaggerated as he is wont to do. He is a man very much at the centre of things, and although I have usually found him amiable, there is something I distrust. I cannot put my finger on it, Grizzel, but after what happened yesterday, I have a feeling of unease, a creeping sensation which I fear will grow apace unless I am determined to suppress it. He sought me out this morning to regale me with descriptions of the Blackfoot but I feel his friendliness is disingenuous. Oh, Grizzel, the winter looms large and all-enveloping and I miss you mightily.

Gideon sat back and read his morbid words. He remained motionless for a good minute before he lifted up the second sheet of his letter, ready to tear it up but then he changed his mind. He would leave his thoughts, look at them later, and make a decision when his clash with Ferguson was not so raw. It was comforting to confide in Grizzel, despite it being at least ten months before she would read his letter. He imagined her poring over it, transfixed by the world he was describing, seeing it as a great adventure, and consequently, in her eyes, he would increase in stature. He allowed his mind to drift and daydream of a time when they would be together until a fierce blast of wind battered the window and broke his reverie.

He glanced around the empty office, registering the other desks with their inkstands and pens. The room possessed a quietness, a peace, totally unlike the men's quarters and he longed to rest his head on his arms and sleep there. He folded his arms on the desk and he dipped forward; he would finish the letter another day.

Thirty-Seven

December 1852

Cold and befuddled, it was some time before Gideon realised he was lost. The snow continued to fall with monotonous softness, muffling all sound as he strained to hear his companions. Surely it was only minutes since they were together, he thought, as he leant forward, peering through the blinding curtain of white. There was nothing on which to fix his eyes. He blinked once, twice, three times, vigorously trying to clear his vision and then he repeated the sequence again and again, terrified that his eyelashes might freeze together. His hands, encased in buffalo mittens, were now numb as were his booted feet, strapped to his snowshoes. He placed his hands in his armpits and stamped his feet as well as he could, and tried to decide what to do.

They had set out earlier that morning, led by the seasoned hunter, James Stewart, who had been waiting for a break in the weather in order to replenish the fort's meat supplies. Dawn had broken cloudless and sharp, its pink light reflecting on the frozen snow, promising easier travelling conditions and the hope of success. Time was running out for the inhabitants of Rocky Mountain House, with food already rationed and hunger continually gnawing at their stomachs. Spurred on by tales of former occupants being reduced to eating the fort's dogs and horses, the Chief Factor had announced the need for a hunting party on the first suitable day.

It had been eight weeks since the Blackfoot had visited to trade and Gideon had witnessed the spectacle of the entire band of traders approach the fort, savouring every moment so that he could write to Grizzel about it. The Company's flag was raised in recognition of the occasion and its cannons fired a salute. Gifts were exchanged and preparations made for the commencement of trading the following day. Gideon, busy at his anvil, had not been present for the actual trading and it was Jamie who had provided him with the details.

All precautions had been taken to ensure that the trading progressed smoothly, with only a limited number of the Blackfoot allowed in the trading shop at any one time. They handed in their pelts through a wooden grating and received blankets, beads, weapons, and alcohol in exchange, based on the value of a large, good-quality beaver skin. This rate was termed 'Made Beaver' by the Company and each hunter at Rocky Mountain House collected goods to the equivalent of two 'Made Beaver' for a buffalo robe while the rarer silver or black fox carried the greater sum of five. The fort also bought horses from the Blackfoot, trading goods worth twenty 'Made Beaver' for one horse. Gideon stored this information away with what he had learnt from Jim Turnbull at Carlton House, as the record-keeping he had been involved in there had consisted of ordering and supplies and not trading.

When trading had finished, Jamie and the other clerks had sorted the piles of buffalo robes and wolf skins and had become anxious about the quantity of pemmican and dried buffalo meat offered. It appeared worryingly inadequate and it was this which made James Stewart leave the fort most days in the following weeks, searching for small game, but his recent news of a buffalo herd spotted near the fort now called for a hunting party. The need was so great that several men were taken away from their normal tasks and handed hunting rifles including, amongst others, Jon Ferguson and Jamie, who Gideon believed to be totally unsuitable. However, the young clerk had assured Stewart that he had had plenty of practice with a gun back home in Perthshire.

They had been hunting for several hours without a sighting of the herd, despite the clarity of the early morning. Now, according to Gideon's reckoning, it was past noon and the light was already fading, hurried on by the steady snow which had rolled in from the north. He shouted, hoping his voice would carry far enough to be heard, but there was no response. His instinct was to retrace his steps but the snowfall had already erased any trace of them. He called again, turning a full circle to maximise his chances of making contact; it seemed only a moment ago that Jon Ferguson had been at his elbow. A creeping suspicion began to take hold of him, that

Ferguson had deliberately engineered their separation in retaliation for Gideon trouncing him, but fear soon replaced all other feelings. He could feel his heart starting to race so he began to count, slowly and with much deliberation, trying to concentrate on his next move. He needed to dig a shelter and wait out the snowstorm as he had done with Joe Kennedy in the winter of 1850, but then there were two of them. Images of his lifeless body being found played in his mind. Who had told him that it was painless to die of the cold? Was it true that blissful sleep drifted into an everlasting one? How would he keep awake with no companion?

Gideon began to scoop out a hollow, stopping to rest and shout at intervals, the snow now falling almost as fast as he could dig. He became lost in the task, his panic abating as he knelt by the edge of the hole, frantically tossing snow over his shoulder. There was no sound except the scrapping of his mittens and his own ragged breaths so, the blow against his back, when it came, flung him headlong into the snow. He was pinned down, his nose and mouth momentarily embedded in icy crystals when, suddenly, he felt a sensation of warm wetness on the side of his neck exposed by his scarf coming loose. He pushed himself up and turned, coming eye to eye with one of the sled dogs he recognised.

'Blue?' he queried, as he disentangled himself from the hound and was rewarded with more licks. Relief flooded through his body; he was not alone in the white wilderness. Man and dog scrambled out of the hollow and Gideon began to shout as loudly as his lungs allowed. Was that a reply? Was someone calling his name? He looked down at Blue and stroked his lean body. Even now, after three years in Rupert's Land, Gideon found it strange to come across a dog with blue eyes and he found it unsettling, as if the dog had a touch of human in him. He had taken to visiting the dogs at the fort, seeking out the friendliest who always appreciated the attention, as an alternative to mixing with the men who gravitated towards Jon Ferguson. Jamie, tired of the teasing and innuendo, had sometimes joined him and appeared to have an easy affinity with the animals. At first, Gideon would take some tasty titbits to share, but recently, food had been too scarce, and now, as his mitten stroked Blue he could feel every bone under the dog's grey-white coat.

Blue began to bark and Gideon reached for his harness to keep him close. The snow was falling thicker now, large sticky flakes, and the shape was almost upon them when a voice was heard calling, 'Blue, Blue, is that you? Where are you, boy?'

'Jamie?' exclaimed Gideon, in disbelief.

The young clerk loomed out of the blanketing white and greeted the excited dog. 'None other,' he announced proudly, his eyes, the only part of his face visible, bright with success.

'Where did you go?'

'What do you mean?'

'Where are the others?' demanded Gideon, feeling aggrieved now that Jamie had appeared.

'Stewart ordered us to split up into smaller groups so that we could cover more ground. We were never that far from the fort.'

'I wasn't told!'

'You must have misheard.'

'I did not mishear! Nobody told me! One minute, I was with the hunting party, and the next, I was alone.'

Jamie's eyes clouded with confusion, an expression Gideon had witnessed many times when the clerk was asked to undertake a new task.

'I don't know what happened,' he responded quietly. 'Don't shout at me.'

Gideon inhaled deeply. 'Sorry, I am so very glad to see you.'

There was an uneasy pause as each man felt wronged. Blue tugged at Gideon's arm, lunging towards Jamie.

The clerk was the first to speak, seeking acknowledgement of his actions. 'I should think you are—Jon Ferguson claimed you had returned to the fort.'

'Jon Ferguson?'

'Yes—you were in his group. Stewart appointed the seasoned men as the leaders.'

Gideon opened his mouth to deny any knowledge of this and then changed his mind. If his instincts were correct, it was best to keep the knowledge to himself. He met Jamie's guileless eyes and thanked him by releasing Blue and shaking his hand as firmly as mittens allowed.

Jamie's mouth curled into a broad smile, masked by the thick scarf which covered most of his face, and pointed to the hollow.

'What are you doing?'

'Isn't it obvious? A'm digging a shelter.'

The clerk examined the hollow and then turned half-circle towards the direction from which he thought he had arrived. 'Snow's getting heavier.'

'Aye,' agreed Gideon. 'We need to hunker down, the light will fade soon.'

Jamie nodded. It was almost the winter solstice, and although the fort was only a few miles away, he was uncertain now of his bearings. 'What about Blue?' he asked hopefully. 'Surely he could lead us home?'

'Want to chance it? I doubt even Blue could find the fort in this blizzard.' Gideon had his back to the wind which had risen unexpectedly, buffeting him with icy blasts. The snow no longer fell in vertical silence but swirled around him in dizzy formations, threatening complete disorientation. His companion's expression was unreadable behind the thick woollen scarf so, in the absence of a response, Gideon continued, 'The best thing is to sit out the storm.'

'What if it lasts all night?'

'We'll wait it out.'

'Have you done this before?'

'Yes, with a seasoned hunter from Carlton House.'

Jamie digested this information for a moment and then began to dig too, and before long, both men and Blue were snug in the shelter, their backs braced against the side towards the prevailing wind. It was quieter in the dip, enabling conversation, and Jamie began to talk, partly to pass the time but also as a diversion to his growling stomach.

'Do you think of home often?'

'Nae,' was Gideon's immediate response, unwilling still to reveal details of his life, but then the lie felt like a betrayal on his lips so he qualified his answer. 'A'm usually too busy to think aboot hame, but if I do, I think aboot the sea.' His companion was disappointed not to hear of the people in Gideon's life and was happy to answer when Gideon posed the same question.

Jamie's reply, when it came, was vehement. 'Never!' he exclaimed, 'my father has disowned me and my mother is not inclined to disobey him.'

Such a declaration, in Gideon's mind, forestalled any further questioning. 'What will you do after this?' he asked, by way of distraction.

Jamie's tone changed, acquiring a wistful quality as he remembered the beauty of the young curate at his local kirk. 'Because I can never go back to Perthshire, I will go to California.'

'To the Sierra Nevada?'

'Aye, it's said you can just pick the gold out of the rivers.'

'Maybe in '49 but that's three years ago. There'll be men like ants all over those mountains.'

'You won't come with me?'

'Nae, prospecting is not for me,' replied Gideon without a flicker of doubt. He was also uncertain how suited Jamie McTavish was to life in a mining camp.

'I thought you might.' The disappointment in Jamie's voice was tangible and his purpose in asking about Shetland became blindingly obvious to Gideon.

'A'm going hame,' he said gently, 'when I've served my time.' Although, as soon as the words had been spoken, Gideon was gripped with a fear of tempting fate, so strong it prevented him from explaining.

'There is someone at home?' demanded Jamie.

'I hope so,' he replied keeping his voice neutral.

'A woman?'

'Aye, the bonniest lass you could lay eyes on.'

'The buffalo carving is for her?'

'Aye, it's finished and will go in the post this spring.'

'You never talk about her.'

'What's to say?' asked Gideon, determined to keep his love to himself. He had neither a likeness of Grizzel nor a token from her to allay his worry that their relationship was so tenuous. Could you build a life on a fledgling affection nourished by a few letters? When he thought rationally about Grizzel and his chance of returning home to find her waiting for him, his heart would clench and it was increasingly easier to keep her locked inside it.

Jamie, who had hoped to find a sympathetic ear so that he could extol the virtues of the curate, Horatio Smith, in confidence, squashed his disappointment and held his peace. There was silence, broken only by the heavy breathing of Blue, for several minutes, as each man contemplated the person they had left behind. Then, Gideon reached out and placed his mittened hand on the dog's body, finding reassurance in the rise and fall of his ribs.

'Let's not be too fixated on the future,' he cautioned. 'We need to concentrate on how we get back to the fort once the storm has passed. He reached into the pocket of his buffalo robe and pulled out his daily piece of pemmican. Blue stirred at the prospect of food and Jamie said, sheepishly,

'I've eaten mine.'

'Here, take this,' instructed Gideon after he had divided his ration into as three equal parts as he could manage. Blue snatched his instantly but Jamie initially refused. 'Take it,' ordered Gideon. 'Where would I be if you hadn't rescued me?'

Thirty-Eight

After eating they dozed, snug in their shared warmth and cocooned against the angry wind. Blue was the first to stir, rising to his feet and sniffing the air. The storm had passed, leaving behind it a cloudless sky as darkness had fallen. Gideon wiggled towards the snow hole's entrance and looked up; a perfect indigo sky arced above him, populated by a myriad of twinkling stars. A large moon, just on the wane, cast silvery light across the newly fallen snow and the drop in temperature had frozen the surface into a hard crust. Beside him, Blue stiffened and growled, so Gideon rotated and adjusted his line of sight. His heart missed a beat.

Three figures loomed large above him, armed with guns, which, by their shape, Gideon recognised as the Company's, pointed unmistakably at the shelter. The brightness of the moonlight allowed three pairs of black, inscrutable eyes to assess him. The seconds expanded to a minute, measured by the thumping of Gideon's heart, when, unexpectedly, Blue brushed past his shoulder and tried to scramble out, his paws slipping as he struggled to find purchase on the hard-packed snow. One of the Peigan hunters reached down and hauled the dog to his feet while the taller of the three men indicated that Gideon should come too. Jamie, who was now wide awake, quickly followed on Gideon's heels, awkwardly slipping as he surfaced. Both men had left their guns in the shelter as an act of peace, an action Gideon was praying would be recognised. The hunters took a couple of steps back and waited.

There was another pause which seemed interminable to Gideon, and then, to his surprise, Jamie spoke.

'Ponoka-si-sahta?' he asked, pointing in a random direction.

All three men shook their heads and pointed to the northwest.

'Rocky Mountain House?' ventured Jamie for, although he had named the North Saskatchewan River, it was vital that they arrived at the correct location on that great waterway.

The three hunters pointed again, and this time, Gideon studied the position of the moon and the North Star. He nodded in agreement and waited, unsure of how to proceed. Would they be allowed to walk away? Blue began to become restless, burrowing his nose into the buffalo robe of the brave who held his harness. A smile softened the sharp contours of the Peigan's face as he produced some pemmican and held it aloft.

'Moki-maani,' he teased as he made the dog leap for it, 'moki-maani.'

One of his companions saw Jamie's envious expression and offered him a piece, before turning to Gideon who took his gratefully. The Blackfoot hunters waited silently, watching the white men chew the tough, dried meat, and then they nodded in satisfaction before they departed as quietly as they had arrived, heading south.

Both men exhaled thankfully, releasing the tension which had made every muscle taut, as they watched the retreating figures grow smaller and smaller.

'How did you know what to say?'

You mean Ponoka-si-sahta?'

'Aye.'

It means Elk River. I asked James Stewart. It's the Blackfoot name for the North Saskatchewan.'

'How did you remember it?'

'I don't know,' admitted Jamie. 'Once heard, I seem to be able to remember words.'

'And pronounce it so it was understood.' After Gideon had spoken, he whispered a silent prayer to God, thanking Him for Jamie's ear for inflection, usually employed to mimic the senior officers.

They stood in companionable silence, waiting for their heartbeats to return to normal, the air sharp in their lungs. Gideon studied the sky.

'You can get us back to the fort in the dark?' queried Jamie, doubt clear in his voice.

'Aye, I can navigate by the stars and the moon is bright. It'll be easier than on a boat in the North Atlantic and I've had a bit of practice at that. We need to go while the sky is clear.'

'I'll get the guns then and we can be off.'

The beauty of the night was breathtaking, the wind had dropped and all was still. Gideon felt they were the only men on earth as they made their way across the wide expanse of white, hoping to reach the trees bordering the Clearwater River. From there, they would meet the old Peigan trail which hugged the river and follow it until its confluence with the North Saskatchewan, and thence, the fort. With each step they took, he began to feel more confident that they would be successful. The moon shimmered in a cloudless sky, strong enough to cast shadows, and his main concern became Jamie who, unused to so much physical activity, might begin to flag.

'Do you ken any more Blackfoot words?' he asked to distract the clerk. If his own legs were feeling leaden he assumed the same was happening to Jamie.

'Iiniiksi is buffalo. It was one of the first words I learnt.'

'From the trade shop?'

'Yes—the plural is iniiksiit. I can only say it. I have no idea how it is written. I thought it wise not to mention buffalo in front of our visitors. They wouldn't like the competition.'

'You have a skill there, Jamie. You could become an interpreter.'

'I've told you, I'm going to the Sierra Nevada—for gold.'

'So you did!'

Jamie stopped to catch his breath. 'I'd never seen so much snow until I came to Rupert's Land,' he announced staring glumly around.

'Neither had I,' admitted Gideon. 'Not too far now, Jamie. Let's make for the trees and then we can rest a bit.'

It was darker amongst the spruce, whose trunks rose high above them, their branches laden with snow, which showered the men when they brushed against them. The lack of light made the going more difficult; the snow was also softer underfoot and very deep in places where it had been funnelled by the wind. Gideon rolled his shoulders, freeing his sweat-soaked shirt where it clung to his back. He turned to see that Jamie was falling behind, the young man more used to pen work than leg work, and temporarily forgetting that he had been rescued by the clerk, Gideon questioned the wisdom of Jamie coming hunting.

'I thought you said we can rest,' called Jamie.

Gideon signalled to him to be quiet and transferred his gun from one shoulder to the other. At his side, Blue tensed and pricked up his ears. He sniffed at the base of the nearest tree and then lifted his leg and urinated.

'What is it?' whispered Jamie, leaning so close that Gideon moved to the side to avoid a further waft of greasy pemmican breath.

He placed a cautionary hand on his companion's arm. 'Wolf?'

It was a logical assumption, the animal being nocturnal and not in hibernation. Both men readied their rifles and waited; although wolf meat was a last resort, it was food and might save Blue from being eaten if circumstances deteriorated further.

The animal emerged from the safety of the trees, a powerful presence in the dappled moonlight. A lone wolf, a young male probably in search of a new pack, he was almost totally black except for the grey markings on his face. For a heartbeat, he looked directly at Gideon, or perhaps Blue, and Jamie seized the moment. It was a clean shot, the wolf died instantly, and both men experienced startling exhilaration. The decision was made without discussion; Gideon, as the strongest, hoisted the carcass onto his back, it would provide a valuable hide at the very least.

Three hours later, they were home, drinking piping hot tea which almost rendered the dried buffalo strips palatable. Their welcome had been muted, with most of the fort's inhabitants asleep, but the sight of the wolf carcass raised the spirits of the men on guard. They had announced to the weary returners that the hunting party had arrived at dusk empty-handed and that there were plans to venture out again the following morning. The Chief Factor had been woken and had come to the kitchen to talk to the two young men.

'What I can't understand is how you became separated,' he said, looking directly at Jamie.

'It was me who became disorientated,' admitted Gideon feeling aggrieved on Jamie's behalf.

'You, Thompson, what were you doing there in the first place?'

'I was helping with the hunt.'

'I never gave you permission to go.' There was a pregnant pause, the Chief Factor's small blue eyes were stern. 'You're the blacksmith—we can't have you getting lost in the wilderness.'

'I volunteered. I had finished the fixings for all the boats, sir.'

The older man masked his surprise at the formality of the blacksmith's speech. He knew Thompson was a Shetlander but there was no trace of dialect as he spoke, only a slight northern isle burr to his pronunciation. Then, there was his friendship with the clerk which was unusual in the strictly hierarchical structure of the Company. The Chief Factor made a mental note to ask the Chief Clerk about Thompson. He studied the young man who met his eyes without flinching which was noteworthy in itself.

'Jamie McTavish showed courage in coming to find me. The storm was upon us so quickly that I lost all sense of direction.'

It was now Jamie's turn to be scrutinised. He sat with downcast eyes, like a chastised schoolboy, reluctant to meet the perceptive eyes of the fort's commander whose questions implied that someone would be held to account.

'Did you volunteer, too?'

Gideon willed Jamie to raise his eyes but to no avail. He kept them firmly focused on his mug of black tea which was rapidly cooling. 'I am considered a fine shot back home and Mr Stewart said he needed every good marksman.'

The Chief Factor leant back from the table, suddenly feeling the effects of his broken sleep; his bed was warm and inviting compared to the hard bench he was seated on. He told himself that he had done his duty, he had investigated the potential loss of two men, two valuable men at that, and Stewart had only been responding to the seriousness of the food scarcity on his own orders. It was too late now to question the wisdom of the Chief Hunter's decision to take the blacksmith and an apprentice clerk with him.

Gideon, seeing the Factor relaxing, hit home. 'Jamie is an excellent marksman. He downed a large wolf with a single shot.'

'You brought the wolf back?'

'Yes, sir.'

'Gideon carried it on his back.'

'The hunt wasn't a total disaster then?'

'No, sir,' they answered in unison, Jamie finally rising his eyes.

The following day, a hunting party left the fort under clear skies. However, James Stewart had been given firm instructions this time; the blacksmith, Thompson, and the apprentice clerk, McTavish, were under no circumstances to join it. They were both needed to apply themselves to their tasks at the fort.

Gideon, on his part, was relieved. He tried to quash his misgivings about Jon Ferguson who had greeted him genially at breakfast, exclaiming how glad he was to see the two lost souls safely returned. The carpenter had raised a guffaw from his close companions with his use of words, especially when he had looked pointedly towards where the officers took their meals. Gideon forced himself not to bristle, reminding himself that bullies were the same wherever they were encountered, but as Ferguson rose from the table, his parting words sent a shiver down Gideon's spine.

'You are like a cat, Thompson—quiet and aloof. But even cats only have nine lives. How many have you used already?'

Determined not to rise to the carpenter's bait, Gideon continued to eat. He raised his eyes, challenging Ferguson's cronies and they quickly averted theirs.

'I asked you a question, Gideon Thompson.'

'A'm not of a mind to answer.' He glanced up and locked eyes with Ferguson.

Silence crept around the room as its occupants watched and hoped that a confrontation was imminent. Any discord or even blows would break the monotony of their existence and it was into this charged atmosphere that James Stewart stepped. He recognised it immediately and shouted, his voice full of authority,

'I want all members of the hunting party out of here, NOW!'

Thirty-Nine

It was three full weeks before a hunting party returned with a kill and Jon Ferguson, who had fired the shot, swaggered around the fort with all the aplomb of a mighty hunter. Many men were unmoved by such a show of bravado as the carcass, when it was uncovered on the sled, was that of an old bull buffalo. Rumours spread that the huge beast had been an easy target, distanced from his herd and enduring his last winter before Ferguson had made his destiny a certainty. Gideon kept well out of the carpenter's way but it was always a tricky balancing act in a small fort.

At times, he questioned himself, worrying that he was experiencing a form of paranoia induced by the claustrophobic living conditions, a version of cabin fever which appeared never-ending. A cheerless Christmas came and went, followed by an equally sombre New Year, when all the men could think about was the growling of their stomachs. They survived January by rationing the old lame mare whose existence could no longer be justified, and by the arrival of February, blowing in icy and clear, the inhabitants of the fort had atrophied into shadows of their former selves. Dull-eyed and hollow-cheeked, their lips cracked and plagued by sores, the men of Rocky Mountain House had become so cloaked in apathy that the first shout of the watchman went unnoticed. He tried again, taking up his bugle, and with superhuman effort, announced their salvation.

A Blackfoot band had arrived for their late winter visit and soon set up camp on the level ground adjacent to the fort. With their travois laden with buffalo robes, pelts, and most importantly, dried buffalo and pemmican, the traders were a sight for very sore eyes. Plagued by malnutrition, the employees of the Hudson's Bay Company summoned their last dregs of energy and trading began. After the customary ceremony, four of the band were admitted through the narrow passage to the trading shop where they handed in their goods in exchange for the prized blankets, beads, guns, and alcohol. Once the exchange had been made, they exited back into the hall where the rest of the traders were waiting their turn. Jamie's fingers ached by the time the whole process had been completed, with every transaction recorded with meticulous precision hour after hour.

Gradually, over the remainder of February and throughout March, the inhabitants of the fort recovered, their spirits rising first, to be followed by steady physical improvement. The days grew longer, the sun shone brighter, and as the ice began to melt on the North Saskatchewan, Gideon began to experience a giddy optimism. Soon, it would be time to load the new boats with skins and provisions and then paddle downriver for six days to reach Edmonton House.

It was the end of April, the launching imminent, with all the boats being floated as more had been built than needed. The empty ones would be used by other forts to take goods to York Factory. Gideon made his way to the river, skirting the large graveyard with its paltry number of marked graves, thanking God, as he passed, that he had escaped such a fate. Most of the graves were now unmarked, victims over the years of the severe weather, and the entire cemetery was neglected and forlorn. Men who are struggling to live have no time for the dead.

As he reached the nearest two boats, he stopped and inspected them, his mind returning to Lerwick where he had often seen the handiwork of Will Cattanach and the other boatbuilders at Hay's Dock. Whether his thoughts could be read on his face or whether it was Jon Ferguson's penchant for picking a fight, he would never know, but before Gideon's opinion had settled in his own mind, the carpenter was roaring at him from a distance of a few yards. Taken aback, Gideon faced his opponent.

'Not good enough for you, Thompson.' Ferguson's face was the colour of beetroot.

'I haven't said anything,' stated Gideon, although he believed that Will Cattanach would have picked fault with some aspects of the boats' finish.

'Why are you looking at them like that then?'

Gideon sighed and spoke without thinking. 'There is no comparison to be made. The sixareens my friends make, are built to withstand the North Atlantic waves for years, whereas these York boats have a life of three to four years and are built for river transport, albeit the most demanding.'

'You're always so bloody superior!'

Gideon shrugged and turned away, refusing to rise to the bait. He walked slowly, one, two, three, steps when the blow hit him on his back between his shoulder blades. He staggered, using every muscle to maintain his balance and swung around, hissing in anger.

'You shouldna have done that,'

The sneer on Ferguson's face, the challenge in his mean eyes, as he leant forward with balled fists was too much to resist. Ten pairs of eyes were rivetted on the carpenter and the quiet blacksmith, expecting a good scrap. It was over in seconds.

Gideon stepped over his prostrate opponent where he lay. Felled by the strength of a right arm muscled by countless hours of striking on the anvil.

Three hours later, Gideon was summoned from the forge by the Chief Factor. He carefully placed the watch he was mending on the bench and walked out into the welcome spring sunshine. The Chief Clerk would have to wait another day for his precious pocket watch to be returned. He crossed the beaten turf of the yard and glanced up at the Company's flag fluttering in the breeze against a perfect azure sky, so vivid that it took a few moments for his eyes to adjust when he entered the dim interior of the Chief Factor's office.

To Gideon's surprise, it was Donald Miller, the Chief Clerk, who was seated behind the imposing pine desk, ready to chastise him. He was about to speak, to argue self-defence, when Miller raised his hand to prevent him.

'I know what happened at the river. There were plenty of witnesses.'

Gideon nodded his acknowledgement.

Miller placed his hands together and steepled his fingers. 'What concerns the Chief Factor and myself is how best to use your talents.'

'Sir?'

'We are aware of your interest in fort procedures other than smithing. This is unusual in itself, and when you left Fort Carlton, it was requested that you return there, if possible.'

Gideon remained silent, watching Miller press his fingertips against his lips while hooking his thumbs under his chin, as if in great thought.

'You realise blacksmiths are in short supply, especially here in the Saskatchewan District.'

'I am aware of that, sir. But perhaps there is a way in which I can serve the Company in more than one capacity.'

Miller rested his hands, still clasped, on the desk. 'Where did you learn your letters, Thompson?'

'At the kirk school and I was fortunate to be under the tutelage of Reverend Murray. He introduced me to reading and I have never stopped.'

'You believe you can fulfil your commitments in the smithy and help with the bookkeeping?'

'Aye, sir. I do.'

'You have finished all the ironwork required of you here?' asked Miller, although he had already checked the inventories.

'Aye, sir.'

'Then I think the best course of action would be for you to travel with the first brigade when it leaves at the end of the week.'

Gideon felt his heart soar. 'To Carlton House?'

'Yes, eventually—you may need to stay at Edmonton for a short while.'

'Would I be posted back here come the end of summer?'

'No—I feel it best for you to work out your service at Carlton.'

A smile was forming, his mouth appeared to curl upwards of its own volition, as Gideon struggled to achieve a neutral expression. 'Thank you, sir,' he responded, 'thank you, sir.'

Miller smiled back. Thompson was an agreeable young man, a good worker, tough and resilient, the kind of man the Company needed. He reminded Miller of himself, twenty-five years earlier, and the lad deserved a break. It was unfortunate that Ferguson had taken against the blacksmith but it was not the first time the carpenter had befriended a newcomer for the relationship to then turn sour. In Miller's opinion, some men were just born nasty and Ferguson was one of them. But he was too valuable a boatbuilder to lose. Privately, the Chief Clerk applauded Gideon's action when provoked too far and he had watched how the Shetlander had looked out for his own apprentice clerk, a sensitive lad who should never have come west.

'That's all,' he said as he indicated that Gideon could leave. 'I wish you luck in your endeavours.'

Gideon rose quickly, eager to be gone. Once he had finished his day's work, he would write to Grizzel. For the first time in months, hope resurfaced. He would be able to take the letter himself to Edmonton and then send it on its way, accompanied by his carving. He was almost out of the door when Miller's voice interrupted his thoughts.

'Thompson, have you finished with my watch yet?'

'By tomorrow, sir—by tomorrow.'

That evening, after he had eaten in peace as a concussed Ferguson was recovering in the small room used as an infirmary, Gideon returned to the forge on the pretext of working on the watch. However, instead of assembling the mechanism, he used the lamplight to examine his carving. Hidden among his tools, where it was safe from curious fingers, the buffalo was wrapped in a scrap of oilcloth. Taking it gently in his hands and unwrapping it, for his right one was throbbing from its contact with Ferguson, Gideon studied the carving for some time. He was pleased with his work, felt he had progressed since the selkie, and imagined Grizzel's delight at receiving it. A decision formed in his mind with such clarity that his heart began to pump. He took up his quill, and using a sheet of paper saved from Carlton House, he began to write.

Rocky Mountain House,
April 1853
My Dearest Grizzel,

My heart yearns for you, for your love,, and if you cannot give me that, for your friendship. With each passing month, you have become dearer to me than I can say. Your silence, though perhaps not of your making, is torture to me and I long to read your words. I pray that, this year, I will receive news of you. You are always in my thoughts, Grizzel.

Gideon had planned to write a longer letter but his hand ached too much. He read what he had written, and unused to baring his soul, he began to worry about whether he had said too much. He laid the sheet down and took up the last letter he had written, baulking at the date. Could he really have abandoned his writing since September? Would Grizzel expect more letters? Yet, what could he have written about? The months since then seemed interminable, a great expanse of cold and hunger, and as Gideon saw what he had written about Jon Ferguson, he marvelled at his own intuition. He would need to mention the carpenter in his present letter, to allay any fears Grizzel might have, but he was reluctant to spoil, what he had decided it would be; a love letter. He stared at the flame, bright behind its glass, as if seeking inspiration, and then, after manipulating his fingers, he began to write.

I am sending you a buffalo this year as a token of my love, carved over the winter, for you to receive as my valentine gift. My sentiments have remained constant.

Though I be beyond the Shetland Sea, my heart will always be with thee.

I have no news to write of except that I am leaving Rocky Mountain House for Carlton House imminently, which pleases me. In my previous letter, if you read my letters in date order, I mentioned a carpenter, Jon Ferguson. I will not trouble you with the details, but suffice to say, I will not be sorry to leave his company.

I will take the buffalo and my letters with me to Edmonton and see them posted. If all goes well, you will receive them before summer is out, Grizzel.

I pray God will keep you safe until we can meet in person.

Sending you the warmest wishes,

Gideon

Postscript,

Please give my regards to Will, and if you are able to, please give me news of my grandparents.

Forty

Carlton House, May 1853

Gideon experienced an overwhelming sense of homecoming as the brigade approached the wooden landing stage. Under him, the water of the North Saskatchewan River flowed sedately on its journey to the sea, while all around him, the dense woodland, freshly green with new growth, was alive with the evening birdsong of spring. On disembarking, his steps increasingly quickened and he began to leave his companions behind, hardly noticing the western sky as a flaming orange sun skimmed the horizon, heralding the end of the day. A light breeze played across his face, cleansing and welcome, it rippled through the prairie grass surrounding the fort and caught the flag which hung limply over the stockade.

He found Jim Turnbull in the clerks' office, his sloping shoulders bending over a ledger. Lost in a world of figures, Jim had not registered the knock so he straightened up with a start at the sound of Gideon's voice, and dislodged his pen and a sheath of papers which scattered to the floor. His pale blue eyes, large and shiny behind his spectacles, lit up with delight.

'You are back!' he exclaimed, clumsily grabbing Gideon's hand whilst simultaneously slapping him on the back. 'You are back!'

'So it seems,' responded Gideon, his hand still in Jim's. He reciprocated with equal enthusiasm, shaking Jim's hand and then took a step back. Both men grinned at each other for a full minute and then shyness overtook them, hot on the heels of embarrassment over their show of affection. The silence stretched out awkwardly, and then, Jim remembered the letter. He turned his attention to a drawer, without giving Gideon any hint of his purpose, so the young blacksmith watched, confused, while Jim rummaged through a pile of paper and envelopes.

'Here it is!' he shouted triumphantly, waving an envelope. 'It's addressed to you.'

'To me?' asked Gideon taking it.

'Yes—it arrived after you had left for Rocky Mountain House and then the winter set in.'

'It's been here months?'

Jim nodded in response and Gideon slowly turned the envelope over. His heart flipped when he saw the handwriting.

'Go on—read it now,' ordered Jim. 'I've got work to do.'

It was quiet in the clerks' office and Gideon acquiesced. Leaning against the end of the desk, he began to read.

Roadside
Lerwick
May 1852
Dear Gideon,

I pray you are in good health and that God has kept you safe in Rupert's Land. It is with deep regret that I must inform you of the death of your grandfather, Matthew Thompson, who died of the congestion of the lungs in October 1851. It also saddens me to tell you of the sufferings of your grandmother, Margaret Thompson, who, as I write, is in her final days and is being cared for by her neighbour, Eliza Moir.

Jim, pretending to work, was surreptitiously watching Gideon. Worried about the contents of a letter, already a year old, Jim was experiencing a cocktail of concern, guilt, and helplessness. He had enjoyed his own bundle of letters, which had arrived the previous year, full of news of his family and friends, and now, as he watched the colour drain from Gideon's face, Jim wished he had made more effort to send the letter on. It was unwarranted guilt, for what could he have actually done? Perhaps he could have found some Cree scouts willing to travel into Blackfoot country? But how would he have arranged that? And there was no guarantee the letter would have reached Rocky Mountain House.

He waited, not wanting to intrude, as his friend slumped onto the nearest chair. Gideon's voice, when he found it, was a strange, tortured version of his usual measured tones. 'My grandparents are dead. Me daa has been in his grave nigh on two years and I have felt nothing. Me grannie, not quite dead when this letter was writ, will be now. All I have done here, all I have endured here was for them.'

Jim shifted uncomfortably behind his desk, frantically thinking of a response. There was no need. Gideon continued to ramble. 'I didna need to come to this God-forsaken land, this wilderness where a man's life can be snuffed out in a snowstorm, where I canna see the sea, where I have known hunger such as I never imagined in Lerwick.'

'The letter is from Grizzel?' ventured Jim, although he had recognised the handwriting.

Gideon raised his head and appeared to drag himself back to the present. It took some time before he focused on Jim, nodded and then added, 'But she didna write it herself.' He was correct for Grizzel, at a loss how to tell him the tragic news, had turned to the Reverend Murray for help and she had copied out the clergyman's words diligently.

Jim could see the letter clearly as it rested on Gideon's knees. 'Read on,' he instructed, 'there is more.'

Gideon raised the paper, for there was only one sheet, and began to read. His expression changed, lifted was the only way Jim could describe it, as he heard Grizzel's voice for she had lapsed into writing as she spoke.

I canna tell you how sorry A'm to tell you this sad news. It breaks my heart for you to be so far from hame in Rupert's Land. I did see your grannie at Eliza Moir's hoose and I ken it brought her comfort to have yer letter. I read it to her twae times. She was very prood of you. I read what you writ aboot me. It made me happy. Dunna wirry aboot Angus Duncan. There is talk o him gyaan ta London wi mi bridder, Will and Kitty. Dunna wirry, A'll be in Lerwick when you come hame, if you writ me and ask me to be.

'Better news?' asked Jim.

'Aye, Grizzel says she'll wait for me.'

'That's good news indeed?'

'Aye, and she'll receive this year's letters before the summer is out.'

'Did you send her a carving?'

'Aye, a buffalo.'

'I'm very sorry to hear about your grandparents. I remember you saying how close you were to them.'

Gideon remained silent, a response was unnecessary. Jim, reluctant to return to the ledger, experienced a growing disquiet as he regarded his friend. The clock on the wall, with its loud uneven tick, marked time and Gideon's expression became progressively more despondent.

'What ails you?'

'What if Grizzel goes to London?'

'You have just told me that she says she'll wait for you.'

'Aye, if I ask her to, but in my last letter, I didna,' Gideon paused and re-phrased, 'I did not ask her specifically to wait for me.'

'What did you say?'

A faint wash of colour tinged Gideon's face as he recalled his words. 'I declared my affection. I am sure Grizzel would understand that I cared for her.'

'Well then?'

'If I'd had this letter,' announced Gideon waving it to the room, 'I would have asked Grizzel to marry me.'

Jim was tiring of the conversation, convinced they could go round in circles all evening. 'You haven't seen the girl for four years, isn't it a bit risky to talk about marriage?'

'You don't understand, Jim. There's this lad, Angus Duncan. He's a boatbuilder like Grizzel's brother, Will, and in the eyes of Janet Cattanach, he is a much better prospect than me.'

'Her mother?'

'Aye, and I'm convinced she will encourage Grizzel to choose him. Also, when Grizzel's friend, Kitty, marries Will, and they go to London, that might tempt Grizzel. Kitty has a way with her, a determination, and she might persuade Grizzel to come with them.'

Jim emitted a heartfelt sigh. 'If Grizzel goes to London, that's her choice.'

'I ken, but she's waited a whole year for a reply to this letter, hoping for a firmer declaration and she won't get one!'

It was true. The carving of the buffalo and his accompanying letters had already left Edmonton travelling with the brigade ahead of his. Gideon had missed the chance to pen a hasty proposal which, in Jim's mind, was fortunate although the latter refrained from sharing his viewpoint. Instead, he asked,

'You have told her that you will definitely return though?'

Gideon tried to recall, with difficulty, the exact contents of his correspondence. His first letters, about his journey, York Factory, and then Norway House were more firmly lodged in his memory than the more recent ones which had been penned against a backdrop of monotony, followed by a struggle to survive. He had admitted affection, of that he was certain, he had made the valentine, writing a lover's verse each time and declaring that his heart was hers, but had he actually clearly stated that he wanted Grizzel to wait for him? Had he ever spoken of the promise of matrimony when he returned to Shetland? He had not. He had been too cautious. The realisation of his mistake came gradually, manifesting itself with nausea deep in the pit of his stomach before his chest tightened, making it difficult to breathe, and his heart quickened. For a couple of minutes, he could not speak, his eyes wide with dismay

'I don't believe I have,' he whispered, almost to himself.

'Don't think about it now. You've had distressing news about your grandparents. You need to settle in—it's been a hard day. Let me finish this task and then, as you say, we'll have a wee dram together, sorry, a peerie dram.'

'I suppose you're right,' replied Gideon, grudgingly. 'There is nothing I can do.' He stood for a moment and looked around the room, apparently studying it as if he had never spent time there.

'Gideon?'

'Aye, I ken. A'm dimsket,' he acknowledged as he walked dejectedly out of the room.

Jim watched him go with a combination of relief and anxiety before returning to the accounts. However, he found his previous concentration elusive and Gideon filled his thoughts. He mulled over several scenarios and played them out in his mind before deciding to bide his time. Gideon was too preoccupied with the contents of Grizzel's letter to be receptive to new possibilities and could well be antagonistic towards Jim taking the initiative on his behalf. His slipping into dialect was testimony to his despondency.

Unbeknown to Gideon, Jim had written to his father and that letter was now on its way to York Factory to catch the summer mail boat. It would reach its destination by late summer or early autumn if all went well. What would his father think of Jim's suggestion? Would he be able to help? Jim believed so, as his father was not without influence. The port of Sunderland was growing apace and was already bustling when Jim had left. The coal staithes were busier than ever with the sea-going colliers loading up, ready to go south, while the shipyards hummed with activity as construction strained to keep up with demand. Jim remembered his father taking him to the staithes when he was a boy and he could always recall the coal dust, the taste of it on his tongue, the air filled with it. He had complained and been chided by his father who had declared that it was such activities which brought wealth.

The more Jim considered his action, the surer he became, especially after the news from Shetland. Gideon had no family there now, he was pining for a girl who could well be married to another by the time he returned, and even if she did wait for him, how would they both feel after a separation of five years? Jim paused after considering the last question, removed his spectacles and rubbed his tired eyes. Yes, that was it. Sunderland needed young men, steadfast, skilful men, of whom Gideon Thompson was one. With employment and good prospects, Gideon would be able to support a wife, whoever she may be, and all Jim needed to do was persuade his friend of the merit of his idea.

With clarity, came concentration and Jim picked up his quill once more and returned to his columns. There was plenty of time. His father's reply would arrive the following summer and that could be the moment to present the opportunity to Gideon. Perhaps a letter would arrive from Grizzel Cattanach in the same mailbag and the decision would be clear-cut. Whatever the outcome, Gideon would know that Jim acted with his best interests in mind, and with that final comforting thought, he dipped the nib in the ink, glanced at the clock and calculated that, within the hour, he would be enjoying a dram with Gideon.

Forty-One

Roker, Sunderland, June 2019

The quietness of the house enveloped her as she walked aimlessly from room to room. Lara was out, no doubt she had met a new beau while Eve had been in Canada, although the signs of her presence were everywhere; a coffee cup by the sink instead of being in the dishwasher, the light above the bathroom mirror still switched on, and the basket by the tumble-dryer half full with the rest of the clothes in the drum, forgotten. It was late, almost midnight, but Eve was functioning on a time of her own, somewhere between two time zones, and not yet ready to sleep.

She returned to the kitchen and plonked herself down at the table noticing, as she did so, a note by the kettle. On investigation, she found it covered a bar of her favourite chocolate, and for the first time since she had landed at Newcastle, Eve smiled. Her niece had written a welcome message followed by the instruction to enjoy the treat. Breaking off a piece of chocolate, Eve ate it slowly and stared out of the window into the night. It was so different from the dark skies she had often experienced while camping with Joel and Nate that she felt an intense flash of longing. Suppressing it, as there was no point in yearning for what had passed, Eve concentrated on the comforting sweetness melting in her mouth and analysed her other emotion.

She felt betrayed. Yes, that was it, she had been betrayed. Alarm bells had rung as soon as she espied Aidan waiting for her at the airport. His face, in fact, his whole demeanour had screamed discomfort, or, as she thought about it now, as she broke another three pieces off the chocolate bar, guilt.

He had hugged her awkwardly, fumbled as he took her suitcase, and appeared uncharacteristically flustered. Her welcoming smile had faded without fully forming, and instead of chatting about her holiday, she had asked,

'What's the matter?'

'Let's get in the car first.'

'That sounds ominous!'

Once they had left the airport and were making good progress on the dual carriageway, south to Roker, Aidan cleared his throat loudly, which immediately irritated Eve in her tired state.

'There have been some changes at work.'

'Have been?'

'There are to be,' he corrected.

'What changes?'

He began with a preamble. 'You know that libraries have recently been under attack due to lack of funds. The local authorities just can't afford the investment any more.'

'Yes,' she snapped. 'Why are you telling me what I know!'

'Don't shout,' he responded using the tone he had perfected to deal with difficult customers.

Infuriated further, Eve was about to use more colourful language when she remembered that he was her boss.

She managed an apology but qualified it by adding, 'Perhaps now is not a good time. I have been travelling for twelve hours.'

'I wanted to give you the heads up,' he explained solicitously, 'before you come to work on Monday.'

'Tell me what exactly?'

'We're going to have to trim some staff.'

'Trim? Human beings aren't hair!'

'Eve—you aren't making this easy!'

'Are you being trimmed?' she asked caustically.

'No.'

'Who is?' She knew the answer before he replied.

Instead of immediately giving her names, Aidan spoke as if he was bestowing a gift on her. 'I thought you and Jennie could job share.'

'Thank you very much.' Her voice dripped with sarcasm.

'Be fair, Eve,' he countered. 'My hands are tied.'

'When does this take effect?'

'September—we have some flexibility. You and Jennie could decide how to split the time. You could divide a week evenly or do three days one week and two days the next. You'd have quite a bit of autonomy, the two of you.' He tried to make the situation sound attractive but Eve was only half-listening.

She was thinking about her contract, signed when she had first worked in the library. Had she been taken on as temporary staff? Could her hours be changed as Aidan had indicated? He was acting as if it was possible. She glanced at his profile, clearly visible, as they were driving through well-lit streets, and had the urge to upset him. He must have known discussions about staffing had been taking place long before she went to Canada, and only now, had he thought to tell her. She changed the subject.

'I had an amazing time in Canada—thank you for asking!'

'What did you find out about your chap?'

'Loads of stuff,' she replied, exaggerating.

'What did you do after visiting Winnipeg?' he asked. 'Your messages became very brief and haphazard.'

'I went on a tour of as many Hudson's Bay Company forts as we could fit in.'

She waited for the significance of her words to penetrate.

'We?' he queried. 'Did your mum's friends take you?'

'No.'

'Who did you go with?'

'Joel and his son, Nate.'

'Who are they?'

'Friends I met. I had the most wonderful time—the best time of my life. The very best. Joel drove us from Winnipeg to Calgary. I even visited his ranch.' Eve wondered whether she should say more and make Aidan jealous, but on reflection, decided that being petty was unworthy of her.

He briefly turned his head to study her before turning his attention to the road. It was quiet, few cars were about as most people were asleep. 'How did you meet them?'

'I met Joel at Calgary airport.'

'You accepted a lift from a man you met at the airport?' Aidan was incredulous.

'Yes—sometimes I can't believe it myself! But I did and it was beyond fantastic!'

'You could have ended up dead in a ditch!'

'I'm not that stupid—I checked him out!'

Eve waited for Aidan to respond with more questions but he chose to remain silent and they were driving along the seafront before he spoke again.

'How old is this Joel?'

'I didn't ask—somewhere near forty.'

'A wrinkly then,' said Aidan who, younger than Eve, was still in his twenties.

Eve laughed despite herself, recalling the deep sunlines around Joel's eyes, and wondered how he would react to the description. With amusement, she thought, and as Aidan regarded the softening expression on her face, he did experience a stab of envy.

He pulled up outside of her house, climbed out of the car and reached into the boot for her case. They stood uncomfortably apart on the pavement. 'Sorry about the bad news.'

She shrugged. 'How will the library manage?'

'Volunteers will make up the shortfall.'

'Oh—great!' She was being replaced by a volunteer.

'I'll be off then.'

'Thanks for the lift—I really appreciate it,' she said genuinely.

'See you Monday then. Have a good rest tomorrow.'

Eve ate another piece of chocolate and checked her watch. It was after midnight, Sunday already, and she should really try and get some sleep, but her mind was buzzing. She took out her phone, the last thing she knew she should do, and brought up the genealogy website. After logging in, she scanned her list of familial matches, restricting the link to fourth and fifth cousins. Disappointingly, only three of them had uploaded their family trees, and on these, there was no mention of the name, Thompson. She continued to assess the other matches and decided that the best way to proceed was to message them through the site. She would start with the first six on her list, omitting those with published family trees. It did not take long, the same brief message was sent to each person explaining that she was trying to find descendants of a Gideon Thompson, born around 1830 in Shetland, who served with the Hudson's Bay Company 1849-1854.

She logged off from the site with a sense of accomplishment. She was, at least, taking some action instead of moping. She reached for the remains of the chocolate bar and ate the last few squares, choosing not to read its calorie content which she knew was more than a quarter of the recommended daily allowance. She reasoned that she had eaten so badly over the previous twelve hours that a meal of chocolate was neither here nor there. The longcase clock in the hall chimed once, and still, Lara had not appeared. Eve decided to make a hot drink and then she would go to bed.

The boiling water had just made contact with the chamomile teabag when her phone pinged. She checked it immediately, hoping it was Joel, but it was a notification that her message had been answered. Eve followed the link, it must be someone who was a night owl or they were in a different time zone. She opened the message. It was from a Linzi Butler, who, by her English, was in the States. It was a chatty answer with details of her forebears, but unfortunately, she had never come across a Gideon Thompson in her own research. She wished Eve good luck, which, at that moment, Eve felt a little short of, and bade her to have a good day.

Eve sipped her tea slowly and worked her way through the pile of mail Lara had collected together. It was depressingly small for an absence of three weeks even though Lara had kept everything; flyers, the free newspaper, a couple of clothes' catalogues her mother had used, some bills, and a bank statement. Eve made a note that she must cancel the catalogues and opt for paperless statements. The only item of any interest was a postcard from a university friend, Vicky; one of the few she kept in touch with, who was holidaying in Crete with her husband. She read it half-heartedly, looked at the stunning archaeological remains at Knossós with a jaundiced eye as they had once planned to go together, and then placed it back on the pile. They had been good friends at the time, both studying Classics, sharing a flat with two other girls, and dreaming of visiting all the great classical sites of Europe. Then everything changed.

Spurred on by her reminiscences, Eve returned to her phone and googled her university supervisor, Leo Jones. His photo popped up immediately accompanied by a list of links. He was now a professor, having moved universities, so she clicked on the link to his new department and composed an email before she lost the courage. After the initial pleasantries, it was brief and to the point; she wanted to explore the possibility of continuing with her thesis. The email completed, Eve drank her tea, which had cooled considerably and decided that she really should go to bed.

The front door key clicked in the lock when Eve was halfway up the stairs. Delighted to have a distraction, she turned and watched Lara trying to creep in quietly.

'I'm here,' she called, starting to descend.

'Sorry, did I wake you?'

'No, I was just going to bed.'

'Welcome home, Auntie,' said Lara, hugging Eve tightly, laughter in her voice.

'You're cold,' remonstrated Eve, as she came into contact with Lara's bare arms. Her niece was wearing the skimpiest top and skirt.

'You sound like Mum.'

Eve shook her head and decided not to pursue the topic of Lara's inadequate clothing. 'It's good to see you, Lara.'

'You too—it's been strange without you.'

Extricating herself from Lara's hug, Eve found herself saying, 'Would you like a cup of tea?'

'Yes, I want to hear all about Canada.'

'You run upstairs and get a cardi, and I'll put the kettle on.'

They sat together at the kitchen table and Eve recounted her holiday experiences. Lara was a considerate listener, asking the occasional question but mainly remaining quiet, allowing her aunt the joy of reliving the events of the previous three weeks. Eve became more animated, her face alive with the excitement of her trip and swept Lara along with her.

'This Joel must've really liked you—he actually asked you to his home. You met his mother!'

'All the Canadians I met were very friendly.'

'Doh!'

'You think he does?' Eve felt like a teenager asking for affirmation.

'Doh!'

'Stop it!'

They both grinned at each other. Eve was the first to collect herself. 'I really must try at least to go to bed.'

She stood up, placed the mugs in the dishwasher, and then pulled down the window blind.

'You're different, Eve—more sparkly!'

'Well, I won't be if I don't get some sleep.'

'Sweet dreams, Auntie Eve!'

Before Eve could respond, her phone pinged.

'Aren't you going to check it?'

'Give me a chance!'

Her heart started to quicken. It was from Joel hoping that she was safely home. She replied instantly saying that she was. Lara rose from the table and stood behind her, her height allowing her to easily read Eve's phone. It pinged again.

'What are you doing up so late?'

'Reply to him,' ordered Lara.

'I'm going to. I'm thinking what to write.'

Lara, her boldness increased by the alcohol she had been consuming although she was far from being inebriated, grabbed the phone, and with lightning quickness, texted, 'Missing you.'

A response arrived almost immediately. Eve held out her hand, the tussle between anger and embarrassment clear on her face, but Lara held the phone outstretched above her head and had the temerity to read Joel's answer first. She wore her poker face.

'Lara,' demanded Eve. 'Don't spoil things.'

'I'm not, see for yourself.'

Eve whipped the phone from Lara and then glanced down. Her heart began to sing as she read his words, 'That makes two of us'

She raised her eyes to meet Lara's triumphant gaze.

'Who was right?'

Still not quite believing what had transpired, Eve whispered back, 'I think you might be.'

Forty-Two

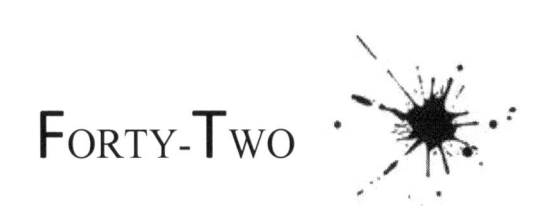

That night, lying in bed with sleep continuing to elude her, Eve had mulled over the significance of the day's events. Threatening to dwarf all other contenders, Joel's reply came top of the list. She had waited until her heart had stilled, and her fingers were under control, before she sent him a single smiley face as a reply. He had responded similarly and she had left it at that, although, every now and then, she had reached for her phone and reread his message. Her conversation with Aidan and his unwelcome news, had lost some of its sting, and by the time she had finally relaxed, her future stretched before her full of possibility.

Eve woke feeling remarkably refreshed as the sun streamed through the gap in the curtains. She glanced at the clock on the bedside table, registered the time and then double-checked. She had been in bed less than five hours. It would not yet be midnight in Alberta. Perhaps Joel was still awake? Her thumbs were balanced over her phone's keyboard when a message came through. Her heart jumped but it was an email informing her that she had another message on the genealogy site. She opened it, glad that she had been distracted. It would become too easy to be permanently attached to her phone.

The message came from a distant familial match, not the closest that she had contacted, and by the formal language, not a young person.

Dear Eve,

I was very interested in your message and feel that I may have some information pertaining to your search. I believe that one of my forebears married a Thompson who had spent some time in Canada, and as far as I know, it would be about the same time as you said. It was my grandfather who was a keen genealogist and I do have his research, although, at the moment, it is in the attic and I will need to wait for my son to come and retrieve it for me. If you bear with me I will be in touch once I know more. I hope I haven't raised your hopes fruitlessly but I was interested when you posted your message.

Yours sincerely,
Winnie Hunter

Eve read the message a couple of times and tried to decide whether it was something or nothing. Thompson was not an unusual name and she had seen many men with that surname in the archives in Winnipeg. Yet, it was a positive reply and Winnie Hunter could well have a connection to Gideon. She had, after all, messaged back immediately, perhaps spurred on by a genuine recollection. However, she had given no timescale as to when she would be able to read her grandfather's papers. Eve began to type.

Hi Winnie,

Many thanks for your reply. It was very prompt. I would be very interested in hearing about your grandfather's research.

Eve

She sent the message and then held the phone in her hand willing a message from Joel to come through. It remained disappointingly silent and then she chided herself. It may be late Saturday night in Alberta but Joel would still need to be up early. There was no weekend in ranching. Reluctantly, she placed the phone down, forced herself to shower and then crept down the stairs to avoid waking Lara, her fingers constantly itching to reach for it.

It was a beautiful day, the sea calm and as blue as the Mediterranean, with the promise of a busy Sunday. Eve pulled on her denim jacket, there was a nip in the air despite it being June, and headed towards the seafront. She paused when she reached the Bede Memorial, the towering carved cross which depicted scenes from the great scholar's life, rising majestically above the Cliffe Park, and made the decision to walk towards the pier and the marina. She would buy a coffee and a pastry at the café there and watch the weekend sailors make ready their yachts.

She had just collected her order and found a sheltered outside table, when her phone began to vibrate in her pocket. It was a message from Joel,

I can't sleep

Eve replied instantly,
Why not?

Followed just as quickly by Joel and a conversation started which lasted the entirety of her breakfast,

Someone has unsettled me.
Who could that be?
A shy Brit.
Me, shy!!!!
Not so shy now she's back home!
True.
What shall I do about it?
It's up to you
A grand gesture?
You've seen the films!
It's not Christmas yet!
Who said it had to be Christmas?
Leave it to me.
Can I wait that long?

No message came instantly back and Eve began to fret. Had she misjudged the banter? She took a bite of her croissant and cast her eyes around the marina. The breeze had picked up, and all around her, she could hear the gentle slap of rigging and the call of cheerful voices. Above her, seagulls circled, watching and waiting, until a couple of fearless ones landed a few feet away from her. An elderly man, sitting at the table next to her, threw them some crumbs and smiled at her when he saw she was looking at him.

'Grand day,' he said.
'Yes, it is.'
'Your phone's wobblin.'
'Oh!' The squabbling of the gulls had masked the sound.

What are you doing?
Having breakfast with an old man and two gulls.
Interesting!
I'd rather be having breakfast with you.
Same here
What are you eating?

A croissant.
No bacon and eggs?
No—not even a pancake in sight.
Back at work tomorrow?
Yes but I've had my hours cut.
How come?
There have to be staff reductions.
Will you manage?
Yes, my sister insists on paying rent for Lara.
That's good of her.
I know.
You could start to do more research.
I've already contacted my old supervisor.
Good girl.
I've also started to search for distant cousins.
Any luck?
Had two answers already.
Wow.
One might lead somewhere.
Ma'am.
Don't you dare!
Ma'am, I want to ask you a question.
A question?
Yep.
Okay.
Would you like to see lots of snow?
Yes.
Christmas in Alberta?
Definitely.

Eve's euphoria lasted all of Sunday. It even continued the following day, allowing her to walk through the library doors with a spring in her step. She bestowed her most cheerful smiles on Aidan who went about his work in a sheepish fashion, stealing surreptitious glances at her when he thought she was preoccupied. She brushed off commiserations from fellow employees with a light hand and comforted Jennie who, originally devastated by her reduced hours, now felt like a traitor because she was looking forward to having more time with her young grandson.

By lunchtime, Eve felt as if she had never been away. Jennie had seen her go into the office and took her chance.

'I was hoping to catch you alone.'

Eve looked up from her bought sandwich, a necessity as Lara had not thought of replenishing the fridge, and waited for yet another apology.

'I feel so guilty because I knew before you. I'm so sorry.'

'Don't be—as long as you are happy to job share, I am.'

'I accepted the reduced hours before Aidan could speak to you.'

'Don't worry about it, Jennie.'

'You're certain?'

'Yes—hopefully, we can be flexible.'

Relieved, Jennie gushed on. 'Any time you want me to cover for you, I will. I'm really looking forward to seeing more of George. Once he goes to nursery, I'll be able to pick him up when it clashes with his dad's shifts.'

'How old is he now?'

'Three months,' replied Jennie, her eyes shining with grandmotherly adoration.

'Planning ahead then!'

Jennie laughed. 'Just a bit.'

'We'll be able to work something out,' said Eve, thinking she had a full nine months before Jennie would have specific commitments.'

'Thanks—I'd better get back. I'm due to relieve Alice on bus passes.'

No sooner had Eve taken another bite of her sandwich than Aidan arrived.

'This is a coincidence,' remarked Eve, 'have you been watching me?'

'It's my lunchtime too.'

'Aidan, you will have already eaten. It must be almost three o'clock.'

'Nothing gets past you, does it?'

Eve smiled sweetly, too pleasantly, in Aidan's opinion. He began to mumble. 'I just wanted to see if you were okay. I thought it might be a bit awkward coming to work this morning.'

Eve regarded her friend and relented. 'That was kind of you but I'm fine.'

He looked at her long and hard. 'I believe you are.'

'In fact, I'm pleased to have an opportunity to talk to you.'

Aidan checked his watch. 'I've got time for a cuppa.'

'Make me one too, please.'

They sat convivially, as they had on numerous previous occasions, but both of them were very aware that the dynamics of their relationship had changed.

'What do you want to talk to me about?'

'I'd like time off at Christmas.'

Aidan regarded her quizzically. 'More than the usual days?'

'Many more.'

'How many more?'

'At least two weeks, maybe more.'

'Impossible.'

'What about these new flexible hours?' asked Eve, raising her eyebrows as she spoke.

The question hung heavy in the air, Aidan procrastinated. 'I haven't put any thought into the rota for December. It's far too early.'

'You usually start in September. Staff have family commitments and I remember how accommodating I've been in the past. I'm not asking for special treatment, but if I can work something out with Jennie and I can take some of my annual leave then, it would be great.'

Aidan appeared to be digesting this proposal. Eve leant forward and gently tapped his hand. 'I'm just giving you the heads up!'

Aidan had the grace to laugh. 'Why do you want so much time off?'

'I'm having a winter holiday.'

'Canada?'

'Yes.'

To his horror, Aidan blurted out, 'What about us?' He had assumed Eve would always be around to be his companion.

Eve spluttered, having just taken a mouthful of tea, and started to cough. He rose immediately and thumped her on the back.

When she had recovered, he admitted, 'That sounded a bit childish! Sorry.'

'We'll always be friends.' Eve said emphatically, 'But there is no "us". We would have got together years ago if the spark had been there.'

'Some people are friends for years and then they realise how important they are to each other.'

'Be honest, Aidan, that's not going to happen. You're just a bit miffed that I've met someone.'

'Have you really?'
'I believe I have.'
'I'm very happy for you, Eve.'
'Thank you.'
'I can't see how it'll work.'
'Aidan?'
'Okay, okay.'
'Drink your tea.'
Eve's phone vibrated on the desk.
'Is that him?'

It would be early morning in Alberta and the first of daily messages had arrived. 'Yes,' she replied joy suffusing her face.

'I'll leave you to it then.'

Eve read her message.

How's it going?
Great.
Great?
I'm sorting out my holidays!
Can't wait.
Neither can I.
Nate says hi.
Hi, Nate.
He wishes you were here.
So do I.
So do I.
Must go—work calling.
Have a good day.
You too.

Eve settled back into her work and her old routine but everything seemed rosier. There was the excitement of making contact with her university supervisor, the anticipation of receiving a reply from Winnie Hunter, and overarching everything, was her relationship with Joel. They messaged twice a day without fail, conversations that ranged from light flirtation to more serious assertions, from politics to everyday life, and with each message, Eve felt that she was taking another step towards him. It did not matter that he was an ocean and half a continent away, the immediacy of their communication brought a closeness which was tangible. At times, she would think of Gideon Thompson and speculate how difficult it would have been for him to keep in touch with home and her heart reached out to him across the years.

Forty-Three

September 2019

A squeal from the hallway told Eve that her dream had come true. She stood stock still, like a rabbit caught in headlights, and then frantically tried to decide what to do. She checked her reflection in the dressing-table mirror, her hair, as usual, appeared to have a life of its own, and her jeans and sweatshirt were clean, which was probably all that could be said of them. She could change, wear something more alluring. Did she have such garments? The idea was dismissed immediately, too difficult to accomplish, so all she did was brush her hair and scrunch it up on the top of her head. Then she descended the stairs and met Lara on the first landing.

'There's a cowboy on the doorstep,' mouthed her niece, her eyes wide.

Eve nodded and eased past her. Lara, only a step behind her, leaned forward. 'You should see his boots!'

Eve only partially heard, all her concentration was focused on the figure framed in the doorway, half obscured by a large parcel.

'Howdy,' he said in his unhurried way, his eyes dancing with delight.

'You're here. You're here. I can't believe you're here!'

Eve would have thrown herself into Joel's arms, if it had not been for the parcel.

'Come in, come in.'

'This is for you.'

Still unable to hug him, as now her arms were full, Eve ushered Joel into the kitchen, followed by her fascinated niece.

Lara, feeling like a spare part but determined to stay, busied herself with filling the kettle and finding three mugs while Eve inspected the parcel.

'Open it,' suggested Joel.

She placed it on the kitchen table and gently pulled away the wrapping to see a section of white wool. 'It's too much, it's too much.'

'That's for me to decide. It's a gift.'

Eve removed all of the wrapping to reveal a Hudson's Bay blanket. She hugged it to her. 'Thank you, thank you.'

Joel grinned. 'You don't have to keep repeating yourself. I did have some difficulty with the folks' accent at the airport but I can usually understand first time.'

Instead of speaking, she hugged him and Joel wrapped his arms around her so tightly it became uncomfortable.

'I saw you admiring them in the shop at Rocky Mountain House.'

Eve wriggled so he released her, but only enough to allow him to meet her eyes. 'That's a mighty firm grip you have,' she commented, as he bent his head and kissed her. She kissed him back enthusiastically, oblivious to Lara leaning awkwardly against the counter.

'A drink, anyone?'

Joel, his attention caught, held out his right hand while still managing to encircle Eve with his left arm. 'Howdy, I'm Joel Baxter and you must be Lara.'

Lara's eyes flicked from Joel to Eve and back again. 'I'll take mine upstairs.'

'No, you won't,' ordered Eve. 'Let's clear the table.'

She folded the blanket neatly and hung it over the back of her chair. 'Sit down.'

They sat around the table, the cafetiere in the centre, and sipped their coffee as if it was a normal Saturday afternoon.

'I didn't expect you until later tonight,' admitted Eve. 'I was going to meet you at the airport.'

'You knew he was coming?' interjected Lara, astonished.

'Yes.'

'You never said anything.'

'I thought you'd be out when Joel arrived.' Even to her own ears her reasoning sounded lame, but how could Eve admit that she had been reluctant to tempt fate. She had imagined all sorts of scenarios which would have prevented Joel from arriving.

'We made it to Heathrow in such good time that I caught an earlier flight. I wanted to surprise you.'

'How long are you here for?' asked Lara.

'Ten days, my foreman wouldn't allow me any longer!'

'How is Jed?' asked Eve, as she saw Lara's puzzlement. She had never told her Joel actually owned the ranch.

'Great, everyone says hi.'

'It's a shame Eve will be at work.' Lara noticed her aunt's expression and asked, 'What else don't I know?'

'I have all next week off plus the first half of the following week. I've swapped days with Jennie. I'm doing all of the half-term holiday so that she can see her daughter in Brighton.'

'Oh,' was all Lara could think to say.

Eve continued, 'We'll probably go away so that Joel will see a bit of the country.'

That night, Eve woke up after only a couple of hours sleep and experienced the strange disorientation of uncertain whereabouts. Then she remembered. She was in Joel's bed, the guest bed in what used to be her parents' bedroom. She gingerly reached out to establish whether he was there and touched a warm thigh. There was no reaction, Joel appeared to be in the deep sleep of the traveller who had reached his destination, so she turned on her side towards him as carefully as she could, and willed herself to go back to sleep.

It was impossible. Her mind was buzzing, electrified by the events of the day, her heart was so full she felt it might burst, and her body was still savouring the passion they had shared together. It had been so seamless, one minute they were bantering and then the next they were revelling in the feel of each other's skin. Afterwards, as she had lain in his arms, she had exclaimed, once again,

'I can't believe you're here.'

'I had to come.'

'Why?'

'My mom said so.'

'Pardon!'

'She said to me, "Son, if I see you looking at that darn phone one more time, I swear I'll grab it and throw it in the trash. If you're so fixated on that girl, go get her! Don't be moping around my kitchen!" That's what she said.'

He kissed the top of her head.

Eve sat up. She could hear Rose's voice. 'Did she really?'

'Yep.'

'So, you're only here because your mother told you to come?'

'Yep.'

'I don't believe you.'

'Believe what you want!'

'I will,' she had replied archly.

'That's my girl,' he said, as he pulled her back into his arms.

She snuggled into him so he kissed her glorious springy hair before searching for her lips and the rest of her body.

The memory of the conversation made Eve's lips curl into a smile. She inched closer to Joel and rested an arm across his chest. He stirred, took her hand in his, and immediately his breathing became deeper. They lay like that for some time, Joel asleep on his back, Eve burrowed next to him. The longcase clock in the hall struck twice, the chime loud in the quiet house. She heard Lara come in from her night out with friends, tired from walking from the nightclub to save the taxi fare, and she could just discern the murmur of voices which told her the group had stayed together. There would probably be two more girls around the breakfast table tomorrow, having spent the night on cushions on Lara's floor or in the lounge. It would not be the first time that Eve was greeted in the morning by the sight of a stranger lolling on the sofa, an arm dangling towards the carpet.

Eve heard the bathroom door click open and shut three times and then the house settled into the peace of the night. Her mind continued to race, revisiting plans for the following day, elated that Joel appeared to be as enthusiastic as her. They would set off in the morning but not too early, and after an overnight in Perth, they would reach Aberdeen the next day. They would take Eve's trusty old Astra estate and share the driving. Excitement bubbled up as Eve picked over Winnie Hunter's recent correspondence.

Dear Eve,

I am delighted to tell you that Duncan and I have retrieved my grandfather's trunk from the attic. It was full to overflowing with folders and documents. I have made a start and believe I have found something. It is a photograph of an elderly woman labelled 'Grandmother Thompson?' on the back. I realise this is not proof of our connection but it's a start?

Hope you are well,
Yours sincerely,
Winnie Hunter

Eve had messaged back immediately.

Hi Winnie,
That's fantastic. Would it be possible for you to scan the photo and send it to me, please?
Hope you are well too
Eve

It was three days before Winnie replied.

Dear Eve,
I am afraid I don't have the means to scan nor do I know how to. Duncan will not be back for a couple of months as I could have given it to him.
Yours sincerely,
Winnie Hunter

Eve replied immediately, not wanting Winnie to feel stressed by her request.

Hi Winnie,
Thank you for getting back to me. Please don't worry about scanning. Have you found any other nuggets of information?
Eve

This time Winnie's message arrived the same day.

Dear Eve,
I have found some letters but there are so many, from different people and eras, that it will take me some time to sort through them.
May I ask, whereabouts in the world are you?
Yours sincerely,
Winnie

Eve, curious about Winnie's rationale behind the question, rapidly typed in her answer.

Hi Winnie,
  I'm in Sunderland, a city in N.E. England.
  Where are you?
  Eve

Four long days later, a message arrived which made Eve's day.

Dear Eve,
  I'm in Shetland. If you are ever coming north I would be pleased to meet you and share some of my findings.
  Yours sincerely,
  Winnie

Hands shaking with exhilaration, Eve typed her response.

Hi Winnie,
  I would love to meet you. I am so thrilled that I'm going to organise a trip to Shetland as soon as possible. Even if we find no connection, it will be wonderful to see where my forebears lived.
  Eve

She had messaged Joel, who had been kept informed about her communication with Winnie and he had been equally positive. She had talked to Aidan and to Jennie, and a week later, she had written.

Hi Winnie,
  I'm planning to come to Shetland at the beginning of next month. I hope to travel with a friend from Canada.
  I am so excited!
  Eve

Winnie had answered, giving tips on where to stay and what to see, before saying how much she would appreciate meeting Eve. There was no invite to actually help sort the contents of the trunk which is what Eve wanted, but at least, she would see the photograph.

The longcase clock began to strike. Eve counted to seven. Surely that could not be? She checked her phone, it was eight o'clock. She had missed the chime. She lay back down and stole a glance at Joel. He had turned onto his side and was watching her.

'Good morning,' she said, feeling strangely shy.

'Good morning.'

'Did you sleep well?'

'I did, thank you.' He continued to regard her intently. 'Do we have to get up now?'

'Yes, we do!'

'Shame!'

She laughed and wriggled out of his reach. 'We need to get going. Also, there might be a bit of competition for the bathroom later. I'm going to have a shower.'

Eve was out of bed before Joel could persuade her to stay. Pulling on her dressing-gown, she glanced back over her shoulder.

'You can join me if you want to?'

Slightly later than she had planned, they were ready to leave. A blurry-eyed Lara surfaced to wish them a good journey and to listen to her aunt's instructions with a touch of petulance.

'I managed well enough when you were gadding around Canada.'

'You mean when you didn't need to text me in the middle of the night to ask which bin was due to be emptied that week?'

'Okay.' Lara lengthened the word.

Eve kissed her niece. 'Go back to bed!'

Lara complied, dragging her feet in their fluffy slippers and disappeared up the stairs.

'Teenagers!' exclaimed Eve jokingly! 'Who would want one?'

'I'd like a couple more,' admitted Joel, eyeing her keenly.

Flustered, Eve pretended not to read any significance into the comment, but later that night, when Joel was once again sleeping soundly next to her, she would re-visit it.

'Come on,' she said. 'We want to get round Edinburgh before rush hour.'

'You have rush hour on a Sunday?'

'Oh, I forgot—it's a Sunday.'

'Too many distractions, I believe.' A voice floated down from the landing. 'And I heard what you said about me!'

'Go back to bed, my lovely niece,' commanded Eve. 'And you, Joel Baxter, come with me.'

'Yes, ma'am,' he replied, his eyes now twinkling. 'We're off on another quest!'

Forty-Four

Shetland, September 2019

Joel sat on his bunk and watched Eve's rapt expression as she peered through the salt-rimed porthole. It was a look he had begun to love in Canada, especially when they were driving through magnificent scenery, but now it did not evoke the same emotion. The Northlink ferry was on the final stretch of its overnight voyage from Aberdeen, a journey which had left one of the cabin's occupants in a state of troubling queasiness. Perhaps if he could actually vomit, he would feel better? Joel tried to concentrate his mind in the hope that he would regain control of his stomach. He had spent half the night sitting in the cabin's compact bathroom, too worried to return to his bunk, and his face, with its sickly pallor was testament to both his jetlag and his seasickness.

Eve, who was transfixed by the view of Lerwick emerging ethereally through the mist, pulled her attention away from the window and studied Joel. His face was a strange colour, his deep tan tinged with yellow, and she experienced a swelling of love so strong that it unnerved her. He smiled dolefully.

'Are we nearly there yet?'

She checked her phone, open as she had already snapped several photos, and said, encouragingly, 'We dock at seven-thirty so not long now.' She came and sat next to him. Joel looked slightly better from the new angle. Possibly the light through the window was accentuating his sickliness? A white sun, almost moonlike, was filtering through the spray covered porthole and she was blocking some of its rays from him. She took his hand and he intertwined his fingers with hers.

'I can't believe you have never been on a boat before.'

'I've kayaked at home but this is a different ball game entirely.'

'True,' admitted Eve. 'You'll feel better once we're on dry land.'

'Sure,' replied Joel, with a total lack of conviction.

The sun had gathered strength, a breeze was dispersing the mist and blue sky widened above them, the colour deepening as Eve drove through Lerwick towards their accommodation on Hillhead. It was still quiet, the town on the verge of a new day, and immediately, Eve liked what she saw. The sea glinted to her left, no longer metallic grey while, on her right, the stone buildings of the town lined the road before crowding up the hill. They came to more wharfs where ferries departed for shorter journeys to nearby Bressay and the Out Skerries, and where holidaymakers disembarked from cruise liners on their tour around the Northern Isles.

'Lerwick means muddy bay,' Eve informed Joel as they stopped at the traffic lights on the Esplanade.

He glanced across the sound to Bressay. 'It doesn't look very muddy to me.'

'The name was coined hundreds of years ago.'

Joel nodded to show he had heard but could not conjure up any enthusiasm.

Eve carried on, unfazed by his disinterest. He would perk up when he had eaten. She regaled him with facts from the guidebook all the way to the Guest House.

'There are about twenty-three thousand inhabitants in Shetland and a third of them live here, in Lerwick.'

There was no response.

'The weather is very unpredictable—you can get all four seasons in a day so we are very lucky this morning.'

Enjoying herself, Eve continued to share nuggets of information.

'We are nearer to Bergen in Norway here than to Edinburgh. The islands used to belong to Norway in the Middle Ages.'

There was no answer. Joel's head had started to loll. 'Don't go to sleep!' she instructed. 'We are almost there.'

He woke with a start, blinked, and looked around him. 'I wasn't asleep.'

Eve smiled knowingly and then turned her attention to studying the houses as they made their way along Hillhead. 'Here we are,' she announced triumphantly as she stopped in front of a solid looking double-fronted Victorian villa, hauling the handbrake on more forcefully than she intended. It was not quite the arrival in Shetland that she had imagined.

An hour later, after a hearty breakfast prepared by their host, Lesley, Eve was ready to explore Lerwick. Joel had picked at his food before stretching his long frame out on the bed, and within seconds, he had closed his eyes. Deciding to give him a couple of hours before she would wake him, Eve crept out of their room buoyed up with excitement and made for the Tourist Office by the Market Cross. She spent some time acquiring a map of the town and several leaflets before strolling along Commercial Street towards Hay's Dock. She did not analyse her choice closely but logic told her that, if Gideon Thompson had worked as a blacksmith in the port, there was a strong chance he would have been employed at the dock.

Eve stood on the quayside and read the information boards, trying to conjure up the bustle of the mid-nineteenth century, becoming more firmly convinced that Gideon would have worked there. She wandered around the Freefield site which, once, had been residential, and then, when she deemed it not too early, she phoned Winnie and arranged to meet her that afternoon. It was not yet ten o'clock so, although she would have preferred to be accompanied by Joel, Eve walked towards the imposing new building which housed the Shetland Museum and Archives. She would visit some of the galleries, mainly those of little interest to Joel, and then, they could return together later.

Once inside, Eve felt like a child in a sweet shop faced with an array of tempting choices. She decided to start at the beginning, and soon, became lost in the displays about the early people of Shetland, learning how the Vikings had invaded, replacing the culture of the resident Picts. She did a double-take when she came across a modelled head constructed from the skull of a young woman who had lived on Shetland five thousand years ago. A pair of vivid blue eyes looked back at Eve, from a face which bore an uncanny resemblance to her Aunt Madge, her mother's sister. 'Creepy,' she said as she stared at the exhibit long enough for fellow visitors to notice, and to stare at her in turn until, embarrassed, she moved onto the Boat Hall.

Confident that Joel would give the boats a cursory glance, Eve spent the rest of her time marvelling at the boat displays. She read about yoals, the boats developed by the inhabitants of Dunrossness and Fair Isle for fishing, which were small enough to be hauled out by hand and stowed above the tideline, and about the larger boats, the fourareens and the sixareens which were four-oared and six-oared respectively. The latter being used for reaching the deep sea fishing grounds. Smaller boats hung from the ceiling of the two-storey hall while a newly built sixareen took pride of place on the lower floor. Eve studied it from prow to stern, itching to touch the smooth wood and to sit in it, imagining Gideon rowing forty miles out from the shore.

The morning flew by, and when Eve returned to the Guest House, Joel was up, showered, and hungry. He gave her a bearlike hug and then demanded, 'Where are we going to eat?'

'We're meeting Winnie this afternoon. She suggested a café on the Esplanade so you and I can have something before she arrives.'

They meandered down to the waterfront, taking one of the closses, the narrow lanes, which led from Hillhead towards the sea, so steep that they had to navigate several flights of steps.

'Not for the old and infirm,' commented Eve as she automatically reached out for a well-positioned handrail, keeping a keen eye on the uneven flagstones under her feet.

'These buildings are old. I like them.' The lane was so narrow in places that they had to walk single-file with Joel leading, still holding Eve's hand which was slightly awkward.

'You do?' queried Eve.

'Yep—do you think Gideon could have lived here?'

'He could have—maybe we will find out?'

The café was bustling when they arrived and there was only one free table, tucked away in a corner. They took it, and as they were sitting down, a grey-haired woman at the next table watched them with naked interest. Eve smiled the polite smile of the stranger, she had become used to people showing interest in Joel, and picked up the menu. The woman showed no sign of returning to her coffee and scone, her focus firmly on them. After a couple of minutes, she spoke,

'Excuse me, you wouldn't be Eve Cummins, would you?'

'Winnie?'

The woman nodded. 'Come and join me.'

Trying to mask her surprise on two counts as Winnie had a soft Home Counties accent as well as appearing younger than she expected, Eve slid onto the chair opposite her distant cousin. Joel was not so circumspect.

'You're English!' he blurted out before Eve managed to introduce him.

'Yes,' she replied. 'Are you disappointed?'

'No, no,' reassured Eve. 'I just assumed you would be a Shetlander.'

'Well, I am by heritage but I was born in England. I came to Shetland in the 1980s and have been here ever since, nursing. I only retired a few years ago. I married and raised my family here so I feel like a Shetlander. I came for a temporary position and I never left.'

'This is Joel, by the way.'

Winnie assessed him. 'You're a long way from home.'

He grinned back at her. 'Just visiting—and coming with Eve on her quest.' Joel turned to Eve as he spoke and his expression told Winnie everything she needed to understand about their relationship.

'I'd better tell you what I know so far. Are you going to order?'

The steaming bowls of homemade broth and bread appeared in record time and Joel narrowly missed burning his mouth in his haste to taste the soup. Eve had waited, eager to hear what Winnie had to say. 'I'm so glad you were here early. It gives us more time to chat,' she said, encouragingly, aware of Winnie's lack of ease. Now, she studied the older woman closely, she realised she was easily into her seventies.

'I had a few things to do in town and I finished early.'

'You don't live in Lerwick?'

'No.'

Eve was taken aback by the brevity of Winnie's reply, she was obviously wary of sharing too much with total strangers. Hopefully, by the end of their conversation, she would feel able to invite Eve and Joel to help sort the contents of her grandfather's trunk.

Winnie took a sip of her coffee. 'My grandfather was interested in genealogy long before it became popular and everything that I have in my possession came from him. I do have a family tree but it could well be incomplete. It's only recently that I have become interested.'

'Is the name Thompson there?'

'No—the only reference, as I said in my message, is on the back of an old photograph. I can go back in a direct line to my great-great-great grandfather.'

'Yes—I remember but I was so sure there must be a connection. Unless the DNA is incorrect.'

Eve watched as Winnie reached into her handbag and retrieved an envelope. Sliding the photograph out, she placed it on the table so it was visible to both Eve and Joel. Disappointed, for the woman in the grainy photograph bore no family resemblance, Eve stated,

'She doesn't remind me of anyone at all.'

'If you have Shetland heritage the link could be elsewhere. Although there are fewer people in Shetland now than in the nineteenth century, we are still talking about a reasonably small gene pool.'

Eve looked sceptical. 'I was so excited about finding the link.'

Joel covered her hand with his, surprised that she was being so naïve. 'All is not lost, honey.' He addressed Winnie and used his casual charm, 'Would it be possible for us to help you to sort through your grandfather's research, please?'

'It's in a complete muddle,' ventured Winnie, remembering her son's warning about strangers looking through family documents. Duncan had been unhappy with her about messaging Eve to say she would be willing to share her findings.

'Did you know Eve's a librarian, Winnie? She's great at putting things in order.'

Winnie regarded the couple opposite her. She had immediately taken to Eve with her bright eyes, friendly face and dishevelled hair. She was reserving judgement on Joel who, in Winnie's opinion, was too handsome for his own good. Long ago, before she had come to Shetland, Winnie had had her heart broken by a tall man with twinkling eyes. The cad had also had a strong jaw, although not quite a square as the man across the table.

Her underlying enthusiasm warred with the misgivings Duncan had raised. Now, she wished she had kept her communication with Eve to herself. Could she arrange for her friend, Jane, to come round and help, too? Watching Eve's eager face, Winnie came to a decision.

'Let's drop into the Shetland Family History Society while I'm in Lerwick and talk to my friend, Jane, who is there today. Then we can arrange for you to come over to me in Scalloway.'

Forty-Five

Eve and Joel were on their way to Scalloway, two days after they had met Winnie, with Joel driving so that Eve could concentrate on the scenery. The delay had been caused by Jane whose commitments at the Shetland History Society had prevented an earlier visit to Winnie's house. She had been extremely helpful to Eve when they had called in at the Society, spending time to help her navigate the 1841 Shetland census where they found a boy with Gideon's name boarding in Lerwick. It fitted with what she had learnt in Canada; boys were apprenticed as blacksmiths as young as eight-years-old. When they had tried to find Gideon again, in the 1851 census, there was no record of him which matched what Eve knew, as he would have been in Rupert's Land. She had wanted to stay longer, being completely at home with the enthusiastic volunteers and their archives, and she was itching to return. That evening, back in the Guest House, she had searched the 1861 census, and again, there was no record of him being in Shetland.

Now, as the car began its descent towards Scalloway, Eve continued to speculate about Gideon as she gazed out of the window, admiring the colourful houses dotted over the hillside. He could well have stayed in Rupert's Land, as did so many others, or had he moved elsewhere? The fact that his name was not recorded in Shetland in 1861 did not exclude the possibility that he had returned there. He could have temporarily been away from home, fishing like many of the Shetland men, or, and she quickly dismissed the notion, he could have died. She would need to spend more time accessing the census for all areas of Scotland and the rest of Great Britain, in the hope that his name could be found. She checked her phone. They were early so she suggested a stroll around Scalloway to Joel, and then she thought, feeling the familiar bubble of excitement rising, that she might find some answers at Winnie's.

A steady rain began to fall as they reached the castle so they nipped into the nearby museum. Eve's eyes lit up with glee as she saw the displays, a treasure trove of information about life on Shetland. For once, Joel did not fidget and shuffle, giving the displays a cursory glance. He became totally immersed in reading about the wartime operation named the "Shetland Bus" which had moved its base to Scalloway in 1942. Shetland fishing boats were used to transport supplies to aid the Norwegian resistance in its fight against Nazi occupation, and to bring fugitives and refugees back to safety in Shetland. He became so transfixed by the bravery of the men involved, making the trips in the dark, challenged by the threat of the treacherous North Sea and of enemy aircraft, always aware that they faced death and danger, that Eve had to drag him away with the promise of a return visit.

Winnie and Jane were waiting for them with a welcome cup of tea. While Joel made polite conversation, between taking bites of the freshly baked scones, Eve's eyes were being continually drawn to the large trunk which dominated the small sitting-room. It must have taken considerable effort to haul it down from the attic, which it had, causing Winnie's son to complain about strained and aching muscles for three full days. Old and battered, with a curved lid reinforced by wooden struts across the top, the trunk had been fastened with two large rusty clasps which Winnie had forced open to find the photograph of 'Grandmother Thompson?'

Winnie had shown Eve several other photographs, while Jane and Joel had carried the tea and scones through from the kitchen. She picked out the one Winnie had shown her in the café. On closer inspection, she could see that the woman was dressed in the style of the 1920s. She tried to hide her frustration, the woman could not be a contemporary of Gideon, and said, for something to say, 'She has a kind face.'

Joel took the photograph from her and tried to see any likeness to Eve. There was none. The woman who stared back at him had narrow, sharp features set in a thin face and he would have called her expression haughty rather than kind. Still, early photographs rarely did their subjects any favours especially if they wore a stern expression. He sat down next to Eve on the sofa and felt the tension emanating from her. He gave her a friendly sideways nudge with his shoulder.

'That's a cool piece of luggage—look at those labels.'

She nodded in agreement. The trunk was covered with different names and date stamps, echoes of its use in the days of steamer travel, and was a historical object in its own right. All the occupants of the room turned their attention to it and Eve took the opportunity to ask,

'Please can we look inside it?'

Jane, being more agile than Winnie, leapt up, equally excited about having a good search through the trunk's contents. They appeared well-organised, consisting mainly of neatly stacked box files in pristine condition. Each box file was clearly identified by the surname on its cover. It was a place to start so they briefly searched through those labelled; Tait, Ibbotson, Hunter, and Angus, taking one box each and scanning for any reference to the Thompsons. There were letters, notes made by Winnie's grandfather, documents pertaining to the relevant branch of the family but no joy in the search for Gideon.

Eve sat back on her heels, her shoulders visibly slumping. Joel, moved to find something, reached back into the trunk and brought out a folder which had been slotted along the front of the box files. He held it up with a flourish so that Eve could clearly see 'Miscellaneous' scrawled across and hastily firmed up his grip as the side had been forced open by its bulging contents. Winnie looked at the frayed blue folder. 'Perhaps that is where the photograph came from? It was loose in the trunk.'

Jane divided the folder's papers between the four of them and it was she who came across the letter. Her eyes shone as she announced, 'I think I have something here.'

Three voices asked in unison, 'What is it?'

'It's a letter from a Matthew Thompson written in 1951 from Edinburgh. Shall I read it?'

She did not wait for a reply and glanced down. 'It's to your grandfather, John, Winnie. Would you prefer to read it first?'

Winnie held out her hand and slowly perused the letter before handing it back to Jane who proceeded to read it aloud in her melodious lilt,

'Thank you for your letter of the sixteenth of last month. I apologise for not responding sooner but it has taken me some time to locate the enclosed. As stated previously, I am not sure where I lie on your family tree, so taking your word for it that we are second/third cousins, I believe the enclosed letters will be of interest to you.

'They are of no sentimental value to me as I prefer to live in the present. My wife found them when she was clearing out my late mother's possessions and chose to preserve them. Interestingly, and to add to the confusion for those looking into family history, my mother was also called Thompson which, of course, is not an unusual surname.'

'A red herring?' interjected Winnie.

'Not necessarily,' replied Jane, glancing over her reading glasses. 'It could be that the connection has come from Matthew Thompson's mother.'

'I'm not aware of any relations coming from Edinburgh,' mused Eve.

'What else does this guy say?' asked Joel as he rose to stretch his legs and did a circuit around the room. He stopped at a glass-fronted cabinet full of curios which appeared to be collected from different parts of the world.

'Nothing more of any significance. He just wishes Winnie's grandfather good luck with his family tree.'

Winnie, who had already read the letter, had stopped listening and was watching the big Canadian who seemed to fill her small sitting-room. She knew exactly what would draw his attention, and as he bent down to see more easily, she said, 'My parents collected most of those—they travelled a lot with my father's work. He was an engineer.'

'What about this one?' he asked pointing to the wooden carving.

'That is one of the odd ones out. I always loved it, and when I was a little girl, I asked my mother where it came from. She said that she didn't know and to ask my grandfather. He didn't know either but thought his father had told him that it came from some cousin. It's just one of those objects that a family hangs on to. When my parents died, I kept it and it came to Shetland with me.' Winnie paused, her mind momentarily elsewhere, and then added, 'I don't think it's a great piece of art.'

'But the person who carved it has captured the animal's essence.'

'Take it out of the cabinet if you want.'

Joel reached behind a miniature gondola and carefully retrieved the wooden buffalo. It was small, fitting the length of his hand, and possessed a beautiful patina, evidence of its age. The carving had been stroked by countless children. Joel ran his fingers down the beast's massive shoulders, feeling the texture of its coat, and knew that the artist had lived among the herds, had lived in North America, perhaps even in Rupert's Land, and he turned to share his excitement with Eve.

Her look of disapproval gave him a start. Its message was clear. Why was he wasting time looking at ornaments when they needed to find the letters? She rolled her eyes back to the trunk. He was about to justify his distraction, to announce that the carving was North American and that it could be a clue, but he changed his mind and gently returned the buffalo to its shelf. He would remind Eve of Winnie's explanation later.

'Winnie,' asked Eve, 'are there any more boxes in the attic?'

Jane suggested, 'Why doesn't Joel climb up and see?'

Eve's smile embraced everyone, even dispelling Joel's tetchiness. 'That would be wonderful.'

Winnie nodded her assent and steered Joel in the direction of the step ladders. Eve held them steady while Joel hauled himself through the trap door. He had no idea what he was searching for, it was like looking for a needle in a haystack. There were plenty of boxes, stacked and neatly labelled, but no other trunks. After some considerable time, Joel gave up. He had opened all of them, despite most being clearly marked, to reveal Christmas decorations, old clothes, bedding, discarded electrical items including an iron and a fan heater, books, and crockery.

He was making his way back to the hatch when he almost tripped over. Righting himself, he reached down and pulled clear an old satchel which had been wedged between two boxes. The leather was old and cracked, stiff where it threaded through the buckles, and it took some time to open it. He lifted the flashlight off the floor and shone it inside. His heart began to beat faster. He took out the first letter. He read the address at the top of the page. His hands began to shake, the light dancing and quivering across the page, as he turned the sheet over and saw the signature.

Forty-Six

Eve could barely contain her excitement as Joel descended from the attic, the satchel slung across one shoulder.

'Eureka!' he had shouted down, 'I've got them.'

Winnie and Jane clustered around the ladder, filling the narrow hallway and making it difficult for him to share the moment of triumph with Eve. He eased the satchel off his shoulder and only paused momentarily before he handed it to Winnie.

Eve, her eyes wide with curiosity, asked for clarification. 'They are written by Gideon?'

Joel nodded, lost for words in the face of Eve's evident delight.

They returned to the sitting-room, all eyes on Winnie as she sorted through the letters. There were eleven, in varying states of preservation, all written by Gideon Thompson in Rupert's Land between 1849 and 1854. Some of the earlier sheets of paper were stained as if they had come into contact with water, not enough to obliterate the writing but some edges had a dried, sand-coloured crinkliness. As Winnie read out the addresses, York Factory, Norway House, Carlton House, Rocky Mountain House, and Carlton House for a second time, Joel believed Eve might burst with anticipation.

'You were correct when we were on the banks of the North Saskatchewan, Eve,' he said, 'about feeling that Gideon had been at Carlton House.'

'Yes,' murmured Eve with a whisper of wonder. Then she collected herself and the researcher in her asked, 'To whom are they addressed?'

'A woman called Grizzel,' replied Winnie.

'That's not a name I've ever heard,' admitted Eve.

'It was quite popular in Shetland. It's a variation of the name Grace.'

'So the letters were written to a girl in Shetland?'

'It would seem so but all the envelopes are missing.'

'How will we find her surname if Grizzel wasn't an uncommon name?'

Jane made a decision. 'Winnie, share out the letters for us to read. Perhaps there will be some clues in them?'

Eve watched Winnie's hands greedily, uncertain of which letter she wanted to read first. If it had been her discovery she would have read them in chronological order, but due to her position in the circle, she received the final two, written in May 1853 and February 1854.

Carlton House,
May 1853
My Darling Grizzel,

If I may be so bold as to address you as such. Your letter has given me hope. I have returned to Carlton House to find it, already over a year old, waiting for me. What sadness it brought me to hear that my grandparents have passed away. It grieves me to know I will never see them again on this earth but the emptiness I feel is tempered by your pledge that you will be waiting for me in Shetland when I come home, if I but say the word.

My greatest fear is that your heart will be stolen by another. The vagaries of the Company's postal service and my movement from fort to fort means that I have missed the opportunity this year to respond to your request that I ask you to wait for me. Another year will pass before you receive these words. I do want you to wait for me and I hope and pray that you will do me the honour of being my wife.

I have little news of my life here in Rupert's Land. It pleases me to be back at Carlton House where the monotony is broken by my friend, Jim Turnbull, and the fort's library. I take heart in the knowledge that I must endure only one more winter for, if all goes well, my beloved, I will be home by the autumn of 1854. It excites yet pains me to know that my return will be only a matter of weeks after you have received this letter.

Your faithful admirer,
Gideon

Eve sat perfectly still after she had finished reading, the letter resting on her lap. She picked it up and as she read it for a second time she was gripped by a feeling of voyeurism. The words were so heartfelt, so private and not meant for a group of people to peruse. She glanced up at the others who obviously had longer letters, and three of them, as they were all engrossed in the small, neat script. Joel was the first to look up, followed by Winnie, and then, Jane. The latter invited them to feedback their findings.

Winnie began, 'The first letter is about Gideon Thompson's journey to Rupert's Land which he describes in detail and his arrival at York Factory. Then, the next two are from Norway House, again, full of details about his life. He refers to Grizzel as his friend and has obvious affection for her. He appears to have carved a selkie as a token of his regard.'

'A selkie?' queried Joel.

'A seal—there are lots in the Shetland waters. You've probably seen them.'

'Mine are all about Gideon's time at a fort called Carlton House,' contributed Jane, noting Eve's increased animation. She turned to the young woman and raised her eyebrows.

'Joel and I have been there, in June just gone. It's weird to think of him there.'

'He writes a very good hand for a blacksmith,' remarked Jane. 'But then again, he would have had some schooling in the kirk school.'

Eve felt a tinge of pride in Gideon and then suppressed it as unwarranted. She had no part in his achievement.

Jane continued, 'These letters are a valuable resource for research about life in Rupert's Land. He describes the severity of the Canadian winters, the cold, the challenges of hunting, the process of trading with the Indigenous Peoples but there are also personal issues. Gideon's admiration for Grizzel appears to deepen, and he is very keen to hear news of his grandparents. He has carved her a black bear this time.'

'Quite a menagerie,' observed Joel, and then his eyes swivelled towards the buffalo in the cabinet. 'I wonder,' he said, almost to himself but loud enough for the others to hear.

He caught Eve's eye and she gave him an apologetic beam. 'Is there any mention of a buffalo in any of the letters?'

'Yes,' responded Joel, flourishing one of the sheets he had been reading in her direction. 'There definitely is!'

'You know!' she exclaimed in mock indignation.

'Yes—it's mentioned in Gideon's letter from Rocky Mountain House.' Joel turned the sheet over. 'Written in April 1853.'

Winnie retrieved the buffalo carving from the cabinet and passed it around the group, each person examining the object with greater interest.

'Are all three of your letters written at Rocky House?'

'Rocky Mountain House,' corrected Joel. 'Yes—he doesn't seem too happy there. It's very bleak and he has trouble with one of the other men.'

'It doesn't surprise me,' said Eve. 'Everyone living in such close proximity. It must have been awful over the winter. But Gideon does go back to Carlton House. My letter is from there in May 1853. It's a sad letter. He must have received one from Grizzel saying she will wait for him to return, if he asks her to, but he has missed his chance. It's going to be a whole year before she receives his reply.' Eve paused, the significance of the delay fully impacting on her. 'It's a marriage proposal and it might have been too late.'

'He's proposed marriage to a woman he hasn't seen for four years! What does the next letter say?'

Eve half-turned to answer Jane, simultaneously realising what she had done. 'I haven't read it yet. I just looked at the date—February 1854.'

She hastily began to read, wanting to check the letter's contents before she revealed them. A tut of exasperation escaped Winnie's lips. 'Just read it out aloud.'

Eve ignored the suggestion. Gideon Thompson had begun to mean so much, her quest into finding more about him having become personal while she was in Canada, that she wanted to cherish his words. As she read, she brought her hand to her mouth in silent exclamation and her face became suffused with amazement.

Carlton House
February 1854
My Darling Grizzel,
Though I be beyond the Shetland Sea
My heart will always be with thee
It is February once again, and as I think of you with love, I repeat the sentiment from my first valentine. It is true that I have not decorated you a card, but by starting my letter with this verse, I trust you will be reminded of my steadfastness.

I have though another gift for you. I have chosen to carve a beaver, perhaps not so majestic an animal as the bear or the buffalo but a creature who works tirelessly to build a home. When I return, I hope to provide you with a home of which you will be proud. I continue to hope and pray that you will have waited for me. God willing, I will receive a letter from you before I embark on my journey home.

Life continues here in Rupert's Land with the same regularity. The end of another hard winter is in sight, although to look beyond the fort's palisade one would question this. It is a frozen, white world, but in a matter of weeks, the first signs of a thaw will come. Jim Turnbull accuses me of being overly optimistic but it is because I am eager to return to you, Grizzel.

Speaking of Jim Turnbull, he had sown a seed in my mind which has begun to grow. Under his tutelage, I have perfected the principles of keeping accounts and he believes I am capable of holding the position of clerk. I may have told you that he hails from the port of Sunderland, a bustling growing town on the north-east coast of England. He confided in me one night, after we had shared a couple of drams, that he had written to his father about me. There is the possibility that I may be able to procure a position as a clerk in Sunderland. What do you think of that, Grizzel? I would not do anything of which you disapproved but I feel that this is an opportunity which needs thoughtful consideration. Would it pain you to leave Shetland? I recall you writing that London beckoned for Will and Kitty.

Do not trouble yourself with worry about the future, Grizzel, but trust that I love you.

Your faithful admirer,
Gideon

'What does it say?' the others asked in unison as Eve stopped reading.

Eyes shining and with a slight catch in her throat, Eve explained.

'Read it out,' demanded Jane, 'there are obviously some clues.'

Joel had not missed the significance of Sunderland. 'Gideon could have returned to England rather than Shetland?'

Eve nodded, her emotional response easing out the objective researcher.

'He could have done,' admitted Jane. 'But he definitely knew a couple called Will and Kitty.'

'Ring any bells, Winnie?'

'I'm trying to think.'

Three pairs of eyes studied Winnie, anxious for a connection. They all had something to say.

'If only we knew Grizzel's surname.'

'It's always harder to trace through the female line.'

'Winnie,' said Jane. 'If Will and Kitty were contemporaries of Gideon Thompson they would probably be four generations back from you. I need to do some research. I must be able to find a link in the Family History Society's archives.'

'Do you want some help?' asked Eve, torn between wanting to be useful and exploring more of Shetland with Joel.

'No dear, you enjoy your holiday on the island and I will try and get back to you before you leave.'

'That sounds like a plan.' Joel's enthusiasm caused Eve to reflect. He was being incredibly patient and they had so few days together.

'I agree,' she said, her eyes lingering on the letters.

'I will take good care of them,' promised Winnie. 'Call again before you leave and you can study all the letters at your leisure.'

'Thank you. I'd really appreciate that,' replied Eve with feeling. It was time to go. The letters did not belong to her, although she believed in her heart that she had a stronger connection to Gideon than Winnie. She was getting closer.

Forty-Seven

Joel leaned back against the springy turf, propped up on his elbows, fighting his inclination to stretch out full-length and rest his head on a welcome tussock. He knew that, if he did, he would fall asleep; it was not yet a week since he had landed at Heathrow and jetlag was affecting him more than he had anticipated. A vista, so beautiful that it deserved the description spellbinding, disappeared as his eyelids drooped, only to reappear as he forced them open. They were on St Ninian's Isle, joined to the west coast of the South Mainland by a causeway of the palest shell sand. It curved in front of him with white-tipped waves licking each side. It was a calm day, the mighty Atlantic tamed, and they had enjoyed a picnic lunch in the gentle breeze.

The problem with having limited time was that each day was packed with activity. The previous day, they had driven to the North Isles, taking the ferry to Yell and then to Unst where Eve was particularly thrilled to be on the most northerly part of the British Isles. They walked hand-in-hand along a boardwalk, protecting the moorland, to the coastal cliffs where the cacophony of birdcall was almost deafening. On their return journey, they explored Yell, visiting the small, fascinating museum, where Eve's eyes lit up when she saw that Gideon's surname occurred several times in annotations. She became convinced that he could have hailed from that island. She had rummaged in her large bag for her notebook, prompting a broad smile from Joel as he remembered, yet again, her habit from Canada.

They had seamlessly picked up the routine of their summer journey across the Prairies, with Eve doggedly searching for clues about her forebear and Joel acting as companion. However, in Canada, he had felt more useful and indispensable, driving the RV while contributing his local knowledge. Now, as he contemplated the sea, which appeared to be ever in view on Shetland, a worm of doubt crept into his thoughts. He tried to unravel the tangle of them but the proximity of Eve rendered the task impossible. He could not deny her magnetism, which had blindsided him at home, as the thousands of kilometres he had flown to see her had confirmed the reality of his feelings. But where did that leave him? It was a far cry from going on a research jaunt to a life together on his ranch. He had less than a week before he returned to Alberta, and without realising it, he voiced his fear.

'Is all this a deal-breaker?'

'Pardon?'

Neatly hiding his surprise that he had actually spoken, Joel swept his arm in an arc, encompassing the sea. 'Is this a deal-breaker?'

A small furrow appeared between Eve's brows. 'What are you asking me?'

'The sea—is it a deal-breaker? You love it so much.'

'I still don't understand what you're asking!'

'Could you live in a place where you are not on a coast?'

She studied his face, trying to read it, without success. If she had understood him correctly, the question was so weighted that any answer was predisposed to cause upset. A light-hearted response would trivialise the seriousness of his inquiry, for there was no sign of playfulness in his eyes. Yet, if she took his meaning and replied firmly in the affirmative, was she being presumptuous? She recalled a conversation they had had on the shore of Lake Manitoba, remembering how quiet Joel had become when she had confessed to her belief that the sea was in her blood. With hindsight, the exchange gained a greater significance.

She stalled and responded with her own question. 'What would you do if I said no?'

Believing that Eve's query was the preamble to rejection, distress flashed briefly in Joel's eyes before he masked it. How could he be so stupid as to rush her? He had had no intention that morning other than to enjoy the day with her. Any discussion of their future together he had planned to leave until Eve visited him at Christmas. She needed to experience life on the ranch in the winter before she made a decision. He would pay for her flight, argue that it was her Christmas present, but he knew she would accept it reluctantly. Then, when would he see her again? Her part-time salary would never stretch to frequent flights to Calgary and he could not neglect the ranch.

'Forget it,' he said, brusquely.

Eve took a deep breath and settled herself, a technique she had learnt on an assertiveness course. She ordered her words carefully before she spoke, determined that Joel would not misunderstand. The hurt in his eyes had given her courage.

'If it was a choice between being near the sea or with the person I loved, I would always choose the person.' She leaned towards him, took his hand, and pulled him upright. They sat, shoulder-to-shoulder, looking out to sea. The brightness of the day had faded, the changing light muting the colour around them, turning the sapphire sea to a soft blue-green. Earlier, Eve had remarked that the sea was as blue and sparkly as the Mediterranean Sea and they had both chuckled, for the air temperature was very different in that part of the world in September.

'I told you that I have contacted my former supervisor, Leo Jones, and he is enthusiastic about me returning to my doctorate. It's a bit too soon to be asking for a greater opportunity but I plan to raise the possibility of a placement abroad.'

Joel turned towards her. 'Anywhere in particular?'

'It would obviously need to be advantageous for my research. This is something I want to do for myself.'

'I understand.'

'Eventually, I might want to stay abroad. Perhaps I could find a teaching position? I would not be the first person to follow this path.'

'Nope,' agreed Joel, as he bent his head to kiss her.

'And if I had a friend native to that country, it would make adjusting easier,' she said, after a lapse of some time.

He tucked one of the myriad waves of unruly hair behind her ear. 'And if that friend filed a sponsorship application for you to become a permanent resident that would be even better.'

'A permanent resident?'

'Yep—but you'd need to be physically present in your new country for one thousand and ninety-five days during the five year period before your friend files the application.'

Eve laughed, delight dancing in her eyes. 'You've been looking up details!'

'Sure, ma'am, I have.' He pulled her to him, wrapping his arms around her.

She stopped laughing and glanced up at him. 'Wow—I'd be in it for the long haul.'

Joel grinned and then he kissed her again.

Later that day, when they were in their room at the guest house, Eve's phone rang. It had stopped by the time she surfaced and scrambled in her bag. Giving Joel a rueful smile, she wriggled out of his embrace and pressed to dial the missed call. He inched towards her, mischief on his face, so she batted him away and stood up.

Winnie answered immediately, her phone obviously still in her hand. 'Eve, is that you?'

'Yes—sorry, I didn't get to my phone in time.'

'I've got great news. We've found Grizzel or, at least, Jane has.'

'Oh!' was all Eve could exclaim in her excitement.

'Jane's here. I'm going to put her on as she can explain it better.'

Jane's soft voice held a hint of triumph. 'I believe I have found Grizzel although I can't be certain without further cross-referencing. However, I am hopeful. I have traced back through Winnie's family to her great-great grandfather. He was Adam Cattanach and he did have an elder sister called Grizzel. I've found her in the 1851 census aged twenty. She was resident in Lerwick, in the Freefield area, and is described as a lacemaker. The period fits but I can't find any reference to Gideon Thompson or a marriage yet.'

Eve hopped from one foot to the other in glee. 'It makes sense. The DNA can't lie so I must be related to Winnie somehow.'

'It seems so. I can tell you more if you wish.'

'Please.'

'The Cattanachs came from Dunrossness, the southern part of the Mainland. Have you been there yet?'

'No.'

'You must go.'

'Tomorrow is our last day.'

'Then you must go tomorrow. There's lots to see and you'd get a feel for where the family hailed from. There is the possibility that Grizzel could be your great-great-great grandmother.'

There was a pause while Eve absorbed the likelihood. 'What can I do to find out more?'

'I suggest you search marriage records. I haven't found anything in the Scottish ones. Perhaps they were married in England? Start with the Central Register Office.'

'I will—but not tomorrow! We'll go to Dunrossness. Can I see where Grizzel lived in Lerwick?'

'Yes—it's by Hay's Dock, where the museum is.'

'I've been there. I went on my first day here while Joel slept off his jetlag.' Eve turned and grinned at him and added, meaningfully, 'We'll go there this evening—we could eat at the restaurant.'

Joel whipped out his phone, ready to make a reservation. 'If Grizzel lived on the dock, surely her family had maritime connections?'

Jane heard his comment. 'Yes, her father was a mariner but he died young, like so many men on Shetland. In both the 1841 and the 1851 censuses, his widow is recorded as the head of the household.'

'Thank you, Jane. You and Winnie have been so helpful.'

'Our pleasure—I'm putting Winnie back on.'

'Hi, Winnie.'

'Eve, I was wondering whether you and Joel would like to come over tomorrow night for some supper.'

'We'd love to.' As she spoke Eve sensed Winnie relaxing.

'Thank you, dear. I'm afraid I was a bit stand-offish after our initial contact. My son was displeased about me corresponding with a stranger and suggesting you come and see the photo in person, especially when he couldn't be here. I became anxious.'

'Winnie, don't worry. He was only protecting you.'

'Quite right too,' shouted Joel.

'Joel, is that you?'

'Yes, Winnie. Eve has her phone on speaker.'

'How lovely,' replied Winnie.

'Looking forward to seeing you tomorrow,' he shouted back.

'There's no need to shout,' mouthed Eve.

'About six o'clock?'

'We'll be there.'

Winnie's voice sounded more assertive as she said, 'I look forward to seeing you too. And Eve—I am very pleased to find that we are related.'

Forty-Eight

Dunrossness did not disappoint despite the dismal weather. A thick mist, a dag, as Lesley had called it as she served their breakfast, refused to disperse. It's eerie fingers clung to them, covering their clothes with a sheen of moisture which, as Eve pointed out, added to the atmosphere. Joel was not so appreciative and he, soon, welcomed the chance to go indoors when they reached their first stop, the Croft House Museum.

They were the only visitors due to the early hour and were able to wander around the house at their leisure. Eve was in her element, her notebook open before Joel had a chance to be fully over the threshold. Immediately, they were taken back to the nineteenth century; a peat fire burned slowly in the hearth of the main room, the but end, as Joel read in the information leaflet, filling the house with its unique smoke. Homemade chairs clustered around it, one of which, was hooded and probably reserved for the oldest member of the family or a guest. As he looked above the fire, he could see hooks for drying mutton and fish and he took a moment to think of how the room must have smelt.

While Eve was talking to the very knowledgeable lady who was on duty, Joel wandered along to the ben end of the cottage, bowing his head to walk through the door. Here, he saw his first box bed up against the side wall, its doors providing both warm and privacy. To the side of it, a sailor's kit bag rested on top of a trunk which reminded him of what Eve had told him when they had passed several crofts in ruins. It had been a precarious existence; crofting alone would not support a family. The menfolk often needed to go to sea in order for them to survive or, perhaps as was the case with Gideon Thompson, go to Rupert's Land. There was a hearth there as well but the fire was unlit. Joel shivered, the cold striking up from the flagstone floor, and went in search of Eve.

Eve refused to leave until she had seen everything although, to Joel's relief, she only gave the barn and byre a cursory glance. He was hungry, even though it was only mid-morning and he had eaten a hearty breakfast, so they drove south to Sumburgh Head, and climbed up to the lighthouse. The mist marred the view but nothing could dim the cries of the gulls and kittiwakes as they wheeled around the cliffs.

'Put your hood up,' they said to each other simultaneously, before Joel grabbed Eve's hand and propelled her into the café just as the drizzle turned to fat drops of rain.

They sat the rain out in comfort, with hot coffee and cake, grinning at each other across the table.

'Are you glad you came?' asked Eve.

'Here, or to Shetland in general?' queried Joel. 'Or to Britain?'

'Well, all of them!'

'Nope,' he teased, although his eyes made a lie of his answer.

'So, you'll be pleased we've only got three days before you fly home.'

Joel sobered in an instant. He took her hands, small and neat, in his large, calloused ones.

'Let's not dwell on that—it might spoil the time we have left. What we have here and now is perfect to me. I have never felt like this with anyone before.'

'Not even Colette?'

'No—we got together when we were students at UW and it sort of grew. Our contemporaries were getting married so it sort of seemed the thing to do. I knew I wanted a family.'

Unable to think of a response, Eve took a sip of coffee.

'Meeting you, on the other hand, was like a thunderbolt. One minute, I was helping this Brit navigate the check-in system, and the next, I was hanging around outside of the Archives as excited as a teenager with his first crush.'

Eve looked at his strong face, deeply tanned by outdoor life. His eyes, more blue than green that day due to his cagoule, stared back intently, willing her to believe his words. She took a deep breath. 'I'm going to say something which might sound stupid.'

'Never!'

'Yes—and I'm being serious.'

'Okay.'

'I felt that I knew you. You seemed so familiar although you came from a totally different world.'

'You mean I'm just your type!' he released her hands and leant back with his arms open.

Eve hooted with laughter, in a very unladylike fashion, causing the couple at a nearby table to turn and stare. Nothing was further from the truth. The idea of falling in love with a rancher from Alberta had been beyond her imagination and she could not quite believe it had happened. Although her heart sang, her head still screamed caution. She fought to regain control and apologised to the neighbouring couple who soon returned to their own preoccupations. Joel was looking at her expectantly, unfazed by her merriment.

'Yes,' she admitted, imbuing the word with more than a hint of uncertainty.

His eyes, alive with mischief, crinkled. 'I'd better up my game then.'

'Might be wise,' she suggested, as she stretched across the table and brushed a kiss across his lips.

'What's that for?'

'For being you.'

The rain had stopped leaving a clearer sky. There was still much to see as Eve was determined to visit the archaeological remains at Jarlshof. It was a short drive from Sumburgh Head, and within half an hour, she and Joel were wandering around the site marvelling at the Bronze and Iron Age buildings. Again, they were alone except for a family with two boys about Nate's age who raced up the steps of the ruined sixteenth century laird's house. Joel watched them wistfully as they waved triumphantly to their parents from the top. Eve, who had been distracted by the foundations of a Viking longhouse, joined him.

'You miss Nate?'

'Sure do,' he replied, squeezing her hand gently.

'Will I see him at Christmas? I'd really like to.'

He drew her to him, wrapped his arms around her, and wanted to shout his thanks to the universe. 'He'd be thrilled to see you. He did nothing but talk about you after you'd left.'

'Nate will be at the ranch?'

'We'll see. If his mom wants him with them we can always fly over to Winnipeg for a few days. Stay with Phil and Rach.'

She hugged him back, by way of answer, and then pointed out that they would be late getting to Winnie's unless they speeded up.

As it was, they arrived in Scalloway without a minute to spare, having visited Quendale Mill and touring the places where Grizzel's family had lived including Hillwell and Rerwick. Eve had insisted that they spend some time in the graveyard, which served the inhabitants of Dunrossness, where she diligently read the names on every gravestone. Discovering her interest in graveyards, Joel had wasted no time in teasing her about her liking for all things genealogical. She had frowned at him, in partial jest, and declared that tombstones were a great source of information. He had chosen to differ especially as, after the rain, a brisk breeze had gathered strength and swept across the exposed landscape.

Now, sitting in Winnie's front room, watching the fire catch in the grate, Joel stretched out his long legs and eased back into the soft sofa. Although only September, the warmth was very welcome, helping to offset the draught which crept under the door. He had noticed what appeared to be a soft toy, an extra-long dachshund made out of floral material, lying to one side, whose purpose became apparent when Jane put it across the door once Winnie had arrived with the pre-dinner drinks.

'I thought a peerie sherry would go down very well before we eat.'

Joel retracted his legs and leaned forward, taking the delicate crystal glass in his hand. He sipped the fortified wine, which was not to his taste, and longed for a beer. He glanced slantwise at Eve who was drinking with enthusiasm, a look of pleasure on her face.

'I haven't had a sherry in ages,' she said. 'I'd forgotten how pleasant it is.' She held up the glass and smiled as the liquid gleamed in the light. 'My mother used to love sherry.'

'Was your mother born in Sunderland?' asked Jane. 'I remember that is the port Gideon Thompson mentioned in his letter.'

'Yes.'

'And your grandparents?'

'Yes, I can remember my Nana showing me the house she was born in. I was quite young. We were on the bus, upstairs because I can remember looking down at it, on the way to my ballet lesson.'

'Excellent — another two generations and we will be back with Gideon Thompson.'

'I suppose we will.'

'Do you know anything else about your mother's family?' asked Winnie.

'Not much—I'd never really been interested in family history until I found the valentine I told you about.'

'You probably know more than you think.'

Eve turned to Jane. 'How come?'

'You will have absorbed information through being part of your family.'

'I suppose so,' replied Eve, sounding unconvinced.

'What did your grandfather do as a living?'

'He was a sailor—in the Merchant Navy.'

'Was he in the Second World War?'

'Yes.'

'Have you ever looked him up in the naval records?'

'No.'

'Who holds the documents in your family—the birth, marriage, and death certificates?'

'I have no idea.'

'Perhaps you could ask an older member of your family?'

'My two elder sisters were the executors of my mother's will but I don't know where any other documents are. I expect they are somewhere in our house—I live in the house which has belonged to our family since the 1950s. I seem to remember my grandparents moved in when they were first married. No, I think it could have been my great-grandparents' home before then.'

'There you go, my dear. You are already piecing the past together. If you search carefully, I am sure you will find out more.'

Eve recalled the box room last time she had been up there without any enthusiasm and her reaction did not go unnoticed.

'Who is the oldest member of your family?'

'My mother's aunt, Ada. She's in her nineties.'

'Mine her for information, Eve. You'll be surprised how much she will know when asked the appropriate questions.'

Satisfied that Eve had been set on the correct path, Jane turned to Joel. 'What do you know about your family history, Joel?'

'Pretty much all of it. Baxters have been raising cattle on our land since the 1890s.'

'But what about before then?'

'I'm not too sure, ma'am.'

'With a name like Baxter you obviously have Scottish heritage.'

'Yes, ma'am. My mom will know something of it, but I prefer to concentrate on the present.'

Winnie nodded knowingly. 'Yet, you are helping Eve on her family history quest?'

Joel coloured slightly. 'When I met Eve, back home, I could be of some help. She was looking into Gideon Thompson who had been based in the Saskatchewan area. I was able to take her to some of the forts.'

Eve witnessed an eloquent glance between the two older ladies and it was her turn to blush. She began to explain, gabbling as she went, about her summer in Canada.

'My dear,' said Winnie, 'I didn't realise you two had just met.'

'How romantic!' said Jane. 'To go on a quest together.'

'I don't think I will do much more research once I know about Gideon. I won't have time. I plan to resurrect my PhD.'

'And Joel will go back to Canada?' Winnie's voice held genuine sadness.

'Yes, ma'am.'

'Then you must take this.' Winnie stood up and walked stiffly to the ornament cabinet. Carefully removing the carved buffalo, she then made her way round the sofa to Joel. 'Here,' she said, placing it in his hands. 'This needs to go back home.'

Eve felt tears well in her eyes as she watched. She caught Jane studying her. 'You've had a good time in Shetland?' she asked.

'The best,' replied Eve, including everyone. 'The very best.'

Forty-Nine

Roker, Sunderland, November 2019

Eve turned the page of the kitchen calendar with a feeling of great satisfaction. It was now November and she could genuinely announce that she would be going to Canada next month. She had managed to negotiate leave for nearly three weeks, by including some of her annual holiday allowance for the following year, as none of the library staff wished for time off in January. Three whole weeks, including the last weekend, to be with Joel. The very thought made her skip around the kitchen as she prepared breakfast.

Lara appeared, sullen and monosyllabic, inwardly railing against her early start. Why did she have more than her fair share of nine o'clock lectures? Several of her friends had managed to escape them altogether. It was one of the downsides of living with her aunt. She had further to travel than most students. Her mother had firmly argued that it was still better to stay with Eve, rather than flat share with her friends, now she was in her second year. Where else would Lara find such comfortable, affordable lodging? In her heart, Lara knew this to be true but she balked at the idea of getting out of bed when it was still dark outside. The prospect of months of winter mornings loomed depressingly ahead.

Eve plonked a mug of coffee down in front of her niece and kindly passed her the two slices of bread she had toasted for herself. Lara took a bite and then remembered her manners. Looking up and seeing her aunt, she realised Eve was already dressed.

'Are you going somewhere?'

Eve raised her eyebrows.

'Thank you for the toast.'

'You're very welcome. And yes, I am going out. I'm going to see Ada.'

'You don't usually go on a Monday.'

'I know but she called me last night and said that she had something exciting to show me.'

Lara rolled her eyes. 'About your bloke, Gideon Thompson?'

'I believe so.'

'Surely, you have enough now!'

It was true that Eve had made considerable progress in her quest to find out as much as she could about the author of the valentine. With the guidance of Jane, she had successfully searched marriage records, and at the beginning of October, she had paid the General Register Office for a copy of Gideon and Grizzel's certificate. It had arrived promptly, and with shaking hands, she had eased open the envelope and unfolded the document. Joy on Gideon's behalf flooded through her when she read the elegant Victorian script.

He had returned home but not to Shetland. He had come to Sunderland and found employment. Grizzel had obviously joined him after waiting for over five years and they were married at Bishopwearmouth Parish Church in the April of 1855. To Eve's surprise, Gideon's occupation was recorded as "Mariner", the same as his father's and Grizzel's. He must have decided not to pursue a career as a clerk. Both fathers were recorded as deceased which caused her to reflect on the two young people that day, proclaiming their love far away from home. The names of the witnesses meant nothing to Eve. Hoping to see Jim Turnbull's name there was perhaps wishful thinking?

One piece of information also fascinated Eve. In the column, "Residence at the time of Marriage" both bride and groom were recorded as living in the same street but with no house number. Had Grizzel found lodgings in the same boarding house? What had their living arrangements been? How long had Grizzel lived in Sunderland before they were married? Eve would need to check the Church of England's marriage regulations in the 1850s. There was so much she did not know.

Later that morning, Ada greeted Eve in an obvious state of excitement, her pleasure at seeing her young relative apparent in her enthusiastic welcome. After a warm hug, Eve was ushered into her great-aunt's stylish lounge where the coffee table was already set, ready for Ada's signature cheese scones and strong coffee. As Eve settled into the corner of one of the green velvet sofas, her attention was drawn by a white envelope.

'Coffee first,' announced Ada, 'it's already on and the scones will still be warm.'

Eve laughed. 'Can't I have a quick look first?'

'No.' With a returning smile, Ada removed the envelope.

'Spoilsport!'

Ada relented a fraction. 'I can fill you in while we enjoy our coffee.'

'I can't wait!'

Ada joined Eve at the other end of the sofa. 'You may not know, but I have a cousin, Janet, who lives in Edinburgh. She's my age and she's in a residential home now. I contacted her son, Mark, to see if he had any family memorabilia and he sent me this.' She waved the white envelope. 'I think you will be very interested in its contents!'

'Why?'

'I believe it tells us how we are related to Gideon Thompson.'

'I think I already know.'

'Oh!'

Guilt washed over Eve as she witnessed Ada's buoyancy deflating. She had failed to keep Ada up to date with her findings in Shetland. Too preoccupied with Joel, messaging each other several times a day, and life in general, Eve had neglected to contact her great aunt. Scrabbling to rescue the situation, she gave a garbled account of discovering the existence of Grizzel Cattanach.

Ada listened attentively and then slowly opened the envelope. She was silent as she passed Eve the photograph, and then she leaned back against the nest of cushions and waited for her great-niece's reaction.

Eve gasped as she stared at the image. It was of a woman well into middle age, dressed in a late-Victorian dress with its high collar and mutton-leg sleeves. Her hair was tightly pulled back into a bun, sitting high on the back of her head, and was fair, although it was impossible to distinguish whether it was blonde or grey or a mixture of the two. There was nothing extraordinary about her, except for her face. Slightly at an angle from the camera, it was round and wore a pleasant expression despite the necessity to hold the pose. A strange sensation shivered on Eve's skin; she was almost looking at her own face.

'Can it be?' she asked, in total disbelief.

'Turn the photograph over,' ordered Ada.

Eve began to read, her voice unsteady, 'Grandmother Thompson (nee Cattanach) a native of Shetland. Her husband was also a Shetlander. In his youth a blacksmith, fisherman, sometime smuggler and a trapper with the Hudson's Bay Co. He settled in Sunderland and sent for his bride-to-be. They brought their family up in Sunderland where Grandfather died at about fifty-years-old. Grandmother lived to a very old age, dying in Edinburgh in her late eighties.'

She looked up at Ada, tears glistening in her eyes. 'Who wrote this?'

'Mark asked his mum. Apparently, it was her grandfather.'

'So Gideon and Grizzel are your great-grandparents?'

Ada nodded. 'And your great-great-great grandparents.'

'How many of those will I have?' Eve did a quick calculation. 'I make it to be thirty-two.'

She was quiet, thinking about Gideon and Grizzel, for several minutes. Ada departed for the kitchen to replenish the coffee. When she returned, she had the coffee jug with her and a small box.

'I thought you might like to see this.' Ada opened the box to reveal a ring, a solid gold band which had once been decorated with engraved flowers and leaves, now almost completely worn.

'Is it yours?' asked Eve, although she knew Ada was unmarried.'

'It belonged to my grandmother, I remember her wearing it.' Ada passed the ring to Eve who studied it closely. The hallmark on the inside was still crisp and easy to read. 'Have you dated it?'

'No, I've never thought to do so.'

'Shall we check it out now?'

'You don't think?' asked Ada, her voice trailing off on the last word.

'You must have an inkling that it could be or you wouldn't have shown it to me,' suggested Eve.

'Let's do it,' agreed Ada.

Eve flicked open her phone and googled hallmarks. She checked the ring. 'I can see a crown which means the ring is made of gold.'

'I think I could have guessed that!'

'Okay,' acknowledged Eve. 'What about the number twenty-two written in numerals?'

'It verifies that the gold is twenty-two carat which is a high grade of gold and indicates that the ring is at least Victorian.'

'You know a bit about old jewellery?' queried Eve.

'A bit about gold,' admitted Ada. 'Newer gold tends to be eighteen or nine carats.'

'This is good. And there's a lion's head which is the mark of the London Assay Office.'

'What's the date?' Ada could not disguise the excitement in her voice.

'It's an S—a rather fancy one. It'll take me a little longer to find the year. They change each year.'

Ada was peering over Eve's shoulder, trying to read the small screen without success. 'Hurry up, Eve. The anticipation is getting too much!'

'You will not believe this!'

'What's the date?'

'1853.' Eve took a deep breath. 'And Gideon and Grizzel were married in 1855!'

'So it could be?'

'It could be but we'll never know.'

'Look at the photo, Eve. Can you see Grizzel's hands?'

Eve strained to make out a wedding band. At times, she believed she could see it, but in reality, the photo was too old to be certain.

'I can't really say.'

'Never mind, it's still wonderful to date the ring.'

Eve held the ring towards the window. The light picked out the worn decoration. She rubbed the tip of her finger across it, the pattern just discernible to her touch. 'Isn't it strange? I found the valentine, the majority of letters were found in Edinburgh, and you have the ring. Precious keepsakes scattered.'

'It's what happens when people die, Eve. You know that. Various members of a family cherish and take different things.'

Suddenly, Eve felt overwhelmingly sad. 'I don't want to think of Gideon as dead.'

'Oh, darling, it was such a long time ago. They had their lives and now you must live yours.'

Eve turned towards her aunt and nestled into her embrace, partly to hide the unexpected well of emotion.

'Be brave, Eve, and live your life to the full.'

She took a moment to compose herself and then she eased out of Ada's arms. 'I will,' she sniffed.

'I want you to have the ring.'

'No, I couldn't.'

'Yes, you can. It's made for a much smaller hand than mine. I haven't been able to wear it for years and I have no daughter to pass it on to.'

'Here, try it on.'

Eve took the ring gingerly and slipped it down her fourth finger, taking care not to place it on her left hand. It fitted beautifully, a warm and comforting presence.

'It might come in useful,' said Ada archly. 'For you and your handsome cowboy.'

Eve's heart fluttered, and to mask her reaction, she eyed her great-aunt sternly.

'How do you know he's handsome?'

'Lara told me.'

'Oh, did she?'

'She did and I can't think of a more wonderful future for this ring than to be worn again as a token of love.'

Eve held up her hand, with fingers splayed, and watched the autumn sunlight dance across the ring's surface. Slowly, she rose from the sofa and moved into the large bay window. Her eyes when they left the ring did not register the panoramic view. Instead, her gaze turned inwards. Thus, on that November morning, Eve succumbed to daydreaming. While wrapped in beams of brightness which glinted the gold, she thought of Gideon waiting on the dock at Sunderland for his bride-to-be.

With his nerves jangling, caught between exhilaration and trepidation, Gideon watched as the schooner from Leith berthed. The minutes seemed interminable before the passengers disembarked and he scanned the crowd frantically. What if he failed to recognise her? What if she failed to recognise him? A man could change considerably from the age of nineteen to his mid-twenties. His fists balled in tension, he felt the rigidity of his jaw, and the trepidation momentarily won.

Then, he saw her, such a small figure in her shawl, carrying a worn carpet bag. Even from this distance, he was aware of her composure. It was apparent in her demeanour, the confident way she was surveying the chaos in front of her as people mingled with dockers rushing hither and thither. It calmed him and he made his way towards her, eager to look into those clear grey eyes which had captivated him. He wound his way through the crowd, raising his arms so that Grizzel could spot him, and for one heart-stopping minute, he panicked, believing he had lost sight of her.

Then, she was standing before him and the years were as nothing. A profound shyness overtook them both when finally faced with the fulfilment of all their longing. Grizzel was the first to recover, having dreamt of little else on the long voyage from Lerwick to Leith and then from Leith to Gideon. She stood on tiptoe and kissed his cheek. His face lit up, he reached for her bag, and linking arms, they walked together into their new life.

Fifty

Alberta, Canada, January 2020

Two months later, on a crisp morning when a white world sparkled under the winter sun, Joel asked Eve to marry him. Disbelief, doubt, and genuine concern that it was too soon caused her to hesitate. Since she had met Joel, her well-meaning sisters and friends, especially Aidan, had been advising caution. Their arguments were sound; she had known Joel for such a short time and exchanging daily messages did not constitute grounds for a solid relationship, she had only been in his physical company for a matter of weeks, although, as the thought flashed through her mind now, the weeks had increased with her Christmas break. Her sisters had metaphorically flocked around her like mother hens, even finding excuses to visit her and to protest about the suitability of her new relationship.

Bemused, but initially pleased by all the sudden attention, Eve had wondered what had sparked such a united reaction. Usually, her three very different sisters found it difficult to agree. Eventually, she traced the root of all the kerfuffle back to Lara. When questioned, her niece had admitted that she had airily announced to her mother that Eve was going to rush off to Canada and marry a cowboy. In her defence, Lara had argued that she had not expected her mother to drop everything and contact her sisters. Lara also argued, when faced with an irate Eve, that going to stay with Joel and his family over Christmas, was sending a very clear message. By this time, Eve's enjoyment of sibling concern had turned to impatience but her sisters' words had firmly lodged in her mind.

Aidan's contribution, also founded on his affection for Eve although he did secretly acknowledge a selfish motive for his behaviour, was worse. He drip-fed his negativity as soon as Eve returned from Shetland, concentrating on how alien life would be for her on a cattle ranch in Alberta. He revelled in checking temperatures, highlighting how cold it was becoming as winter approached; he quoted average monthly snowfall from previous years and raised concerns about how a city girl would take to rural life. One day, he went too far and Eve rounded on him declaring that she was only going for Christmas. He had reacted huffily, did not apologise, and had walked away with a throw-away remark that Alberta was a very long way from the sea.

All of this foreboding, flooded back to her as she studied Joel's earnest face and then, just in time, as his eyes clouded with disappointment, she remembered. She remembered the joy of seeing his tall figure waiting for her at Calgary Airport and the absolute bliss of being encircled in his arms. She recalled the delights of Christmas, the welcome she had received from all the gathered Baxter family, the thrill when she saw Nate, in Winnipeg, who said little at first but leaned into her as soon as he climbed into the truck's cab, and most of all, the ease of being with Joel. Clarity came to her coupled with certainty. She would live anywhere, even on the moon, if she could be with him.

'Yes,' she declared.

'Phew!' he exclaimed as he literally swept her off her feet and hugged her so tightly she feared for her ribs. 'That took you a bit too long to answer.'

'Sorry—you know me. I'm Little Miss Cautious.'

'I do, ma'am. And I wouldn't have you any other way.'

She looked at him with such love that Joel felt his heart flip. 'I'm getting cold. Let's go back to the hotel.'

They were in Banff, enjoying a few days on their own before Eve was due to leave. Having reached its zenith, the low sun was already sinking, casting long shadows as they strolled through the town crowded with winter holiday-makers. Happy faces were everywhere, glowing from activity in the magnificent mountains; couples like themselves, families with excited children, tired after the morning's exertions, and older people who were taking their time on the wintry sidewalk. Eve experienced a moment of illumination; she would grow old in Canada and found the thought profoundly moving. Last Christmas, such an idea was inconceivable, yet now, it was becoming reality. She looked up at Joel.

'When do you want to get married?'

'As soon as possible! Why wait?'

Eve could think of several mundane reasons, riding on the back of her sisters' advice and on the red tape involved in marrying a foreigner, but she pushed them to one side.

'I agree. Why wait?'

Giddy with excitement, Eve arrived back at the hotel and beheld her surroundings through a euphoric haze. The welcoming fire appeared to burn brighter, the sighing and shifting of its logs louder, the decorations on the enormous Christmas tree more dazzling, and as she walked across the foyer, she knew she too, glowed with radiant happiness. Her ecstasy carried on unabated throughout the following day when they stopped off in Canmore and reached dizzying heights as Joel placed an exquisite ring on her finger.

Together, they had chosen a gold ring set with the precious gemstone, Ammolite, found only in Alberta, and now, as Eve sat in the departure lounge of Calgary Airport, fighting back tears, she twiddled the ring so that it caught the maximum light. Iridescent green, deep and lustrous, mingled with shimmering blue, both woven with flashes of intense red. Then, absently fiddling with it, Eve's thoughts moved to how different her present experience was from the last time she had waited at the airport. Bereft at going home, she had hoped that Joel would appear at the last minute, only to be disappointed. This time, they had been together until she went through security as late as possible, and ahead of her, the future stretched, inviting and beguiling. She would be back at Easter, Joel had already booked her flight and life was wonderful.

It was not to be. As the world reeled in shock with the spread of Covid-19, Eve's dreams of travelling to Canada that Easter were shattered. England was in total lockdown. Travel was banned, like millions of people, she could not work and an unimaginable time commenced. As the pandemic increased its hold across the entire globe, any chance of Eve seeing Joel that year receded. They were fortunate in that they did not lose any loved ones to the virus, and for that, they were eternally thankful, but between lockdowns, restrictions and quarantine in both countries, their hopes continued to be shattered.

Fluctuating, at times, between optimism and despair, Eve would remind herself about Gideon and Grizzel. She was lucky to have daily contact with Joel, and as she told him often in their chats, she was descended from hardy stock who possessed great patience and steadfastness. If they could wait, she could wait. He would laugh and they would talk of their time together, both past and future, and then they would make plans which were regularly thwarted by developments beyond their control.

Eve threw herself wholeheartedly into her research; keeping in frequent contact with Leo Jones, using online resources during the lockdowns, and making the most of reference facilities during the times when restrictions temporarily eased. She was not alone at home as Lara continued to live with her, receiving her tuition online, and they settled into a comfortable routine, alternating their academic work with walks along the beach and the occasional binge on box sets.

Joel's life continued as it had, ranching being one of the safest occupations in a pandemic, and he escaped the infection, as did Rose and the men. Riding out on Rocky and watching the seasons change, it was initially hard to believe that the world was in the grip of a potentially deadly disease. Yet, as it continued to spread in waves and mutate, causing problems in the meat-processing industry, interrupting the supply chain, and threatening the sustainability of his herd, Joel's face developed an expression of perpetual anxiety.

The year 2020, which had begun so amazingly for Eve and Joel, ended dismally with no prospect of respite. Christmas was a miserable time, compared to the previous year, as Eve and Lara celebrated it together. Reluctant to leave her aunt alone, Lara had chosen to stay in Roker rather than return home at the end of term. By the time Christmas Day was on the horizon, unnecessary travel was banned from one area to another so there was no chance of visiting Berkshire. An emotional video call took place between Lara and her parents early on Christmas morning and between Eve and Joel later in the day to accommodate the time difference, both emphasising the surrealness of the situation and their lack of freedom. It truly felt, on that day, that the world had been turned upside down.

One particularly tedious February day during the second lockdown in England, the monotony was broken by a package from Winnie. She had decided to give Eve Gideon's letters. During the following days, Eve read them many times and took comfort from reading his words.

Then, as the winter days lengthened and the first snowdrops valiantly pushed through the hard earth in Eve's small garden, hope was restored. A medical breakthrough, achieved in record time, promised greater freedom. When Eve received her first vaccination, enthusiastically despite never liking needles, she felt an incredible surge of optimism. Her chats with Joel became livelier, they dared to make tentative plans, and as spring turned to summer, the separate jigsaw pieces of their lives came together to make a complete picture.

The arrangements for Eve to finalise her research in Canada were in place. Lara had graduated and was about to embark on her own post-graduate study. She would stay in the family house in Roker sharing it with three fellow students. Eve had already resigned from her job in the library after the first lockdown, once it was obvious there were not enough hours for both her and Jennie. There was nothing to keep her in England and when, in early August, it was announced that five additional Canadian airports were designated to accommodate fully vaccinated international travellers, Eve began to pack.

On the evening of a mellow autumn day, she arrived in Edmonton, her calm exterior masking her inner turmoil, worried that, at the last minute, something would go wrong. Her fingers clamped around her passport and papers, her vaccination details and her quarantine plan, so firmly that even the tired customs' official at the end of his shift, tried to put her at ease as he checked that everything was in order. It failed to help and it was not until Joel walked towards her that Eve began to believe. Seeing him only on a screen for almost two years, she had forgotten how tall he was compared to her and how he moved with such languid grace. He stopped when he was a couple of strides away from her, his eyes saying what his arms could not. Taking the handle of the largest suitcase she was allowed, he pulled it along behind him, keeping the distance between them as they walked into the soft golden sunlight. The pandemic was not over, but whatever the future held, they would face it together.